SHIELDING RILEY

Delta Team Two, Book 5

SUSAN STOKER

CHAPTER ONE

"So, you're ten?" Porter "Oz" Reed asked his nephew, wracking his brain to try to come up with something to talk about with the little boy currently standing in his living room.

Logan nodded, but didn't elaborate.

The kid had just been dropped off at his apartment by Texas Child Protective Services. Oz had discovered his sister was dead...and she'd apparently had a child. A kid he'd never known about. Oz was an uncle.

The problem was, he knew next to nothing about kids. How the hell could he be a parent to a ten-year-old? Inwardly, he was freaking out but trying not to let this kid see he was floundering. Logan had to be traumatized after abruptly losing his mother then getting dropped off at a stranger's house and being told it was his new home.

Doing the math in his head, Oz realized that his sister had to have been pregnant the last time he'd talked to her, probably at their dad's funeral, but she hadn't mentioned it to him. It was crazy that he hadn't even known about his nephew, but he supposed he shouldn't be surprised.

After he'd learned Becky was spending the money he'd sent her on drugs—and was using while at their dad's funeral

—he'd kind of lost it. Yelled at her. Told her she was throwing her life away. That she needed to get her head out of her ass. It was no wonder she hadn't told him she was pregnant.

And his nephew looked exactly like his sister, except for his eyes. They were gray like his own. Becky's eyes had been hazel. But the little boy had his mother's hair, brown and wavy—short to Becky's long—and it was obvious he'd also inherited the Reed height. At six-five, Oz towered over most people. His sister hadn't been a slouch at five-eleven. He didn't know how tall a ten-year-old boy should be, but he had a feeling Logan was taller than most other kids his age.

"Are you hungry?" Oz asked, trying again to communicate with the boy.

Logan shook his head and refused to meet his gaze.

Mentally sighing, Oz tried to think of something else to say. At the best of times, he wasn't exactly great with kids. It wasn't that he didn't like them, he just hadn't been around them often. He'd never felt like much of a kid himself. With his childhood, Oz had grown up fast.

His eyes drifted down to the plastic bag in his nephew's hand. He frowned. "What's that?" he asked.

Logan's eyes met his for a second before dropping to the floor again. "My stuff," he said with a shrug.

"Your stuff?" Oz echoed, confused.

"Yeah. I don't have a suitcase and this was all I had to hold my stuff."

Oz stared at his nephew. Then it hit him—all Logan had in the world was in that bag. A damn garbage bag.

Anger welled up inside him. Anger at his sister. Anger at the people from Child Protective Services. Anger at the entire situation. He was the last person who was qualified to raise a kid. But he was all Logan had left in the world, he needed to get his shit together and figure this out.

"Right," he said, doing his best to control the anger in his tone. He strode over and sat on the couch near Logan, not missing that the kid sidled away from him, putting plenty of room between them.

"When's your birthday?"

"October twenty-second."

"What's your favorite color?"

"Blue."

"Do you like sports?"

"Yeah."

"Favorite food?"

"Don't have one."

Oz sighed. "I know this is weird. And...I'm very sorry about your mom."

"Why? You didn't even know her. Didn't even know I existed. Why would *you* care?"

As much as Oz didn't like the kid's attitude, he couldn't blame him. And he had a point. "I care," he said.

"Could've fooled me," Logan muttered.

"The relationship between me and your mom was strained, I won't lie. I hadn't had any contact with her since before you were born. She was doing some stuff back then that wasn't good. I'd just joined the Army and wasn't living in Texas anymore. I wanted to help her, but she had to want to help herself."

"Drugs," Logan said sadly.

Oz hated that his nephew knew that. "Yeah. I guess she didn't kick the habit," Oz said regretfully.

"She was trying to stop," Logan said.

Oz stared at his nephew, not sure he could believe him. It wasn't that he thought the kid was lying, but adults hid a lot of shit from their kids, and if Becky wanted her son to think she was trying to quit, she probably could've hidden the worst of her habit from him.

"I know you don't believe me, but she was. She went to a program and everything. We were doin' good," Logan said.

"What happened?" Oz asked, hating himself for asking.

He should be asking Child Protective Services, not a ten-year-old kid. But the question had popped out.

"Someone broke into our apartment. Killed her. Stole anything they could sell. I was at school."

"Shit! I mean...shoot, I'm sorry," Oz said, making a mental note to try to curb his swearing.

Logan made a sound in the back of his throat.

Looking at his watch, Oz saw that it was after nine. It seemed odd that CPS would drop a kid off so late in the evening, but it was what it was.

Then something else occurred to him. He had a two-bedroom apartment, but the second bedroom was currently a catchall room for his shit. He had a set of weights in there and a ton of boxes. He definitely didn't have a bed for a ten-year-old kid.

"I have no idea what your schedule's been, when you go to bed and that kind of thing," Oz said. "But it's getting late and you've got to be tired."

Logan didn't respond.

"Since I didn't know about you, I don't have your room set up, so you can sleep in my room tonight and tomorrow we'll see about setting up your bedroom."

"I don't want your bed," Logan said, sounding fiercer than he had since Oz had known him...which admittedly was only about forty-five minutes.

"It's a good thing," Oz said, refusing to rise to the kid's bait. "Because I'm not giving it to you. I'm a big guy and that California-king bed fits me perfectly."

"I'm not sleeping in it with you!"

This time, Oz heard fear in his nephew's tone.

He tamped down his dismay at what that fear meant. "And I wouldn't ask you to. You're not a baby, and you need your own bed, just like I do. I'll sleep out here on the couch. You'll be safe in my room."

Logan frowned, and Oz saw his eyes go from the couch to

Oz's large frame and back to the couch. "You won't fit," he said finally.

Oz shrugged. "Trust me, this isn't the worst place I've slept in. Not even close. I'll be fine."

"Is it comfortable?" Logan asked, not dropping it.

"Not particularly."

"Is your bed comfortable?"

"Yup. Extremely."

"I don't understand," Logan said in a tone that nearly broke Oz's heart.

"What don't you understand?" Oz asked gently.

"Why you're giving me your comfortable bed when you'll have to sleep out here on the uncomfortable, too-short sofa."

"Because you're in a new place and are probably overwhelmed. You're missing your mom, and are probably very sad about what happened to her. Because I'm your uncle, and it's my job to look after you now, and because I care about you. I know that might be hard to believe, considering we just met tonight, but you're my flesh and blood. I regret not knowing about you until tonight, but now that I do, I guarantee that I'll do whatever I can to make your life easier, not harder. And that starts with tonight, giving you a nice bed to sleep in and a space of your own until I can get your room set up."

Logan's head came up and he stared at Oz for a long moment. Then he asked, "Aren't you afraid I'm gonna look through your stuff? Steal something?"

Oz shrugged. "If you want something in my room or bathroom, help yourself. There's nothing in there that I'd be pissed about you taking. Although I have to say, you've got some growing to do before you'll fit into my clothes or shoes. I don't have any nudie magazines, and I'll make sure I remove my pistol before you go to sleep."

Logan's eyes got big. "You have a gun?"

"I'm in the military, so yeah, I have a gun."

"Have you ever killed anyone?"

Oz shifted uncomfortably. But he didn't want to lie to his nephew. "Yes. But if it helps, they tried to kill me first." He couldn't tell what his nephew was thinking. For just a second, Oz thought he saw interest in Logan's eyes, but then his expression blanked and he shrugged.

"How about we get you ready for bed. You have pajamas in your bag?" Oz asked.

Logan nodded.

"Okay. Come on. I'll show you where everything is."

Almost thirty uncomfortable minutes later, Oz was back in his living room, feeling more emotions than he'd felt in a very long time. He was worried, heartbroken, and pissed at his sister. He couldn't believe Becky had a son and hadn't tried to reach out. She'd been living in Austin for years, according to Logan, so close to Fort Hood. Oz wasn't sure she'd even known where he was, but he still couldn't shake the anger.

Logan hadn't said much as Oz changed the sheets on his bed so the kid would have a clean place to sleep. He hadn't unpacked his fucking garbage bag of clothes in front of him, and it was obvious he was waiting until Oz left to get settled.

He wanted to hug the kid, tell him that he was safe, but they were strangers. He didn't think his nephew would find his embrace comforting. And asking if he was expected to sleep in the same bed as him? God...had someone abused him?

Oz had so many questions, and no answers.

He supposed they would come in time, but he needed his nephew to feel safe and loved now. Not a week, month, or year from now.

For the next hour, Oz paced the small living room, his mind whirling with everything he needed to do. He had to get ahold of his commander and let him know about his situation. His team needed to know as well. He knew without a doubt, Trigger, Brain, Lefty, Lucky, Doc, and Grover would do whatever they could to help him. Not to mention Gillian, Kinley, Aspen, and Devyn.

He also needed to get a family care plan set up with the Army; it was especially important since he was Delta Force.

An FCP would ensure a service member's family was taken care of when a soldier was deployed. And since Oz deployed more frequently than the average soldier, and since he was now essentially a single parent, the plan needed to get filed as soon as possible.

The FCP was essentially written instructions and legal documents for when he was sent off on a mission. It would specify where Logan was to go and who would be his legal guardian while Oz was overseas. It also contained medical care information, contact information for everyone who would assist with Logan, important documents like life insurance papers, financial details, and guidance on the everyday activities of the child. Of course, Oz didn't know anything about Logan's preferences or life yet, but he would.

The thought of leaving Logan while they were getting settled wasn't pleasant. For the first time in Oz's life, something else was more important than the Army.

It was surprising that he felt that way so soon, but he hadn't lied to the boy. He cared about him. He was his family. That meant something to Oz.

Oz knew Logan would come first from here on out.

He'd talk to his team and commander about what having Logan in his life meant as far as missions went. He wasn't ready to quit the team, not by a long shot, but he needed to be a stable force in Logan's life.

The pain in his nephew's eyes was as clear as day. More than just from his mother dying. He hadn't had an easy life, and that hurt Oz more than he could say. He wanted to give Logan everything, starting with stability and the knowledge that he was now safe. That he had a home with his uncle.

Oz sighed, his head spinning. He had a lot of shit to get done and he wasn't sure where to start. Tomorrow, he'd need to see about getting Logan added to his Tricare account and make sure he was covered healthcare wise. Then he needed to see about getting him enrolled in school. He'd probably need a physical as well.

And that started Oz thinking about how Logan might be tall, but he was extremely slender. He began to worry that he hadn't been eating well...which made him think about what he had in his own pantry.

"Shit," Oz exclaimed, getting up to check. What did little boys even eat? What did *Logan* like to eat? He had no idea.

As he searched his nearly bare pantry, the thought of being responsible for his nephew's well-being was suddenly overwhelming. What did he know about being a parent? Nothing! More than one girlfriend had accused him of being completely clueless when it came to other people.

He'd been called a selfish bastard when he hadn't bothered to call a woman after getting home from a mission. He had a hard time remembering his girlfriends' favorite foods, their favorite flowers, or even their birthdays. How the *hell* could he take care of a kid?

Knowing he was panicking, but unable to stop himself, Oz walked down the hallway and put his ear to his bedroom door. He heard nothing. It had been forty-five minutes since he'd left Logan inside, and he quietly turned the knob and peeked in.

His nephew was in the middle of his king-size bed, his legs and arms completely outstretched, as if he was trying to take up as much room as he possibly could. Weirdly, he had on a pair of pink pajamas with unicorns. They were too short, only hitting him about mid-calf, and his stomach was exposed where the shirt had ridden up. Oz assumed they were second-hand and maybe all his sister could afford.

But most importantly, Logan was fast asleep. Oz could hear his slight snores from where he stood in the doorway.

Making a decision he was sure he'd probably regret, Oz left the bedroom door open and headed for the front door of his home, which he also propped open, then made a beeline for his neighbor's apartment. Riley, that was her name.

They'd never had a real conversation, just exchanged greetings here and there. But he wasn't sure where else to turn at this hour. He could probably call Gillian or one of the other women who were dating his teammates, but he didn't want to disturb them so late. Besides, he could hear the TV on in Riley's apartment, so he was pretty sure she was still up.

And after what had happened earlier that evening, Oz hoped Riley would be willing to help. He'd overheard his neighbor kicking her verbally abusive boyfriend out of her apartment. Oz had stood in the hall to make sure the man left without getting physical, and at the time, Riley had seemed grateful.

He wouldn't go inside her apartment, that wouldn't be safe for her, but more importantly, he wanted to keep an eye on *his* apartment.

Knocking on her door, Oz held his breath. A good Delta operative knew when to ask for help—and he hoped Riley would be willing to lend him a neighborly hand.

CHAPTER TWO

Riley Rogers couldn't sleep. After kicking Miles out, she'd cleaned her apartment for hours. Her ex was a slob. Dirty dishes in the sink, never throwing his trash away, leaving used glasses and plates with old food on her coffee table while he played his stupid video games. Disgusting.

After cleaning, she paced, thinking about everything that had happened that night. Her argument with Miles, his threats...and her neighbor.

Miles had scared her. She'd been afraid he would refuse to leave, might even get violent with her, but when she'd opened her door and had seen her huge neighbor standing there, clearly listening, Riley was relieved.

Porter had stood there with his arms crossed, glowering at Miles, and magically, her now ex-boyfriend had backed down and left with only a few more threatening words.

Her neighbor had actually said his name was Oz, but she figured that was a nickname because she'd gotten his mail in her box once by mistake, and it had been addressed to Porter Reed. She'd been happy to introduce herself tonight...because God forgive her, she'd eyeballed the man more than once. It was wrong. She'd been in a relationship, but she couldn't help it. Every time she'd seen the man, he was polite and helpful, which was already nothing like Miles.

Riley was so tired of dating losers. She wanted a partner. Someone she could rely on as much as they relied on her. But instead, she found parasites, people who wanted her to make all the money while they hung out and watched TV or smoked pot. And the few soldiers she'd dated from the nearby Army base hadn't been much better. At least they went to work, but they hadn't cared about her as a person, only as someone they could have sex with now and then. It was depressing.

But then there was her neighbor. Tall, muscular, and with shoulders so broad she couldn't see past them when she was behind him. He had brown hair, like hers, and unique gray eyes. Riley didn't particularly like being shorter than most people she met, but there was something about Porter that made her want to rest her head on his chest and have him protect her from the world. Which was just stupid.

Still, thinking about how he'd stood like a sentinel at his door, making sure Miles knew he was there and watching, made her shiver in delight. He'd protected her, a stranger, when few men in her past ever had.

She'd been on the verge of doing something stupid—like asking if he wanted to come over for a cup of coffee or something—when an official-looking man had walked down the hall with a small boy at his side. He'd told Porter that the boy was his nephew, and that he was handing over custody of him.

The look of shock on Porter's face made her think he was finding out he was an uncle for the first time. Which was both surprising and heartbreaking. The two had disappeared inside his apartment, and she hadn't heard anything from them since.

And she'd listened.

The walls in this apartment complex weren't all that thick. She frequently heard his TV and music playing, just as he probably heard every harsh word Miles had flung at her while they'd dated. It was embarrassing, but in a way, it had been the catalyst for finally kicking him out. Knowing her neighbor had heard some of the things Miles had said to her in the past, and she still hadn't broken up with him, was pretty humiliating.

Riley knew she wasn't the most beautiful girl on the block. She was pretty ordinary, actually. At five-four, she was shorter than most women, but her weight was average. She wasn't super skinny, and she wasn't overweight. She had her problem spots—her thighs and ass, mostly—but all in all, she was content with her looks.

She didn't have a lot of friends, didn't have any family, and spent most of her life behind the doors of her apartment. As a transcriptionist, she worked from home and relied on the internet to get jobs. She received audio files from doctors, authors, and anyone else who needed their words typed out, listened to the files, typed what was said, and sent the documents back.

She was lucky enough to have many repeat customers, which kept her income steady. She didn't make a ton of money, but it was enough to keep a roof over her head, her bills paid, and food on the table.

She'd met Miles online, as she had a few of her previous boyfriends, and was done going that route. She hadn't had any luck so far, and while the internet allowed her to work from home, it obviously wasn't conducive to finding true love.

She probably needed a nice long break from men in general. It was very likely the tenants on her floor thought of her as the weird neighbor, anyway. The one they never saw and who didn't have any friends. So be it.

That was better than being the girl who was murdered by her abusive boyfriend she refused to leave.

Sighing, Riley was about to head to bed when she heard a knock on her front door.

Freezing, her heart beating out of her chest, Riley wondered if Miles had returned. He'd done it before, come crawling back after a fight, begging for her forgiveness and telling her how much he cared about her. Whatever. She wasn't falling for it this time. It was obvious he'd just wanted a place to hang out, sitting on his ass and being lazy. She was well and truly done with him.

Tiptoeing to the door so she could look through the peephole to see who was knocking at this hour of the night, Riley was shocked to see her neighbor, the gorgeous Porter Reed, standing on the other side. He looked agitated and kept glancing back down the hall toward his apartment.

Without thought, Riley took the chain off and unlocked the deadbolt before opening the door.

"What's wrong?" she asked without preamble.

"I... What do boys eat for breakfast?" Porter blurted.

Riley blinked. "What?"

"I...uh...you saw that I just got custody of my nephew. He's sleeping—I've got the bedroom door open, and the one to the apartment, so I haven't left him alone—but I got to thinking about the morning, and he didn't want anything to eat tonight, but I have no idea what he's going to want for breakfast in the morning."

"What do *you* eat?" Riley asked.

"Um...a protein shake, usually," he said sheepishly.

Riley couldn't help but wrinkle her nose in disgust.

"I know. I figured he wouldn't want that, but I don't know what he *would* want."

"Do you want to come in?" Riley asked.

"Thanks, but I can't. I need to watch my apartment and listen in case Logan wakes up."

That's right, he'd said that, but Riley was completely thrown by him showing up at her door and asking such an easy question. "Right, sorry. Um...let's see...cereal, Pop-Tarts, pancakes, maybe scrambled eggs, granola bars...he looks like he's probably not all that picky."

But instead of her words making her neighbor feel better, they seemed to stress him out all the more.

"Shit," he said under his breath. "I don't have any of that. Not even eggs. I need to go to the store—*fuck*, I can't go to the store with him in the apartment! I can't leave him alone. Should I wake him up and take him with me? I really don't want to. I'm not sure the kid even likes me. He'd probably like me less if I woke him up in the middle of the night to go to the freaking store. Damn it."

Riley's heart melted for the man. It was obvious he wanted to do the right thing for his nephew, but had no idea what that was at the moment. "Wait here," she ordered.

She hadn't meant to sound so abrupt, but instead of getting upset with her—or telling her to shut the fuck up and not tell him what to do, which is what Miles would've said—he merely nodded. His lips were pressed together in agitation and his forehead was furrowed with stress lines.

Riley left her door standing open and she walked quickly back inside her apartment. She headed for the kitchen and grabbed one of the reusable grocery bags she kept handy for trips to the store. Opening her pantry, she filled the bag halfway with odds and ends that she thought a kid might enjoy. Luckily, Riley wasn't a health nut, so she had plenty to choose from.

Then she opened her fridge and threw in the carton of eggs, which had six left, a half-eaten container of cream cheese and the half-gallon jug of milk, which had just enough left in it for a bowl of cereal. She grabbed the package of bagels from her counter, and the three-fourths-full box of Froot Loops.

At the last minute, she threw in two bananas and three apples. The bag was overflowing by the time she was done, and Riley worried that she might've gone overboard, but decided the man and boy next door needed this food more than she did, and she wanted them to have plenty of options.

She rushed back to her door, hoping Porter hadn't left. He was still there, standing with his back against the wall across from her apartment. He didn't look any less stressed; if anything, he looked *more* concerned.

"Here," she said, holding the bag out to him.

But instead of reaching for it, Porter just stared at it in confusion. "What's that?"

"Breakfast stuff," she said. "It's all been opened, sorry, but I had several things that I'm sure your nephew will eat. You can find out in the morning what he prefers. I threw in some granola bars—the soft kind, the hard ones are disgusting—eggs, bagels, cream cheese, cereal, cheese sticks, some fruit, and peanut butter, just in case nothing else appeals to him. All kids eat PB&J sandwiches, I think. There's also some other junk in there—don't judge, I have a sweet tooth."

"I can't take that," Porter said, still not reaching for the bag.

"Why not?"

"Because, it's your food."

"Porter, it's fine. I'm not wasting away, as you can probably see."

He frowned at that. "There's nothing wrong with your size," he told her.

Riley wanted to bask in his approval, which was ridiculous, but she couldn't remember the last time Miles had complimented her. "Uh-huh. Anyway, I've got plenty of food. This should tide you over until you can talk to your nephew and find out what he likes to eat. I'm assuming you're going to get him enrolled in school, and you'll need to figure out if he wants to eat the school lunches or if he wants to pack his own, so you'll need lunch food as well. And dinner stuff. Chicken fingers, hamburgers, pasta, that sort of thing. Most kids eat a ton, so I'm sure this won't last long."

The more she spoke, the more the rattled look in Porter's eyes increased. Riley realized she was freaking him out.

Taking a chance, she stepped forward and put a hand on his arm. "Porter?"

He blinked. Then said, "No one calls me that."

"Oh, um...sorry."

"No, it's fine. How did you even know that was my name?"

"Your mail was delivered to my mailbox once. I'm sorry, I can call you by your nickname...Oz, right?"

"I kinda like you calling me Porter," he admitted.

"Okay," Riley said. She couldn't be imagining an attraction between them...could she? Now wasn't the time or the place, but she couldn't help liking how his entire attention was on her when she spoke. He wasn't looking down at a phone, wasn't checking out her boobs, wasn't looking past her at her TV, which was on low inside her apartment.

His eyes flicked down to the bag she was still holding then back up to her face. "I really shouldn't take your food."

"It's fine," Riley insisted, holding the bag out once more.

"I feel horrible about it."

"Don't. It'll give me a reason to get out of my apartment tomorrow," Riley said. "I'm only sorry I don't have any doughnuts or cinnamon rolls. I'm sure your nephew would love those."

"Logan. His name is Logan. And he's ten."

Riley smiled and breathed out a sigh of relief when Porter reached for the bag of food she'd collected.

"I'm really sorry for bothering you. I panicked," Porter admitted a little sheepishly.

"It's okay. I'm glad you did. I work from home, so I'm pretty much always here. If you ever need anything, please don't hesitate to come over. I can also give you my number so you can text if you want. I know how scary it can be for a kid to move in with strangers."

This time the concern on his face was directed at her. "You were a foster kid?" he asked.

Kicking herself for bringing it up, Riley nodded. "Yeah. My parents struggled a lot, and I went in and out of foster homes for most of my life. They'd get their shit together and get me back, then they'd spiral and I'd go back into the system. I probably had seven different families I lived with. Most were good, but it was just hard to not know how long I'd be there, and if or when my parents would get me back."

"He only had a garbage bag to hold his stuff," Porter admitted.

Riley knew about that all too well. "That sucks. Most kids don't have a suitcase or a duffle bag when they enter foster care. They have to bring whatever belongings they can fit into a plastic trash bag. Can I give you a tip?"

"Please do."

"Wash his clothes as soon as you can. The smell of that damn plastic permeates clothes easily, and it sucks to have to smell it all the time as you're going about your day."

Porter looked horrified. "I will. Tomorrow when he wakes up."

Riley nodded.

"You truly don't mind if I need help? I'm totally out of my depth here."

"Are you planning on keeping him?" Riley couldn't help but ask.

"Of *course* I'm keeping him. He's my nephew. He doesn't have anyone else to look after him."

"I'm sorry if I offended you," Riley said quickly. "It's just that a lot of people wouldn't want their lives disrupted by a kid who isn't theirs."

"Disrupted? I think *he's* the one who's had his life disrupted, not me. I hate that I didn't know about him before now. I hate that I never reconciled with my sister before she died. I'd like to think she got her shit together, but looking at

Logan, and seeing the pain in his eyes, I'm not sure she did. I would *never* give up my nephew. No matter how hard his sudden appearance in my life is for me, it's got to be ten times worse for *him*. He's staying."

The warmth in Riley's belly grew. She loved how fierce Porter was about his nephew. He didn't say he loved the boy, but that wasn't surprising; he'd just met him, and hopefully love would come in time, for both man and child. "Then I'm happy to help."

"Thank you," Porter said with a heartfelt sigh. "And I feel stupid that I have no idea what a kid eats for breakfast."

"Cut yourself some slack. There will be a lot of things you don't know about a ten-year-old, but you'll learn quickly."

"I hope so." Porter stood up straighter, and Riley could almost see the confidence returning. "I'll pay you back for this," he said, gesturing to the bag.

"No need."

"There's every need. Will you...do you want to meet Logan?" Porter asked.

"Of course."

"I mean, not now, he's sleeping. At least I hope he is. But maybe tomorrow? We have a lot of running around to do. I need to get him added to my benefits and see about school and stuff, but maybe you want to come over for dinner?"

Riley eyed him. "Are you nervous about being alone with him?" How she knew that, she couldn't say, except that she felt as if she could read this man. Which was crazy since they'd just officially met.

"A little. Tonight's conversation didn't go so well. I know his favorite color is blue and his birthday's in October."

"One day at a time," Riley told him. "That's all you can do."

"I know. So, dinner? Or is that too much?"

"I'm happy to come over," Riley said with a smile. It

wasn't as if she needed to check her social calendar or anything. "Do you want me to bring something?"

"I got it. If nothing else, I can grill up some hamburgers. Six?"

"Sounds good. Oh, and do you want my number?"

"Yes."

Riley waited, but he didn't move. She frowned. "Do you want me to go get a piece of paper to write it down?"

He smiled...and seeing the wrinkles form at the sides of his eyes made her want to run her fingers over them. The man was gorgeous. She had no idea how he was single, but it appeared that he was.

"Just tell me your digits. I'll remember them," he said.

So Riley rattled off her number, not quite sure she believed that he'd remember it.

Chuckling, Porter said, "The Army trusts me with super-top-secret info that can never be written down. I think I can remember seven numbers, my grocery fairy."

Riley knew she was blushing at the nickname. And of *course* the Army trusted him with some of their most secret information. She had no idea what he did, but with the way his arms bulged with muscles, she guessed he was probably some sort of elite soldier. She'd lived in the area and dated enough soldiers to recognize someone who did more than push papers or stand around holding a rifle. "Right."

"Thanks again. You're a lifesaver," Porter said. "I'll text you tomorrow to make sure you haven't changed your mind about coming over."

"I won't change my mind," Riley said with one hundred percent confidence.

He gave her a small chin lift, then headed back to his apartment.

Riley couldn't help but stare at his ass as he went. The man was built like a mountain. Tall and unwavering. For one second, she thought about their size difference and how, at over a foot taller than her, it would really hurt if he decided to hit her, but she shook her head and banished the thought.

She couldn't assume every man she met was going to hurt her, that was defeatist thinking that belittled her own self-worth.

Instead...she imagined how it would feel to have her neighbor over her while she was flat on her back in bed. He'd surround her, make her feel small and dainty for sure.

That was a much better thought. A surprising one, since she'd never really felt all that sexually attracted to Miles.

She was still standing in her doorway when Porter stopped at his own and looked down the hall at her. "Riley?" he asked.

"Yeah?" she answered, ready to answer whatever question he had.

"You're way too pretty and good for that asshole you kicked out tonight. He's the idiot for not seeing what an amazing girlfriend he had. Good night."

And with words that blew her mind, Porter entered his apartment and shut the door behind him.

It took a second for Riley to move, but then she closed and locked her own door before putting her back to it and sliding down until she rested her ass in her foyer.

Porter's words echoed in her head. She'd already felt good about her decision to break up with Miles, but her neighbor's opinion solidified the decision. He thought she was pretty. And an amazing girlfriend. Riley was pretty sure she could go weeks on the high his words gave her.

She had no idea what might happen between them, if anything. Instinctively, she knew Porter Reed was a good man. She'd been wrong before, but something told her she wasn't wrong about him.

It would feel good to be around a man who freaked out about not knowing what to feed his nephew, rather than getting all pissed off about a stupid computer game or running out of drugs. The fact that he wasn't afraid to say thank you or to ask for help was another bonus.

Smiling to herself, Riley got up off the floor and headed for her bedroom. She needed to gather up Miles's stuff he'd left at her place and arrange to get it back to him, but for now she was exhausted. She had a few jobs she needed to get done tomorrow, go to the grocery store and restock...and then apparently she was eating dinner with her neighbor and his new charge.

Suddenly her life seemed much more exciting than it had even a few hours ago. Riley couldn't wait for tomorrow to come.

CHAPTER THREE

"A kid?" Doc asked in disbelief the next afternoon.

Oz nodded. The day had been nonstop so far. He'd been even more grateful for his neighbor's generosity that morning when Logan had eagerly eaten a little bit of almost everything she'd provided. He started out with a bowl of cereal, then he'd eaten a granola bar, and even some of the scrambled eggs Oz had made. It was obvious the kid hadn't eaten in a while, and Oz made a mental vow to make sure he always had enough food in the house.

Conversation had been stilted and awkward, and mostly one-sided, but Oz wasn't daunted. It would take some time for things to get more comfortable between them, and in the meantime, he just had to provide a safe home for Logan.

They'd gone to post, and Oz had gotten Logan added to his official record, and he now had his own military ID. Oz had asked his nephew if he wanted to go to school on or off the Army base, and without hesitation, Logan had said off.

Oz had no idea if that was the right decision or not, as he knew nothing about how good the local schools were, but he was determined to give Logan as much choice as he could with how things went in his new life.

They'd gone to the post hospital so Logan could see a physician and they could get the paperwork needed in order to officially enroll Logan in the fifth grade. They still had to go to the grocery store and then the furniture store. At the very least, Logan needed a bed. He also needed clothes and toys and shit, but that would probably have to wait for another day.

Oz had taken Riley's advice and washed all of Logan's clothes that morning, and he'd gotten upset with how little the boy owned all over again. He couldn't understand how CPS hadn't boxed up all his stuff from the apartment he'd lived in with his mom. Where had all her stuff gone? His? Was it sitting in a storage unit waiting for Oz to claim it? He needed to talk to Logan's caseworker, but again, other things took precedence.

Oz hadn't had time to introduce Logan to his Delta teammates before he was shuttled off on a tour of the motor pool, including all the tanks that were parked there, by one of the admins who worked in their building. Oz felt a pang in his gut when the first smile he'd seen on his nephew's face had been directed at the man who'd asked if he wanted to see a tank up close and in person, but he pushed that aside. He knew it wouldn't be an easy road gaining Logan's trust, but he'd be patient. The reward when it finally happened would be greater than anything Oz could imagine. He just knew it.

"I know, it's crazy," Oz replied to Doc.

"Out of all of us, I never would've thought you'd have the first kid," Trigger quipped.

Oz snorted. "Right? I mean, you, Lefty, and Brain are the ones with women, not me."

"You okay with this?" Grover asked. "You need anything?"

"I actually need everything," Oz said honestly. "But I'm working on it, thanks. My neighbor came to my rescue last night."

"Your neighbor...?" Lucky asked.

"Yeah. Riley Rogers. Last night was crazy, not only because Logan was dropped off at my doorstep so late, but Riley finally kicked out her asshole boyfriend. He went to her place and started in on her almost immediately. The walls in my complex are super thin, so I hear them a lot. He was berating her for pretty much everything. She works from home—I'm not sure what she does—but he was telling her she was lazy and a bitch for not letting him hang out at her place more."

"Guess he doesn't work?" Trigger said dryly.

"Apparently not. Anyway, Riley'd finally had enough and broke up with him. He didn't take it well. I stood by my door just in case he decided to get physical, but as I'd hoped, when he saw me there, he left without touching her."

"You think he's gonna stay away?" Lefty asked.

"No clue. But I'm just glad she finally got up the strength to kick him to the curb. She's way too pretty to be treated like a piece of shit," Oz said.

"So, you said she came to your rescue? Sounds like the opposite to me," Brain observed.

"Right. Anyway, after the asshole left, the CPS worker showed up with Logan. She saw and heard what was said. When Logan fell asleep, I realized that I didn't have anything for him to eat in the morning, and I couldn't leave him to go to the store. So I went next door and asked for Riley's help. She ended up giving me a bag full of breakfast stuff. I think the only thing missing was doughnuts."

"That was pretty nice," Doc said.

"You gonna pay her back?" Lucky asked.

"I would if I thought she'd let me. But I have a feeling she's kinda prickly about that sort of thing. I *did* invite her over for dinner tonight. I figure maybe if Logan and I aren't alone, things will be less awkward."

"So you thought inviting a stranger over for dinner, a

woman at that, would make things less awkward?" Trigger asked, his brow shooting up in skepticism.

"Uh...shit. Yeah?" Oz said.

"Right. Okay. I'm sure it'll be fine," Lefty said.

Oz wasn't so sure now, but he wasn't going to uninvite Riley. That would be extremely rude. And he had something else he needed to talk to his friends about. "Logan said he preferred to go to school off post, which I'm cool with, but I'm still going to need to fill out a family care plan. The commander has given me some time to figure out all the details, but I'm not gonna be able to deploy with the team until it's done. I just...I don't have anyone I can leave Logan with when we're gone...and I was wondering if you guys thought Gillian, Kinley, and Aspen might be willing to be listed?"

"Absolutely," Trigger said without hesitation.

"Of course," Lefty agreed.

"I'm sure Aspen would be honored," Brain said.

"And I know Devyn wouldn't mind being a backup if needed," Grover added, talking about his sister, who'd started hanging out with the other women.

Oz breathed a sigh of relief. "Thanks. I was planning on calling them as soon as possible to ask in person, but I'd appreciate if you'd give them a head's up. Let them know what would be required of them if we go on a mission."

This next part was harder, but Oz pushed through, not one to put off awkward conversations. "If, God forbid, something happens to me...I'm gonna want one of you guys to take him in. I don't want him to go into the system. He's had enough hardship in his life, and I can't stand the thought of him being shuffled around from foster home to foster home. Did you know kids in the system sometimes don't even have a suitcase to carry their shit? They have to use a garbage bag. It's horrible."

Trigger stepped forward and put a hand on Oz's shoulder.

"First of all, nothing's gonna happen to you. We've all been together a long time, and while shit happens, we're constantly looking out for each other. If you die, something's gone terribly wrong, and we're *all* probably fucked. Secondly, of course we'll look after your nephew. Logan will *never* go into the foster system. The kid's probably scared, worried, and unsure about his future with his uncle. He's your family, so he's our family too. Go ahead and put me and Gillian down as his guardians if something should happen to you."

Oz took a deep breath. He loved his friends. "You probably should talk to Gillian first," he said.

"Nope," Trigger said immediately. "She'll be on the same page as I am on this one. Logan might not know it yet, but he lucked out when he was placed with you. It sucks about his mom, but he's gonna have a good life here. He not only has you, but he's got all of *us* now."

"Um...we're done with the tour." The sergeant who'd taken Logan for a tour of the tanks and other large trucks on the base stood in the doorway.

Oz turned to see his nephew staring at him with a look he couldn't interpret. "Great. Thanks for your help, sergeant."

"Anytime. Later." And with that, the other man turned and left the room.

Oz held out his hand. "Come here and let me introduce you to my best friends, Logan."

The boy cautiously shuffled forward, but didn't come close enough to be touched. Oz wasn't offended. It would take time for him to learn to trust him. "These are the men I work with on a daily basis. And when I'm deployed, they're the people who have my back, just as I have theirs. This is Trigger, Lefty, Brain, Lucky, Doc, and Grover. Those are their nicknames and what we usually call each other."

His teammates all said hello to Logan.

The boy looked at each of them, then up at Oz. "What you do is dangerous?"

Oz wasn't sure he wanted to get into this now. It was too soon. He didn't want to scare the hell out of the boy. But he'd obviously overheard at least part of his conversation with the team. If he ignored the question, it might make Logan even more nervous.

Crouching so he could be eye-to-eye with the boy, Oz nodded. "Sometimes, yes. We're special forces. Do you know what that is?"

Logan's eyes widened and he nodded.

"We get sent on highly specialized missions. To rescue people, to track down bad guys, to help other countries when they have something that needs to be done that their military can't do. But you see these men behind me?"

Logan's eyes skittered to his friends, then back to Oz.

"They're the best of the best. We've been working together a very long time, and I trust them with my life, literally. We're always extremely careful. I can't guarantee that I'll never get hurt, but you need to have confidence that we one hundred percent will do whatever it takes to get home. Trigger's married, and Lefty and Brain have girlfriends. Grover's sister lives here too. So we all have very important reasons to come home."

Logan seemed to take that in before saying, "And if you die, then someone else will take me in?"

"Yes, my wife and I will," Trigger answered.

Oz kept his eyes on his nephew, trying to read his expression, without luck. When Logan didn't respond, Oz asked, "Are you okay with that?"

Logan met his gaze and shrugged. Then whispered, "Why?"

"Why what?" Oz asked.

"Why would he take me? I'm a stranger."

"You're not a stranger," Trigger said kindly. "You're Oz's nephew."

"But he didn't even know about me until yesterday," Logan insisted.

"That doesn't make you any less my family," Oz told him. "I know we have a lot to learn about each other, and I haven't wanted to overwhelm you, but it's obvious we need to talk about this. I'm upset with my sister, your mom. She didn't tell me about you and I don't know why. I wish I had tried harder to repair our relationship. She was older than me, and when I graduated from high school she was making lots of really bad decisions. Decisions that I knew were going to get her in trouble. I was going into the Army and didn't want any of her bad choices to affect me. I was selfish and only concerned about myself."

"That's not fair, Oz," Grover said. "You were young."

Oz shrugged, but didn't look away from Logan. "It's been over ten years since I've seen or talked to Becky. And now I won't ever get the chance. I'll regret that forever. But you know who I'm *not* upset about?"

Logan shook his head.

"*You.* I hope you'll eventually be comfortable enough to tell me all about your life. About your mom. The good *and* bad. We're all more than the bad decisions we've made in our lifetime, and while your mom might've done some dumb stuff, I'm confident she loved you.

"These guys are my family. We might fight and get upset at each other, but we'd never turn our backs on one another. If and when Trigger and Gillian start having kids, they'll be like my nieces and nephews too. I'd take their kids in without question, just as they'll do for you. You'll always have a place to live, Slugger. You'll never have to worry about that again. Okay?"

Logan nodded.

"Right." Oz stood and faced his team. "I'll call Gillian, Kinley, and Aspen soon. Thanks."

"You need anything, let us know," Lucky said.

"Assuming you won't be making PT at oh-six-hundred. I'll talk to the commander about moving it to oh-eight-hundred after you get Logan off to school," Trigger said.

Oz closed his eyes for a second, then met his friend's gaze with gratitude. "Thanks."

"Of course."

Working out was mandatory for all soldiers, but for their Delta team, it was also a time to bond, to talk through shit. And because he wouldn't leave Logan alone in his apartment, Oz hadn't been sure what was going to happen with that. Moving the workout time until after he'd dropped Logan at school would be a weight off his shoulders.

It was still just settling in that his entire life was about to change. Not in a bad way, but being a single father wasn't easy.

Oz had a newfound respect for all the single parents in the world. Work, school, shopping, everything was more difficult when you had to make sure your child was cared for and wasn't left alone.

"You ready to hit the stores?" Oz asked Logan.

The boy merely shrugged. It seemed as if that was his favorite mode of communication.

"Great. We've got a lot to get done before dinner tonight. My neighbor's coming over, she's the one I told you about this morning, who made sure we had stuff to eat for breakfast."

Logan's expression didn't change, he just shrugged again.

Oz mentally sighed. It wasn't going to be easy to break through his nephew's shields, but he'd do it...eventually...he hoped.

CHAPTER FOUR

Riley held the casserole carefully as she made her way down the hall toward Porter's apartment. He'd said she didn't need to bring anything, but it felt weird to show up with nothing. So she'd made a green bean casserole. It was a risk, Porter's nephew might hate vegetables—hell, *Porter* might hate them —but this dish was one of her favorites. She'd put crispy onions on the top and used extra cheese as well, to try to entice the guys to eat it.

She knocked on the door and stood in the hallway feeling slightly awkward and seriously nervous. Was this a good idea? Probably not. Riley was way too interested in her gorgeous neighbor. Hadn't she just decided she was done with men for a while? And now here she was.

Just as she'd decided it might be best to go back to her apartment and hide, the door opened and Porter was standing in front of her.

Thoughts of retreat flew from her brain as she got a good look at her neighbor. He looked stressed. There were lines around his mouth and the smile he gave her was strained.

"Hey," he said.

"Hi," Riley returned. Then she lowered her voice. "Are you okay? Is Logan all right?"

"We're good. It's just been a stressful afternoon," Porter told her. Then louder, he said, "Come on in. You're right on time. Dinner's almost ready."

Riley let Porter take the dish out of her hands and she entered the apartment. The setup was the same as hers, but reversed. Her kitchen was on the right after entering the main room, Porter's was on the left. The hallway in her place went to the left, his went to the right. She was somewhat surprised to find Porter's place was immaculate. She supposed she'd stereotyped him and figured it would be a mess, simply because he was a guy, but after thinking about it, she should've suspected it would be neat since he was in the Army.

Logan was sitting in the living room watching TV.

"Logan, this is Riley Rogers. She's our neighbor."

The boy didn't even look up.

"Logan," Porter repeated. "It's rude to ignore someone when they're introduced to you."

His nephew reluctantly looked away from his show over to where she was standing. "Hey."

"Hi. It's nice to meet you," Riley told him.

Logan merely shrugged and turned his attention back to the show.

Porter whispered, "Sorry," as he headed for the kitchen.

"It's fine," Riley said in a low tone. "I take it things are a little rough right now?"

To her surprise, Porter put the casserole dish down and rested his hands on the countertop. He lowered his head and sighed.

Her heart went out to him. She hadn't known this man for very long, but it was obvious he was struggling.

"I think he hates me," Porter said. "He's barely said more

than a dozen words to me since we left post this afternoon. He communicates via grunts and shrugs. I saw him smile only once today, and that was at a random soldier on base who was showing him around, and not at me.

"We went to the store and I bought a shit-ton of stuff, but I have no idea if he likes any of it because all he did was sulk as he followed me around the store. I bought furniture, and again, he could hate it for all I know, because not one iota of emotion crossed his face the entire time." Porter looked up at Riley, and she saw the frustration and sadness in his eyes. "I don't know what to do."

Riley wasn't exactly an expert on kids, but she did know some of what Logan was probably thinking. She'd been in his shoes. Pawned off on strangers while her parents tried to get their lives back together. She put a hand on his arm. "You just need to be patient."

"I know," Porter said, keeping his gaze locked on hers. "But I care about this kid so much already, and it's only been a day! I want him to know how sorry I am that I didn't know about him before, and that he's safe with me."

"Have you told him that?" Riley asked.

Porter blinked. Then shook his head. "Not quite. He overheard me talking with my team today about how they'd take care of him if anything happened to me. I made sure he knew that my friends were like my family, and they were now his family."

Riley struggled to find the right words. She wasn't sure she was qualified to help this man and his nephew, but she wanted to try. "When I was taken away from my parents the first time, I was terrified. I didn't know where I was going to live, what I was going to eat, where I was going to sleep. I was placed with a very nice family, who were great to me, but it wasn't what I was used to. It wasn't my home. I didn't know them. Then, just when I was getting comfortable again, I was picked up and brought back home to my parents. I was happy, but also felt extremely guilty because I'd begun to like it at that other house. My parents tried hard, but they fought a lot. It was uncomfortable in my house. I constantly had to be on my best behavior so I didn't set either one of them off.

"The second time I was taken away, it was a little easier, but still scary. That family wasn't as nice as the first one, but I didn't have to worry about being smacked around or not having enough to eat, like I did at home. The feelings of guilt were still there. Every time I got shuffled around, those feelings came back. I was confused, and it was always scary having to move in with strangers, even if they were nice.

"Cut Logan some slack, Porter. You two aren't automatically going to be best buds simply because you're related by blood. And I know you're a guy, but you're going to have to tell him how you feel. A lot. He probably won't reciprocate. But get over it. Talk to him about how you felt about your sister. Tell him that you care about him. That you're glad he's here even though it means a lot of changes in your life. If you open up to him, I think he'll eventually return the favor. But trust takes a while."

Porter shifted, and before she knew what he was doing, she was in his embrace.

She was a foot shorter than he was, but somehow they still managed to fit together. Her cheek rested on his chest, and when his arms went around her, she felt absolutely surrounded by him. She could tell Porter had probably taken a shower before she'd come over. He smelled fresh and clean. Even his T-shirt smelled as if it'd just been laundered.

Riley had never been a touchy-feely person, mostly because her parents didn't hug her a lot, and she'd learned to keep people at arm's length. But instead of feeling uncomfortable...she felt as if she'd come home.

Just as she moved her hands to return his hug, Porter stepped back. His cheeks were rosy, as if he was embarrassed.

"I'm sorry," he said.

"For what?" Riley asked in confusion.

"For touching you without asking first."

Movement out of the corner of her eye caught Riley's attention. She turned her head to see Logan standing just outside the kitchen.

"It's okay," she told Porter.

"It's not," he said with a shake of his head. "It's never okay to touch a woman without making sure *she's* okay with it. I just...I'm glad you're here. I'm sorry all that stuff happened to you, but it makes me admire you more than I already did. And you're right, I'm just being impatient. I need to curb that and just go with the flow. What did you bring us?"

For a second, Riley was thrown by his quick change of topic, but then she realized that he'd seen Logan watching them too.

"Green bean casserole. And before either of you wrinkle your noses and say you don't like it, trust me, you'll like mine." She turned and looked at Logan. "You want to know what's in it?"

Logan shrugged.

Riley took that as a yes. "Of course it's got green beans, but you'll hardly be able to taste them because I doubled the amount of cheese in there. And it's got cream soup, and sour cream, and I even put extra onion crunchies on top. You ever had those, Logan?" she asked. She hadn't mentioned it actually contained cream of *mushroom* soup, because that tended to freak people out if they didn't like mushrooms. She hated the things, and she freaking loved cream of mushroom soup. It tasted nothing like the fungus she refused to think about eating.

Logan said "no" in a small voice.

Riley decided it was a good thing that he'd even spoken to her. She smiled. "You'll love 'em. They're like potato chips, but crunchier. And they make your breath super stinky. It's awesome."

That won her a little smile from the boy. Riley glanced at Porter—and froze when she saw how he was looking at her. He also had a small grin on his face, and for a second she thought he was going to hug her again. But then he turned to his nephew.

"We'll have to make sure we brush our teeth right after dinner so we aren't knocking each other over with our breath. Although...it might be fun to see who has the worse breath. We could always breathe on each other and see who falls over first."

Porter's teasing was extremely cute, and Riley was thrilled to see another smile form on Logan's face.

"Thanks for bringing something," Porter said. "You didn't have to. I actually made a salad to go with our burgers. I wanted to make sure Logan had some greens to go along with his protein."

And just like that, Riley's heart swelled in her chest again. Porter might not think he was doing a good job with his nephew, but from where she was standing, he was doing everything right.

"Awesome," she said.

"Dinner will be ready in about five minutes, if that's okay."

After Riley nodded, Porter turned to Logan again. "Go wash your hands. Then please come back and help us set the table."

Without a word, Logan turned and walked out of the kitchen. When he was out of earshot, Porter took a step closer, but he didn't touch her again. Riley didn't feel crowded in the least.

"Thanks for coming over. I appreciate it. I think having someone else here as an icebreaker is good. Makes things easier."

For who? Riley thought, but nodded instead of voicing her

question, deciding it didn't matter. Seeing Porter vulnerable was interesting. Intimate.

"I know you heard Miles," she said instead.

Porter's brow furrowed. "Who?"

"My boyfriend...well, my ex-boyfriend. The walls in our apartments are thin, and I know he was loud whenever he was yelling at me." Riley wasn't sure why she was bringing this up, except she didn't want Porter to think badly of her. To think she was a pushover. "He wasn't always like that. At first he was super nice and helpful. But when I told him that he couldn't hang around my place every day because I had to work, he started getting resentful. And jealous, I guess. He assumed I must be cheating on him. But I really did need to work."

"You don't have to tell me this," Porter told her when she took a breath.

"I just... You had to hear *everything*. And I know it took me too long to kick him to the curb, but I kept hoping that things would change. That he'd trust me when I said I wasn't seeing anyone else. But when he started calling me names and scaring me, I was done."

"I was proud of you," Porter told her, his intense gray eyes swirling with emotion. "No one deserves to be told they're trash."

"Thank you." Riley hated that he'd heard that part, and deep down inside, she sometimes felt as if she *was* worth less than those who'd had an idyllic upbringing. Who had big important jobs. But she tamped down those feelings—and blurted something she'd had *no* intention of bringing up. Ever. "And I'm not frigid."

Porter's eyebrows flew up.

Riley closed her eyes in mortification, but forged on. "I know you had to overhear him saying that more than once... and definitely when I kicked him out last night. But it's not true. The one time we slept together, it wasn't good. For either of us," she said, forcing herself to open her eyes and meet Porter's gaze. "I think I knew he was an asshole even then. He didn't have a job and always wanted me to pay for everything. I have no problem splitting the costs of meals and stuff when I'm dating, but he showed absolutely no inclination to pay for *anything*. When I stopped wanting to eat out or buy him stuff, that's when he started showing his true colors—"

"Riley, stop," Porter said, interrupting her blabbering.

She flushed.

"I wouldn't believe *anything* that asshole said, even without you explaining anything about your relationship. Anyone who yells at someone like that isn't worth giving the time of day to. I'm sorry you had to go through that, but as I said, I'm proud that you kicked him out. That couldn't have been easy."

"It wasn't," Riley agreed. "He was pretty scary. Have I thanked you for standing outside your apartment yet?"

"You don't have to thank me for that. Bullies usually back down when someone stands up against them. They only like to pick fights with people they think they can overpower."

"I'm done."

Riley turned to see Logan standing in the doorway of the kitchen again. The boy could really move silently. She made a mental note to remember that in the future and not get into deep conversations when he might appear and overhear.

"Great. Come over and I'll show you where everything is in here," Porter told his nephew.

Riley stood out of the way as Porter pointed out the silverware drawer, where the cups, plates, glasses, and bowls were. Watching him with his nephew was extremely touching. He was good with the boy. He didn't talk down to him, even while making it clear that he expected Logan to help with things around the apartment.

Logan carefully carried three plates to the small table next to the kitchen, then came back for more.

"Does this need to be heated up?" Porter asked.

Riley looked over to see her neighbor holding the casserole dish she'd brought. "No. It should still be good to go."

"Excellent." Then Porter took the aluminum foil off the top and leaned over and inhaled deeply.

He turned to Logan, who'd just come back into the kitchen. "Come smell this, Slugger. We're gonna have the worst breaths ever after we eat this!"

The boy didn't exactly smile, but his lips definitely quirked upward. He walked toward his uncle, and the man and boy stood side by side as they leaned over her green bean casserole.

"This is henceforth going to be known as onion casserole in this house," Porter declared, using what Riley could only describe as a "kingly" tone.

She chuckled.

"What do you think, should we put the entire dish on the table, or put it in bowls here in the kitchen and bring those into the other room to eat?" Porter asked Logan.

Logan shrugged, but then said, "I think bowls."

"Great idea," Porter agreed immediately. "I don't like my food touching on my plate. And I know that's weird, and everyone always tells me that it all mixes together in my stomach, but I don't like mixing tastes."

Logan looked up at his uncle in surprise. "That's what Mom always said too."

Porter smiled down at Logan, but Riley could see it was sad. "Yeah, I think I learned it from her. Drove our dad crazy. He used to yell at us when we wouldn't eat something because it had been 'contaminated' by something else on our plate. I had forgotten Becky and I had that in common. Thanks for reminding me."

Man and boy stared at each other for a moment, before Logan nodded and looked away.

It was a small step toward what would hopefully be a good relationship between them.

Riley reached up and grabbed a bowl from the cabinet, discretely squeezing Porter's upper arm in support as she passed.

Dinner was a little awkward, but Riley still couldn't remember a meal she'd enjoyed as much in a very long time. Watching the dynamic between Porter and Logan was interesting. The boy snuck glances at his uncle whenever he thought he wouldn't be seen, and Porter was going out of his way to try to be entertaining. Logan didn't say much, but it was obvious he was listening to everything he said.

Riley was relieved when both had two helpings of her green bean casserole, now known as onion casserole. As she suspected, the cheese and other ingredients masked the taste of the green beans. The dish might not be all that healthy with the other stuff added in, but at that moment, it didn't matter.

She also noticed that Logan subtly shifted the salad on his plate farther to the side so it wouldn't touch his hamburger... just like Porter had done.

Both man and boy ate way more than Riley could've ever finished. If Logan ate a bit too fast, no one commented, and Porter did his best to keep up a steady stream of conversation about nothing in particular. Logan didn't really participate, only answering in shrugs and grunts when he was asked a direct question, but at least he didn't ignore his uncle altogether.

After dinner, when Logan began to head to the couch to watch TV, Porter stopped him. "Dishes need to be done, Slugger."

Logan turned to look at him.

"I don't know how things were in your mom's house, but I've always thought it's only fair that whoever cooks, doesn't also have to do dishes. You're in luck, because I have a pretty kick-butt dishwasher, so you can simply load it up and let the machine do all the work."

Logan stared at his uncle for a long moment, and Riley held her breath. When the boy finally shuffled into the kitchen, she let out a relieved sigh.

Learning the ins and outs of a new household was hard, she knew that firsthand. Figuring out what you were expected to do as chores and what might set off the people living in the house could be scary. She suspected Logan was being extra compliant right now to protect himself. She figured there would be times when he'd be disobedient and disrespectful, but she was glad tonight wouldn't be one of those times.

Riley sat at the table as Porter helped Logan load the dishwasher. He gave the boy helpful hints on how to place the dishes inside, then he showed him where the tablets for the dishwasher were and how to operate it.

"Good job."

"So if I make dinner, you'll load the dishwasher?" Logan asked.

It was the first full sentence Riley had heard the boy say, and it was beautiful to hear.

To Porter's credit, he didn't make a fuss out of Logan finally speaking. "Yup. You like to cook?"

"Not really. But sometimes if you want to eat, you gotta make it yourself."

And just like that, Riley's good mood took a dive. She didn't like that Logan had ever had to fend for himself as far as meals went. Obviously, Porter didn't either.

Porter crouched in front of Logan so he could look him in the eye as he spoke. He did that all the time, which she thought was extremely thoughtful. "Unfortunately, that's true.

But as long as you're with me, that won't happen. Honestly, I don't much care if you do the dishes or not, I really just want you to learn to be polite and responsible, and helping out around the house is a part of that. But even if you throw a tantrum and refuse to help me, I'll still feed you. I'll still make sure you're safe and cared for. I love you, Logan. I know we just met, but you're my nephew, and every time I look at you, I see my sister, which is a great thing. I'll teach you everything I know about cooking—which admittedly isn't a lot—but I guarantee that when you're in charge in the kitchen, I'll do all the cleanup. Deal?"

Logan nodded.

Riley's heart melted for what seemed like the hundredth time that night. Seeing how great Porter was with his nephew was making it really hard to look at him as nothing but a neighbor. She was impressed with him, and he wasn't even *trying* to impress her. He was just trying to be the best uncle he could.

And the fact that he'd taken her advice, at least in a small way, and flat-out told Logan that he loved him also impressed her.

She watched as Porter stood. "You want to show Riley your new room?"

Predictably, Logan shrugged, but he walked out of the kitchen and said, "I can show you my room, if you want."

"I'd love to see it," Riley said with a smile. What she really wanted to do was stay with Porter. To talk to him. Help soothe him, because even though his lips were quirked upward, it was obvious he wasn't all that happy. She couldn't blame him. The small details Logan was inadvertently revealing about his life were heartbreaking. And she had a feeling they didn't know the half of it.

Riley glanced back at Porter as she and Logan headed down the hall to his room, and she saw he'd dropped his head and was gripping the back of his neck with one hand, the other fisted by his side. She hated seeing him so stressed but there wasn't anything she could do about it other than entertain Logan for a while to give Porter some time to collect himself.

Logan led her to his room, the second bedroom, which she used as a home studio back at her place—and she gasped in surprise at what she saw. Porter had transformed the room into a space perfect for a little boy. Riley had no idea what Porter had used this room for before Logan arrived, but now it had a full-size bed, a set of drawers, and a small desk against one wall. There was a bookshelf, which was mostly empty, and she could see clothes hanging up in the open closet.

And everywhere she looked, there was baseball paraphernalia. On the wall was a poster of a Texas Ranger pitcher, and a rug shaped like a baseball sat on the floor. Riley saw a bat, ball, and glove in the corner of the room. The comforter even had the logo of the Texas Rangers on it. The nickname Porter had given his nephew made a lot more sense now.

"So...you like baseball, huh?" Riley asked.

Logan nodded. "Yeah. Shin-Soo Choo is my favorite outfielder. He's amazing and has caught some crazy flyballs. He even saved a kid from getting a foul ball in the face once. And he bats and throws left-handed, which is cool. He's from South Korea and has three kids. All their names start with A, which is awesome. Get it? A for awesome. He led all active major league players in career hit by pitch with one hundred and thirty-two."

"What's hit by pitch?" Riley asked, thrilled the kid was actually talking. It was obvious baseball was his passion.

"It's when the batter is hit by a pitch," Logan said completely straight-faced.

Riley wanted to laugh, but she held back and nodded instead.

"As long as the batter did his best to avoid being hit, he then gets to go to first base automatically. And in two thousand nineteen, he was the eighth oldest player in the American League."

Riley's head was spinning, but she gamely tried to keep up. "So your uncle knows that you like baseball and got you all this stuff, huh?"

Logan nodded and looked at the floor. "When he washed my stuff, he saw my Texas Rangers T-shirt."

"I have a feeling Porter's pretty observant."

"Yeah. He has to be since he's special forces."

That was news to Riley, but it didn't really surprise her. He'd talked about "his team," and while she'd just assumed he was talking about the men he worked with on the Army base, it made sense that they were as close as they were because they weren't just regular soldiers.

Then Logan surprised her by saying, "My mom talked about him a lot. Said she was proud of him."

Sitting on the edge of the bed, Riley wasn't sure she should discuss Porter behind his back, but since Logan was talking, she went with it. "He seems as if he's a guy anyone would be proud of."

"I'm not sure why he's being so nice to me. If he didn't like my mom, why would he like *me*?"

Riley's heart broke for the boy. "He liked your mom," she said immediately. "Sometimes adults have arguments and they stop talking, but that doesn't mean they don't still care for each other. And he's nice to you because he loves you. You're his nephew. He might not have talked to your mom in a long time, but that has nothing to do with *you*, Logan. And I know if he'd known of your existence, he would've reached out and fixed the relationship with your mom."

"She wasn't the best mom," Logan said softly.

"Mine wasn't either," she admitted sadly. When Logan looked up at her, as if he needed to know he wasn't alone in how he felt about his mother, she went on. "She and my dad hit me sometimes. And they forgot to buy food. And they didn't wash my clothes, so kids at school made fun of me. Someone would report them and the authorities would take me away. I'd live with foster families until my parents stopped drinking and got themselves back on track. Things would be okay for a while, but then they'd start drinking again and the same thing would happen. But you know what? I loved them anyway. They hurt me, ignored me, and made me feel sad, but they were still my parents."

"What happened to them?" Logan asked. He'd sat on the bed and was facing her with his legs crossed, his elbows resting on his knees.

Riley lay back and stared at the ceiling. "I got old enough to take care of myself, so I could wash my own clothes and make my own food. I learned to steal money from them so I could go to the grocery store. I worked really hard and graduated from high school and moved out. Four months after I moved away, they died in a drunk-driving accident. They were coming back from a bar and had drank too much. They drove off a bridge and their car sank. Even with all their faults, they didn't deserve that."

"I loved my mom," Logan admitted. "I didn't understand why she was so mean when I was little, but she got better. She stopped doing drugs and we were doing good. I miss her."

Riley sat up and reached for Logan. Then she remembered what Porter had said earlier, about getting permission to touch, and asked, "Can I give you a hug?"

Logan didn't respond verbally, but he did scoot closer to her and initiate the hug himself.

Riley wrapped her arms around the skinny little boy. She had no idea what had gone on in his house, but the love he still had for his mom was easy to see.

They sat on his bed with their arms around each other a

few minutes, until Logan seemed to get control over his emotions.

Not wanting him to be embarrassed, Riley said, "Your uncle is a good man. It sounds like he and your mom had a hard childhood too. I have no doubt he'll do whatever he has to in order to make sure from here on out, your life is as easy as he can make it. Including buying you a bed, baseball stuff, and clothes. But that doesn't mean you have to forget your mom. That you don't love her any less. You can love more than one person. And you know what else?"

"What?" Logan asked, looking up at her with huge tear-filled eyes.

"I bet he'll want to know all about your mom. He feels awful that he didn't get in touch with her for so long. I know he won't mind you talking about her." Riley made a mental note to make sure she talked with Porter about what she'd told his nephew. He could get mad at her, but it was obvious Logan wanted, and needed, to talk about his mom.

Logan nodded.

"I like your room," she said.

"Me too," Logan admitted softly.

"I live right next door," she told the little boy. "If you ever need anything, you're welcome to come over anytime."

"Thanks. Riley?"

"Yeah?"

"Can you tell Oz that I'm tired? I think I'm gonna go to bed."

"You sure?" Riley asked, hating that he might not want to hang out with his uncle.

"Yeah. I need to brush my teeth. I'm gonna go to school tomorrow and I want the other kids to like me."

"They will," Riley said, realizing that Logan was nervous about starting a new school.

He shrugged.

"Okay, I'll tell him. Thanks for talking to me and showing me your room," Riley said.

Logan nodded.

"See you later."

"Later," Logan said.

Riley got up and headed for the door. She closed it behind her and walked down the hall toward the living room. When she got there, Porter was standing by the large window that overlooked a green courtyard behind the apartments. There were picnic tables, a few public-use grills, and a volleyball court no one ever used. And since it was dark, there certainly wasn't anything interesting going on outside. So why he looked like he was studying the courtyard as if there would be a test later on, she had no idea.

When she entered the room, he turned to face her, and Riley felt horrible about the sad look on his face. She knew immediately he'd been listening to her conversation. "You heard?" she asked softly.

Porter nodded. "You were great with him."

"I think I remind him of his mom. You know, because I'm female," she said, wanting to make Porter feel better.

He shook his head, and that reminded her a lot of Logan. "No, it's not that. It's just you."

"He'll come around," Riley told him. "He's just unsure about everything right now."

"I'm sorry about your parents," Porter said.

Riley swallowed hard. She realized he'd not only overheard what Logan had said about his childhood, but that he'd heard what she'd said too. "Thanks. I'm just glad they didn't kill anyone else that night. And honestly, it was kind of a relief. My mom had been putting a lot of pressure and guilt on me to give them money. I feel horrible that I was relieved I wouldn't have to worry about them hounding me anymore."

"Don't be," Porter said. "Because you're right, they never would've stopped begging you for cash. When someone is

46

addicted, they can't think about anything other than how they'll get their next hit or drink."

"Your sister?" Riley asked gently.

"Yeah. It was bad. I wasn't even eighteen, and she did all she could to get me to give her money I'd earned from my jobs. At first I did, thinking I was helping her, but all she was doing was using it to get more drugs. I felt horribly guilty when our dad died, and I joined the Army and refused to send her any more money, but like you said, it was a relief when I cut her off. But now I can't help but think about Logan and what his life was like."

"It sounds to me as if she'd finally gotten herself together," Riley said. "That things were better."

"Yeah," Porter agreed.

"I'm sorry for telling him he could talk about his mom—" Riley started.

But Porter interrupted her. "Don't be. It was smart. I never want him to think he can't talk about her. You're right, for all her faults, she was still his mom and he loved her. I'd never take that from him. And I'm actually interested in getting to know the woman she'd become, instead of remembering the drug addict she was when I last knew her. Thank you for making the suggestion. I owe you."

She shook her head. "No, you don't."

Porter chuckled, but it wasn't exactly a humorous sound. "I do. I have a feeling that I'll owe so many people over the next eight years. I hadn't realized how hard it is to be a single parent."

"I'm happy to help in any way I can."

He stared at her for a long moment. "You mean that, don't you?"

"Of course," Riley assured him.

"Earlier, you said you worked from home. What do you do?"

"I'm a transcriptionist. I take what someone records and

type it out for them. I have a few doctors on my client list, and I type up their notes on patients. I also transcribe authors' books that they're writing...well, that they're recording. And also lectures, that sort of thing. There're more and more automated programs coming out that will do the same thing, but I'm hoping there will always be a demand for humans to do it. I'm more accurate than machines, and with the medical field, there's the matter of security."

"You like it," Porter said. It wasn't a question.

Riley nodded anyway. "Yeah. Since I don't have a college degree, I had a hard time finding a job I loved and was qualified for, but I've gotten faster and better at transcription over the years, and I've got a decent client list now. I'll never get rich doing it, but it keeps a roof over my head and keeps me busy."

"The Army has a thing called a family care plan. It's mostly for single soldiers with kids, and it spells out what's to be done with the children when they're deployed or if something happens to them. My friends and their girlfriends have already said they're happy to step in while I'm deployed, or if something happens to me, and we've changed our schedule so my workday starts a little later, so I can make sure Logan gets to school all right, but..." His words trailed off.

"But what?" Riley asked, intrigued.

"Never mind. It's stupid."

"Porter, *what?*"

He shook his head. "We just met. Asking you to do anything would be a huge imposition. And, if I'm being honest, I like you, Riley. And I don't want you to think I'm taking advantage of you in any way, or my interest in you is only because of Logan."

Riley blinked in surprise. He was interested in her? Her fingers tingled, and she couldn't help but feel goose bumps breaking out on her arms. She tried to remind herself that she was taking a break from dating, but she knew if this man asked her out, she'd say yes in a heartbeat. He wasn't like Miles or any of the other jerks she'd dated over the years. She knew that down to the marrow of her bones.

"Ask," she ordered.

"I was just thinking that sometimes I have meetings that run long. Or that I might not be able to get home before Logan does. I don't want him to be a latchkey kid, like Becky and I were. I was wondering if you'd mind keeping an eye on him after school until I could get home. It would only be for a couple hours on weekdays."

"Of course I will."

"I know it's a lot to ask, and if you're busy with your work then I can think of something else. I'm sure the school has some after-school programs or something. Shit, I should've thought about that first before bothering you."

His words were quick and running together. Riley smiled. "Porter, I said I would. It's fine. I like your nephew. I don't understand his obsession with baseball, but I can pretend to like to watch it if he wants."

Porter let out a long breath and stared at her so long, Riley squirmed. "What?"

"Thank you."

"You're welcome."

"I'll pay you for your time, of course."

Riley held up her hand. "No, you won't."

"Yeah, Rile, I will."

"Here's the thing...if you start paying me, then I'll feel like your employee. And it'll make our friendship, relationship, neighborship, whatever you want to call it, feel uneven."

"You're right," he said after a second or two. "But you'll need to come over *here* when Logan gets home and eat my food. I'll get Netflix so you won't be bored, and I'll get a TV for Logan's room and get the premium sports channels so he can watch baseball in his room, and you can watch whatever you want out here. You can use my wi-fi. I'll upgrade it to the fastest speed available, so if you need to work here, you can."

"Porter, it's fine. Seriously."

He moved closer then, and didn't stop until he was standing right in front of her. Riley had to tilt her head back to keep eye contact with him. He slowly reached for her, giving her time to step away, to reject his touch. She didn't move.

His fingers curled around the back of her neck, and his thumb caressed the skin just below her ear. "Seems I have a lot of regrets lately. Not contacting my sister, not knowing about my nephew's existence...not getting to know my neighbor before now."

Riley knew she had a stupid grin on her face, but she couldn't help it. Then she sobered. "I like you, Porter, but I'm also a little gun-shy after dating some seriously not-good men."

He nodded. "I get it. I'm going to be busy with trying to figure out how to raise a kid, so I'm not sure how much time I'll have to be more than a friend, anyway."

"So maybe we can take things one day at a time. Not rush into anything," Riley suggested, mentally wincing at how lame she sounded.

"Deal. And for the record, I'm nothing like that asshole Miles. I will *not* raise my voice to you or Logan."

"I know. You're a good man," Riley blurted, repeating what she'd told Logan.

Porter winced. "Not all the time, but I try." He took a step back, and Riley hated how cold she felt without the warmth of his hand on her neck and without him standing close.

"I'm going to make sure I'm home when he gets here for at least a week, but if you wanted to come over and hang out with us, that might help make him more comfortable. Then when it's just the two of you, it won't feel so weird or like you're his babysitter. It sounds as if he's used to being on his own a lot, and I don't want him to think I don't trust him or anything."

And again, Porter's insight and concern about Logan was extremely touching. "Sounds good."

"I'll text you with his bus schedule. I do appreciate your help."

"Of course. You're doing a good job with him. I know it's only been a day, but seriously, you are. The bed, the baseball stuff, the food and chores, it's all good."

"I'm making shit up as I go," Porter admitted.

"Which makes it even more impressive. I'm gonna go and let you have some time to yourself. I'm guessing you aren't used to making small talk all day."

He laughed. "Never talked so much in all my life."

"Enjoy the rest of your evening."

"I'll walk you home," Porter said.

Riley laughed. "It's just down the hall."

"Yup," Porter agreed.

Knowing she wouldn't be able to talk him out of it, and secretly loving how protective he was, Riley headed for the door. He walked the short distance with her to her own apartment, then put his hands in his pockets and nodded at her awkwardly. "Thanks again. Your casserole dish will be clean and waiting for you tomorrow."

"So I can fill it with something else?" Riley teased.

"If you want," Porter said with a smile.

Immediately, she began to think about what else she might make that the guys next door would like. "I'll see you later."

"Later," Porter said, sounding exactly like his nephew had earlier.

Closing the door, Riley listened as Porter's door closed and his television came on. She hadn't really thought too much about how thin the walls were before last night, but as she stood in her apartment now, she knew with certainty that Porter *had* heard every single word Miles had ever yelled at her. It was embarrassing, but she pushed it to the back of her mind.

Her neighbor had admitted he liked her, regardless of what he'd overheard.

Smiling to herself, Riley headed for her bedroom. Her life had changed quickly, but she was used to that. Although it was nice that this time, it seemed to be for the better.

CHAPTER FIVE

Oz was hot, tired, and irritated after the training session he and his team had participated in that day. Yet nothing could dampen his excitement when he thought about heading home. It was an odd feeling. In the past, he never looked forward to the end of the day and going back to his empty apartment. He liked training. He liked crawling around in the dirt and baking in the Texas sun. But now he had Logan to look forward to seeing.

His nephew had only been living with him for a week and a half, but Oz's life had completely changed in that time. He loved hearing how his days at school went. He was still settling in, and Oz knew the kids at school hadn't been completely welcoming to Logan, but the boy was working on it, and Oz couldn't have been more pleased when Logan had started a conversation about the best way to make friends.

They weren't exactly chummy yet, but Oz took pleasure in the fact that Logan was at least talking to him now.

Then there was Riley.

When he'd asked his neighbor if she wouldn't mind looking after Logan in the afternoons until he got home from work, he'd done so out of necessity, but also because he was truly interested in getting to know her.

She and Logan seemed to be growing closer by the day. He might have been irritated that they'd bonded so easily, while he and his nephew were still somewhat tiptoeing around each other, getting used to their new normal, but Riley was so outgoing and friendly, he couldn't get upset.

Oz had been able to convince her to stay and have dinner with them each night, though inevitably, she'd go back to her own place right after they ate. She'd told him that she wanted him to have one-on-one time with Logan. He supposed she was right, and he wanted that time with his nephew...but he found himself disappointed to see her go each evening.

Riley Rogers was funny, compassionate, pretty, interesting, and Oz wanted to spend more time with her.

A lot of things about being a single father were a surprise to him, but one of the most frustrating was how hard it was to cultivate a new relationship. He couldn't leave Logan by himself, and the kid was pretty much always around, so the opportunities to let Riley know he was already interested in more than a neighborly relationship were slim.

But this weekend, Grover was having a get-together at his house. He'd just bought an old farmhouse on a bit of land. He needed help cleaning up the property and tearing down an old barn, and the team never passed up any opportunity to get together outside of work.

"So, ten o'clock tomorrow?" Lefty asked Grover. They were all standing in the parking lot chatting before they headed home.

"Yeah. But really, any time works. I'll probably get up early and start, but you guys can come over whenever," Grover said. "Devyn is spending the night with me and she's going to make sure we're fed."

Lucky seemed to perk up at that. "I can get there as early as you need me," he said.

Doc chuckled. "Out of the goodness of your heart, right? The fact that Grover's sister will be there has no bearing on what time you show up to help."

Everyone chuckled. It was no secret that Lucky was interested in Devyn, but, so far, she was doing her best to keep him at arm's length.

"For the record, and as I've told you before, I'm perfectly all right with you going out with my sister," Grover said. "The thing about Devyn is that when she's scared, she goes overboard trying to pretend everything's all right. She's always been that way. And ever since she's moved to Texas, she's done nothing but pretend."

"What's she scared of?" Lucky asked.

"I have no clue," Grover said on a sigh, running a hand through his hair. "I trust you with my life, so I certainly trust you with my sister's. As far as I'm concerned, you have my heartfelt support if you wanted to try to convince her to go out with you. All I ask is that you have a care...and let me know if you find out anything worrisome."

"I can do that," Lucky told his friend solemnly. "But, you have to remember that Devyn isn't five years old anymore. She might be your little sister, but she's also a grown woman."

"I know. But I can't help but remember the sick little girl when I look at her. We thought we'd lose her to the leukemia, and it's hard to shake that feeling, even years later. And that's part of the reason I haven't demanded she tell me what the hell is going on," Grover said. "I haven't wanted to say or do anything that will make her decide not to confide in her older brother. Anyway, what about the rest of you? Any idea when you might come over?"

"Gillian and I will probably be there closer to eleven. It's the weekend, and I don't get too many mornings where I can lie in bed being lazy with my wife," Trigger said with a grin.

"Kinley and I'll be there around ten," Lefty said.

"Same for me and Aspen," Brain added.

"I can get there around eight or nine," Doc volunteered.

"You gonna bring your pretty neighbor?" Trigger asked Oz.

He nodded. "I'll try." Oz had told his friends all about Riley and how helpful she'd been.

"So her hanging around has been working out?" Lefty asked.

"Extremely much so," Oz told his friends. Even he was surprised at how well things were going. One night he'd been agonizing over who to put down as the secondary emergency contact for Logan's school, and she'd volunteered. She'd reasoned that since she was home most of the day, she could easily get to Logan's school quickly if she was needed.

"Gillian's looking forward to meeting her," Trigger said.

"I think she's eager to meet Gillian and the others too," Oz said. "Although she's nervous about coming face-to-face with *you* guys."

"You told her what you do?" Lefty asked.

"No. But I think Logan might've said something. Remember when I told him at the office that we were special forces? I think he passed that along. She's made a few comments about my teammates that make me think she realizes we aren't regular Army," Oz said.

"Are you worried about that?" Doc asked.

"Not in the least," Oz said honestly. "The woman is looking after my nephew. I trust her. I just haven't had time to sit down and talk to her without Logan being there."

"You found out any more information about where all his stuff is?" Trigger asked.

Oz shook his head. "No. I called CPS, and they said they'd get back to me. It makes no sense that they'd take a kid out of his own house with only a garbage bag of belongings."

"You want me to make some inquiries?" Grover asked.

"Thanks, but no. Logan's okay for now. I mean, I wish I could get him some mementoes of his mom and shit, but he's not hurting for clothes or toys or anything. I'm just irritated at the secrecy."

"When kids are involved, there's always secrecy," Lucky said. "I mean, I don't know firsthand, but the government is generally pretty close-mouthed when it comes to anything with kids."

"Yeah. Anyway, Logan's good. I think he'll enjoy getting out and getting some fresh air tomorrow. I do worry about him being around all the equipment and stuff though," Oz said.

"Don't worry. We'll watch out for him. He'll be fine," Grover assured him.

"Any word about Somalia?" Oz asked Trigger. He'd been worrying about the increasing tension over there. It was part of the reason they'd been training so hard lately. He usually loved going on missions, but the potential timing for this one wasn't great. He wanted more time to bond with Logan, to reassure him that he was safe and, even if Oz was deployed, he would still be taken care of and wouldn't return to the system.

"Nothing new since this morning," Trigger said. "We're still on standby. You know I'll let you know as soon as I find something out."

Oz nodded. He didn't want to think about leaving...even as he felt guilty that a tiny part of him was kind of looking forward to it. Being a single dad was *hard*, and heading out on a mission would give him a break. Which was why he felt guilty. It had only been a week and a half and he was already looking for a reprieve. It was so confusing, being responsible for another human being. He *wanted* to see Logan, liked having him in his life, but not having time to himself was taking a bit of getting used to.

Glancing at his watch, Oz saw that it was already five-thirty. He'd sent Riley a text letting her know he might be a little later getting home today, and she'd been okay with hanging out with Logan until he got back.

"See you tomorrow," he called out as he headed for his white Ford Expedition. It didn't take long to navigate the roads to his apartment complex. The good thing about living in Killeen was that there wasn't as much traffic as in Austin or the bigger cities.

Jogging up the stairs to his floor, Oz looked forward to finding out if Logan was having a good Friday. What he'd learned at school...and particularly, if he'd made any friends yet. The latter worried Oz. He wanted his nephew to look forward to going to school, not to dread it because of a lack of friends.

He couldn't stop thinking about Riley either. At least part of his impatience to get home had to do with her. He knew she was great with kids, was a hell of a cook, and was a very hard worker. But he wanted to find out other, more personal stuff. Was she a dog or cat person? Did she like to do outdoorsy stuff or was she content to hang inside? Did she like surprises, did she go all out in decorating for the holidays, was she a bed hog? Things he typically found out from dating a woman.

And Oz definitely wanted to take Riley on a date. Wanted to pamper her, show her his appreciation for all her help. He'd already learned that when she stood and stretched after dinner, she was about to say her goodbyes. While he appreciated her trying not to wear out her welcome and giving him time alone with Logan, he hated to see her go.

When Oz entered his apartment, he immediately knew it was empty. He didn't hear Riley's laughter or Logan's higher-pitched voice. There was no tantalizing smell of anything cooking coming from the kitchen.

Just before he began to panic, Oz saw a note propped up in the middle of the table.

He picked it up and read Riley's feminine handwriting.

. . .

We're going stir crazy inside. We went down to that little park across from the apartment complex. Logan's going to show me how to throw a baseball. Pray for me! Lol I didn't want you to worry if you got back before we did. I thought you guys could have a junk food/frozen food night—chicken nuggets, French fries, pizza rolls. I brought over my air fryer for you to borrow. See you soon.

-Riley

Oz realized he was grinning. Then he sobered. It sounded like she wasn't planning on joining them for dinner, and that thought was depressing. She probably had other stuff to do.

Shit...maybe she had a date?

He dismissed that thought. He didn't think she'd take Logan to the park if she had to get ready to go out later, but then again, he didn't know how long it took Riley to get ready for a date. The possibility was there that she *did* have a date. She was pretty damn amazing, and any guy would be lucky as hell to call her his girlfriend.

With that thought fresh in his mind, Oz didn't hesitate to turn and head for the door once more. He stunk from being out in the hot sun all day while training, but he didn't want to wait a minute longer than necessary to see Riley and his nephew.

He crossed the parking lot and headed for the small park across the street. It was nothing more than an open stretch of grass with a swing set and slide. But the large open area next to the playground was perfect for throwing a ball back and forth. Making a mental note to take Logan out here more often, he headed for the only two people in the park.

As he approached, he saw Logan pull his arm back and let loose a pitch toward Riley.

She held up the baseball glove in her hand—and closed her eyes as the ball approached.

Oz could see what was about to happen seconds before it did, but he couldn't move fast enough to stop it.

The ball swerved a little, and because Riley had her eyes closed, she didn't move the glove to catch it.

Instead, it hit her cheek, bouncing off and landing in the grass nearby. She let out a small noise of distress and immediately fell to her knees, cradling her cheek with her hand.

Oz was by her side within moments of her being struck. "Let me see," he ordered, putting his hand over hers on her cheek.

Riley shook her head. "Give me a second."

"I need to see how bad it is," Oz told her.

She looked at him, and he saw tears in the one eye she had open. His stomach clenched.

"I'm okay," she said, and Oz could literally see her trying to pull herself together. His admiration of her increased.

"I'm sure you are. But please, let me just look at it for a second?" He needed to see if her cheekbone was broken or if the ball had busted any blood vessels in her eye.

Slowly, Riley lowered her hand, and Oz's gaze ran over her cheek. It was red, and she'd probably have a black eye, but nothing seemed out of place or swollen yet. He very gently probed the skin of her cheek, noting how soft it was in the process. "Can you open your eye?"

She nodded and slowly opened the eye on the side of her face that had been hit. Besides the tears, it looked okay. Letting out his breath, Oz gave her a small smile. "You're okay. You're probably gonna have a shiner, but it doesn't look or feel as if anything's broken."

"Are you a medic?" she asked.

"Well, no. Doc's the go-to guy as far as medical issues on the team, but we've all had training."

She nodded, then her gaze flicked behind him. "Logan," she whispered.

Turning, Oz looked for his nephew. He was still standing where he'd been when he'd thrown the ball—and he looked frozen in place. His eyes were wide and his face was as white as a sheet.

Immediately concerned, Oz stood.

The second he did, Logan took a quick step backward.

Instinctively, Oz stilled. Not wanting the boy to turn around and run—which it was obvious he was ready to do—Oz put his hands out to his sides, trying to look as nonthreatening as possible. "She's okay, Slugger."

Logan didn't respond. He kept his eyes on Oz's hands.

And that killed Oz. Not because of his nephew's fear, but because of what it *meant*. "I'm not mad. Neither is Riley. Accidents happen. She's okay."

Then Riley was at his side, doing what she could to reassure the boy. "I obviously suck at this baseball thing. Your favorite outfielder would be mortified with me," she said, trying to lighten the situation.

But Logan didn't relax. He stayed right where he was, every muscle taut and ready to bolt.

"Look at me, Logan," Oz ordered gently. He waited until Logan had raised his eyes to meet his gaze. "It was an *accident*. Riley's okay. You're okay. I'm not mad. Everything's fine."

Logan blinked, and Oz was glad to see his words were finally sinking in.

"I didn't mean it," Logan said softly.

"I know you didn't."

"I didn't mean to throw it so hard."

"I shouldn't have closed my eyes," Riley said. "You told me to keep my eye on the ball, and I didn't. This is all *my* fault, not yours."

Logan's shoulders relaxed a fraction, but it was obvious his guard was still up. "Are you going to spank me?"

There was so much Oz wanted to say. His mind was whirling with all the reasons why Logan was so completely terrified, but all he said was, "No."

"I'll go to bed without dinner," he offered.

"Not necessary," Oz told him. "There are plenty of times I've made a mistake, but that doesn't mean I needed to be punished for them. I'm going to come closer. Don't run, please," he told his nephew. Then he turned to Riley for a second. "You okay?"

"I'm good," she said immediately. She'd put her hand back up to her cheek, and it was obvious it still hurt, but she was doing what she could to downplay it. For Logan's sake. His admiration for her rose tenfold, and he was immensely grateful. "I'll get you some ice as soon as we get back to my apartment. Just hang in there another few minutes."

"I'm okay," she told him. "Take care of Logan. He needs to know you aren't going to hurt him."

Oz knew that, and the thought of his nephew being scared of him was extremely upsetting. The thought of anyone putting their hands on this boy made his fists clench. But he immediately relaxed and opened his hands, not wanting to scare Logan any more than he already was.

He took a step toward his nephew, then another, relieved when the boy didn't bolt. He got within six feet of Logan, then got down on his knees and sat on his heels, hoping the position would help the boy feel safer. "It was an accident, Slugger," he repeated. "It happens."

"I hurt Riley," Logan said, his lower lip quivering.

"You did," Oz said. Then added, "But she's okay."

"I deserve to be beaten," Logan whimpered.

"No, you don't," Oz said, memories welling up inside him. "What would that do? You already apologized and said you didn't mean to do it. Riley's already admitted that she should've kept her eyes open and at the very least dodged the ball. What would me or Riley hitting you accomplish? Would it take back what happened?"

Oz waited until Logan shook his head.

"Would it make you feel less guilty?"

"No."

"Would it make Riley feel better?"

"Maybe," was the answer that time.

"It most certainly would not," Riley said from behind him. Oz could hear that she'd moved closer, but she wasn't crowding him or Logan.

"My dad used to hit me and your mom when we were young. It didn't happen all the time, he usually just yelled at us. But every now and then he'd surprise us by being violent. He'd smack me when I didn't want to eat something he'd made for dinner. He'd punch me in the back when I didn't move fast enough for him. He'd backhand me in the car if I said something he didn't like. All that hitting didn't do anything but scare me. And make me sad. Did your mom hit you when you messed up?" Oz wasn't sure he wanted to know the answer.

But he was deeply relieved when Logan shook his head. "No. Sometimes her boyfriends."

"Right. I need you to listen to me, Slugger. Are you listening?"

Logan nodded.

"I will *never* hit you. Ever. No matter what you do. I might speak to you in a very stern voice that might be a little scary. I might ask you to take a time-out so we can have some space away from each other, so we can both calm down. I might even make you do extra chores around the house. But I will never raise my hand to you. It's *never* okay to strike someone smaller or weaker than you. Ever. Women, children, or even men. I'm not going to go so far as to tell you that you should never hit anyone in your entire life, because sometimes you have to stick up for and protect yourself, and others around you. But you should never raise your fists or kick anyone who can't defend themselves."

Oz prayed his words were sinking in. The last thing he wanted was Logan to always be tiptoeing around him, afraid he was going to be beaten or screamed at if he did the slightest thing wrong. Oz had grown up that way, and it had sucked.

Several moments went by, until Logan finally asked, "Promise?"

"I promise," Oz said, making a cross over his chest as he said it. "On my honor as a soldier, I will not hit you. No matter what."

Then his nephew's lip began to quiver again. "I didn't mean to hurt you," he told Riley, right before he burst into tears.

Riley had moved around Oz before he could get off the ground. She wrapped her arms around the little boy and rocked him back and forth. "I know you didn't. I apparently just stink at baseball. If we ever go to a game, you'll have to make sure to watch out for foul balls so they don't hit me."

Logan nodded against her.

Oz came up beside Riley and reached for her face. He gently ran his thumb over her red and slightly puffy cheek. The mark looked way too much like she'd been punched in the face, and it made him extremely uncomfortable.

"Logan? We need to get Riley back and get some ice on her face."

His nephew looked up at him and nodded. He took a step away from Riley and wiped the tears from his cheeks as he regained his composure.

"Will you go grab the ball and her mitt before we go?" Oz asked.

Logan nodded again and jogged toward the baseball, behind where Riley had been standing while they'd been playing catch.

Knowing he only had seconds before Logan would be back, Oz said, "The same goes for you. I might be bigger and stronger, but I won't hit you either, Riley. I won't scream insults at you or belittle you. I admire you way too much to do anything that would hurt you."

"I know," she said.

Their gazes stayed locked, and Oz swore he saw more than friendship in her eyes. But then Logan was back, interrupting the moment. Without thought, he held out his hand to his nephew.

When Logan looked down at his hand and hesitated, Oz mentally kicked himself. *Too soon*, he told himself. Dropping his hand, he said, "Come on, let's get home. I don't know about you, but I'm starving. I've been out in the sun all day and could use some junk food." That was a lie. Oz never ate junk, but for his nephew, he'd do just about anything.

"You do stink a little," Logan said.

Oz was about to respond...when he felt a small hand slip into his own.

His heart swelling, Oz smiled down at his nephew. "Yeah, well, you spend all day crawling around in the dirt and see if you smell like roses afterward."

"Do you like it?" Logan asked.

Oz couldn't stop himself from reaching for Riley's hand. She'd scared the hell out of him when she'd fallen to her knees, and he needed that connection with her. She'd gotten hurt because she'd been playing with his nephew. Then she'd been right there at his back, trying to console Logan, make him feel safe. Nothing felt more right than standing between the two of them, their hands connected, as they walked back toward his apartment.

"I don't like it, I love it," Oz responded to Logan's question. He hadn't known his nephew long, but he could barely imagine a time when this kid wasn't in his life. And every day, they seemed to get more comfortable with each other.

Every day, Logan asked more questions, opened up about his likes and dislikes. It was exciting and scary at the same time. "I hope when you get older, you can find something to do that you absolutely love. That you're passionate about."

They chatted about bugs, dirt, and what they thought the worst smells in the world were as they headed back to Oz's apartment. When they reached the door, Oz dropped Logan's and Riley's hands as he reached for his key.

"I'll just head back to my place," Riley said.

Oz turned to stare at her. "What?"

"I'm gonna go home," she repeated, indicating her door with her thumb.

"No," Oz said resolutely, pushing open his door and reaching for Riley's arm.

She let him pull her into his apartment but as soon as the door was shut, she said, "Porter, I—"

He cut her off by turning to Logan. "Will you go to my bathroom and grab the blue bottle of pain reliever in the cabinet next to the sink?"

Without a word, Logan ran toward his uncle's bedroom.

"Seriously, I'm fine, Porter. You guys need some time."

"Wrong. We need to take care of you. Make sure you're okay. Logan needs to do it because he's the one who hurt you. I need to do it because the thought of you being next door and hurting tears me up inside."

She blinked. "I...I'm just your neighbor."

Riley didn't sound as if she was one hundred percent sure about that, which he liked. A lot. "Wrong," Oz told her without hesitation. "You're so much more than *just* my neighbor. I know things are a little weird because you're helping me with Logan, but let me be clear. I want to go out with you, Riley. I want to take you out to dinner, flirt with you, see if you taste as good as you smell, and show you in every way I can think of that I'm interested in you *not* because of what you've done for me and Logan, but because of who you are as a person."

"Oh...um...okay," she stammered.

"Okay?" he asked. "You'll go out with me?"

She gave him a shy smile and nodded.

"And you'll let me pamper you a bit tonight? I hate that you got hurt. The fact that you were totally out of your element throwing that ball with Logan, but did it anyway to try to make him happy, means the world to me. But maybe no more baseball throwing with him for a while, at least until I teach you how to catch. I'll do a better job of taking him outside and playing with him."

"I don't need to be pampered."

"Fine. I'll just play doctor with you then," Oz teased.

She blushed and gave him another small grin.

"Besides, if I have to eat this crap tonight, you do too."

She chuckled. "You might find you like it."

"Doubt it."

"Famous last words."

"Here it is!" Logan said as he ran up to them with the small bottle in his hands.

"Thanks, Slugger. Let's get Riley settled on the couch, and we'll put together an ice pack for her and get her something to drink so she can swallow the pills. Then you can help me get dinner ready."

"Chicken nuggets. Yum!" Logan said with a wide grin.

"Oh, yeah, yum," Oz said with as much enthusiasm as he could muster. He heard Riley snicker quietly. He put his arm around her and pulled her against his side. He enjoyed hearing her laugh turn to an inhale as he touched her.

She was soft in all the right places, and he loved how she fit against him. He helped her to the couch—not that she really *needed* help; it was just a blessing to be able to touch her and have his arm around her for once. When she was settled, he put a hand on Logan's shoulder and led him to the kitchen.

"Let's see what damage two guys can do in here, shall we?" he asked his nephew.

The smile on the little boy's face reminded him so much of his sister's, Oz had to close his eyes for a second.

He would treasure every minute he had with this kid because he knew all too soon, Logan would grow up and move out on his own. He'd missed the first ten years, but he'd do whatever it took to make his nephew feel safe, loved, and protected for the rest of his life.

CHAPTER SIX

One of the reasons Riley had been leaving right after dinner each night was to try to keep herself from falling so hard and fast for Porter. But it was obvious that hadn't helped. The man was lethal. Good-looking, considerate, and an amazingly good father, even if he'd been thrown into it unexpectedly.

She'd intended to entertain Logan for an hour or so until his uncle came home, then leave them to their frozen-food dinner.

Of course, that's not how things turned out.

Her face was still throbbing and the memory of the immediate pain that had bloomed in her cheek as the baseball hit her was still very fresh in her mind. She'd been appalled that Logan had been so scared of being disciplined for something that had been an accident. But she had to admit that Porter had done an amazing job of soothing his nephew, of reassuring him that he'd never hit him.

Then when he'd told her the same thing, Riley was a goner. She knew he was partially referring to Miles with his declaration, and while that embarrassed her, she decided to focus on the meaning behind his words rather than shame for her past decisions.

Riley always seemed to fall hard and fast for men. She tried to curb her enthusiasm when she began dating someone, but she tended to want to see the good in people. And she was lonely. But after Miles, easily her worst boyfriend yet, she'd been determined to be on her own for a while.

Of course, that was before Porter stormed into her life with his adorable nephew.

Now he wanted to take her out. She hadn't even hesitated to agree. He was unlike anyone she'd ever dated, in all the good ways.

And spending time with Logan was fun too. The boy was smart, and every day she learned something new about him. As she sat on the couch and listened to Porter and Logan talk about the best way to make an ice pack and what would be the most comfortable for her, she smiled, only wincing slightly at the pain it caused.

Her phone buzzed with a text, and Riley frowned as she read it.

Miles had been a pain in her ass ever since she'd kicked him out. At first he was full of apologies and saying he was sorry, but that had morphed into him calling her all sorts of names for ignoring him and cussing her out over text. She'd hoped he'd get the message that they were well and truly done, but he wouldn't stop harassing her.

Riley had searched her apartment from top to bottom and put everything she'd thought was his in a box and placed it in the mail room. She'd told Miles what she'd done and told him to come and get it before someone stole it. She'd noticed the next day that the box was gone, but Miles hadn't stopped texting and calling.

Now he was saying that she hadn't given him back everything, that he wanted to come over and find his shit himself. Which wasn't happening. Riley wasn't stupid. She wasn't going to let him back into her apartment. He'd try to claim stuff that wasn't his and probably rob her blind.

She knew Porter would help her if she asked, but she was too embarrassed to involve him. Miles would *definitely* say lots of horrible shit if he saw Porter helping her, and she'd die of mortification, even if Porter didn't believe anything Miles said.

She could handle Miles on her own. He'd get tired of harassing her sooner or later, she just had to wait him out.

She ignored the text, just as she had most of his others.

The differences between her ex and Porter were night and day. She tried to imagine what Miles would've done if he'd seen her get hit in the face by a baseball, and decided he'd probably laugh and tell her she should've ducked.

Remembering the fear and concern in Porter's tone and touch as he'd knelt next to her on the ground made Riley close her eyes briefly to stem her emotions. It had been a very long time since someone had been so concerned about her well-being. Her parents had loved her in their own way, but they'd never been very touchy-feely. They were too busy getting drunk or trying to defend their parenting skills to the authorities to bother doing something as common as hug her.

"Here's some water, Riley," Logan said as he very carefully handed her a glass.

"Thanks, Logan. I appreciate it."

He stood there staring at her.

"What?"

"Oz told me to make sure you took the pills and didn't try to pretend you were all good."

Riley chuckled. It seemed Porter knew her pretty well already. She didn't like taking any kind of drug, even if it was just Aleve. But she didn't want to worry Logan more than he already was, so she opened the bottle and shook out two pills. She put them in her mouth and washed them down with the water.

"Good girl," Porter said from her right.

God, that sounded amazing.

71

Riley needed to get herself together.

"We put ice in a bag, then wrapped it up with a pillow-case. A towel is too thick so you won't feel the cold so well, and paper towels get wet and soggy. Oz suggested the pillow-case. If it gets too wet, just let me know and I'll get a new one." Logan's tone was full of both concern and excitement. It was obvious he was worried about her, and still remorseful.

Riley reached for the ice pack. "Thank you for taking such good care of me," she told the boy.

"We're making chicken nuggets, pizza rolls, and cheese sticks for dinner," he informed her.

Riley already knew that, but nodded anyway. "Sounds good."

"I've never had pizza rolls before," Logan admitted.

"You're gonna like them," Riley assured him. She had no idea if he would or not, but she wasn't going to say anything to discourage him. She'd found out over the last week and a half that Logan was pretty guarded, but when he tried some-thing new, especially food, he was usually pleasantly surprised.

Porter lifted his hand to scratch his face, and Riley noticed that Logan visibly startled, scooting out of the way of his uncle's arm. Porter saw his reaction too, but he didn't say anything. It was still going to take some time for Logan to trust that when his uncle said he wouldn't hit him, he was telling the truth.

Riley wasn't surprised. She'd had a very hard time trusting people for a long while after she'd moved away from home. She'd believed her parents when they said they were going to try harder. That she wouldn't be taken away again. And time and time again, they'd lied, fallen back into their old behav-iors of drinking too much and neglecting her. She'd trusted the wrong people in her early twenties, and even now that she was twenty-eight, she'd still trusted Miles when he said he was going to get a job.

But somehow, she knew Porter was telling the truth when

he'd told her and Logan he wouldn't hurt them. He oozed goodness from every pore, and it was refreshing.

It would take a few rounds in the air fryer for all the food to be cooked, and after asking permission, Logan wandered off to his room to wait. That left Riley and Porter alone in the living room.

"Does it still hurt?" Porter asked as he perched on the edge of the couch next to her.

"Just a little," Riley said.

"I know the ice is probably uncomfortable, but keep it on your face as long as possible. It'll help with the swelling, and hopefully it'll make the black eye you'll probably have not as dark."

"Okay."

Porter looked down at his lap then. "He was so scared."

Riley knew exactly who Porter was talking about. "He was," she agreed.

"He thought I was going to beat him," Porter whispered.

Riley nodded.

"I mean, I'm not an idiot, I know that happens all over the world. But I *hate* that he learned that in my sister's home. Becky tried to protect me from our dad, but it never worked, he'd just smack her around, then start on me. I begged her to stay out of his way when he got into one of his moods. We had some long talks about how when we grew up, we'd never let anyone treat us like that again. I can't believe she hooked up with men who were just like our dad. And to let them hit her kid?" Porter shook his head. "It makes me so sad."

Riley reached out with her free hand and put it on Porter's thigh. It wasn't a sexual touch; she wanted to comfort him. "You can't blame your sister. Drugs are horrible, but once someone is hooked, it's so hard to get off them. And nothing matters, not eating, not doing what they need to be safe, and, unfortunately, not any children they might have. And a lot of people are dishonest. Becky could've started dating a man who she thought would help her kick her habit, or who would treat her and her son kindly, but then found out he wasn't anything like she'd thought. And once in an abusive relationship, especially if someone is hooked on drugs, it's not that easy to get out. Cut her some slack, Porter."

He took a deep breath and covered her hand with his own. "I'm guessing you're talking from experience, which I *also* hate."

"Things with Miles didn't get that far. And you're right, I've been in an abusive relationship in my past, and one of the hardest things I've ever done was finally ending it and getting away. I swore I'd never date anyone like that again...then I met Miles, and we both know how that turned out."

"But you kicked him out before things went too far," Porter said.

"Yeah. But I don't have a kid. And if I did, and if I'd lived with Miles, it wouldn't have been as easy to simply leave," Riley argued, still wanting to make her point.

"I'm beginning to understand more, and I've only had Logan for a short time. I've been very judgmental about anyone who does drugs, and I'm just starting to see that everything isn't always black and white. I do feel better because Logan says that Becky had changed recently. I just hate seeing the fear in his eyes when he looks at me or when I move too fast."

"Give him time. He watches everything you do very carefully. He mimics you all the time. He'll learn that you have nothing but his best intentions at heart. You'll earn his trust before long, I know it."

Porter studied her. "Will I earn yours?" he asked.

Riley blinked. "I trust you."

"Do you?" he asked with a tilt of his head. "There are times I think you do...then I'll ask an innocent question about the texts you've been receiving, and you deflect the conversation, hoping I'll drop it. I also see you watching me just as carefully as Logan, as if you're waiting for me to turn on you."

Riley sighed and tried to pull her hand back, but Porter held it tightly. She was embarrassed that she was sitting here preaching about trust and being patient, and he'd seen right through her.

"I'm gonna earn your trust too," Porter repeated confidently. "You'll see that I can be your safe haven. That if you give me all of you, I'll do everything in my power to protect you. From me, from assholes who think they can take advantage of you simply because you're a woman, and even from your own self-destructive thoughts. I'll treasure you exactly how you are, because I happen to think you're pretty amazing."

Riley stared at Porter, unsure she was really hearing him right.

The air fryer buzzed, letting them know the first batch of food was done. Porter held her gaze as he leaned forward, and Riley closed her eyes.

She felt his lips touch her forehead lightly, then he stood.

She opened her eyes and watched him stride into the kitchen. He unloaded the first batch of food, putting it into a bowl and sticking that into the oven to keep it warm, before he dumped another bag of food into the basket and restarted the air fryer.

He came back into the living room and asked, "Do you need anything? Something different to drink? And don't ask for alcohol, it wouldn't be a good idea right now. I've got more water, tea, and I might be able to scrounge up a soft drink from somewhere."

"I'm good with the water Logan brought me earlier," she told him.

"Okay. I'm gonna check on Logan. When I come back, are you still gonna be here?"

Riley raised an eyebrow. "You think I'd sneak out while you were with your nephew?"

Porter studied her for another long moment. "Maybe," he said. "I know you were gonna go back to your place if I didn't pull you into my apartment before you could really protest. And for the record, that was out of character for me. I don't usually haul women around to places they don't want to be."

"If I didn't want to be here, I wouldn't be here," Riley told him. "My cheek might be throbbing, I might not want to make a scene in front of Logan, and I might be a foot shorter than you, but I would've put up a fight if I truly didn't want to come inside."

Porter smiled. "Noted. If the air fryer goes off, the last batch of junk to go in is right beside it. Just dump what's in there into the bowl in the oven and add the new stuff."

"I know how to use my own air fryer," Riley said with a smile.

"Are you sure I can't grill up a steak? It won't take long," Porter asked, looking like a little kid begging for a piece of candy.

"You'll live if you eat one meal of frozen food," she informed him.

Sighing and acting like she'd just taken away his favorite toy, Porter said, "Oh, all right."

Riley couldn't help but chuckle. And that made her cheek throb. "Ow," she complained, but didn't stop smiling.

Immediately, Porter's demeanor changed. "Maybe I should call Doc and see if he can come over and look at that cheek. You might be hurt worse than I thought."

He made a move to get his phone, which was sitting on the kitchen counter, but Riley stopped him. "I'm fine. Promise. I'm just going to be sore for a while."

"Okay, but if you don't feel any better by the end of the night, if that ice and the pills don't take the edge off, I'm calling Doc."

Riley already felt better than she had when they first got back to his apartment, so she knew his treatment was working, but she agreed anyway. "Okay. Go check on Logan."

Porter eyed her for a long moment, then nodded and turned to head down the hall.

Once he was out of her sight, Riley leaned back against the couch cushion and sighed. She'd thought her evening would be pretty boring; she'd say hi to Porter when he got home, then she'd go back to her apartment and read or watch TV while listening to the muffled sounds of her neighbors getting settled for the night through the thin walls. But instead, she'd gotten hurt, Porter had more than taken care of her, they'd learned that Logan had a ways to go before he'd be able to trust again, and Riley had agreed to go out on a date with the neighbor she had a massive crush on. It was crazy how fast things in life could change.

Forty minutes later, Riley smiled at the two males sitting across from her. After staring at the pizza rolls suspiciously, Logan cautiously nibbled on the corner of one. His eyes had widened and he'd declared them "delicious." He and Porter had inhaled the chicken nuggets, pizza rolls, and the cheese sticks. Porter had even dug out a package of French fries from the bottom of his freezer and air fried those as well.

"I have to admit...that was pretty darn good," Porter said.

Riley could only smirk at him.

Then he turned to Logan. "But don't get used to it. We need to balance out the crap we eat with good stuff. Tomorrow, we'll load up on vegetables to balance out our bodies again."

"Okay," Logan said.

Riley could only shake her head at the kid in surprise. Most children she knew balked at eating any kind of vegetables, but obviously, Logan thought pretty highly of what his uncle said and thought, even after only a week and a half.

Then Porter turned to her. "What else can that air fryer do?"

"Apple chips, cinnamon rolls, banana s'mores, French toast sticks, hamburgers, grilled-cheese sandwiches, sweet potato tots...even pineapple cake. There are a ton of recipes on the internet for all sorts of things. Meatballs, pork chops, catfish, baked potatoes, salmon, corn on the cob, even spanakopita."

"Spank-a-ko-whatas?" Porter asked with a smile.

"Not spank, *span*-akopita. They're Greek and sooooo good," Riley informed him.

"Is there anything your air fryer can't make?" Porter asked.

She thought about it for a second before saying, "Soup."

Everyone laughed.

"Right, that would probably be bad," Porter said.

"Although I have a few Crock-Pots I could loan you if you wanted to give a soup recipe a try," she told him.

Porter held up a hand. "I'm a half-decent cook, but I'm not going to push my luck. Besides, I'd never leave a Crock-Pot on while I was out of the apartment. That's asking for trouble."

Riley wasn't surprised. Porter seemed to take safety very seriously—including hers—which pleased her to no end. Her cheek felt much better after holding the homemade ice bag on it before eating. She'd seen both Logan's and Porter's eyes flick to the red mark on her face more than once, but neither mentioned it, which she was grateful for.

"So, Logan, tomorrow we're going over to Grover's house...you think we should invite Riley?"

Riley gaped at Porter. "What?"

"He's got a barn he needs to take down at the house he just bought, because it's a safety hazard, and everyone's getting together to help him. Gillian, Kinley, Aspen, and Devyn are going to be there. Want to come?"

"Me? Um...I'm not sure," Riley stuttered.

"Oz said I could help the men," Logan said excitedly.

Her eyes met Porter's. "Is that a good idea? I mean, is it dangerous?"

If anything, his smile got wider.

"What?" Riley asked.

"I just love that you're so concerned about him. It'll be fine. We aren't going to do anything that would put him or any of us in danger," Porter told her. "It'll be good for you to get some fresh air. And I'd love for you to meet my friends."

Riley really wanted to go, but it made her nervous too. He'd told her all about the other women. It was obvious he liked and respected them, which made her feel good—but also scared her to death. What if his friends didn't like her?

She must've been quiet for too long, because Logan added his pleas to his uncle's.

"I don't know anyone either," he said. "We can hang out together if no one likes us."

The sad thing was that it sounded like Logan truly thought that was a possibility. "Who wouldn't like you?" she asked him. "You're sweet and considerate, and I'm sure you'll be a huge help to the guys." She looked at Porter. "Are you sure?"

She didn't have to elaborate on what she meant. Was he sure *he* wanted her there? Was he sure he wanted her to meet his friends? That seemed like a big step, even more than going out on an official date.

"I'm sure," he said, the two words somehow conveying exactly *how* sure he was about everything happening between them.

"Okay."

"Great!" Porter said. "I told Grover we'd be there around ten. Is nine-thirty okay to leave?"

"Of course." Riley almost opened her mouth to ask if he wanted her to make breakfast for them all, but she stopped herself at the last minute. She was beginning to enjoy spending time with these two guys a little too much. She was already in over her head, and if or when things between her and Porter didn't work out, it would be extremely awkward to live right next door to him. It would tear her apart to see him bring another woman home. To see Logan every day but not be able to share his life.

Shaking her head, Riley did her best to push those thoughts to the back of her mind. She and Porter weren't really dating yet, even if he *had* asked her out. She already had them breaking up and was getting depressed about it. She was being ridiculous.

"Be sure to wear clothes you wouldn't mind getting dirty," Porter told her. "Grover has some four-wheelers he said we could take out for a ride if we wanted. There's a trail that butts up against the property he bought."

"Jeans and a T-shirt okay?" Riley asked. "Is that what the others will be wearing?" The last thing she wanted was to show up in jeans if everyone else was in sundresses or something.

"I have no idea, but they aren't going to be dressed like they're meeting the queen of England or anything," Porter told her with a chuckle. "Stop worrying. They're going to love you."

Riley stopped the snort that wanted to escape. Guys were all the same. They were so sure a group of women would get along just because they were the same gender. She knew better. Guys were much more laid-back about meeting new people. They just went with it. But Porter bringing a chick into his inner circle was probably a whole different thing.

"They are," Porter insisted. "Trust me."

There was that trust thing again. He knew how hard it was for her to trust others, but when Riley glanced over at Logan, she saw he was nodding. If the boy could trust his uncle, she could too. She nodded as well.

Porter beamed. "Great. Logan, will you please help me bring the dishes to the kitchen?"

Riley stood up. "You guys cooked, I'll clean up," she volunteered.

"Nope. You brought over the air fryer. And I definitely need to do something more than sit on my butt after eating all that stuff. Logan and I will take care of it."

She couldn't exactly argue when he'd all but said he wanted to spend time with his nephew.

"I'll just get going then," she said as she stood.

To his credit, Porter didn't protest, simply eyed her for a long moment, probably trying to read her mind and make sure she wasn't leaving because she was uncomfortable or wasn't having a good time, and truly *did* need to get going instead. He must've seen something in her expression that reassured him, because he nodded and said, "I'll walk you to your place."

"Seriously, Porter, it's just next door."

"A man always makes sure his lady gets home safely," was all he said. Then he turned to Logan. "You good for a few minutes here on your own, Slugger?"

Logan nodded. "I don't think a velociraptor is gonna swoop down in the two minutes it'll take you to walk Riley home and kidnap me," he quipped.

For a second, Porter stared at his nephew, then he burst out laughing. "Right. I just didn't want you to get nervous in here by yourself."

Logan had laughed along with his uncle, but then he got serious. "I was alone at my other place all the time. In the last couple years, Mom worked a lot."

"I get that," Porter said. "But it's not in my make-up to leave a kid to fend for himself. I don't doubt you're responsible enough to be all right on your own, I just don't like it. It makes me uncomfortable. Having Riley come over to hang with you after school isn't because I don't trust you or because I think you're going to get in trouble, it's for my own peace of mind. Okay, Slugger?"

Logan nodded. "Okay. And...I like having her here."

Riley felt like crying again. Without even trying, Porter was showing his nephew how much he cared about him. Explaining his actions, and not making Logan feel as if he was a burden or a baby.

"Okay, so if a T-Rex or any other kind of dinosaur happens to come by in the two minutes it'll take me to walk Riley to her door to make sure there aren't any scary dinosaurs hiding over at *her* place, use your baseball bat to fend them off until I can come and help, yeah?"

Logan smiled. "Okay, Oz."

"And if you can get these dishes loaded into the dishwasher, and go through the apartment and gather up all the trash so we can bring it down to the dumpster, I'd appreciate it."

Instead of being annoyed that he was being given chores, Logan's shoulders straightened as if he was proud to be helping out. "I can do it."

"Thanks. I'll be right back," Porter said as he walked up to Riley and took her elbow in his hand and steered her to the door.

"I had fun today, Logan," Riley said. "I promise to catch the ball with my glove next time instead of my face. See you tomorrow."

"Bye," Logan said as he concentrated on carrying all three of their plates to the kitchen without dropping them.

Riley walked alongside Porter as he led them out of his apartment and down the hall to her own. She pulled her key out of her pocket and unlocked her door. Porter didn't move away from her as she did so.

When the door opened, however, he didn't push inside or in any way make her feel uncomfortable. Not that Riley was uncomfortable around him in the least. She wouldn't have had a problem if he'd wanted to come inside, but she knew they were both aware that Logan was alone next door. And even with all Porter's teasing about velociraptors, he wasn't comfortable leaving him by himself for long.

"Take another painkiller before you go to sleep," Porter ordered gently. "And it probably wouldn't hurt to ice that cheek again tonight, as well."

"I'm okay," Riley insisted.

"I don't like to see you hurting," he said softly.

She shrugged. "It's a part of life," she said philosophically.

"Doesn't mean I have to like it," he retorted. Then he placed his palm on her non-hurt cheek. "Thanks for agreeing to come tomorrow."

"Are you really sure you want me to come?" she asked once again.

"Absolutely. I haven't gotten to spend as much time with you as I'd like. And while I'll be working on the barn with my friends, so we won't be together all day, I'll still get to hang out more than just the couple hours we've gotten in the evenings."

Her skin prickled with delight.

"I'm not going to just dump you off with the ladies all day, either. I really do want to take you out on the four-wheeler. Do you have any problems with that?"

"Nope. I'm looking forward to it."

"Good."

She saw Porter's eyes darken right before he said, "I'd like to kiss you goodnight."

Swallowing hard, Riley licked her lips and nodded.

His head came down slowly, giving her time to change her mind. But there was no way Riley was going to do or say anything that would make Porter back off. She'd dreamed of this moment more times than she was comfortable admitting.

His hand was still on her face, and when his lips brushed against her own, their position felt very intimate. She rested her own hands on his waist and stood on her tiptoes to try to make things easier on him. Riley felt his other hand rest on the small of her back...but then she couldn't think about anything but how good his lips felt on her own.

He didn't crush her to him. Didn't force his tongue into her mouth. At first he merely sipped at her lips, nipping and running his tongue along them, as if he was learning her taste. But the second she opened her mouth to him, he didn't hesitate to accept her invitation.

He deepened the kiss, making Riley's head spin.

She'd been kissed a lot in her life, but nothing had turned her on as much as Porter's kiss. She could feel her nipples hardening under her shirt, and she couldn't get close enough.

Riley pressed her chest against his and opened her mouth wider. Trying to get more of him. His tongue dueled with hers, and when he tilted his head to get farther inside her, Riley's hands clutched at the material of his T-shirt.

She groaned when their movements tweaked her cheek.

Porter immediately lifted his mouth from hers.

Riley didn't want to let him go, she tried to keep contact with him, but he was too tall and too determined to make sure she was all right.

"Did I hurt you?" he asked gruffly. His lips were a little swollen from their kiss, and Riley wanted nothing more than to pull his head right back down to hers.

"No."

"You moaned," he said, informing her of something she already knew.

Closing her eyes, Riley leaned forward and rested her forehead against his chest. She could feel his heart beating hard under his shirt and she kept hold of the material. His hand had fallen from her face as she'd leaned forward, and she could feel him lightly caressing her back.

After a moment, she got her composure back and lifted her head. She didn't step out of his embrace though. Riley had no idea what she was going to say, but she shouldn't have worried. Porter said exactly what she was thinking.

"That was pretty damn amazing."

She nodded. "Yeah."

"I've never really liked kissing. I mean, it's always kind of been a means to an end for me." Porter winced. "I know that sounds bad, but it's true. With you? I feel as if I could kiss you for hours and never get bored. I love feeling your body react to my touch and caresses. It's such a fucking turn-on."

Riley could feel how his own body had reacted to their kiss. His erection was hard against her belly as she remained plastered to his front. She liked knowing she'd turned him on so much.

Licking her lips, she could still taste him on her skin.

He groaned. "On that note, I'm gonna let you go," he said, and dropped his hands. But it still took him a second to actually step away from her. His eyes roamed her face, then flicked down her body, resting a moment too long on her chest before he met her gaze again. Riley was keenly aware that her hard nipples were visible through her shirt. She'd always been a bit top heavy and self-conscious of her breasts. But seeing the approval, and desire, in Porter's eyes made her want to arch her back and preen a bit.

His hand came up and he ran his thumb over her sore cheek once more. "Thanks for being so good to Logan. You were very brave, and I know you downplayed how much pain you were in for his benefit. Means the world to me."

"He's a good kid," she said.

"He is. I'll see you in the morning. I'm gonna see if I can get Logan to eat something semi-healthy for breakfast. After that dinner we had, he'll need some protein and some veggies to make it through the day tomorrow. You too. Don't eat Pop-Tarts and doughnuts in the morning, okay? Maybe make yourself an omelet or something."

God. She'd never had someone be as concerned about her well-being as Porter.

"Okay."

"Okay." Then he ran his thumb over her lips one last time before finally stepping backward. "Lock the door," he ordered.

Knowing he'd stand there until she was safely locked inside, Riley smiled at him once more, then shut the door. She put the chain on and locked the deadbolt before she heard his footsteps going back down the hall.

Through the wall, she heard his own door open and shut then heard him talking to Logan. She couldn't make out the words, but even the low rumbly sound of their conversation soothed her. She was glad they were getting along better, and that Logan seemed more comfortable in his new environment with every day that passed.

He hadn't made many friends at school yet, which concerned her, but she hoped that with time, that would change. Logan was a little shy, but funny and sweet, and she couldn't imagine anyone not wanting to be his friend.

Riley headed for her bedroom. She took two more painkillers and soaked a washcloth in cold water and held it to her face. She was too tired to get an icepack together, so she made do with several rounds of the cold washcloth.

She changed and climbed into her bed, suddenly exhausted. She'd had a long day with work, playing with Logan, getting hurt, then enjoying the company of both Porter and Logan throughout dinner.

Then there was that kiss.

Logan made her feel beautiful and cherished, and those were things she hadn't felt much in her life. But that wasn't why she was falling for him. It was seeing how amazing he was with his nephew that had her melting inside. Anyone who could treat a scared kid the way Porter did, was someone who would treat their girlfriend with respect. At least she hoped so.

Tomorrow she'd get to see Porter interacting with his friends, and that would further show her what kind of man he was. Was he someone who would act all macho around his closest friends, or would he be the same man she'd gotten to know over the last week or so? Time would tell.

CHAPTER SEVEN

Oz hadn't been nervous to bring Riley over to Grover's house. He'd told his friends he'd be bringing her before he'd even asked if she wanted to go. He'd been pretty sure he could convince her. He also knew without a doubt the other women would like her, just as she'd enjoy their company. It was hard for him to understand why she couldn't see how amazing she was, but he supposed her upbringing had a lot to do with her nervousness. It seemed to him that the people she'd let into her life had abused her trust. Her parents. The men she'd dated. And because of her experiences, she hadn't been complimented that often. He vowed to change that.

Well, he'd do whatever he could to help her blossom. Riley didn't *have* to help him with Logan. Didn't have to help him with meals. Didn't have to be so welcoming and open to both him and his nephew. But she'd done more to help him than she'd ever know.

When Logan had first been dropped off, Oz had floundered badly. He wasn't sure he'd be able to be the kind of role model his nephew needed, despite his determination to try. But with Riley's help, and the help of his teammates and their women, he was beginning to get into the groove of being a parent. He knew he'd screw things up in the future, but for now, he didn't think he was doing too badly.

Looking over at Logan, Oz smiled. He was working side by side with Trigger at the moment, raking old, moldy hay toward the big bay door that had been carefully dismantled earlier. Grover had plans to use the doors in a project in the house. Both Logan and Trigger were chatting behind the masks they wore to protect their lungs, and the structural integrity of the building had been triple checked before anyone had gone inside.

Doc had promised Logan that later, he could sit inside the bulldozer and help actually knock down the building, and the boy had been ecstatic about the prospect. Every day, Oz saw his nephew open up, and even in the short time he'd been around him, the kid seemed so much more relaxed.

But every now and then, like yesterday when Riley had been hurt, Oz saw what the effects of past abuse had done. Made him extremely wary and watchful. And while Logan had begun to open up to Oz...it still seemed as if he was holding something back. He didn't talk about living at his mom's house very often, and when asked direct questions about how what his life had been like, he clammed up.

His nephew was keeping something from him—and Oz hated it. He understood that Logan was cautious about sharing anything about his mom that might seem derogatory, but Oz knew he couldn't fully deal with everything he'd been through if he didn't talk to him. Next week, he was going to see his commander about the possibility of getting Logan in to talk to a child psychologist. If Logan wouldn't talk to Oz, maybe he'd open up to someone more qualified to help him.

Oz also hadn't had any luck in figuring out where all Logan's stuff had gone. He'd shown up with only a fucking plastic bag of clothes; he *had* to have more stuff than that. But he was getting the runaround from CPS. It was bullshit and frustrating, but Oz hadn't wanted to rock any boats and risk them taking Logan away from him.

So he'd let it drop, but the many questions he had about his sister's situation and what had really happened remained. All he knew was that there had been a home invasion, and she'd been killed. The perpetrator hadn't been found and the detectives were still investigating.

He needed to know that whoever had murdered his sister would pay for what they'd done, but so far, all he'd gotten were reassurances that they were looking into the case and would let him know if they found out anything.

But today was a day for fun, and yes, working hard out in the sun to take down Grover's barn. They were actually having a good time and it was refreshing to be outside, even if it was hot. Oz glanced over at the house and saw the women were still sitting on the large covered porch. Grover had bought some of those awesome wooden rocking chairs that were outside all Cracker Barrel restaurants.

Riley had been quiet and nervous when they'd arrived, but he could see her laughing at something one of the others said, and he smiled

"She's good for you," Grover said from next to him.

Turning to face his friend, Oz nodded. "You know, I'd been aware of her for quite a while. I mean, I could hear her in her apartment puttering around, and I'd seen her in the hallways of our apartment complex, but I never really gave her much thought, beyond anger on her behalf when her douche ex yelled at her. I regret not trying to get to know her earlier, but now I realize that she probably wouldn't have given me the time of day if it hadn't been for Logan."

"You think she's with you because of him?" Grover asked with a frown.

"No! I mean, I don't think so. I just think after things with her ex ended so badly, she was ready to be done with men. She's said as much. I'm not sure she would've been open to starting a new relationship. But I honestly have no idea what I would've done without her."

"You know the other women would've stepped up," Grover admonished.

"I know," Oz said, "but Logan may've felt more like a burden. It's easy for Riley to come over from next door. And she's...she's been where he is. I think they've bonded because of that."

"Because she spent time as a foster kid?"

"Yeah." Oz had told his friends all about Riley and what she'd been through.

"Kinley was too," Grover reminded him.

"I know. But I can't exactly go to Logan and be like, 'Here, you'll like Kinley because she had a shit childhood just like you,' Oz said with a frown. "Riley and Logan just naturally clicked, and I'm grateful for it."

"It's hard to believe this sometimes, but I think everything happens for a reason. It can be difficult to understand what that reason is when you're in the midst of whatever shit life has thrown at you, but later, after some introspection, it all makes sense," Grover said.

Oz thought about that for a moment. He wasn't happy that Becky had died before he'd been able to reconcile with her, but he now had Logan in his life. He had no idea what would happen in the future, but for now, he hoped that Grover was right.

"How's Devyn doing?" Oz asked.

Grover sighed and shook his head. "Not good. She's keeping something from me, and it's killing me. We used to be really close, but now she won't talk to me, and I don't know why. I talked to my mom, and she's worried too, but Devyn also refuses to talk to Mom. So I'm just trying to keep my eye on her."

"You know she's not that fragile kid with leukemia anymore, right?" Oz asked gently.

"Yeah, although a part of me will always want to protect her. She'll always be my little sister."

"And Lucky? Were you honest when you told him you were okay with him dating her?"

"Absolutely," Grover said without hesitation. "I love you guys. And if Lucky or Doc ended up with her, I'd be over the moon. But she's being standoffish. It's driving him crazy."

Oz couldn't help but chuckle. "It's probably good for him. The man's been lucky with just about everything else in his life, it's about time he has to work for something."

Grover grinned. "True. It'll be interesting to see who has more patience."

"For what it's worth...I think he's getting under her skin," Oz observed.

"Yeah. Maybe he can find out what's wrong. I'd be forever in his debt if he did," Grover said.

"Ever hear anything back from that woman over in Afghanistan?" Oz asked.

Grover frowned and shrugged. "Sierra? No. And just between us...it's not sitting well with me."

"She was a firecracker. Not too much over five feet and going toe to toe with you," Oz recalled.

"Yeah, which makes it even more suspicious that she just blew me off," Grover said. "If she didn't want me to email her, I would've thought she'd just tell me after the first time I tried to get in contact with her when we got home.'"

"Have you looked into what's up with that?"

Grover shook his head. "Not yet. I mean, it's kind of an ego killer that she seemed friendly while we were there, and then the second I left, she blew me off. I've put it off because I'm not sure I really want to find out she's all good and just wasn't that into me."

"What if something *did* happen to her, and she literally can't return your emails?"

"I know. That's why I'm gonna talk to the commander and

see if he can make some inquiries. If she's ghosting me, she'll never know I checked up on her and I can move on. But if not..." Grover's voice trailed off.

Oz wasn't sure what his friend could do if anything was wrong, but it was something to worry about another day. Today, the sun was out and they had a barn to raze.

"Hey, Oz, look what we found!" Logan called out as he held something up.

The kid was holding up the carcass of the biggest rat Oz had ever seen. "Gross," Oz muttered to his friend before giving his nephew a big smile and thumbs-up.

Grover chuckled. "Yeah, I'd found a few of those, which is why I gladly let Trigger and Logan take over the raking job."

"Smart man," Oz told him.

Grover clapped Oz on the back and headed over to help Doc with something on the other side of the barn. Lefty wandered up minutes later and stood beside him. "So, Riley was a foster kid?"

"Yeah. I mean, kind of."

"Kind of?" Lefty asked, one eyebrow raising.

"Her parents lost custody of her several times, and while they worked to take care of whatever CPS told them they had to fix, she lived with other families."

Lefty whistled. "That's tough. I don't know which is worse, not having parents, or to be taken away from them every couple years while they worked through their shit."

"I know. Then they died when she was eighteen, and she's been on her own since then. I know she and Kinley didn't have similar situations growing up, but I'm hoping they'll have enough in common that they'll click as a result," Oz said.

"Just because they were both foster kids doesn't mean they're gonna be besties," Lefty warned.

"I know. I just...I want Riley to like them. She's content

being by herself, but I think she would really blossom with some friends who truly understand her."

Lefty gestured to the porch with his head. "I don't think you need to worry about her making friends."

Oz looked over and saw the women were once again laughing together about something. He relaxed a bit. "I knew they'd get along," he said more to himself than the man standing next to him.

"They're all good people. Everyone needs friends. I don't know what I would've done without all of you by my side during all those months when Kinley was in WITSEC. You kept me sane when I wanted to tear the country apart looking for her. Gillian had Ann, Wendy, and Clarissa before she hooked up with Trigger, but they were either already married with kids or dating. I think Kinley and Aspen have been good for her. And I know Kins feels blessed to have Gillian, Aspen, and even Devyn in her life."

Oz couldn't believe they were standing there chatting about women's friendships, but it didn't feel weird in the least. Not when he was doing it because he wanted to make sure Riley was comfortable. "Thanks, I appreciate the reassurance."

"No prob. But I'm not going to start talking about periods and other women's shit with you," Lefty said with a grin. "Come on, let's get this barn taken down so we can get a beer and hang out with our chicks."

Oz chuckled. "Sounds like a plan. Will you help me keep an eye on Logan? I don't want him to get hurt."

"Of course. We've all got eyes on him. He'll be fine."

Oz nodded and looked back at the porch one more time, before turning his attention to the old rotting boards around him. The sooner they got the barn taken down, the sooner he could check on Riley and hopefully take her on that four-wheeler ride he'd promised her.

* * *

Riley laughed at something Gillian said. She'd been fairly quiet so far, letting the other women talk around her, but she truly was enjoying herself. Everyone was down-to-earth and very welcoming, which had been a relief.

She hadn't been sure what kind of reception she'd get from the other women. She'd felt like an outsider most of her life. Because of the way she'd been raised, because she only had a high school education, because she worked from home instead of in an office...for so many reasons.

But with Gillian, Kinley, Aspen, and Devyn, she didn't feel uncomfortable at all. They were all sitting on the porch watching the men take down the barn. She couldn't help but let her eyes linger on Porter. He'd taken his shirt off, and she felt as if she needed a fan to cool herself down. His shoulders were broad, and every time he picked something up, his muscles rippled sexily. She couldn't decide if she liked his arms better, or his back, or his abs.

"Wipe the drool off, girl," Gillian teased as she leaned over and nudged Riley's arm.

Startled, she glanced over at the other women and saw they were all looking at her. Blushing, Riley could only smile and shrug.

Everyone laughed. "Don't feel bad, seeing Trigger shirtless makes me want to drag him off and have my wicked way with him," Gillian told her.

"Gage is still trying to make up for lost time while I was in WITSEC," Kinley said with a small, secret smile.

"I think that was the bravest thing I've ever seen anyone do," Gillian told her. "Seriously. *And* you left before you'd healed from being beaten and thrown off that bridge. You're either crazy or bulletproof."

Kinley winced. "Probably more of the former than the latter."

Riley shifted in her seat. "But you're okay now?" Porter had told her the basics of what the other women had been through. It was just another reason that she'd felt a little unworthy to be around them.

"I'm good. Before a storm, I've noticed that my bones seem to ache, but luckily the weather's pretty good around here," Kinley said with a smile. Then she got serious once more. "I hear we've got a lot in common when it comes to our upbringing."

Riley knew immediately she was talking about being a foster kid. "Yeah. But my stays were only temporary until my parents got their act together and could get me back."

"I'm sorry, but that doesn't sound any better than my situation," Kinley said. "I mean, yeah, you still had your mom and dad, but you never knew when you'd be taken away again, and it had to hurt knowing they kept doing shit that would get you removed from the house."

It had. Kinley had hit the nail on the head with her observation. Riley had often wondered why they hadn't loved her enough to do whatever it took to ensure she'd never get taken away again. They kept falling back on their old habits. "Yeah, there were many nights I lie awake wondering why I wasn't able to go home yet. Why my parents hadn't immediately done what was required to get me back," Riley said.

"That sucks. I used to pray that the families I'd go to would want me enough to adopt me, but it never happened. I couldn't figure out what it was that I'd done wrong every time I was moved to another home," Kinley said.

"And I wondered why my parents loved alcohol more than me," Riley reciprocated.

Kinley leaned forward and reached out her hand. Riley took it, somehow feeling so much better when the other woman squeezed it gently. "It sticks with you, doesn't it?" she asked softly.

Riley nodded.

"It gets better. I know that's kinda trite, and I don't mean it to be, but with the right man," she paused to look over at the barn, then continued, "and with the right friends, it's amazing how much of your past you can forget when you're finally happy and content."

Riley had searched for that contentment for ten years, and still hadn't found it. Although she had to admit that the time she'd spent with Oz and Logan had done a lot to make her believe she could finally be happy.

Kinley gave her hand one last squeeze then sat back.

"I have a question," Gillian said.

"Shoot," Riley said.

"Not for you. For Devyn."

Everyone looked over at the other woman. Riley had been intimidated when she'd been introduced to Devyn. She was tall, almost six feet, and had beautiful long blonde hair and the bluest eyes she'd ever seen. She'd thought that Devyn had to be a model or something, and when she'd said as much, Devyn had laughed and said she was "only" a vet tech at a local veterinarian clinic.

"I want to know why you really moved to Texas," Gillian said in a gentle tone, but one still filled with determination.

"You know why," Devyn said. "My boss wanted to date me and I didn't reciprocate his feelings. When he got physical with me and pushed me into an exam table, I was done. I needed a fresh start. It took me way too long to finally find a job here, but now that I have, I'm happy."

"I'm sorry, that had to have sucked, but why here? I mean, you're good at what you do. I would think any number of vet clinics in Missouri would've hired you. Was your boss that much of a dick that he somehow blocked you from getting another job? And you've got two brothers who still live in Missouri, wouldn't they have helped you?"

Devyn was quiet for a long moment. "Let's just say the

timing was actually really good. It gave me a perfect excuse to leave town and make a fresh start."

Riley didn't like the sound of that. Not at all.

"What does that mean, though?" Kinley asked. "I also remember you didn't want to talk to your mom one day when Grover had her on the phone."

"Look, I like you guys, but I don't really care to talk about myself that much. I'm fine. Everything's good," Devyn said, sounding a little desperate.

Riley could tell that all *wasn't* fine with her, but she didn't know her enough to feel as if she could push.

Apparently Gillian didn't have as many reservations. "I get the feeling you haven't had much luck with guys in the past. And I know you felt stifled growing up and that you missed out on a lot because of your leukemia. But you can trust us. And the guys too. Especially Lucky. He'd do anything for you."

"That's what I'm afraid of," Devyn muttered.

"You've got a *lot* of people who would do just about anything to protect you. Your brothers, Lucky, the guys on the team, us...you just have to let us in," Gillian insisted.

"Sometimes the people who are supposed to protect you are the ones who hurt you the most," Devyn said quietly.

Riley knew what she meant. She'd experienced that first-hand with her own parents.

It was obvious the other women didn't like what they were hearing, and Kinley opened her mouth to say something, but Devyn sat up, straightened her shoulders, and asked Aspen firmly, making it clear she was changing the subject and was done talking about herself, "How's Brain doing with remembering all the languages he thought he'd lost after your ex beaned him in the head?"

Aspen hesitated, as if she really wanted to go back to Devyn's troubling comment, but then she gave her friend a small smile and went with the change of subject. "It's amazing, really. Once he really started remembering, everything seemed to come back almost at once."

Riley had heard about Brain's temporary amnesia when it came to all the foreign languages he knew, but she didn't know that Aspen's ex had hurt him. Porter had skipped that part in the story...probably because he didn't want her to worry about Miles. "What happened to your ex?" she asked.

Aspen sighed. "He died the same night he tried to kill Kane. Got electrocuted."

"And the asshole got a hero's burial," Gillian grumbled.

"Seriously?" Riley asked.

"Yup. It was my word against a dead man's," Aspen said. "A dead man who had several Army commendation medals and who'd never been reprimanded for anything in his career."

"That truly sucks," Riley said. "I could write a letter to someone, letting them know that he wasn't as great as he seemed, if you thought it would help."

All four women stared at her with wide eyes.

"I mean...if you wanted me to," Riley stammered.

"Thank you," Aspen told her. "But it's okay. I can't say that I'm happy with how it all played out, but I'm fine, and Kane is all right, and we're happy. I'm satisfied with that."

Riley admired the other woman. She wasn't sure she'd be as gracious if she'd been in her shoes. Thinking about what had happened to Aspen, how it had been her ex who'd hurt Brain, predictably got her thinking about Miles and how he hadn't stopped texting and calling her. It was getting harder and harder to ignore his messages. In his latest, he was bitching that she had one of his video games. She'd looked through all her CDs and DVDs and hadn't found the stupid thing. But Miles hadn't stopped harassing her about it.

She hadn't thought about it before...but what if he saw her with Porter? Or Logan? And decided to go after them?

She shuddered. She didn't even want to think about someone else getting hurt because of her bad choices.

But she didn't have time to dwell on it as Aspen began speaking again. "Besides, Kane and I have better things to think about than my asshole ex..."

Everyone leaned forward when she didn't continue right away.

"Yeah? Like what?" Kinley asked impatiently.

The smile on Aspen's face was huge when she said, "I'm pregnant."

There was complete silence for a beat as her words sank in. Then everyone leaped to their feet and surrounded Aspen.

"Oh my God! Congrats!" Gillian gushed.

"That's so awesome!" Kinley told her.

"Better you than me," Devyn said with a chuckle.

"Congratulations," Riley said with a smile as she gave the other woman a small hug.

When everyone got settled in their chairs again, Gillian asked, "Were you trying? I mean, no offense, but you aren't even married."

"Yeah, we've discussed getting married a few times, though he hasn't officially asked me yet. We had a talk about kids, and we agreed that we both wanted them. I've had weird periods my whole life and my gynecologist told me once that it might be more difficult to get pregnant. We decided that I'd go off birth control and we'd take things one day at a time. I swear to God Kane has like, super sperm or something, because I'm pretty sure I got pregnant almost immediately."

"That's so cool. What does that mean about your job?" Devyn asked. "You just started that new paramedic gig with the ambulance service around here, right?"

Aspen wrinkled her nose. "I did. And I feel horrible about it. I mean, isn't that any manager's nightmare? They hire someone, and then they get pregnant? But I'm determined to work as long as possible, and as long as it's safe for me and my baby. I love what I do, and I'll go back to it after the baby is born. I do feel kind of cheated though."

"About what?" Kinley asked.

"I don't get to have 'hurry up and get home, I'm ovulating' sex," Aspen said with a grin.

Everyone laughed. When they'd gotten themselves under control, Gillian asked, "So...when's the wedding?"

Aspen shrugged. "I don't know. Kane said even though we weren't doing things in the conventional way, he didn't want to deprive me of the whole proposal thing. I'm perfectly all right with a low-key wedding. My parents, and his, will want to be there, but I don't want to spend the money on the dress, huge reception and all that. Will you guys be upset if we don't have a reception?"

It was obvious to Riley that Aspen was worried about it, but everyone immediately reassured her.

"No way. You have to do what's right for you," Devyn said.

"We get to see you every day, we can celebrate with you any way you want," Gillian reassured her.

"I don't think you guys need anything for the house or anything in the way of presents to start your life, so we'll just buy you all the baby things," Kinley added.

"I think you should do what's right for you and Brain," Riley added. "If you try to please everyone else, it'll just be more stressful, which isn't good for the baby."

"Very true," Aspen said with a smile. Then she turned to Kinley. "When are you and Lefty getting married?"

"As soon as we can plan a trip to San Francisco. He's already upset that it's taken as long as it has. He's about ready for us to elope to Vegas, I think," Kinley said with a smile.

"I mean, honestly, it's not a bad idea," Gillian said. "With their jobs, I know they all feel a bit of pressure to get married sooner rather than later. They just want us protected."

"I know. But I think we're going to see if we can't get to

San Francisco in the next month or so. We just want to be married. Is it bad that I just want it behind me so we can get on with our lives?" Kinley asked.

"I don't think so. When you find the person you want to spend the rest of your life with, you want that life to start as soon as possible. As least that's the way it was with me," Gillian said with a smile

"I totally agree," Aspen said. "And now that I'm pregnant, I'm guessing my proposal will happen pretty soon, and he'll get right on arranging some sort of quick ceremony."

Riley was relaxed enough that she felt comfortable asking, "Because they're in the Army?"

Four pairs of eyes swung her way, and she felt as if she'd said something wrong because of the way they were studying her.

"You don't know what they do?" Gillian asked.

Scared she'd really fucked up now, Riley swallowed hard. "Um...they're in the Army. I don't know what their exact jobs are though. Doesn't everyone have a specific...um...MOS, I think that's what it's called?"

"Yeah, military occupational specialty," Aspen said. "I was a Sixty-Eight Mike, for example." She looked at the others. "Do we tell her? I'm not sure of the etiquette here."

Riley felt sick. *Tell me what?* She felt as if she was ten years old again and sitting on the sidelines while everyone else ate lunch with their moms on Mother's Day at her school. Always an outsider.

Gillian leaned forward and rested her elbows on her knees. "Tell us about you and Oz," she asked.

Feeling as if she was in the hot seat and not understanding why, Riley felt extremely uncomfortable. "He's my neighbor. I'm helping out with Logan until he can get home from work during the week."

Gillian impatiently waved her hand. "Right, but are you

dating? I mean, Oz hasn't brought a woman to one of our get-togethers before."

Riley was unsure where she stood with the other women, but she was suddenly a little irritated. "I'm not sure what you want to know. Do I like Porter? Yes. I think he likes me back. As far as if we're dating...it depends on your definition. We've eaten together almost every night since Logan came to live with him. He kissed me last night, and said he wants to take me out. But we still don't know each other very well...as evidenced by whatever it is I don't know about his job that you guys are being so secretive about."

"I'm sorry we're being so mysterious," Aspen said. "But their jobs aren't something they talk about a lot. Someone saying something to the wrong person can literally be a matter of life and death."

Riley gaped at her. "Then you shouldn't tell me. I'm really no more than Porter's neighbor. If it's something super-secret that he does, then I don't want to know. At least not right now. And not from you guys. The last thing I'd want is to put him in danger."

"I appreciate that, Rile," a deep voice said from her right.

Turning, Riley saw Porter standing by the side of the porch. She had no idea how long he'd been there, but he'd obviously overheard at least some of their conversation.

He turned to the other women. "And I appreciate you following OPSEC protocol. I'll take it from here." He held out his hand to Riley. "How about that four-wheeler ride I promised you?"

Riley looked from his hand to the barn. To her surprise, it was mostly disassembled. She'd been so focused on the conversation with the other women that she hadn't even noticed. Porter had put a shirt back on, but his temples shone with sweat. She'd never been much of an outdoorsy girl, but seeing the evidence of how hard Porter had been working turned her on even more than she'd been while watching him without his shirt.

"Do you guys need anything before I go?" she asked the others.

They all smiled at her.

"We're good," Kinley said. "Go."

Riley looked at Aspen. "Does he know about...you know?"

The other woman winked. "Probably not, since he hasn't said anything. Feel free to tell him though. Kane and I will let the cat out of the bag for the other guys while you're gone."

"Do I know what?" Porter asked, looking concerned. "Are you all right?" he asked Aspen.

"I'm fine. Now you both have something to tell the other. If I were you, I'd go while you still can," she teased. "I'm guessing you don't have a lot of time to yourself now that Logan is around. While he's being entertained by our guys, it's the perfect opportunity for some alone time with Riley."

"If you're sure you're okay," he said.

"I'm sure. Go on," Aspen ordered.

Porter walked around to the stairs and held out his hand again.

She immediately stood and headed toward him. She stopped at the top of the stairs and looked back at the women. "You'll still be here when we get back? I'd hate for you to leave without getting the chance to say goodbye."

"We'll be here," Gillian told her. "Promise."

Riley nodded and went down the few steps until she could take hold of Porter's hand. His warm fingers closed around hers, and while she was still nervous about what the women were discussing and what he might have to say, she still trusted him.

As they walked toward a four-wheeler sitting alongside the house, Riley asked, "How's Logan?"

"He's great. Hanging out with my friends has been good

for him, I think. He seems more relaxed than he's been since moving in with me."

"Good," Riley said on a relieved sigh. If anyone needed this, it was Logan. She hoped he could see the true friend his uncle was to the other guys, making Logan more comfortable with his new situation.

Porter stopped by the machine. It hadn't seemed that big when she was sitting on the porch, but now that she was next to it, it looked huge.

"You'll be fine," Porter said as if he could read her mind. He picked up a helmet and strapped it on her head. Riley couldn't help but feel tingles when he touched her. She loved being this close to him. Then he put on his own helmet and threw his leg over the seat. "Come on, Rile. Climb up behind me and hold on."

She wasn't sure exactly how to get on and hoped no one was watching her clumsy attempt at mounting the machine. She heard Porter chuckle but ignored him. When she was finally seated behind him, she suddenly got shy. She lightly put her hands on his sides.

"I said, hold on," Porter told her, taking her hands and curling them around his stomach.

Riley scooted forward to make her position more comfortable. She was now plastered against Porter's back, and he pressed her palms flat against his belly. "I'm not going to break," he said. "And the last thing I want is you falling off backward. So hold on, sweetheart."

Fall off backward?

Riley gripped Porter tighter and ignored another chuckle.

He started the four-wheeler and the sound of the loud engine made it clear they wouldn't be talking while he drove.

"Hang on!" Porter reminded her one more time over his shoulder, then pressed on the gas and the machine lurched.

Riley squeezed her eyes shut as they shot forward.

CHAPTER EIGHT

Oz loved the feel of Riley's hands around his waist. He knew she was terrified when they'd first set out, but the longer he drove on the trail around Grover's property, the more she relaxed. He felt her rest her cheek on his back, and he reached down to squeeze her hands.

Grover had told him about a spot a few miles down the trail that would be perfect for having a talk. There was a small creek nearby and while there might be a few other four-wheelers that came through, they'd have all the privacy they'd need.

He wasn't exactly surprised that the matter of him and the others being Delta Force had come up, but he was pleased the other women were being cautious in talking about it. But as far as he was concerned, he wanted Riley to know. Not only was she looking out for his nephew, she was quickly becoming very important in his life.

Oz would've been more freaked out about how fast he was falling for her if it hadn't been for his teammates. He'd seen how quickly they'd bonded with their women, and they were all still going strong. Trigger was married, and he knew Brain was going to ask Aspen to marry him soon. He'd talked with them about how he might do it, and they'd all offered their suggestions. Lefty was also itching to get Kinley to San Francisco, where his parents lived, so he could officially marry her as well.

So Oz's feelings for his pretty neighbor didn't seem so out of place when he thought about the circumstances that had brought his friends together with their women.

Riley leaned into the turn with him, and he couldn't help but feel proud of how quickly she'd picked up the subtle nuances of riding the bike. It wasn't quite the same as riding a motorcycle, but he liked that she was in tune with his movements.

He kept his eyes open for the spot Grover had told him about and was relieved when he recognized the pull-off immediately. He eased the four-wheeler off the side of the trail so it wouldn't be in the way of anyone else who rode by, then cut off the engine.

He turned and smiled at Riley. "So?" he asked. "Do you like riding?"

"I love it! At least with you driving. I don't think I'd be comfortable taking the wheel."

"You'd do fine," he reassured her. "Hop off and I'll show you why we stopped here."

Oz waited until Riley had swung her leg over the back of the machine and stood before climbing off the seat himself. Riley took a step and swayed on her feet.

"Easy," Oz warned, catching her around the waist with one arm.

"My legs feel like Jell-O!" she exclaimed.

"Just take it easy, you'll get your land legs back," he said.

"Land legs?" she asked with a laugh.

Oz unclipped his helmet with one hand, not wanting to let go of her for even a second. He placed it on the seat then reached for Riley's. Without taking his gaze from hers, Oz placed her helmet next to his own. Then he took her face in his hands. His thumb brushed against the slight bruise on her cheek. The ice she'd used yesterday had done a great job in reducing the severity of the broken blood vessels. "Does it hurt?" he asked.

Riley shook her head. "No. And I used some foundation to hide the slight black eye I had this morning. It was really more a dark circle under my eye than anything else."

Oz drank her in. If he didn't know what had happened the day before, he would've just thought she wasn't sleeping well or something.

Then he did what he'd been thinking about doing all day. He tilted her chin up with one finger and dropped his head.

Riley went up on her tiptoes to meet him halfway. Her body pressed against his own as she used him for support. As much as he wanted to devour her, Oz did his best to keep the kiss light and easy. He nipped at her and ran his tongue over her plump lower lip. He loved that she immediately opened to him. She tested his resolve as her tongue came out and licked over his own lips. But he pulled back, keeping his arms around her, and smiled.

She pouted. "You call that a kiss?" she asked.

He chuckled. "For now, yes. I want to show you something, and we need to talk. If I kissed you the way we both want, we wouldn't get to either. And this four-wheeler would look more and more like a good place to take you."

Riley blushed at that, but she eyed the bike next to her with interest.

"Lord, woman, have some pity on me," Oz begged as he kissed her forehead. "Come on, Grover said it wasn't far from here."

The small chuckle that left her lips made him smile. She seemed to be as eager for him as he was for her. He walked them into the trees, holding branches out of her way as they went. He heard the stream before he saw it.

Riley inhaled with pleasure as soon as she saw their destination. Someone had put a bench in the shade under the trees. At the moment, it wasn't more than a strong trickle as Texas hadn't gotten much rain lately, but Oz couldn't deny that it was still a beautiful place. There were birds chirping overhead and the trees threw plenty of shade on the area.

He led Riley over to the bench and, after he'd tested it to make sure it would hold their weight, urged her to sit. He took a seat next to her and kept hold of her hand.

"It's so beautiful," Riley said, looking around in awe. "Maybe you can convince Brain to bring Aspen here to propose."

"Great idea," Oz said.

Riley blushed. "I mean, if he wants. I didn't mean to presume anything."

"You aren't presuming anything. Brain wants his ring on Aspen's finger more than anything, but he also doesn't want to rush her."

"Um...you remember how I asked Aspen if you knew about something?" Riley asked.

"Yeah. She said she's okay, but is she really?"

"She's pregnant," Riley blurted.

Oz stared at Riley for a second before breaking out into a huge smile. "No shit?"

She returned his grin. "No shit. I don't really think he'd be rushing her if he asked her to marry him."

"That's awesome. I didn't know they were even trying."

"I got the impression that they weren't, not really. I guess they had a conversation about kids and how they both wanted them, and they agreed to let nature take its course. Well, according to Aspen...Brain's sperm are apparently just as smart as he is."

"He's gonna be even more impatient to marry her then," Oz said. He wasn't upset that Brain hadn't told him and the others yet. He figured that if Aspen had told the girls, Brain was probably at that moment telling the guys. Oz couldn't help but feel pleased that Riley had been included in Aspen's big reveal.

"Marriage isn't required for a baby to be born," Riley teased.

"It's not, but it goes back to what the ladies were hinting at before we left," Oz said.

Riley's brows furrowed in concern. He decided not to beat around the bush.

"I'm fairly certain Logan told you that we're special forces. We're Delta Force, Ri. We get sent on shorter specialized missions when we're deployed. They're usually pretty dangerous, and I know Brain's gonna want to make sure both Aspen and his child are taken care of, just in case. He's already had a close call and knows what's at stake."

He tried to read what Riley was thinking, but her face was blank.

"That's it?"

"What's it?" Oz asked.

"That's what they were talking about? That you guys are special forces?"

"I guess, yeah."

"I *did* already know that," Riley said. "Logan let it slip when he showed me his room," Riley said.

"Special forces is one thing, but Delta is kinda different. More intense and dangerous than, say, the Army Rangers."

"More dangerous?" Riley asked, frowning.

"Yeah, but we're good at what we do. *Very* good." Oz watched as Riley digested what he was saying.

"I guess I didn't realize that you guys being special forces...er...Delta Force...was what the others were talking about earlier," Riley said. "I mean, it's obvious how close you all are, and honestly, while I'm not thrilled that you guys go on dangerous missions, I'm thinking you've got the best people you can have at your back."

This was going a lot better than Oz could've imagined.

Not that he knew what her reaction might've been, but he'd heard from other Deltas how their girlfriends hadn't taken the news of their jobs that well. Some had even been hysterical, thinking their men would die every time they went on a mission. He should've known Riley wouldn't react poorly.

"I trust them with my life, and vice versa. We're as careful as we can be, but that doesn't mean there isn't a risk. And I wouldn't be surprised if Brain and Aspen were married before we left on our next mission."

"Will that be soon?" Riley asked.

"It's possible. I won't be able to tell you where we're going or how long we'll be gone. But there's some stuff going down, and we might need to step in and lend some assistance."

Riley stared at him for a long moment. Then she nodded. "Okay."

"Okay?"

"Well, it's not *okay*, but nothing I say will change what you do, and I wouldn't want it to. It's obvious you enjoy your job and that you're good at it. Where will Logan stay while you're gone?" she asked.

"Thank you," Oz said softly, bringing her hand up to his mouth and kissing the back. "You have no idea how much your support means to me. And I've got a family care plan filled out in regards to Logan. Gillian has offered to let him stay with her until we get back."

Oz didn't know why he suddenly felt guilty about that. He wanted to explain that he'd set up the arrangements before he'd gotten to know her, but he let it go. The last thing he wanted was to put a girlfriend on his FCP, then break up with her. Not that he was planning on breaking up with Riley, but it still felt too early in their relationship for something as huge as looking after his kid when he was gone.

"I think she's a great choice," Riley said, and Oz couldn't read any resentment or jealousy in her tone. "You have great friends, Porter."

"I know," he said. "And they're now your friends too," he told her.

"They are, aren't they?" she asked with a small smile.

They sat in silence for a moment, simply listening to the birds singing and the water babbling over the rocks in the stream.

"Porter?" Riley asked after a minute.

"Yeah?"

"Thanks for bringing me here. And by here, I mean to this stream, but also to Grover's house in general. I don't get out much, and it's been a nice change of pace."

"You're welcome. I wish I had thought to bring a picnic lunch or something. It's not much of a date so far."

Riley grinned up at him. "It's the best date I've had in a very long time," she admitted softly. "You shared your friends with me. I got to be included when Aspen told the others about being pregnant. You were honest with me about what you do—and don't worry, I won't say anything to anyone, not that I know anyone I'd tell, but still—and you introduced me to four-wheeling. I appreciate that you didn't drive crazy to try to impress me, that would've just scared me to death. You've shared so much with me, and I've got absolutely nothing and no one to share with you. I know this is a one-sided thing between us, but I'm still grateful."

"I don't want your gratitude," Oz told her honestly. "And nothing is one-sided. You don't get it. I'm totally out of my element with Logan. I don't know how to be a parent, especially to someone who's lost his mom. Yeah, Becky was my sister, but I didn't even know her. I mean, I knew who she was when we were growing up, and I knew who she was when I stopped communicating with her, but I have no idea about Becky, the mom to Logan. Sometimes I think I don't *want* to know, that it would just piss me off hearing how Logan was treated, but then there are times I think she cleaned up her act and was a good mom.

"Anyway, I'm babbling, but you don't have to bring anything to our relationship other than you. You staying with Logan in the afternoons makes me able to relax and not worry about him. And there's nothing better than coming home to the sound of your laughter. You've helped make my apartment a home, Ri, and I can't thank you enough for that. So no more thinking we're on unequal ground, okay?"

"I'll try, but I can't help thinking that anyone would've stepped up like I have. And hanging out with Logan isn't a hardship, not at all. He's wonderful, and even in the short amount of time he's been with you, I've seen changes in him...for the better. He's respectful and he doesn't take his eyes off you. You might not think you know what you're doing, but it doesn't matter, because from where I'm standing, you're doing everything right."

"I still want to take you out on a real date," Oz told her.

"Okay, but this feels like a real date to me," Riley insisted.

"So we're officially dating, right?" Oz asked.

Riley blushed and nodded.

"And we're exclusive?"

"I hope so," Riley said.

"We are," Oz said firmly.

She smiled. "Maybe we need to seal it with a kiss?"

"Great idea," Oz agreed, lowering his head.

How long they sat on the bench making out, Oz had no idea. It was taking all he had not to slip his hands under Riley's shirt and pull it over her head. He wanted to touch her all over. To see her hard nipples without her shirt and bra being in the way. But he also didn't want to disrespect her by taking her right here on this hard bench. He wanted their first time to be in his bed. He wanted to take his time and show her exactly how into her he was.

The sound of four-wheelers coming down the trail interrupted their peaceful solitude.

Riley pulled back and her eyes were glassy. Her lips were

plump from his kisses, and it took everything within Oz not to lower his head once more.

She licked her lips and blushed when she looked up at him.

"God, you're pretty," Oz said, running the backs of his fingers against her pink cheek.

"And you're hard to resist," Riley told him.

He gestured to his lap with his head. "The feeling's mutual. I'm not sure I've ever been this hard just from kissing someone before."

His erection was pressing against the zipper of his cargo pants, and was definitely uncomfortable. Oz was a little embarrassed about pointing out his need, but he also wanted to make sure Riley knew how she affected him. She lit up in his arms, and he knew together they'd burn the sheets if and when they ever got there.

"I've never wanted someone like this," she admitted. "I'm usually ambivalent about having sex. Which is why Miles and I only tried once."

"That doesn't make you frigid, as he accused, it makes you smart. And I'm guessing it means you haven't had great sex in your past. And you should know, even if it makes me sound over-the-top macho and conceited, I can't *wait* to show you what you're missing. I'm gonna do my best to ruin you for anyone else."

"I don't think it'll be hard," Riley told him.

"Oh, it's hard all right," Oz blurted, then winced as soon as the words were out.

But luckily, Riley laughed. "I walked right into that, didn't I?" she asked.

"What I'm trying to say is that what I feel with you isn't like anything I've experienced before. I respect you, look forward to sitting across the table at dinner and talking about your day. I enjoy spending time with you outside the bedroom, and that hasn't happened to me in a very long time.

I love kissing you, and I'm happy to keep doing so until you're comfortable with anything more."

"I've never met a man like you," Riley admitted.

"Good," Oz said immediately. "Because I've never met a woman like you either."

The sound of the other vehicles faded.

"As much as I want to sit here and make out with you some more, we should probably get back. Make sure Logan's good," Oz said.

Riley nodded. "You think Aspen and Brain have told everyone else yet?"

"Probably. Normally they would've waited until I was there, but I'm sure Aspen was confident you'd let me know."

"I still don't get how they can be so welcoming. For all they know, we're just friends."

"They know better," Oz said as he stood. He took her hand in his as they headed back to the four-wheeler.

"How?" Riley asked with a cute little tilt of her head.

"Because I've never brought a 'friend' to one of our get-togethers before. I never wanted a woman I wasn't serious about to get any ideas."

He felt Riley stumble a bit at his words, and Oz took the opportunity to wrap his arm around her waist and pull her against his side.

"And you're serious about me?" Riley asked.

He was impressed with her courage to ask the question. "Absolutely. One hundred percent serious," he said. Then without missing a step, he leaned down and kissed her on the lips. It was a quick, teasing kiss, but no less potent than the long, slow, deep ones they'd shared earlier.

"Well then. I guess it's good that I feel the same. This would've been extremely awkward otherwise."

Oz burst out laughing. "Yeah, it would've been, wouldn't it?"

She smiled up at him, and Oz swallowed hard. She was so

beautiful. The sunlight was playing peekaboo in the trees and when a strand of light caught her brown hair, it sparkled. Her hazel eyes seemed more blue in the sunlight and green in the shade. Oz knew he'd never get tired of learning new things about her. She'd keep him on his toes, and he loved that.

He helped her buckle her helmet once more, sneaking another kiss as he did. Then he climbed on and fastened his own helmet. This time when she put her arms around him, she didn't hesitate to plaster herself to his back. Her hands flattened against his belly once more, and her fingertips played with the hem of his shirt.

He pressed against her hands and took a deep breath. Before he started the engine, Oz turned to look at her. "Careful, Rile. You're playing with fire."

"It feels kinda good to be a bad girl," she teased. "Are you saying you don't like this?"

He did. He loved the feel of her fingers exploring him. He wished she'd slip them under his shirt and against his bare skin. Hell, he already knew he'd have fantasies later about her taking his cock in her hands and jerking him off while he drove. Of course that wasn't smart, safe, or very private on this public trail, but none of that seemed to matter to Oz's very eager dick.

"You know I love your hands on me, but I'm begging for mercy. The last thing I want is to show back up at Grover's with a hard-on," Oz told her honestly.

He felt her breathe out a sigh of frustration. "You're right. And I'm too much of a chicken to actually do anything out here. I'm more of a behind-closed-doors-sex kind of girl."

"I'd never do anything that would embarrass you," Oz told her. "I might talk a good game, but I've never been an exhibitionist." He picked up her hand, kissed the palm, then placed it back on his stomach, a few inches higher than she'd had it a second ago.

Getting the hint, she moved her other hand up and clasped her fingers together. "Home, James," she quipped.

"Yes, ma'am," he replied with a smile, then started the engine.

The trip back to Grover's house seemed even more intimate than the ride out had been. Riley held him tighter, and he drove a little slower, wanting to draw out their time together. He loved his nephew, but he made a mental note to do whatever he could to carve out time to take Riley on a date as soon as he could. He knew his friends wouldn't mind looking after Logan to give him that alone time either.

He was still smiling, thinking about how much he'd love having Riley all to himself again soon, as they pulled into Grover's yard. All the guys were on the porch with the women now, and everyone was smiling and laughing. He'd been right, Aspen and Brain had most likely shared their big news. Oz knew it wouldn't be long until they were married. If *his* woman was pregnant, Oz wouldn't wait a second longer than necessary to put a ring on her finger. In the military, being married meant a hell of a lot more protection and stability for his spouse.

"Come on," he told Riley after he'd parked the four-wheeler and they'd put their helmets on the seat. "Let's go celebrate with our friends."

The huge smile on her face told him everything he needed to know. Riley wanted to belong, wanted to be part of the group. What she didn't know was that she already was, without doing a damn thing but being herself. He saw Gillian mouth "you know now?" to Riley, and couldn't help but chuckle at how blatant his friend's wife was about asking if he'd told her he was Delta Force.

But he saw the pleasure in Riley's face when she nodded. He knew she felt accepted, and it made him want to kiss her again, right then and there in front of everyone. But instead, he simply shook his head at Gillian's antics when she clapped her hands with excitement.

Then Brain said, "It's about time you got back."

Before Oz could ask him what the big hurry was, Brain got down on one knee in front of Aspen.

Oz heard Riley gasp, but all he could do was smile.

"I wanted to wait until everyone was here. I've been trying to think of something romantic and over-the-top to do when I proposed, but nothing seemed right. Except doing it here and now in front of all our friends. Marry me, Aspen. As soon as possible. Now that you're pregnant, there's no need to wait. And I'm not asking just because you're going to have my baby. I just want you, and our little one, protected as soon as possible."

Aspen grinned. She immediately nodded. "Yes, of course!"

Everyone around them clapped and cheered as Brain stood and took Aspen into his arms. He spun them around in a circle, then leaned down to kiss her.

Oz looked down at Riley. She was grinning from ear to ear. He reached out and took her hand in his. She was now a part of their inner circle. He just had to be patient to make it a more permanent thing. And the fact that the idea didn't freak him out went a long way toward making him know, down to the marrow of his bones, that she was it for him.

For him *and* Logan.

CHAPTER NINE

Oz was pleased with his purchase. He'd stopped by the mall on his way home from work to get Logan a present. The reason *behind* the gift wasn't as pleasurable, however. They'd been informed that they'd be heading out to Somalia tomorrow. So he needed to prepare Logan and let him know he'd be staying with Gillian while he was gone.

It was another upheaval in the boy's life, and Oz was more than aware that it wasn't fair. Logan deserved a stable home, and with Oz, he wouldn't get that. But he *was* loved, and that would have to be enough for now.

It had been just over a week since they'd taken Grover's barn down, and Logan seemed more and more comfortable in his new home. He didn't seem as easygoing outside their apartment, but the boy wouldn't say what, if anything, was wrong. Oz had decided to just go with the flow and not push the boy too hard to open up. If something was going on at school, he hoped he'd tell him or Riley about it sooner rather than later.

Brain and Aspen had gotten married the other day. He'd left for lunch, and when he arrived back on post two hours later, he was wearing a ring and was married. They'd gone down to the courthouse and had a short and easy ceremony. They weren't planning on having a reception, but instead promised to have a huge baby shower closer to the time when she was due.

Things with Riley were going great. She stayed for dinner every night, and then he'd walk her to her apartment and make out with her for a while before reluctantly leaving her to enjoy a couple hours with Logan before it was time for him to go to sleep.

The situation wasn't exactly ideal, but Oz was trying to be patient. Because of how much time they'd been spending getting ready to deploy, Oz hadn't had the heart to ask one of his friends to come over and stay with Logan while he took Riley out. She understood, but it still bothered Oz.

And now he'd be gone for an indeterminate period of time, and he just hoped Riley wouldn't give up on him before they'd even really started dating. It was hard enough to have a relationship as a special forces operative, add in a child and things got exponentially more difficult. But Oz had never given up in his life, and he wasn't about to start now.

He unlocked his door to a beautiful sound. Laughter.

Logan and Riley were in his living room, and they hadn't heard or noticed him coming in. Their heads were bent over her phone and it sounded like they were watching a video. As he watched, Riley sat back and nodded at his nephew. Logan hopped up and began doing some sort of weird dance; it looked more like jerking and undulating than actual dancing. It only lasted about fifteen seconds, then they were both laughing again, and Logan came forward to check out the video Riley had made.

The laughter began once more, and Riley said, "That's perfect, Logan! Good job!"

"What's perfect?" Oz asked.

Both boy and woman startled at hearing his voice, then Riley laughed again.

"Hi! We didn't see you come in!"

That much was obvious, and Oz smiled at her. "What'cha doin'?"

"Oh, it's a dance challenge on TikTok," Riley told him.

"Which means nothing to me," Oz said ruefully. "What's TikTok?"

"It's an app, and *everyone* posts stuff on there," Logan informed him.

"Ah," Oz said. He had a lot of learning to do about what was cool for kids these days. One thing Logan living with him had done was make him feel completely out of touch with popular music, TV shows, and fashion.

"We'll do some more tomorrow," Riley told Logan.

"Okay."

Oz cleared his throat. He needed to break the news that he'd be leaving, but he hated to disturb the mood. Deciding to put it off for just a while longer, he walked back to the door, where he'd left the present for Logan. All kids liked presents, and while this was more on the practical side than something frivolous, he hoped his nephew would still like it.

"I got you something today," he said as he wheeled the suitcase into the room. He'd gone to the mall—which was a huge sacrifice, because he hated that damn place—and had found the perfect suitcase for Logan. It was white and decorated to look like a baseball. It was a bit smaller than Oz would've liked, but he couldn't pass it up.

Logan stared at the suitcase for a long moment.

But instead of being pleased with the gift, he looked as if he was about to cry.

"Slugger?" Oz asked, concern blossoming through him.

"I *hate* you!" Logan cried in a tone Oz had never heard from him before. It was full of pain and anger, and it was clear the lighthearted mood he'd walked in on had been obliterated.

Logan didn't give Oz a chance to reply, he ran past him and to his room, slamming the door as hard as he could.

Wincing, Oz looked from the hallway to Riley, then back to where his nephew had disappeared. He literally had no idea what to say, because he had no idea what he'd done wrong.

Riley stood and walked toward him slowly, her brows drawn in concern.

"I don't understand what just happened," Oz admitted.

Riley took both of his hands in hers and asked gently, "Why a suitcase?"

"Because we just got word that we're being deployed tomorrow. He has to go to Gillian's while I'm gone, and I didn't want him to have to use a damn plastic bag again."

Riley's face smoothed out, and she put one of her hands on the side of his face. "The first time I was taken out of my parents' house, I had to use a garbage bag to put some stuff in because we literally didn't *have* a suitcase. I was confused and scared about what was happening. But after a while, I settled into the foster home I was in. Until one day, my foster mom came home with a suitcase. She told me I had to pack, that I was leaving. I didn't know where I was going, all I knew was that suitcase signaled another change in what was a very confusing time. I...I think Logan saw the suitcase and thought you were kicking him out. That he has to leave."

Oz blinked in shock, then shut his eyes as agony coursed through his body. He hadn't meant for Logan to think he was being kicked out. Not at all.

He'd fucked up. Big time.

Opening his eyes, he lifted Riley's hand from his cheek, kissed the palm, then immediately turned and headed down the hallway.

He knocked on Logan's door and heard his nephew yell, "Go away! I'm not done packing yet!"

Knowing he had to fix this—now—Oz opened the door.

Logan was standing in front of his closet, ripping his shirts and pants off hangers and throwing them behind him toward the bed.

"Logan, stop and listen to me," Oz said in a low, anguished tone.

"No! I won't! You made me think you wanted me, that I was here to stay! But I should've known better! Mom always said you were so great, but obviously she didn't know you at *all*!"

Oz was done. The pain in his nephew's words ate at his heart. He loved that Becky had mentioned him at all to her kid, but he needed Logan to understand what had just happened.

He walked into the room and turned Logan so he was facing him. He held his arms tightly, but not painfully, so he had no choice but to look at him.

"I bought you that suitcase because I thought you'd like it. That it would remind you of me. *I'm* the one leaving, Logan, not you."

The boy had been struggling to get out of his uncle's grasp, but at his words, he stilled.

"That's right. I have to head out on a mission tomorrow. We never usually get a lot of notice, and this time is no different. I knew it was coming, but I had hoped to have a couple more weeks with you before it did. I've arranged for you to stay with Gillian while I'm gone, because you obviously can't stay here by yourself, but when I get home, *you're coming back here*. I'm not kicking you out. You're a part of me, and I'm *never* letting you go. I love you, Logan—so much it scares the hell out of me."

"I don't have to leave?" Logan asked quietly.

"No. Not for good. Just while I'm deployed," Oz said. "I'm so sorry. The suitcase was a stupid idea. I wasn't thinking. I should've known how it would make you feel. I'm not very good at this uncle thing yet, and I'm probably going to screw up a lot more. But my heart is in the right place. I'd never do anything to hurt you on purpose. I love you, Slugger. Can you forgive me?"

"You're apologizing?" Logan asked uncertainly.

"Yes. When I mess up, I'm gonna apologize. It's what men do when they make mistakes. I'm sorry I made you feel as if I *don't* want you here. I *like* coming home to you. You've made my life not so lonely. Please tell me you forgive me."

Logan nodded, but his forehead scrunched up. "Is your mission gonna be dangerous?"

Oz sighed. "I won't lie to you, Slugger, almost every mission has an element of danger to it. But you've met my teammates, they have my back. We all have big reasons to come home safe and sound. Trigger's got Gillian, Lefty has Kinley, Brain has Aspen and now his unborn baby. And the other guys have family and loved ones too. We aren't out there being crazy and unsafe."

"How long will you be gone?" Logan asked.

Oz let go of Logan's arms and crouched in front of him. "I don't know. I wish I did. Sometimes our missions are over quickly, and other times they take longer. It could be a few days, or it could be a month or more. If I knew, I'd tell you. That's the hard thing about what I do. One of the *good* things about my job is that while I can't tell you where I'm going or how long I'll be gone, the guys in the regular Army are gone for a lot longer than I should be. Sometimes they're deployed for a whole year."

"A year?" Logan asked, his eyes wide.

"Yeah. But I won't be gone that long," Oz said.

"Promise?"

"Promise. I'm gonna need to ask you a favor while I'm gone, though."

"What?" Logan asked suspiciously.

"Please don't play catch with Riley. We both know she can't catch worth a darn."

Oz was relieved to see a small smile cross his nephew's face. They both turned to look at his doorway when they heard a small sniff. Riley was standing there wiping tears off her face.

"Riley?" Logan asked. "Why're you crying? What's wrong?"

"I'm okay," she told him. "I'm just glad that you and your uncle aren't fighting anymore."

Logan looked at the floor for a second, then up at Oz. "I'm sorry for saying I hate you. I don't."

"I'm glad. We do need to figure out how we're gonna get your stuff over to Gillian's, since the suitcase was obviously a bad idea. And now that I think about it, it wouldn't work that well anyway since it's so small," Oz said. "How about this... I've got an extra duffle bag. It's not very fancy and it probably still has sand in it from the last time I was deployed, but we could fit a lot of your stuff in there."

"You'd give me one of your duffle bags?" Logan asked.

"Of course. But remember, I warned you. It might be a little stinky."

"Cool!" Logan breathed.

Oz chuckled.

"Oz?"

"Yeah, Slugger?"

"I wanna use your bag but...can I look at the suitcase? I've never had one before."

"Of course," Oz told him. "It's yours. You can put whatever you want in it. Shoes, all the bathroom junk you use, even your pillow if you want." Oz had been surprised at the amount of gel, shampoo, and deodorant the ten-year-old seemed to need. He didn't even remember brushing his hair when he was Logan's age, but things had changed over the years, that was for sure.

"The extra duffle bag is in the back of my closet. Go grab that and the suitcase, and we'll clean up the mess in here and figure out what you need to get you through at least a week at Gillian's. If I'm gone longer than that, she can bring you back here to get anything else you need. Okay?"

"Okay!" Logan said. He hesitated for just a second before dashing out of the room.

For a moment, Oz thought he was going to hug him, but he knew that was too much to hope for this soon. Especially after such a colossal misunderstanding.

"You did good," Riley said softly.

Oz stood up from his crouch on the floor and looked at the clothes strewn around the room. He shook his head. "No, I fucked up."

"And then you fixed it. Porter, if you think other parents are perfect all the time, you're so wrong. Look at my own. They messed up all the time, and yet I still loved them. Yes, I wish things had been different when I was growing up, but they were doing the best they could at the time. I know it's different since they were alcoholics, but still. And you apologized. I can't remember my mom or dad *ever* telling me they were sorry when their actions got me taken away. They blamed the Child Protective Services employees for being incompetent, they blamed each other, they raged about how unfair it was that they had to prove their worthiness of being parents. But not once did they sit me down and tell me they were sorry."

"I can't get the look of betrayal in his eyes out of my brain," Oz admitted.

Riley looked down the hall, checking for Logan, before walking toward Oz. She put her arms around him, pressing her cheek to his chest. "Cut yourself some slack. You did something you thought he'd like. You couldn't have known."

"I should've," Oz grumbled, but wrapped his arms around Riley and held her to him.

"I wish you were my uncle," she complained, "and I'd had your apartment to go to when I needed it."

"I'm *not* your uncle," Oz said definitively. "But you can still come to my apartment any hour of any day if you need to."

Riley tilted her head up and rested her chin on his chest. "Thanks," she whispered.

"I hate that I have to leave before I got to take you out on a date," he told her.

"I'm counting four-wheeling as a date," she told him.

"Fine. Then before I could take you out on a *second* date," Oz said.

"You'll just have to make sure you come back safe and sound so you can do that then," Riley told him.

He knew she was worried about it, and it felt good. "I'm gonna come back to you, Ri."

"Promise?" she asked, echoing Logan's question from earlier.

"Promise," he said with a small grin.

"You guys aren't gonna start kissing, are you?" Logan asked from the doorway.

Riley jerked in his arms, but Oz held her tightly. He looked over her head at his nephew. He had one of his old duffle bags in one hand, the end dragging on the floor, and the baseball suitcase in his other. "We might. That gonna bother you?" he asked, curious as to what Logan thought about him being with Riley. If he hated the idea, it wouldn't make him give up on the possibility of dating his neighbor, but it might make him change how he went about it.

"No. As long as I don't gotta watch," Logan said as he came into the room.

Oz smiled down at Riley. "Well, there ya go," he said softly.

Riley was blushing, but she licked her lips and said, "All right then."

Not able to stop himself, Oz leaned down and touched her lips briefly with his in a chaste kiss. He wanted more, but he needed to make sure Logan was good with everything that happened. Oz still felt horribly guilty about making him think for even a second that *he* was going to have to leave.

Riley smiled up at him, then took a step back and put her hands on her hips. "Looks like we've got some folding to do. I'll start with the shirts. Logan, you get your pants. Put the ones you want to take in one pile, and when you're done, you can go through my stack and decide which shirts you want to pack and which we can hang back up."

"What do you want *me* to do?" Oz asked.

The naughty look in Riley's eyes almost made Oz pick her up and carry her into his own bedroom, but he simply smiled back.

"If that bag really does have sand in it, can you see if you can dump it out? I'm sure Gillian doesn't want a beach in her guest room. And if you have any Lysol around, you might spray it too. Logan might think it's cool to smell like a stinky soldier, but I'm sure his teacher and his classmates might disagree."

If Oz didn't know that Riley was single and childless, he might've thought she'd been doing this mothering thing for years. She seemed to know exactly what to say and do to make Logan relax. She was a godsend, and he itched to make sure she knew how important she was to him.

Two hours later, Logan was packed and they'd eaten one last meal together. The minutes were ticking down too quickly, and before Oz knew it, Riley was saying it was time for her to get back to her own apartment.

She gave Logan a long, heartfelt hug and told him that he could call her whenever he wanted to. Even if it was the middle of the night. Her reassurance seemed to make him feel better, although Oz couldn't help but think of all the things that could go wrong that would make his nephew need to call Riley.

"I'm gonna walk Riley to her apartment, okay, Slugger?"

Logan nodded absently. He was used to the routine by now.

"I'll be right back. Go ahead and get ready for bed, and I'll come in when I get back to say goodnight. If you've got any other questions for me, I'm happy to answer them."

Logan walked to the end of the hallway, then abruptly ran back toward Riley. He gave her one more fierce hug, then turned and ran back toward his room.

Riley sniffed, and Oz hated knowing the two most important people in his life were sad because of him.

He intertwined his fingers with hers and walked her out. They went down the hall, and he held on as Riley unlocked her door. This time, he didn't stand outside as usual. He urged her inside and, as soon as the door shut, he took her in his arms again.

They stood locked together for a long moment. Oz could feel her fingers digging into the muscles in his back as she held him close.

"Ri?" he asked into her hair.

"I'm okay," she mumbled without lifting her head.

Oz chuckled. "Why don't you look at me and try to convince me of that?" he asked.

She tilted her chin up, and he sighed at seeing the tears in her eyes. He brushed his thumbs right under her lashes. "I'll be back before you know it. Just think about all the work you'll get done without also having to do my job as a parent half the time."

"I'm gonna miss you both," Riley said softly. "I look forward to meeting Logan's bus, and he's just so...interesting. Thinking about the endless days of transcription without the reward of seeing either of you at the end of them is kind of depressing."

"You could go hang out with Logan at Gillian's place. I'm sure she wouldn't mind."

"I know, and I'm sure I will, but I'm gonna miss you too, Porter."

His heart swelled in his chest. "I'll miss you too, Ri. I've gotten used to seeing you every day."

"I hate not knowing where you're going or when you'll be back."

Oz tensed. This was one of the hardest things about dating. He wanted to reassure her, tell her that they'd be working with the Somali military, that they wouldn't be doing anything on their own, but he couldn't divulge any details.

"But I'm so freaking proud of you," Riley went on. "Even without knowing anything about what you're doing, I want to tell everyone I know, which isn't that many people, how amazing you are and that you're out saving the world. Keeping us safe. Doing what so many others wouldn't be able to do."

God. This woman. "Thank you," Oz said quietly.

"No, thank *you*. I'm gonna worry every second you're gone, but you'll be okay, I know it. I'll kick your teammates' asses if you aren't," she mock threatened.

Oz chuckled.

Then one of her hands snuck up to his neck and into his hair. She pulled at him and went up on her toes.

Not able to keep from teasing her, Oz asked with a grin as he resisted her obvious signal, "Something you want?"

Riley growled. "Yes. You."

That one word had Oz's cock immediately stiffening. *He* knew she didn't mean that the way it sounded, but his dick didn't. His dropped his head and gave Riley what she wanted. What they both wanted.

He took a step forward, then another, until her back was against the wall. One of his legs went between hers, and he pressed his thigh against her hot core. She moaned into his mouth as he kissed her, and the hand in his hair tugged hard.

He felt one of her legs inch up his own, opening herself to him.

Oz held her against him with one hand at the back of her neck, and the other he plunged under the hem of her shirt. He palmed one of her of generous tits.

Riley pulled her mouth from his and her head hit the wall. "Yessss," she hissed.

Oz couldn't stop himself from pulling down the cup of her bra and pinching her nipple between his fingers. In response, she arched her back, thrusting her chest toward him, and the leg hitched around his thigh tightened.

Looking down, Oz licked his lips and swallowed hard. She was absolutely beautiful, and she came alive under his touch. He pushed his hips into her belly, letting her feel how much she was turning him on, before he lowered his head once more.

They made out against her wall for several minutes. Long enough for Oz to pull down the material covering her other tit and fondle that one too. Long enough for him to actually be able to smell Riley's arousal, and long enough for him to realize that if he didn't stop, he'd most likely come in his pants right then and there.

Letting go of her nipple was surprisingly difficult, but he finally moved his hand to her hip. He tightened his grip on her nape before he lifted his head and straightened her bra and shirt. Riley protested, raising her chin and trying to keep her lips on his. But he was too tall—and he really needed to stop.

They were both panting, and a flush had worked its way above the collar of her shirt. Oz couldn't wait to see if that flush went all the way down her chest.

"We need to stop," he said after a moment.

"I know," Riley agreed. "But I don't want to."

Oz smiled at that. At least they were on the same page.

"Guess I'm not frigid after all," she said with a small smile and blush.

Oz snorted. "I told you that you weren't."

She smiled, then sighed. "You should get back to Logan. I'm sure he probably has more questions."

"If you need anything, don't hesitate to call my commander. Or Gillian. And if Miles doesn't stop texting you, you need to call the cops and file a restraining order against him."

Riley jerked in surprise. "You know about that?"

"Yeah. It's hard to miss, since your phone is always buzzing. I looked at it the other night when it vibrated, and you were busy with Logan. I won't apologize for it, Riley. It was locked, but I could see the previews of the texts. For the record, I think it's probably smart that you're ignoring him, especially if you don't have that game he wants, but if he escalates, don't hesitate to call the cops. Okay?"

"I will. And I don't *have* his stupid game. I've looked everywhere for it. At this point, I'm ready to go buy the damn thing and give it to him. I just want him to stop. To go away. I don't know where he left the damn thing, but it wasn't here."

Oz rested his forehead against hers. "I'm not supposed to say anything but...I don't think we're going to be gone too long this time. Tensions are escalating where we're going, but we're going in as advisors. The government doesn't want us engaging in any firefights. We're going to train some of their units and then hopefully come home."

Riley nodded. "Okay."

Oz could feel some of the tension in her body release.

"Be safe while I'm gone," he said.

"I will. Be safe while *you're* gone," she returned.

Taking a deep breath, and knowing one of them was going to have to make the first move to separate, he stood up straight. Oz ran his hand over her hair then couldn't help brushing his thumb over the spot on her cheek where the baseball had hit her. "And no playing catch with Logan, got it?"

She smiled weakly. "Got it."

"I'll see you soon," Oz said as he dropped his hands and took a step back. Riley didn't move from her spot against the wall. He knew he'd never be able to walk into her apartment again and not remember the hottest make-out session he'd ever had.

"Be safe," she said again.

Oz nodded. He lifted his chin in goodbye, then reached for the doorknob. He didn't look back as the door closed behind him and he headed for his apartment. He needed to get back to Logan and make sure the kid was one hundred percent sure that he would be coming back to him. He'd had enough losses in his life, Oz was determined not to be another.

Usually the night before a mission, he was solely focused on maneuvers and logistics of what was about to happen, but tonight was all about making sure the people he loved would be all right.

Loved...

Did he love Logan?

Yes, absolutely.

Riley?

Oz mentally nodded. It was crazy, but he thought he loved her too. He wasn't ready to marry her, but if he lost her, he knew without a doubt he'd have lost something precious, and he'd always mourn what could've been.

Oz made a decision right then and there, standing in the hallway of his apartment complex, his hand on his own doorknob. When he got back, he was done tiptoeing around his relationship with Riley. Logan approved, or at least he wasn't opposed to the idea, if his reaction to them hugging was any indication. They had amazing chemistry, and Oz *liked* Riley.

She was funny, thoughtful, and he'd never been so attracted to anyone before.

If Riley Rogers thought he was intense now, she hadn't seen anything. When Oz wanted something, he went after it one hundred percent. It was how he'd gotten through Delta Force training, and how he'd managed to survive several missions no one should've come back from in one piece.

His determination to not only give his nephew an amazing life, but to show Riley how much she was starting to mean to him, grew tenfold.

He hadn't wanted to go on this mission, but he had a feeling it was just the push he'd needed in regards to his relationship with Riley.

Smiling, Oz opened his door and locked it behind him. As he headed for Logan's room, he mentally swore to do whatever it took to make his relationships with both his nephew and his neighbor stronger.

CHAPTER TEN

Riley looked at the calendar over her desk for what seemed like the hundredth time that afternoon. It had been three days since Porter had left, and she'd never felt lonelier. She'd been used to being by herself most of the time before Porter and Logan had come into her life, but now she couldn't seem to concentrate. She worried about Porter, wondering where he was and if he and his teammates were all right. She worried about Logan, and if he was okay at Gillian's house.

She worried about Miles, and how he'd been threatening to come over and break her door down if she didn't give him the game he claimed he'd left at her apartment.

Thanks to the latter, every little sound made her jump, and she was slightly ashamed of how needy she felt when just a month ago, she was perfectly content to stay inside her apartment day and night.

It wasn't too surprising that when her phone rang, Riley jumped yet again, almost knocking her laptop off the table in front of her. Nervously chuckling at herself, she looked at the display and saw Gillian was calling.

Her heart immediately started beating hard in her chest.

Was something wrong? Had she heard something from the Army about the guys? Riley clicked on the green button.

"Hello?"

"Hi, Riley, it's Gillian."

"What's wrong? Are the guys all right?"

"Nothing's wrong, I'm sorry for scaring you. I haven't heard anything from Trigger or the team. I'm calling about Logan."

Shit. Riley hadn't even thought that something might be wrong with Logan. "What about him?" she asked.

"He's fine," Gillian said quickly. "He's a really good kid. Quiet. Almost too quiet. I can't get him to engage with me hardly at all. I was wondering if you would mind if I brought him over after school today? I think seeing you would do him a lot of good. You know, getting him back into his routine."

"Of course," Riley said, sighing in relief. She couldn't deny that she'd missed the boy, and she'd love to see him.

"And...this might be too much to ask, and I understand if you say no," Gillian continued. "But I'm thinking maybe it would be better if he went back to sleeping in his own bed at Oz's apartment. He seems...lost. And I *hate* seeing him this way. I'm not trying to pawn him off on you or anything, I really like having him here, but he's said more than once that he misses you, so I just thought—"

"Yes," Riley said, interrupting her. "I have no problem with you bringing him back over here for good. I can sleep over at Oz's apartment and get him on the bus in the mornings. But...will we get in trouble with the Army? Porter told me that he'd filled out paperwork that says Logan would be staying with you."

"I have no idea," Gillian said, not sounding worried in the least. "But it's more important to do what's right for Logan than to follow the family care plan to the letter. He's being cared for, and he'll be safe. That's all that matters."

Riley had the brief thought that with Miles threatening to

come over, maybe Logan wouldn't be as safe as Gillian thought. But then again, her ex wouldn't know she was next door with Logan, so they should be okay. "All right. But if Porter gets mad, you have to help me explain," Riley said.

"Oz isn't going to get mad, especially not with you," Gillian told her. "He's crazy about you...*and* Logan. He'd be more upset if he came home and found out how much Logan was struggling."

"True," Riley said.

"He should be home from school before long, so we'll be there in about forty-five minutes or so. That should give him time to pack his things. Will that be all right?"

"Of course!" Riley told her. Mentally, she was trying to decide if they had enough to eat or if they needed to go to the store, but decided between her apartment and Porter's, they'd be all right for at least tonight. "I appreciate you calling. I know I'm not Logan's mom, but I'd like to think I'm his friend, and I don't believe he's uncomfortable. I'm sure it's not you."

"I'm not offended," Gillian reassured her. "He's had a tough time of it lately. And getting into a routine is important. He's used to you and his new room now. I'll see you soon."

"Drive safe," Riley said.

"I will. Bye."

"Bye."

Riley hung up and stared into space for a minute, wondering if Logan was going to be okay...and missing Porter all the more. He'd know what to do to help his nephew feel better. Even though he was new at the whole parenting thing, he seemed to catch on very quickly. He wasn't perfect, evident by him springing a suitcase on Logan, but he'd immediately rectified his mistake. He'd talked to his nephew, apologized, and made sure the boy knew he hadn't meant to upset him.

Riley shook her head and stood. She had a lot of stuff to do before Gillian arrived with Logan in under an hour. She had to pack, figure out what they were going to eat for dinner, shoot off a few emails to let clients know when they should expect their transcriptions to be returned.

But as she hurried into her bedroom, Riley was smiling. She was looking forward to getting back into her routine of working during the morning and spending the afternoon with Logan. She wouldn't get to see Porter for dinner, but at least she wouldn't be alone anymore.

* * *

Two hours later, Riley was sitting next to Logan on Porter's couch. The little boy had given her a huge hug when he'd seen her, and it felt awesome. Gillian hadn't stayed long, just long enough to make sure Logan knew she wasn't dumping him off, and that he had her phone number in case he needed anything.

Riley had made them both a snack, homemade pizza bagels, and now she wanted to see if she could get Logan to open up a little more.

"So...you okay?" she asked.

Logan nodded.

"Gillian's nice, yeah?"

"Uh-huh."

Right, so this conversation wasn't going well so far. Logan had never been a chatterbox, but she hadn't had this much trouble getting him to talk to her since the first couple of days she'd hung out with him.

"I miss Porter," she told him honestly. "Which feels weird because we haven't known each other that long, but something about him being here makes me feel safe. And he's funny, even though he doesn't try to be funny. I like knowing he's right next door just in case, and now that he's gone, everything's really quiet."

"He snores," Logan said quietly, looking down at his fingers in his lap. "Well, not really snores, but breathes really deeply. I can hear him from my room. Knowing he's here, that I'm not alone in the apartment, makes me feel safe too."

Riley did her best to keep her tone even. "Were you alone in your other place a lot?"

Logan shrugged. "Mom worked nights. So she left after dinner and usually didn't get home until right before I went to school."

Riley felt horrible for both Logan and his mom. She couldn't imagine how that felt, to leave your little boy home alone—day or night—while you went out and worked.

"She used to leave at night all the time to hang out with her friends, but she stopped doing that. She had a really hard time finding a job, and the only one she could get was at night."

Riley scooted closer to Logan. "I'm sure she didn't like leaving you."

"She didn't," Logan agreed. "She apologized lots, but said she trusted me to be good while she was gone." He looked up at her. "I know she wasn't the best mom, I'm not stupid, but she changed. Wasn't doing drugs as much."

Riley felt so bad for the little boy. She knew it wasn't easy to just up and quit using drugs. But it sounded like his mom had been trying. "She loved you," she told Logan.

He nodded.

"I'm very sorry she died," Riley said quietly.

It was several moments before Logan responded. "Me too. But does it make me a bad person to say that I like it here better?"

"Oh, Logan. No, it doesn't. There were many times when I was sent to a new foster family that I felt the same way. I liked most of those houses a lot. They were clean, and I didn't have cockroaches crawling over me when I slept. I got to eat regularly, no one forgot to buy food. And I didn't have to listen to my parents screaming at each other when they were drunk. I remember feeling sad when I had to go back home. I loved my parents, but while they did their best, they weren't very good at taking care of me."

Logan nodded as if he completely understood what she was talking about. Since it felt as if he was opening up to her a bit, Riley asked, "So, you're happy to live with your uncle, and you like Gillian...is there anything else going on that you don't like right now? How's school going?"

Riley saw his bottom lip quiver before he got control over it, and she knew she'd hit the nail on the head.

He shrugged.

Riley decided the best way to get Logan to open up was to continue to let him know that they probably had a lot of common experiences. "When I was around your age, I had a best friend. We were really close. But one day, she just decided she didn't like me anymore. She was hanging out with one of the popular girls in school instead, and they made my life unbearable for many years. They made fun of me and no one wanted to eat with me at lunch. They said I smelled, and they made oinking noises at me when I walked by. It was horrible. I hated going to school."

"What happened?" Logan asked quietly. "What did you do?"

"I was sent to another foster home around that time, and because it was kinda far away from where my parents lived, I had to enroll in a new school. That was hard too, because I didn't know anyone, but I kinda liked it because I didn't have to deal with my ex-best friend and her new group of mean girls. When I went back to my parents' house, I told them I wanted to keep going to the new school, and they actually filled out the paperwork I needed to make that happen."

Logan looked up at her then. "I hate my school," he

admitted. "Most of the kids are mean. Not just to me, but to everyone."

Riley didn't know what to say. She wanted to tell him that he could change schools, but it wasn't her place to decide that. And she didn't know if he was just feeling sad that he'd had to leave his old school with friends he might've had there, or if there really was something more going on. She felt completely out of her league in helping him with this particular problem, and it sucked.

She scooted closer to the boy and put her arm around his shoulders. "I'm sorry," she said softly. "I don't know why kids are so mean to each other. I'd like to say it'll get better, but I don't know if it will. Maybe you can see which other kids are being treated badly and try to make friends with them? I mean, if you're feeling bad, I bet they are too, and they might welcome a new friend."

"Maybe," Logan said with a shrug.

"And, if you truly hate your school that much, I bet if you talked to your uncle, he'd look into seeing if he could switch you."

"I already told him I didn't want to go to the school on the Army post," Logan admitted.

"So?" Riley asked.

He looked up at her, and the hope in his eyes was almost painful to witness.

"I mean, people change their minds all the time. It's not the end of the world."

He nodded.

"Think about it. You opened up to me and that went okay, right? Talk to Porter, Logan. He loves you and would hate to know you were unhappy and didn't tell him. I'm not saying he'll be able to magically make all your problems disappear, but sometimes talking to someone makes things seem not quite so bad."

"Okay," he said softly.

"Okay," Riley agreed. "Now...what should we do this afternoon? Want to go to the park and play catch?"

He opened his eyes wide and shook his head. "Oz told me not to throw the ball with you no matter how much you begged."

Riley chuckled. "I'm not *that* bad."

Logan's eyebrows went up.

"Right, okay, so I am. But I want to do something with you that you like. And you like baseball. So...what do you suggest?"

Logan thought about it for a moment, then he said tentatively, "What if we set up a target and I practiced throwing balls at it? You could watch and help me gather up the balls after I throw them."

"Perfect," Riley beamed. It didn't sound all that exciting to her, but if Logan was happy, she was happy. "I think we need to go to the grocery store, but for tonight, how does hotdogs smothered in chili, cheese, and baked beans sound?"

Logan smiled. "Yummy!"

"Good. Go get your balls and bat and we'll head across the street to the park."

They stood, and Logan headed toward his room to gather his things. But he turned before going down the hall. "Riley?"

"Yeah?"

"I'm sorry your friend did that to you."

"Me too."

"And thank you for letting me come back here. I like Gillian. She's really nice. But she's not you."

Riley felt her eyes tear up. "You're welcome. I missed you a lot."

Logan nodded then spun and headed for his room.

Riley took a few deep breaths to get her emotions back under control, then went to Porter's bathroom to grab some sunscreen. If they were going to go outside, even though it was late afternoon, she wanted Logan to be protected.

* * *

Later, after she'd watched Logan pitch a million balls (it wasn't that many, but it felt like it), and after they'd eaten their questionably nutritious dinner, and after they'd watched a rerun of *Wheel of Fortune* on TV, Riley told Logan it was time for bed. Tomorrow was a school day, and while she knew he wasn't excited to go, he still needed to be rested.

"Where are you going to sleep?" Logan asked.

Riley shrugged. "Here on the couch."

Logan frowned in confusion. "Why? You can use Oz's bed."

Just the *thought* of sleeping in Porter's bed made Riley yearn for things she wasn't sure would happen. "I'm okay out here."

By the stubborn look on Logan's face, she knew he didn't like that. "Okay. You can have my bed, and *I'll* sleep out here on the couch."

"It's fine." Riley tried to tell him, but he was having none of it.

"No. It's not fine. You're a female and should have a comfortable bed. If there's something wrong with Uncle Oz's bed, then you should get my bed and I'll sleep on the couch. It's not as if I haven't done it before."

His words made her proud and kind of weepy at the same time. "There's nothing wrong with your uncle's bed. It's just that...it's *his* bed. And I feel weird using it."

"But he's not here. What does it matter?"

There was obviously no way she was going to explain to a ten-year-old that the sheets probably smelled like Porter and it would make her want the man more than she did already. But she really liked how concerned he was for her.

Knowing she was going to regret it, she said, "I guess it doesn't matter. You win, I'll sleep in his room and you can stay in yours. Okay?"

"Okay," Logan said happily. "You don't have to get up in the morning. I set my alarm."

Sometimes the things he said made her so sad. She remembered how she'd learned to set her own alarm when she was around his age, because there was no way her parents would be awake after drinking all night to get her up for school. She figured the same was true of his mom. After working all night, she probably didn't get up with him either.

"It's okay, I'll probably head to bed not too long after you do. Besides, I want to make sure you get a healthy breakfast and see you off to the bus."

"Okay." Logan got up and disappeared down the hall, and Riley heard the water turn on in the small hall bathroom.

Closing her eyes, she tried to get herself together. It was too late to do laundry. She should've done it when she'd first come into the apartment with Logan. Now she was going to have to sleep in Porter's bed, under his sheets, and imagine how awesome it would be if he was there with her.

She took her time cleaning up the already clean kitchen and putting everything back in its place before she headed down the hall. She knocked lightly on Logan's door.

"Yeah?" he asked.

She peeked her head in. "All good?" she asked.

He nodded. "Uh-huh."

"Okay. Sleep well. I don't know if I snore or breathe loud, as I've never had anyone tell me I do, but I'll leave my door cracked open so if you need anything in the middle of the night, you can come get me."

Logan hesitated, then nodded. "Thanks. I...I know I'm being a pain, but I just like it here."

"You aren't a pain," Riley told him. "Promise. And I like you being here too. Now, go to sleep. Pancakes okay for breakfast?"

"Awesome," he said with a smile.

"Good night, Logan."

"Night, Riley."

She shut the door, leaving it open a crack before taking a deep breath and heading down to Porter's room. She'd put her bag inside earlier, and when she pushed open the door, she had to take another calming breath.

It looked as if Porter had just left. The covers on the bed were pulled back, as if he'd thrown them out of his way when he'd woken up the day he'd left to go off and save the world. There was an easy chair in one corner of the room and the top drawer of his dresser was partway open. She wandered into the attached bathroom and couldn't keep a smile from her face.

Porter might be a hotshot special forces soldier who was meticulous in most aspects of his life, but he was anything but stereotypically neat with his bathroom.

A towel was thrown over the shower bar instead of being hung up neatly on the rack on the wall. Shaving cream remnants were in the sink and his toothpaste didn't have the cap on it. It was weird, but seeing how messy the sink was made her feel better somehow.

Riley worked quickly, cleaning up the room, lining up the mouthwash bottle, shaving cream, and bottle of vitamin C on the counter. She closed the toothpaste so it wouldn't dry out and put his toothbrush back into the holder thing next to the sink. The towel over the bar was dry, so she folded it and hung it on the rack next to the shower.

It felt a little awkward being in Porter's personal space, but she couldn't deny she liked it. She went out into the room and grabbed her bag, digging inside to get the oversized T-shirt she liked to sleep in. Then she went back into the bathroom and changed.

If it felt weird being in Porter's space, stripping in a room where he was frequently naked was even more strange. Closing her eyes, she could picture Porter easing his underwear off before stepping over the bathtub into the shower.

Could almost see him rubbing the towel over his body, probably impatiently and not very thoroughly, to dry himself.

Shaking her head, Riley did her best to get control over her imagination. She was here to look after Logan, not lust after her neighbor. She managed to brush her teeth and find a clean towel for the morning before heading back into the bedroom.

Riley climbed into the bed and pulled the covers up to her chin. The mattress was comfortable and his sheets were extremely soft. She made a mental note to ask him where he'd bought them, then immediately rejected that idea. She wasn't going to tell Porter she'd slept in his bed—no way. Of course, Logan would probably let the cat out of the bag at some point, but she wasn't going to volunteer the information.

It felt too...intimate. She didn't think he'd mind her staying in his apartment while he was gone, especially since it was in Logan's best interests, but she didn't want him to get upset that she'd invaded his personal space.

Then again, he certainly hadn't seemed reluctant to invade *her* personal space the other night. When he'd had her up against the wall and his hands had roamed under her shirt.

Inhaling deeply, Riley felt surrounded by Porter. His slightly musky and earthy scent was all over his sheets and pillows. She knew when Logan had suggested she sleep in here, this was what would happen. That she'd get turned on simply by being in Porter's space. By lying in his sheets. Where he'd probably jerked off...

She refused to think about him being with another woman here. He'd told her that he hadn't dated anyone in a very long time.

As she pictured him, her hand moved without her really thinking about it. Brushing over her hard nipple before resting on the waistband of her panties. She glanced at the door, then closed her eyes. Logan was fine. He was asleep. She could do this.

Slipping her fingers under the elastic, she opened her legs wider and turned her head into the pillow. Once again, Porter's scent engulfed her. She began to stroke her clit, thinking about how amazing his hands had felt on her the other night.

It didn't take long. It had been a while since she'd masturbated, and being surrounded by Porter's scent seemed to push her over the edge even faster.

Riley imagined what it would be like to be in this bed *with* Porter. To have his hands between her legs, to stare up at him as he ever so gently entered her, being careful not to hurt her. He'd take her slowly at first, making sure she orgasmed before he took his own pleasure. Then he'd fuck her hard. Pounding into her, each thrust pushing her farther up the bed until she had to put her hands over her head to keep from hitting the wall.

He'd throw his head back, and she'd see the veins pulsing in his neck as he exploded deep within her. He'd growl out her name as he came, holding her hips in place as he pressed himself as far inside her body as he could get.

That was all it took. Riley's vivid imagination, and the frantic strumming of her clit, pushed her over the edge, and she let out a small whimper as she came. Her body shook with pleasure and she panted with exertion.

She removed her hand from between her legs and closed her eyes as she lay there, replete...and feeling extremely guilty. God, she'd just masturbated in Porter's bed.

But she couldn't deny she felt amazing.

And sleepy.

It had been a long day, and Riley was exhausted.

She fell asleep with Porter's scent in her nose, feeling content that Logan was safe. She prayed that Porter would return uninjured as well. She'd gotten used to both man and boy, and was looking forward to another date with Porter.

CHAPTER ELEVEN

Oz was dirty and tired, but very happy to be back in Texas. They'd been gone for eight days, and he'd never felt such an intense anticipation to get home as he did after this deployment.

Some of what he was feeling must've shown on his face, because Trigger nudged him with his shoulder and said, "It's different, isn't it?"

"What is?" Oz asked.

"Returning home when you know you've got someone waiting for you."

"I'm not sure anyone is waiting for me," Oz said.

"Liar," Trigger said with a smile. "I saw the way you and Riley looked at each other when we were at Grover's house. I'd say she's probably going to be very glad to see you."

Trigger wasn't wrong. Oz tried to hide his smile, with no luck.

The phone in Trigger's hand rang, and he was still grinning when he answered it. "Hey, Di, we just landed... Okay... all right...I'm sure it's fine. I'll tell him. See you soon. Love you."

"Gillian okay?" Oz asked.

"She's fine. But you should know...a few days ago, Logan went back to your apartment."

"What?" Oz asked, panic rushing through him.

"Hang on, don't freak. I don't know all the details, but apparently Gillian called Riley and asked if she'd be all right staying with him at your place. She agreed, and Logan's been taking his original bus to your place every day after school."

All sorts of scenarios ran through Oz's mind. He had no problem with Riley staying at his apartment with Logan, but he wondered why the change? Had Logan given Gillian problems? Was he sick? All sorts of negative scenarios flew through his head. And when he double checked his phone, he didn't have any messages waiting from Riley, telling him what was going on.

He was definitely freaking.

"Go," Trigger told him. "We'll take care of things here. But we still need to have the after-action review tomorrow," he warned.

Feeling grateful, Oz nodded at his friend and team leader. "I owe ya."

"Whatever," Trigger said. "But drive safely. You won't do anyone any good driving like a bat out of hell and getting into an accident. Logan's still at school right now, anyway. So go home, find out from Riley what's going on, and for God's sake...take a fucking shower. You stink."

Oz waved at his friend, but a shower was the last thing he was worried about. He needed to get home. To make sure Logan was all right. And Riley too. All thoughts of the mission they'd just completed flew from his mind.

He didn't remember the drive from the post to his apartment, except that it seemed to take too long. He took the stairs two at a time as he ran up to the second floor. It took three tries to get the key into his lock, and when the door finally swung open, he dropped his duffle bag on the floor and bellowed, "Riley!"

There was no answer, which worried him even more. In the back of his mind, he knew he had no reason to be so concerned, but the change in plans definitely bothered him.

He did a quick search of his apartment to make sure she wasn't sleeping, only hesitating when he saw a bag on the floor of his bedroom that definitely hadn't been there when he'd left. The room smelled like honeysuckle, which again, it hadn't a week ago. It was a smell he associated with Riley. He'd complimented her on the way she smelled a while back, and she'd told him it was her lotion, something called Aerin Mediterranean Honeysuckle. He didn't care what it was called; he just knew it would always remind him of her.

He turned and headed back for his door. He wrenched it open, prepared to go next door to find Riley, but stopped in his tracks when the woman he was desperately looking for was standing right in front of him.

He took hold of her shoulders and pulled her into his apartment.

"You're back!" Riley said with a huge smile. "I heard you through the walls. When did you—"

Oz cut off her words with his lips. He devoured her as if he were dying of thirst, and she was a huge glass of water. And she didn't resist. Riley opened her mouth and let him in, giving as good as she got.

Pulling away with a gasp, Oz held Riley by her shoulders and ran his eyes down her body. "Are you all right?"

"Of course I am. Are *you*?"

"Yes. Is Logan okay? Why did he leave Gillian's? Is something wrong?"

"He's good. I guess you already know that I've been staying here with him," Riley said dryly.

Turning, Oz pulled Riley into his living room and set her down on the couch before speaking. "Trigger got a call from Gillian, but she didn't tell him much. Only that Logan was back here with you. What happened?"

"Nothing major," Riley said calmly. "Gillian didn't think he was very comfortable at her house and thought he'd like it better being back here. And she was right. This apartment might be new to him, but it's home. And with things being rough at school, it's like a refuge. I was happy to stay with him until you got home."

Oz breathed out a sigh of relief, then what she'd said penetrated. He sat on the couch next to her. "Things are rough at school? How? In what way?"

"I think you should talk to him about it," Riley said after a moment's hesitation.

Oz shook his head. "No. I need to know what he told you. I have no idea how to get him to trust me. I mean, I think on the surface he does, but I can tell he's holding back. And he obviously feels comfortable with you, if he was okay with you being here and he opened up about whatever's going on at school. Please, tell me so I can help him. I'm afraid if I have to wait for Logan to tell me, things will get worse."

Her face gentled. "He's just not making friends like he should. I guess there's a group of kids who are pretty mean, picking on him and some others, and he just feels lonely."

Oz let out a deep breath. "But he's not behind academically?"

"Not as far as I can tell. I've helped him with his homework and it doesn't seem to be too difficult for him. I'm pretty sure it's just the fact that he's the new kid and the others aren't that welcoming that's frustrating him."

"Right. I'll see if I can get him to talk to me," Oz said. Then he took Riley's hands in his. "And you're good? How's the situation with Miles?"

Riley wrinkled her nose.

"That bad?" he asked.

She shrugged, and he knew she would downplay whatever it was Miles was doing now. "It's okay. He still thinks I'm holding one of his games hostage."

"Is he still texting?"

"Yeah."

Oz ran his thumb over the back of her hand. "Thanks for looking after my nephew for me. I honestly never dreamed I'd dump so much on you that night I came over to ask what the hell I was supposed to feed him for breakfast."

"He's a great kid, Porter. And I like spending time with him."

"So...you've been staying here. In my room?"

He watched as a blush bloomed across her cheeks. "I'm sorry. I hadn't planned on it, but when Logan realized I was going to sleep on the couch, he questioned me about it. Didn't understand why I didn't just stay in your room."

"I could smell you in there. Honeysuckle."

Her blush deepened. "I brought my lotion over because my skin's been really dry lately. Sorry."

"Don't be. I like it." Then something else occurred to him. "You've been sleeping in my bed..."

She bit her lip and nodded.

"God, that's *such* a turn-on," he said quietly.

Riley's big hazel eyes were fixed on his own, and he could see her breathing had sped up. He loved the thought of her there. In his space. Using his pillows. Her bare skin against his sheets. He felt his dick twitch in his pants, and his head began to lower.

She tilted her chin up to meet his lips when they heard someone at the door.

Riley backed away from him and looked toward the door. Oz turned his head in time to see Logan walk into the room. The relief at seeing his nephew smiling and in one piece was overwhelming. Oz leapt up from the couch and headed for Logan.

Without thought, he went down on a knee and hugged him tightly.

"You're back," Logan muttered into his shoulder.

"I am, Slugger. It's so good to see you. I missed you!"

"You did?" Logan asked.

Oz pulled back. "Of course I did. I missed throwing the baseball around with you. Making dinner. Even working on those pesky word problems. Being here with you is *much* better than lying around in the dirt and eating MREs for dinner."

Logan crinkled his nose. "You do smell pretty bad."

Oz burst out laughing. He'd forgotten all about the fact that he hadn't showered in days. He'd been so intent on getting to Riley and Logan that nothing else had penetrated.

"Sorry, Slugger. I was too impatient to get back here to check on you and Riley. How was school?"

He didn't miss Logan's subtle grimace before he said, "Fine."

"Right. I'm thinking there's some stuff we need to talk about. I'm not mad that you wanted to come back here instead of staying with Gillian, but we should discuss it. And I'm not getting happy vibes from you about school. Not to say school is always fun, but it's necessary so you can grow up and be smart and not a doofus."

Logan's lips twitched, but Oz kept going.

"But for now, I'm just happy to be home and that you're good. How about if I shower and then we go throw the ball around a bit? Then we can have some dinner before we chat about everything that happened while I was gone. Okay?"

"I'll get my stuff packed and head back to my apartment. Get out of your way and let you have some uncle-nephew time," Riley said, standing from the couch.

"No!"

Oz and Logan both said the word at the same time.

Oz grinned at his nephew before turning back to Riley. "Why don't you come with us to the park? You can critique us. I'm sure you've been working hard this week. Why don't Logan and I make *you* dinner tonight?"

"Like you haven't been working hard," Riley muttered. Then said louder, "I don't know, you guys need some bonding time."

"We're good. Aren't we, Logan?" Oz asked, hoping the kid would agree with him.

"Yeah, we're good. Please, Riley? Stay?"

Oz knew she wouldn't be able to resist that puppy-dog face, and he was right.

"Oh, all right, but only until after we eat."

Standing, Oz smiled huge at her. He'd missed her too. Of course he'd missed his nephew, but not in the same way he'd missed Riley.

"I'll go change and get my baseball stuff together," Logan said as he dropped his backpack in the middle of the hallway and headed toward his room.

Oz shook his head but left the backpack where it was. Then he walked over to where Riley stood. He took her face in his hands. "Sorry I stink," he said.

She chuckled. "It's okay."

"Tell me, did you shower here? Or wait until Logan had gone to school before going back to your apartment to get ready?"

He saw her swallow hard, and the blush that had faded from her cheeks returned.

"Here," she admitted softly.

The thought of her being naked in his shower was erotic as hell. "Tell me you slept naked," he pleaded.

Riley laughed. "No way in hell. Not with your nephew down the hall."

"Darn," Oz complained.

"You're crazy," she said, shoving him gently. "Go shower. You really do smell pretty bad."

"So if I wanted to kiss you again, you'd tell me to go to hell?" he teased.

"No. But by the sounds coming from your nephew's room,

154

he's about two seconds from coming back. He's gonna be impatient to get to the park, so you'd better get your butt in gear."

Oz loved this. Loved the teasing banter with Riley. He didn't feel as if he had to watch every word he said with her. "Maybe I should get you just as stinky as me, then you wouldn't mind that I haven't showered in days."

"I don't mind it now," she admitted. "It means that you were out there in the world doing what you could to make it a safer place. I admire what you do, Porter. It makes me proud to know you."

Even not knowing what the hell he'd been doing, or where, she was still proud of him. That made Oz more determined than ever to keep her.

He kissed her, making sure not to touch her with any part of his dirty black cargo pants and uniform top. He glanced at the hallway, not seeing Logan, and felt safe enough to nuzzle her ear and say, "I'm gonna go shower, and imagine you being in there, wet and slick with my soap. Then I'm gonna jerk off to get rid of this hard-on I can't seem to lose since coming home to you. I want you, Riley. Whenever you're ready, though. No pressure."

Then she blew his mind by pulling back so she could meet his eyes, and saying, "I want you too, Porter. And turnabout is fair play."

Oz frowned. "What?"

"You masturbating in the shower. It's only fair...since I've been doing the same thing in your bed."

Oz almost choked. The thought of her getting herself off in his bed was enough to make him reach down to grab hold of her hand. He'd taken two steps with Riley in tow, his only thought to pull her into the shower and take her the way he'd been dreaming of for weeks, but Logan appeared in the hallway, blocking them.

"Got my stuff!" he announced. Then frowned. "You're

supposed to be in the shower," he accused. "It'll be dark if you take too much longer!"

Oz heard Riley giggle behind him, and she dropped his hand. He felt her pat his arm. "Go on, He-Man, we'll be waiting right here."

"Later," he warned her in a low, husky voice.

"Can't wait," she admitted.

As much as he didn't want to leave her, he walked past Logan and ruffled his hair. "I won't take too long," he told his nephew. "Why don't you pick your backpack up off the floor and maybe start on homework while you're waiting. That way, you don't have to do it later."

"All right," Logan said in a tone that revealed he wasn't too happy to do any kind of schoolwork right then, but he wasn't about to disobey either.

Oz looked at Riley and felt his cock twitch. It was definitely time to get in the shower. But he consoled himself with the thought that soon, he'd have her in his bed—while he was there too. He couldn't wait.

CHAPTER TWELVE

It had been two days since Porter had returned from his mission. Riley couldn't believe how forward she'd been with him the other night. And she still blushed when she thought about telling him that she'd masturbated in his bed.

But she felt comfortable around him. Not all that shy. Too bad things hadn't worked out for them to enjoy anything more than short make-out sessions the day of his return. After dinner that night, when Porter had asked Logan about leaving Gillian's house, she'd felt like they really needed to hash things out between just the two of them.

And while they'd both protested her leaving, Riley went home. She didn't want to overstay her welcome. So she'd said goodbye to Logan, and Porter had walked her to her apartment like he always did. He declined to come inside, saying if he did, it would be a hell of a long time before he got back to Logan. So instead, he kissed her almost desperately in her doorway and left her with a long carnal look that promised good things to come.

Porter had been in meetings throughout the next day, and then he'd told her that he'd be late coming home tonight. He'd sounded guilty as hell about asking if she'd make sure

Logan got something to eat for dinner, and she'd done her best to reassure him that she truly didn't mind. That she liked hanging out with his nephew.

Still, Riley was looking forward to seeing Porter again. She wanted him. Was almost desperate for Porter to get his hands on her. Riley had no idea how they'd manage it, but maybe instead of her going back to her apartment, they could wait until Logan was asleep and she could finally experience being in Porter's bed at the same time as he was.

She should've felt guilty about wanting to have sex with Porter while Logan was there, but the boy had told her just that evening that he didn't mind if she dated his uncle. That he would really like it, actually. It was a bit awkward that he'd brought it up, but she couldn't deny she was grateful.

So now, she and Logan were both waiting for Porter to get home. Riley, because she wanted in his pants, and Logan because he simply enjoying being around his uncle, even if he hadn't verbally said as much.

They were watching *Wheel of Fortune* when they heard a commotion in the hallway.

"Open the damn door, bitch!"

Riley tensed, recognizing that voice. Miles.

"I swear to God if you don't open this door, I'm going to break it down, Riley! You've been ignoring my texts and calls long enough. This shit ends right here and now!"

By the tone of his texts, and the mean voice messages he'd left, it was obvious he was getting more and more irritated with her.

"Let me in so I can find my shit myself. You're so fucking incompetent, I'm sure you're just not looking in the right place!"

Riley shook her head in frustration. She truly didn't have his stupid game. She'd searched her apartment from top to bottom and had told him it wasn't there. But he didn't believe her. She'd thought he'd eventually get tired of harassing her and go away. Obviously she'd been wrong.

Logan made a sound from next to her, and Riley's guilt increased tenfold when she saw how scared he looked. Then the little boy stood up and reached for her hand. He pulled her to her feet urgently and dragged her around the couch. He pointed at the small space between the wall and the sofa. "You go first!"

Riley frowned. "What?"

"Hide! There's room. I already checked it out. If you lie kind of sideways, you'll fit. You're small."

Riley wanted to cry. He'd already checked it out?

She opened her mouth to say that it wasn't necessary for them to hide. That they were safe inside Porter's apartment and Miles didn't know they were there—when her phone started to ring. It was sitting on the kitchen counter, and it rattled and vibrated as it pealed out with the loud, old-school ringtone she'd programmed in.

"I *knew* it!" Miles hollered from the hallway. "I knew you were fucking your neighbor! Two-timing whore!"

Then seconds later, Miles began pounding on *Porter's* door. "Open up, bitch! I know you're in there! I can hear your phone ringing!"

"Riley!" Logan cried in a low, urgent tone.

Without thought, she moved. She didn't think Miles could get inside, but what if he did? She should be brave and tell Logan to hide while she faced her ex, but he sounded *pissed*. And she honestly had no idea what he'd do to her if she actually opened the door or if he somehow managed to break it down. So...hiding absolutely seemed like the right thing to do at the moment.

She lay on the floor then turned onto her side and wiggled into the small space behind the couch. She might be slight at only five-four, but it still wasn't exactly easy to wedge herself into the hiding spot. The couch moved away from the wall a bit farther, but she hoped it wouldn't be enough for Miles to notice if he did get inside.

Riley scooted all the way forward, giving Logan space to hide behind the couch as well. Her breaths sounded loud in her own ears as she panted with fear.

Miles hadn't let up pounding on the door. Her phone continued to ring as well. It allowed five rings before the voice mail kicked in. Then Miles obviously hung up and called her back. Over and over, her phone rang as he harangued her from the hallway.

She couldn't understand why he was so desperate to get a game back. Yeah, he was into his video games, but this was crazy excessive.

Miles called her every name in the book, and Riley felt horrible that Logan had to hear the vile things he was spewing. At no time while they'd been dating—maybe except for that last day, when she'd had enough—had she ever thought Miles would do something like *this*. He'd been verbally abusive, more so toward the end, but not physically violent.

Now, every other word out of his mouth was a threat to her well-being. He'd also started in on Porter, calling him a freak, a Neanderthal, Bigfoot. He accused her of sleeping with him while they were dating, saying she'd regret cheating on him.

Everything he said was completely ridiculous, but it was obvious Miles was on a roll and beyond irrational. Riley had no idea if he was drunk or high or what, but as bad as he'd been before, this was *not* the man she'd dated.

The door sounded like it was shaking on its hinges. She didn't have a good vantage point of the door from her spot behind the couch, but she figured it would be obvious if the locks gave way.

She closed her eyes and flinched with every beat of his fist on the door. Any second now, he'd break through...and if he found her, she had no idea what he'd do.

Riley was shaking now. Her nerves getting the best of her. She felt Logan's hand around her ankle and concentrated on that. She had to keep herself together. For *him*. If Miles did somehow get inside, she wouldn't let him put one hand on the boy. No way in hell.

Then as suddenly as the commotion started—it stopped.

Riley could still hear yelling in the hall, but it was muted now, as if from a distance. And Miles was no longer beating on the door, thank God.

Before she could crawl out from behind the couch and try to figure out what was going on, and what she needed to do next, Riley heard the door to the apartment fly open. It hit the wall in the foyer, and she froze. She could hear someone racing into the living room. Luckily, whoever it was kept going. She heard the person go down the hall where the bedrooms were located.

Within seconds, the person was back, and she heard him say, "Fuck!"

Porter.

He was back.

Riley wiggled forward enough so her head was sticking out from behind the couch. She saw Porter standing near the entrance to the hallway. He ran a hand through his hair in agitation and was staring at her phone on the kitchen counter.

"Porter?" she whispered as she did her best to wiggle out from behind the couch.

His head whipped around, and he was on the move the second he saw her.

"Riley!" he exclaimed. He had a hand around her biceps and was helping her stand before she'd even processed he was right there in front of her. "Where's Logan?"

"I'm here," Logan said as he scrambled backward to get out from behind the couch.

Porter kept his hand around her arm and towed her to the

other end of the sofa to get to his nephew. He went down on his knees, taking Riley with him, and he wrapped one arm around the boy and the other around Riley. He buried his head on Logan's shoulder and shuddered.

"Porter? We're okay," Riley said, trying to soothe him. The second she saw him, she realized they were safe, that he wouldn't let Miles touch either of them.

"Give me a second," he mumbled into Logan's shirt.

"Logan did good," Riley told him. "Found us a place to hide just in case Miles managed to get in. Speaking of which...where is he?"

She felt Porter take a big breath, then he lifted his head and looked at her. "One of our neighbors called the cops. They got here at the same time I did. They hauled him down the stairs, hopefully to the back of their cop car, and I came in here to check on you guys. You're okay?"

Logan nodded.

Porter put his large hand on the side of Logan's neck and rested his forehead against his nephew's for a moment. Then he nodded and slowly stood, helping Riley to her feet as well.

"Right, so...apparently ignoring your ex didn't work out so well."

She couldn't help it. Riley chuckled. She couldn't believe she found *anything* about this situation humorous, but Porter's words were the understatement of the year. Then she sobered. "I should talk to him."

"No!" Porter bit out. "No way in hell. I don't want you anywhere near that asshole."

Riley raised her eyebrows and gestured to Logan with her head as she said, "Language."

"It's okay," Logan said from between them. "I've heard bad words before. That guy at the door said a lot of them. I don't know what some of them meant, but it was obvious they weren't nice."

Riley bowed her head and sighed. One more thing she regretted.

Then Porter's hand was on her cheek. "Look at me, Ri," he ordered.

She opened her eyes and looked up into Porter's. The gray was a lot less stormy now than a few minutes ago. "I don't want you anywhere near that guy."

"I know, but maybe I can convince him I really don't have his stuff," she told him.

Porter pressed his lips together. "He's gonna believe whatever he wants. Seeing you, especially right now, isn't a good idea. But you're gonna have to give a statement to the cops."

"Okay," she agreed.

Porter looked down at Logan. "Slugger?"

"Yeah?" Logan said.

"Good job on getting both you and Riley to safety. I walked right through this room and didn't even think about looking behind the couch."

Instead of looking proud of himself, Logan simply looked upset as he nodded.

Riley wanted to know what that was about, but someone cleared their throat in the doorway.

Porter moved faster than she'd ever seen him move before. He put himself in front of her and Logan, between them and the person at the door. But it was merely a police officer, not Miles or someone who might be a threat.

"It looks like you found them," the officer told Porter.

"Yeah, they're good," Porter said.

"We're gonna need a statement."

Riley nodded and took a deep breath. She tried to step around Porter but he stopped her by putting an arm around her waist. Looking down at her, he said, "If you need more time, it's fine."

"No, I'm okay. I really just want to get this done so we can relax. I was looking forward to tonight."

"Me too," Porter whispered. Then he kissed her forehead and nodded at the officer.

The next hour was spent telling two different police officers what had happened, including her history with Miles. They asked if *they* could look through her apartment for the game Miles was apparently still bitching about, and she agreed. She had nothing to hide, especially not his ridiculous game. She told the officers she was willing to give Miles fifty bucks to buy a new one, but Porter told her under no circumstances was she giving her ex even one penny.

By the time Porter closed his door behind the last officer, Riley could barely keep her eyes open.

"Come on," Porter told her.

She followed him without comment as he towed her into his room, then to his bathroom. He turned on the water in the tub and, when it got warm, put the stopper in. He squirted a healthy amount of his body wash under the stream before turning to her.

"I know it's not a fancy Jacuzzi tub, and it's not one of those super-deep luxury jobs, but I think you need a nice, long, hot soak."

Her eyes watered. She couldn't ever remember a time when she'd been pampered like this.

He took her face in his hands and tilted it up. "I was so scared when I couldn't find you. I think tonight took ten years off my life."

"Mine too," she admitted.

"You relax. I'm gonna sit with Logan for a while and make sure he's okay."

"He said he'd already scoped out that hiding place. I bet he even tried it out, to make sure he'd fit," Riley told Porter.

He frowned. "I'll talk to him. Will you stay tonight? Not for sex...I just...I want to hold you. Prove to myself that you're all right."

"I'd like that," she said. And she would. She could take a

bath in her own apartment, but she liked being here with Porter and Logan. And the thought of sleeping in Porter's bed with him was too enticing.

Porter leaned down, and she went up on her tiptoes. The kiss they shared was intimate and gentle instead of passionate and explosive. It was as if Porter knew she needed soft right now. She hated that she'd brought danger to his doorstep, and that Logan could've gotten hurt because of her. The cops had told her that they thought Miles finally believed his game wasn't in her apartment, but she had no idea if that would keep him away. He'd been over-the-top pissed tonight—and it scared the shit out of her.

Pushing that thought away, she brought herself back to the moment. To Porter's lips on hers. He eased away from her and ran a hand through her hair. "I'll put one of my T-shirts on the bed for you. I have no doubt it'll cover you all the way to your knees. But if you want something from your place, just let me know, and I'll run over and get it."

He was always so sweet to her. "Your shirt is fine." Riley had a feeling once she put his shirt over her head, she wasn't going to want to give it back. Even if nothing ever happened between them, which she doubted would be the case, she wanted something to remember this moment. How cherished she felt. How wanted and cared for.

"Take your time in the bath," he ordered before stepping away from her. He closed the bathroom door, and she closed her eyes and sighed, backing up to the counter and holding onto it with her hands as she leaned her ass against it.

Tonight had been bad. Scary. She'd planned on sleeping with Porter, but not *sleeping* sleeping. Though she couldn't deny the thought of cuddling up with him and falling asleep in his arms wasn't immensely appealing.

Riley had no idea how long she was in the bathtub, but she felt much steadier when she finally climbed out. Better yet, she smelled like Porter. She cracked open the bathroom door with only a towel around her and saw the room was empty. She grabbed the T-shirt Porter had left for her on the bed and scurried back to the bathroom.

She was more than ready to make love with Porter, but not as anxious for him to see her in all her naked glory just yet.

She put the T-shirt over her head and smirked at how it did indeed cover her almost down to her knees. She brushed her teeth and hair, then headed for the door. She wanted to lie down, but first, she'd make sure Porter knew she was out of the bathtub and decent.

She headed for the living room—and stopped when she looked inside Logan's bedroom.

Porter was sitting on the floor, staring at Logan, who was sound asleep on his bed.

"Porter?" she whispered.

He looked up and immediately stood. The heat in his eyes almost scorched her as he took her in from head to toe.

"Is he okay?"

Porter nodded and left the room, pulling the door almost shut. Then he put his hand on the small of her back and walked with her back to his room.

Once they were inside, he closed his own door almost all the way, leaving it open about four inches, then finally spoke. "I just...once he fell asleep, I couldn't leave. I love that kid so much, and I hate that I missed out on years with him. He told me tonight that he hates his school. That there's a group of kids in his class who are mean, not just to him, but to nearly everyone. I'm thrilled he finally opened up, but I hate that I can't do more to help him."

"I think tonight showed him that he could rely on you to be there when he needs you," Riley said.

"Yeah, I guess. But I think he's still keeping stuff from me."

"Porter, he's not going to tell you every little thing that's bothering him. You have to give him more time," Riley said gently.

"I know, but it still tears me up to feel like he's hiding something."

Riley realized she wasn't the only one who needed pampering tonight. Porter had recently gotten back from a mission, which had to have been stressful, and now he had a kid to look after. Tonight had scared him, he'd admitted it earlier, so he needed her to be there for him just as she'd needed him.

"Go change," she ordered. "Then come to bed."

He smiled tiredly. "Any other night, those words would have me immediately sporting a hard-on."

"It's a good thing we already decided we weren't going there tonight then, isn't it?" Riley said.

"I'm glad you're here. And that you're all right," Porter told her.

"Me too. Now go. I'll get the lights."

He nodded, then turned and headed for the bathroom.

Riley turned off the overhead light and climbed under the covers. It didn't take long for Porter to finish up and join her. She caught a glimpse of his wide shoulders, a smidgen of chest hair, and long, muscular legs before he lifted the sheet.

Then she was in his arms. His skin was warm and smooth, and while she knew she should feel shy, being with him simply felt right. The shirt she was wearing drifted up her leg as she turned into him and hitched up her knee, resting it against his thigh.

He sighed deeply, and Riley felt the tension seep out of his body. *This* was what she needed. What they both needed. She didn't feel awkward, wasn't worried about what she should be doing or how she touched him. They were simply two adults soaking each other in.

"You smell like me," he murmured.

"I know."

"I like it better when you smell like you," he told her.

Riley smiled. "Noted."

A minute went by where neither of them spoke. Then Porter said, "I like this. A lot."

"Me too."

"I'm sorry I didn't get home earlier."

"Uh-uh," she scolded. "Miles was gonna do what Miles was gonna do, no matter what. It's done. I'm okay. Logan's okay. You're okay. We're moving on."

She felt Porter smile against her hair. "All right, Ri."

"What's on tap for tomorrow?" she asked.

"I've got more meetings to wrap up the mission we just got back from. I need to deal with Logan's school, because if he's unhappy, I gotta see what I can do to fix that. I'm about done trying to deal with the red tape about any stuff Logan might have left at Becky's place. I hate it, but he doesn't seem to really miss anything he might've had from before, so I'm going to move on with that. I also want to update my family care plan and get you listed as the person Logan will stay with when I get deployed again...if you're okay with that?"

"Of course I am. He's easy. It's not a hardship to be with him when you're not here, Porter."

"I just don't want you to think he's the only reason I want to be with you. I'd want you even if he wasn't in the picture."

"I know. It's weird that not too long ago, I was ready to be done with men for a very long time. Then I met you and Logan. Now I can't imagine not seeing you guys every day."

"Do you regret how fast we're moving?" he asked.

"No." And she didn't. Porter was so different from anyone she'd ever dated, it wasn't even funny. She'd be a fool to put the brakes on when she was happier than she'd ever been.

"How's your job going? Are we putting a crimp in your time?"

"No. I'm good," Riley told him, pleased that he'd asked. "I haven't really changed how many hours a day I work, I just work *different* hours now. It's nice to put my computer and headphones away in the afternoons and just chill with Logan, and you when you get home."

"Good. The last thing I want is for either of us to mess with your livelihood."

And that was just another reason why she was head over heels for the man in her arms.

Neither said anything else, and Riley loved the feel of Porter's fingers at the small of her back. He absently caressed her as he held her against him. Eventually, he relaxed completely under her, and Riley realized that he'd fallen asleep.

Smiling as she heard his deep breathing—that wasn't quite snores, but definitely not exactly quiet—she closed her eyes herself. She supposed some women might be annoyed by the noise he was making, but it made Riley feel not quite so alone. Like Logan, she liked knowing he was right there, just in case.

CHAPTER THIRTEEN

It took Oz a few seconds to remember where he was and who was in bed with him. But when he did, he couldn't help but smile. Yesterday had been tough. He hadn't been there when Riley and Logan needed him, but his nephew had done a great job in keeping his head together and hiding both him and Riley.

Oz had been exhausted by the time Logan finally fell asleep. After the emotionally tough homecoming, and then the talk he'd had with his nephew about how much he hated his school, Oz had been done in.

Falling asleep with Riley in his arms was exactly what he'd needed. Nothing about last night was awkward, even though it was the first time they'd shared a bed. He'd been too tired to do anything more than briefly think about slipping the shirt she was wearing over her head, but then her low, soothing voice had eased him into sleep.

He had another long day ahead of him. He and the rest of his team had to finish the report on everything they'd done and said while in Somalia, and while he usually didn't mind the intense AARs, this one seemed more irritating than usual.

Oz knew it was because he wanted to be home with Logan and Riley.

He'd asked Brain if the feeling of impatience with the job ever went away, and his teammate had only smiled and shook his head. "You learn to deal with it. But it helps when your woman is cool about how much time the Army takes away from her."

And Riley *was* cool with his schedule. She'd gone out of her way to reassure him, and to make sure neither he nor Logan ever felt like a burden. Oz knew he should be doing more to show Riley how much he appreciated her, but he was at a loss as to how to accomplish that.

She was so good at using small gestures to remind both him and Logan how often she thought of them. She'd even bought them matching cafeteria trays the other day...so their food wouldn't touch when it was served. It was a cute gift, and a practical one. He'd felt a little silly eating from his tray, but he loved the smile on Riley's face when she saw they were actually using them.

Things had moved fast between him and Riley, but he knew deep in his bones that she was it for him. It helped that his team was completely supportive. No one questioned him. No one warned him to slow things down. Trigger, Lefty, and Brain had been there. And Oz was determined not to let any crazy terrorist, hit man, or ex hurt his woman.

Thinking about her ex-boyfriend made Oz tense. Miles was not only an asshole, he was stupid for letting Riley go. The man had no clue how amazing she was. But Miles's loss was Oz's gain, and he'd do everything in his power to make sure the man stayed way the hell away from his family.

His family...

He should've been freaking out by even thinking those words, but instead he felt content. *This* was why he did what he did. So his woman and kid could be safe from the evil in the world.

Riley shifted against him, and Oz looked down. Her lips were pursed and he could feel her smooth, silky leg against his thigh. It didn't seem as if either of them had moved much during the night. He felt well rested, and the longer he lay there next to her, the more turned on he got.

But instead of feeling as if he had to have sex right that second, he simply enjoyed the intimacy of waking up with another person.

Movement out of the corner of his eye caught his attention, and Oz looked up to see Logan standing in the doorway of the bedroom. "Morning, Slugger," Oz said. "Join us?"

Even though he'd kept his voice low, Riley stirred against him.

"You both have clothes on, right?" Logan asked.

Riley obviously heard his question, because she shifted against Oz nervously. The slide of her bare leg against his own belied his next words.

"Of course. Come 'ere."

Logan walked into the room and climbed onto the bed. He lay down perpendicular to them at their feet, propping his head on his hand and staring at them.

Oz moved into a sitting position, keeping his arm wrapped around Riley so she had no choice but to sit up with him. The covers kept their lower halves hidden from Logan, and luckily, the appearance of his nephew had killed Oz's morning erection.

"You sleep okay?" Oz asked Logan.

The boy nodded, but it was obvious there was something on his mind.

"Things are crazy right now, but I promised you last night that we'd go visit the other schools in the area to see if there's one you like better. I know you didn't really want to go to the one on post, but you might like it if you gave it a try," Oz told him.

Logan nodded again.

"Is there something else on your mind, bud?" Oz asked.

"I just...is it ever okay to keep secrets? I mean, like, really big ones?" Logan asked.

Oz felt Riley tense against him, but he did his best to not overreact. He wasn't sure he was qualified to navigate these tricky waters, but he gave it a shot. "That's a hard question to answer without knowing the secret, but the way I see it, secrets have a way of growing bigger and bigger with time. Sharing them with someone you trust can help make them feel not so overwhelming."

Logan dropped his hand and flopped onto his back and stared at the ceiling as Oz continued.

"The thing is, some secrets are okay, like the one Riley kept from us when she bought us those cool dinner trays. We knew she was keeping something from us, but when we saw our surprise, it was exciting and fun," Oz said. "But other secrets can be harmful. Either to the person keeping it, or to the person who it's about. Those aren't the good kind."

Logan nodded and said, "But knowing who to trust is hard."

Oz hated the uncertainty in his nephew's tone. He wanted to tell the kid that he could absolutely trust him—then demand to know what secret he was keeping. But he took a moment to think about his answer.

Riley beat him to it.

"When I was your age, no one knew about the situation with my mom and dad. I was the new kid at school, since I had to switch to a different one when I got removed from my house, and didn't have any good friends I could trust. Then one time, my teacher asked me to stay in for recess. I was scared to death, thinking I was in trouble. But she put her arm around me and told me that she'd noticed I'd been struggling with my schoolwork, and she asked if anything was wrong. If everything at home was okay. I cried, and I told her how I was living with strangers and was waiting on my parents to come and get me when they were allowed to. And you know what happened?"

Logan looked over at her. "What?"

"My teacher gave me more time to get my work done. She had no idea what was going on with me, and because I told her, she was able to cut me some slack. Every day, she asked how I was doing and made sure I was okay. Her attention helped. A lot. It was hard to trust her with my secret, but after I did, I felt a lot better. I didn't tell my classmates, but even just that one person knowing, and giving me extra time to get my work done, made me feel a lot better."

Logan nodded and turned his head to look back up at the ceiling.

Oz wanted to beg him to share whatever he felt was such a big secret, but he also wanted him to come to him on his own. To trust him enough to tell him whatever was weighing on his mind. He looked at Riley and could tell she shared his concern, but was willing to give Logan time to think about what they'd said.

He squeezed her shoulder and felt her fingertips press into his chest in return. He loved how they could communicate without words.

"I was thinking...Killeen has a youth baseball program. Would you be interested in checking it out?" Oz asked Logan.

His nephew sat up on the bed. "Really? Like, for me to play, not just watch?"

"Yeah, really. And of course for you to play."

"But isn't it expensive?"

"I have no idea how much it costs, but I have a feeling you're gonna be really good, Slugger. You've got a great throwing arm, and you have no problem hitting the ball when I pitch it to you. If you want to play, I'll figure out a way to make sure that happens."

Logan's eyes got big, and he nodded slowly, as if he was

afraid if he showed too much enthusiasm, his greatest desire would be snatched away.

"Okay then. I'll do some research, and we'll see how to join a league and when they meet. If we can get you in, we'll start as soon as they'll let you," Oz said.

Logan smiled then. A huge, carefree smile that Oz had never seen on his face before. "Awesome!" he shouted, then scrambled off the bed and headed for the door.

"Where ya going?" Oz asked.

"I need to check my baseball stuff. Make sure it's clean and I'm ready for practice when it starts!" Logan said without looking back. He disappeared out the door before Oz could respond.

"I think he's excited," Riley said dryly.

"Ya think?" Oz asked. Then he moved quickly, turning so he was hovering over Riley, who was suddenly flat on her back, blinking up at him in surprise. "You're beautiful."

He wasn't surprised when she blushed. "Yeah, right. I just woke up and my hair's probably a disaster."

"It is," Oz agreed, smiling when she wrinkled her nose at him. "But it got that way because you slept in my arms. In my bed. All night. Therefore, it's the prettiest thing I've ever fucking seen."

"Porter," she whispered.

"Last night meant the world to me," he told her. "I needed that. The connection with another human being. With *you*. But it also solidified the fact that I want this," he gestured between them with a hand, "to happen. You and me. Dating. Making love. Trying to figure out how to raise Logan to be a well-adjusted, normal kid. Thinking about all the ways I can fuck him up scares me to death. But together, we make a pretty good team. Tell me you want this too. That you want to be mine. That me having a kid doesn't scare you away."

"It doesn't scare me away," Riley said immediately. "I've always wanted a big family."

Oz's cock surged at hearing that. She obviously felt it, because she smiled shyly up at him.

"Fuck. Right. Okay, we don't have time right now for me to show you all the ways I fucking *love* that idea. But barring any other disasters, ex-boyfriends going crazy, or the Army calling me on a mission tomorrow, I'm gonna make sure you know how much you mean to me tonight. I want to sink so far inside you that neither of us knows where one ends and the other begins. I want to watch you orgasm so hard, your eyes roll back in your head, then fall just as hard myself. It's gonna happen, Ri. Here. Ever since you told me you'd masturbated in my bed, I swear I can smell you on my sheets. I need you. And not just for sex, although I have a feeling that's gonna be out of this world. But because you're *you*."

"Um...wow," she said quietly.

"I know. That was a lot. But fuck it. Life's too short not to go after what you want. And I want you, Riley Rogers. All of you."

"I want you too."

"Good. Now...as much as I love you in nothing but my shirt, I'm gonna have to ask you to please put your jeans on before we go out there and feed my nephew."

Riley giggled. "I can do that. But you have to put a shirt on. Seeing you bare-chested might be too much for my libido to handle."

Oz burst out laughing. "Right." Then he got serious. "This is gonna work between us," he declared.

"I hope so. I haven't wanted something this badly in a very long time."

"It will. Do you want me to make the pancakes this morning, or you?"

"I'll do up the batter if you cook them. Logan likes it when you make shapes and I suck at that. Mine just look like weird blobs."

"Deal." Then Oz leaned down and kissed her forehead.

"I'd kiss you properly, but I've got morning breath. And if I start kissing you now, I might not be able to stop," he admitted.

Riley smiled. "I don't think I've ever had a guy admit that his breath might be bad."

"I'll be your first in a lot of things," Oz said confidently. After some of her past comments, he had a feeling no guy had ever taken the time to truly satisfy her. And he was definitely ready to take that on.

Oz pushed off her and rolled to the side. He caught a glimpse of her bare thigh and red panties before he forced his eyes away. The more time he spent with Riley, the more time he *wanted* to spend with her. And he could honestly say that had never happened in the past.

"I'll use the bathroom in the hall," Riley told him.

"Thanks for staying last night," Oz said from the safety of the bathroom doorway.

"Thanks for *letting* me stay," she returned.

"You've got an open invitation," he blurted. He hadn't intended to invite her to practically move in, but she was already spending a hell of a lot of time in his apartment. He might as well make sure she knew how welcome she truly was.

She pressed her lips together and nodded.

Oz was a bit disappointed. He wanted her to immediately agree and start discussing which drawers she could use. But then again, that wasn't Riley. She'd use caution because she wouldn't want to impose.

But Oz had a feeling she'd never be an imposition.

"Time's ticking," he teased. "Go get the batter ready. I'll check on Logan and make sure he gets ready for school and isn't too engrossed in his baseball stuff."

"Enjoy your shower," Riley said with a smile, then she climbed off the bed, slipped on her jeans, and headed for the door.

Oz watched her until she disappeared into the hall then forced himself to close the bathroom door. He'd definitely have to take care of himself in the shower, but with the way he was feeling right now, and with the memory of Riley in his arms still fresh, he knew it wouldn't take long for him to orgasm. Riley had him wrapped around her little finger, and she had no clue. And Oz freaking loved that.

* * *

It was hard for Riley to focus on her work when she arrived back at her apartment. It had taken an hour or two for her to really get into the groove. Thoughts of Porter and Logan were at the forefront of her mind. She couldn't believe she'd spent the entire night in Porter's arms. It had been better than her fantasies. He'd been warm, but not too hot, and having him next to her made her feel safe. Safer than she'd felt in a long time...maybe ever.

If she'd gone back to her apartment, she probably would've had nightmares of Miles breaking down her door and putting his hands on her. But instead, she'd slept like a baby. Porter wouldn't let anyone hurt her. It was comforting and thrilling at the same time.

And Logan was still breaking her heart. She hated that he'd scoped out a hiding place just in case he needed it. He shouldn't've had to do that. He should've felt safe with his uncle. But since Porter was a stranger, and Logan had obviously had a difficult childhood up to this point, he'd felt the need to come up with a contingency plan, just in case things went south.

And then that morning, when he'd talked about secrets... Riley had wanted to scoop him up and hold him tight and tell him that he could absolutely trust her and his uncle. But he obviously needed more time. She just hoped it wouldn't take too long. She had a feeling both man and boy needed each other, and the faster Logan could come to the realization that he could trust Porter, the happier they'd both be.

Though, she knew better than anyone that trust couldn't be forced. Porter would have to somehow prove to his nephew that no matter what, he could depend on him.

It was after lunchtime when something out of the corner of Riley's eye caught her attention. It was her phone. When she was working and wearing headphones, she always turned on the flash alert on her phone to let her know when she got a call. Not that she really got that many, but when she did, she wanted to be able to answer.

She pulled her headphones off and picked up her cell. Wary, because she didn't recognize the number, Riley answered.

"Hello?"

"Is Riley Rogers there?"

"Speaking."

"Hi. This is Principal McClain. There's been an incident with Logan Reed, and we haven't been able to get ahold of his guardian. You're listed as an emergency contact."

Riley's heart felt as if it had stopped beating. "Is Logan okay?"

"Yes, he's fine. But we need someone to come to the school to pick him up. He's been suspended, effective immediately."

What the hell? Suspended? Riley had a million questions, but she was already on the move. She had no idea what had happened, all she knew was that she had to get to Logan. "I'm coming. Are you sure he's all right?"

"Yes. Come to the front door. You'll need to be buzzed in, then come straight to the main office. It's to your right when you first enter." The man's voice was no-nonsense and unemotional.

"Okay. I'll be there in ten minutes."

"See you soon," the principal said, then ended the call.

As she raced down the stairs, Riley tried to call Porter but the call went straight to voice mail. He'd told her once that when they were in meetings, everyone turned their cells off so they could concentrate. It made sense, as they weren't sitting around talking about the weather, they were probably talking about some highly sensitive, super-secret national security stuff, but at the moment, she was stressed out that she couldn't reach him.

Putting her phone in her purse, Riley raced to her car in the complex parking lot. The Toyota Camry was old, and definitely not fancy, not compared to Porter's Expedition, but it safely got her where she needed to go, so it worked for her.

In eight and a half minutes, she pulled up to Logan's school. She parked in a visitor's parking space and jogged up to the doors. She was buzzed right in and hurried to the office. She needed to see Logan for herself. Make sure he was really all right.

On one side of the room, a boy sat against the wall. He had red hair and was holding an ice pack to his face. But instead of looking upset about his injury, the kid had the audacity to smirk at her when she entered.

Riley's skin immediately crawled. The boy might be the same age as Logan, but he reminded her all too much of the bullies she'd dealt with when she was his age. This kid didn't seem as if he cared about anything, certainly not about hurting someone else's feelings.

Turning her attention from the boy to the secretary, she said, "I'm Riley Rogers. I'm here about Logan Reed."

"You can go on into Mr. McClain's office. Logan is in there."

Nodding, and ignoring the kid who she could feel staring at her, Riley pushed open the door, trying not to feel weird about being in the principal's office. She was an adult, but some things never changed, she supposed.

Logan was sitting in a chair with his legs dangling off the

floor. His head was lowered but he picked it up when she entered—and the look of abject fear on his face when he met her gaze made Riley's steps falter. Was he scared of *her*?

She went straight to him and knelt on the floor in front of him. Her hands rested lightly on his knees. "Are you all right?"

Logan nodded.

"You sure?"

He nodded again.

Riley wanted to say more. Wanted Logan to talk to her, but it was obvious he was closed off at the moment. She'd have to find out what was going on from the principal.

"Thanks for coming so quickly. I'm Dr. Leonardo McClain," the man said, holding out his hand.

Riley wanted to roll her eyes. He was purposely using his title. She supposed he wanted to make sure she knew he was the important one here, the one with the doctoral degree. And Leonardo? Not Leo? That seemed pretentious to her as well. But she gave him the benefit of the doubt. Lots of people didn't have nicknames.

She shook his hand and said, "Riley."

"Right." Leonardo took a seat then gestured to Logan. "We had a major problem here today. Mr. Reed hit Gary Wittingham, another boy in his class, hard enough to leave a bruise on his face."

"Why?"

The principal blinked.

Riley didn't break eye contact with him.

"I don't think it matters why. The point is that we don't tolerate any kind of physical aggression at our school."

"I understand that, and I think that's a very good policy to have. I would still like to know why Logan hit this other kid. Context matters."

"Actually, it doesn't," Leonardo said pompously.

Riley was done with his attitude. She turned to Logan. "Why'd you hit Gary?"

For a second, she didn't think he was going to answer her. He looked down at his hands in his lap, refusing to meet her gaze when he finally said, "He touched Lacie."

Riley frowned. "What?"

This time, Logan's voice was stronger and he looked up at her. "He touched Lacie. She's in my class, and she's fat, so no one really talks to her much. But she's been nice to me. At recess, Gary was making fun of her. Talking about her...*boobs*." The last word was whispered, and it was obvious Logan was embarrassed to even say the word, much less actually talk about that part of a girl's anatomy. "Then he shoved her against the wall, out of sight of the teachers, and put his hands on her. *There*. I could tell Lacie was really scared. I told Gary to knock it off, and he asked me what I was gonna do about it. So I punched him. Lacie ran off crying. Gary went straight to the teacher and tattled on me for hitting him."

Riley saw red. She wasn't upset with Logan. No, she was extremely pissed that the adults had failed not only Lacie, but Logan as well.

She stood up straight and stared at the principal. "Right, so you're suspending Logan for protecting another kid?"

Leonardo didn't even flinch. "No, he's being suspended for hitting another child. As I said, we have no tolerance for physical violence here."

"But sexual harassment *is* acceptable?" Riley shot back.

The principal looked startled for a moment, then he said, "The kids here are too young to even know what that is. Logan should've gotten a teacher to handle the situation. Violence isn't the answer."

Riley wanted to tear her hair out. "So you're saying Logan should've left Lacie alone with this bully—who was touching her *private parts*—to go get a teacher? That's ridiculous! There's no telling what the kid could've done to her in the time it took for Logan to get help."

"We can't have kids hitting each other," the principal insisted.

"You can't have them sexually assaulting each other either," she barked back.

A commotion in the outer office stopped her from saying anything else.

They heard the secretary say, "You can't just—"

Then Porter was there.

He went straight to Logan, just as Riley had, and put his hand on his shoulder. "You okay, Slugger?"

Logan nodded, but his gaze was back down in his lap, refusing to meet his uncle's.

"What's going on? I was in meetings and couldn't answer my phone, but when I had a break, I saw that the school had called several times, as had Riley. I figured something was up and headed straight here. I called on my way but your secretary wouldn't tell me what was going on. Just that Riley was here and Logan was in trouble."

"Please sit, Mr. Reed," Leonardo said.

"I prefer to stand," Porter said in a steely tone.

Riley couldn't help but admire his steadfastness.

"Right, I'm Dr. Leonardo McClain, the principal."

"I figured that. Can someone please tell me what the hell's going on?"

Riley saw Leonardo frown, and she assumed it was because he didn't like Porter swearing. But this was definitely a time for a few swear words , and Porter didn't even know what had happened yet.

She decided to cut through the crap and let Porter in on the shit-show. "Logan witnessed a kid named Gary touching a girl's chest, and he hit him. *Doctor* McClain doesn't care *why* he hit the bully, just that he did. So he's suspending him." She couldn't keep the disdain from her tone.

Riley watched as Porter's entire body locked tight. She could see the muscle in his jaw working.

He.

Was.

Not.

Happy.

"Look at me, Logan," Porter ordered his nephew.

Reluctantly, Logan lifted his chin and looked up—way up —into his uncle's eyes.

"Is that what happened? You were protecting that girl?"

"Yes, sir."

Riley hadn't ever heard Logan call his uncle "sir," and it was obvious how terrified Logan was that he was in trouble.

Porter squeezed Logan's shoulder again gently, then looked at the principal. "So you're suspending my nephew because he hit someone who was assaulting one of your students. What's happening to the other kid? I'm assuming that's him sitting out in the other room."

"His father is coming to pick him up and take him to the hospital to make sure he's not hurt worse than our nurse thought," the principal said.

"And?" Porter barked.

"And he's going to have to apologize to the girl in question."

Riley thought Porter's eyes were going to bug out of his skull. "You can't be fucking serious."

"I'm going to have to ask you to watch your language," Leonardo said.

"You *aren't* kidding," Porter said with a shake of his head. "You're seriously going to make this little girl—who was probably terrified when Gary touched her—face her abuser and accept his *forced and insincere* apology. That's the dumbest thing I've ever heard. What are you going to do about protecting her and other girls from this jerk from here on out? And I'm assuming your lame reasoning means the other kid isn't being suspended?"

"He didn't hit anyone," Leonardo said a little less sanctimoniously.

"Right. He just touched a girl inappropriately without her permission. That's *so* much better. How long is Logan's suspension?"

"A week," the principal said.

Porter nodded. "Come on, Logan. We're done here."

Riley could tell Porter was barely hanging on to his control, but she couldn't help respecting him more than she had already. He wasn't going to hang around and let the pretentious Dr. McClain talk down to him for another second.

Logan stood. His shoulders were slumped and it was obvious he was dreading being alone with his uncle. Porter kept a hand on his shoulder as he walked him out of the principal's office.

Gary still had a smug look on his face as he sat against the wall, and Riley could tell that Porter hadn't missed it. But he didn't say a word as he headed for the exit. His stony silence was a little intimidating even to Riley, and she knew without a doubt that he wasn't a violent man.

It wasn't until they were outside the building that he spoke. "You're coming with us," Porter told her.

Riley didn't question it. She'd figure out how to get her car back to the apartment complex later. It wasn't as if she went out a lot, she could go without it for a while. She just hoped the school wouldn't have it towed.

Proving he was as alert as ever, Porter said, "I'll get one of the guys to bring your car home."

Riley simply nodded.

Porter opened the car door for Logan and waited for him to climb inside. Before he shut the door, he said, "I'm gonna talk to Riley for a sec, Slugger. Just hang tight."

He waited for his nephew to nod before shutting the door.

Then he took Riley's arm and led her around the back of the car. He stopped when they were directly behind the vehicle—then he pulled her into him so fast, Riley's head spun for a second.

But she didn't hesitate to latch onto him. She could feel Porter shaking as he held her.

"Porter?"

"I'm okay," he said. "I'm just *really* pissed off right now."

She kept her mouth shut, not sure what to say to help him. All Riley could do was hold him tight.

It didn't take long for Porter to get himself under control. He lifted his head and said, "Thank you for getting to him as fast as you did. I'm sorry I wasn't reachable."

"It's okay. That's why you put me down as an emergency contact."

"This being a parent is a lot fucking harder than I ever thought it could be. I'm not sure I'm gonna survive it," he admitted.

"You will," Riley said.

He sighed. "Okay, Logan's freaking out, and I need to get him sorted. Thanks for coming with us."

"Of course."

Then Porter took her hand in his and led her around to the passenger side of the SUV. He waited until she was situated in the seat before going back around to the driver's side. Without a word, he started the engine and pulled out of the lot.

Riley thought they were going straight home, but she realized pretty quickly that wasn't Porter's destination. She had no idea where he was going, but she didn't say anything.

She was pretty shocked when he pulled into a strip mall and parked right in front of an ice cream shop.

After Porter turned off the engine, he started to climb out. "Come on, don't just sit there," he said, when neither Riley nor Logan moved.

Confused about where Porter's head was at, Riley did as he asked and got out of the car.

He led them into the shop, bought them all huge bowls of ice cream, then found a small table at the front of the store.

Logan looked like he was going to cry, but he still didn't say anything. He took a few bites of the sugary treat, but it was obvious he had no appetite.

"Okay, so, I think I'm calm enough to talk to you about what happened now," Porter said. "If I'm understanding everything right, there was a girl on the playground who was being touched by this Gary kid, and she didn't like it. So you hit Gary to get him to stop and he tattled on you. Right?"

Logan nodded. "Lacie's shy. She's also fat. I'm not saying that to be mean, she just is," he said. "She's bigger than the other girls in my class. Gary makes fun of her all the time. Oinks at her and stuff when the teacher can't hear him. It makes her really sad. She's been nice to me, not like Gary or a lot of the other kids. He took her around the corner of the playground at recess where the teachers couldn't see him, then he pushed her against the wall and squeezed her...you know. Lacie was scared, I could tell, and she told him to stop but he wouldn't. She started crying. So I went over there and told Gary to stop too. He said no. Then told me to make him. So I did."

Logan's words were rushed, as if he wanted to get everything out before his uncle started yelling at him.

Porter reached out and put his hand on the back of Logan's neck, leaning forward so they were only a few inches apart. "I'm proud of you, Slugger."

Logan looked shocked. "Huh?"

"I'm proud of you," Porter repeated. "You didn't have to intervene. You could've ignored what was happening. But you didn't. You stepped in to help Lacie when she needed it. You know that your mom and I weren't on good terms, but she managed to raise a very good kid. I know she made mistakes, but I couldn't be happier with what you did."

"But I *hit* Gary."

"You did," Porter agreed. "And the jerk deserved it. No one should touch *anyone* in their private places without their consent. You know what consent is?"

"Yeah. It means without them saying it's okay," Logan said.

"Right. I don't care if someone is five years old, or ninety-five. It's *never* okay. And that goes for men and women, girls *and* boys. It's never all right. Ever. You did the right thing, and I will always have your back when it comes to you protecting others from something like that."

"But...I'm suspended," Logan said, lip quivering.

"Yup. Which just gives us time to figure out what other school to enroll you in."

Logan looked hopeful. "Really?"

"You aren't happy with the school you're in, and there are other schools in this area. Not a lot, but some. We can go visit them and see if we can find one you'll like. I'd already told you I was open to you switching, but I wouldn't let you go back to that asshole's school now even if you wanted to."

Riley saw Logan's eyes fill with tears. She reached over and put her hand on Porter's arm, wanting to feel connected with both of them. She was proud of what Logan had done too, and she was so relieved that Porter was praising him instead of yelling at him. Not that she thought he'd be mad at his nephew, but suspension was a serious thing.

"I know nothing about the last few months has been easy on you, Slugger. I want to do everything in my power to help you feel at ease. I don't expect you to be perfect, but will insist on you being respectful and a good person. And so far, I've been overwhelmed at the kind of young man you're becoming. You could be bitter and mean, like that Gary jerk, but you aren't. You have compassion and empathy for others, like Lacie. That will take you far in life, and while I hate that I didn't know you before, I'm so very pleased to have you with me now."

Logan didn't respond, but the tears overflowed from his eyes. He shut them tightly, as if he was ashamed.

"Don't be embarrassed by crying, Slugger," Porter told him, wiping away his tears with his free hand. "I'd much rather you show emotion than go through life like a robot."

"Do you cry?" Logan asked.

Porter nodded. "Yeah. I've seen a lot in my lifetime, so it takes a lot to move me to tears, but when it happens, I don't try to stop them."

"Like when?" Logan asked.

Riley was seeing a side of Porter she hadn't expected, and she was just as interested in his answer as Logan.

"I was on a mission. We were in a very poor country, and while I know we have privileged lives here in the United States, it still didn't prepare me for what I saw. We were patrolling, and we went around a corner and there was an alley. I looked down it, to make sure there weren't any bad guys lurking there, and I saw a little boy, probably about your age, although he weighed about thirty pounds less than you; he was extremely skinny. He was standing over a pile of about ten dead dogs. He was trying to sell them as meat.

"It was the saddest thing I'd seen in a very long time. I was sad for the boy for having to do that, and for those dogs. I cried for at least an hour after seeing him. I had to keep patrolling, so I couldn't stop and let my grief out. But those tears wouldn't stop. The other guys didn't make fun of me. They didn't tell me to 'man up' or some other ridiculous macho thing. They silently supported me and let me feel what I felt. I want you to always do the same. If you're happy, or sad, or frustrated...you can cry. It doesn't make you less of a man, got it?"

Logan nodded.

Riley felt tears on her own face. She couldn't imagine the kinds of things Porter had seen while on his missions. She'd just assumed they were all dangerous and he spent his time shooting things, but it was obvious she'd done him a disservice.

"Riley's crying now," Logan said.

Porter turned and, without taking his hand from Logan's neck, reached for her face. His thumb brushed a tear off her cheek.

"Oz?" Logan asked quietly.

Porter turned his attention back to his nephew. "Yeah?"

"I thought you were really mad."

"I was. I still am. But not at you, Slugger. I'm mad at Gary's dad for not teaching him to respect others. I'm mad at your principal for not having Lacie's back. I'm mad that you got suspended. But I'm not mad at *you*."

"Riley was mad too," Logan said.

"She was, huh?" Porter asked.

"Uh-huh. Her face got really red, and I wasn't sure what she was gonna do. It was probably good you got there when you did."

The look Porter shot her way made Riley squirm uncomfortably in her seat. Logan was right. It was a good thing Porter had arrived when he had, because she was about to go off on *Doctor* McClain.

"It's good she has your back," Porter told his nephew. Then he studied Logan's face for a long moment before asking, "You good?"

"Yeah."

"Great. Our ice cream's mush now, but I'm not gonna let it go to waste, are you?"

"No way!" Logan said with a smile.

Riley was relieved to hear the lightness in his tone. He'd obviously been scared to death about what Porter was going to say or do to him. And now that it was clear he wasn't in trouble, that his uncle was proud of him for what he'd done, it was as if ten pounds had been lifted from Logan's shoulders.

Then Porter turned to her. "*You* good?" he asked.

"Yeah. Are you?" she returned.

"I'm getting there," he told her. "Just need to spend some more time with my two favorite people and I'll be better."

It took everything in Riley not to pounce on Porter right then and there. Today had made it crystal clear that she'd fallen for him. He was trying so hard to be a good parent to Logan, and from where she was sitting, he was doing an amazing job.

They finished eating their melted ice cream and headed back home. Riley wasn't sure where things were going next with her and Porter, but she knew where she *wanted* them to go. Though she also didn't want to overstay her welcome.

She shouldn't have worried. As they were walking down the hallway toward their apartments, Logan asked, "You're staying for dinner, right?"

"Yeah, you're staying, right?" Porter echoed.

"I was going to let you have some guy time," she told them. "You need to talk about schools and figure out what happens next."

"We've got time to talk about that, right, Slugger?" Porter asked.

"Right. And you said I could help you make tacos. I want to stir the meat!" Logan said.

"All right, all right. You've convinced me," Riley said with a chuckle.

"Here's the key, go ahead and open the door," Porter told his nephew. Logan took the key and ran ahead of them.

Porter leaned in, so his lips were against her ear, and said, "You want to stir *my* meat?"

Riley choked on a laugh. "Porter!" she exclaimed.

He was grinning from ear to ear, and Riley couldn't help

but be relieved. The day had been pretty emotional, and she loved that he could tease her after everything that happened.

Then he got serious. "Stay. I need you. I was so pissed off today it took everything I had not to lay into that asshole. I feel bad for Lacie, but I can't let Logan stay there. Not with people like McClain running that place."

"I know, I was ready to rip him a new asshole myself," Riley said.

"So you'll stay?"

"For dinner?" she asked.

"Yes. And the night."

Riley bit her lip uncertainly, then blurted, "I want you. I'm not sure I can sleep with you again and keep things PG."

"PG," Porter said with a chuckle. "You're cute. And I'm up, literally, for anything you want to do. You can call the shots tonight. I won't go further than you're ready for."

"And if I'm ready to go all the way?" Riley forced herself to ask.

"Then I'm gonna ruin you for all other men," Porter said with confidence.

"I think you already have," Riley admitted.

Porter opened his mouth to say something, but Logan interrupted. "Got it!" he called out. "Come on! I'm hungry!"

"That kid's always hungry," Porter mock grumbled. "We just had ice cream, for God's sake."

"You know you don't care. He needs to put on a few more pounds anyway," Riley said.

"You're right. Ri?"

"Yeah?"

"I'm not taking you staying lightly. I know things have been fast-forwarded, with you staying here with Logan and being with us every night. I wouldn't ask you to stay if I didn't want a long-term relationship with you. If I didn't see us working out in the long run."

His words soothed something within Riley she hadn't

even known needed soothing. "Same. I love Logan, but I wouldn't be with you just to have him in my life."

"Good. I'll walk you back to your place later so you can grab some overnight stuff."

Riley wanted to blush at that, but she wasn't embarrassed in the least. She wanted to be with him. Wanted to be intimate with him. She'd never been as happy as she'd been with Porter. He was everything she'd always wanted in a partner.

"Okay," she told him with a huge grin.

"Fuck, it's going to be a long evening," Porter complained.

"I've heard that anticipation makes pleasure more intense," Riley told him.

"Oh, it's gonna be intense all right," Porter told her with a wicked look in his eyes.

"Behave," Riley said with a swat to his arm. "Your impressionable nephew is watching."

Porter didn't reply verbally, just smiled at her instead. He put his hand on the small of her back and gently herded her to his door. But his fingers slipped under the hem of her shirt and rested on her warm skin, making her shiver. He wasn't playing fair, but then again, the reward for them both at the end of the evening would be well worth the foreplay. She hoped.

CHAPTER FOURTEEN

Oz's emotions were all over the place. He was still reeling from the fact that Logan had been suspended for protecting a little girl from someone touching her sexually. It was insane that a fifth grader had done that at all, but it was even crazier that Logan was the one being suspended as a result. Oz hadn't lied, he was as proud as he could be of his nephew, but it still angered him that Logan had been punished for doing what was right.

On the other hand, he was almost giddy at the thought of Riley spending the night again. He couldn't stop thinking about her. How she'd gone all mama-bear with that asshole principal. When he'd asked her if she would be his emergency contact, he honestly hadn't thought she'd ever need to step in. But she'd been amazing.

The evening had been good. Logan seemed lighter somehow, more open. He'd smiled and laughed throughout preparing tacos, and after dinner, had sat down with Oz and they'd looked up all the schools in the area and discussed pros and cons. Of course, they didn't know what the kids were like who attended them, but they could visit each one to check that out.

They also talked about baseball, and Logan was still excited to start, but he also expressed concern that he might not be as good as other kids his age who'd been playing longer. Oz reassured him that he'd help him practice to get him up to speed.

Eventually, after walking Riley back to her apartment so she could pack a bag, they'd moved to the living room and watched television together. As the minutes ticked by, Oz became more and more aware of the sexual tension between him and Riley.

Logan was oblivious, lost in the action on the screen, but Riley was slowly driving him crazy...and she knew it too. Her hand on his thigh strayed into dangerous territory a few times, and he had to physically shift her so her back was to him, his arms wrapped around her, to keep those wandering hands still.

But of course, that put her delectable backside against his crotch, and his cock was more than happy with the new position. His arm lay between her heavy breasts, and he played with her fingers as they half-reclined on the couch.

Just when he didn't think he could stand lying there a second longer, the show ended and Logan stood.

"I'm going to bed. Oz?"

"Yeah, Slugger?"

"Um..." His gaze went to Riley, then back to Oz.

Oz stiffened. He didn't like the look in his nephew's eyes.

"Can I talk to you tomorrow? Just you?"

"Of course. Is something wrong?" Oz asked.

"No. I mean, not really. But I think I'm ready to tell you my secret."

"Okay, Slugger. You can talk to me about anything, I hope you know that," Oz told him.

"I wasn't sure until today. Thank you for not being mad at me."

"I would've been more upset if you hadn't done anything

to help Lacie," Oz reassured him. "Get some sleep. I called my commander and he let me take tomorrow off so we could get the school thing narrowed down. We'll talk in the morning."

Logan nodded. "You don't need to come tuck me in tonight. I'm good. You can hang out with Riley."

For a split second, Oz had a glimpse of the future. Of a teenaged Logan giving him a manly chin lift as he headed off to his room for the night. Of Oz heading to his own room to find Riley waiting in their bed. It both saddened him that Logan would grow up before he knew it, and excited him to think Riley might be with him for the long haul.

"How can he seem to be maturing right in front of our eyes? He hasn't even been here that long," Riley said with a small shake of her head.

Oz wasn't surprised she was on the same wavelength.

She tilted her head back so she could look into his eyes as she said, "You're a very good influence on him."

"You aren't worried about what his secret is?" Oz asked.

"Not really. I mean, *he's* obviously worried about it, but I'm more emotional over the fact that your support of him today was the push he seemed to need to finally trust you. He wouldn't be willing to open up to you if he didn't feel that trust."

"I'm sorry he doesn't want to talk to you about it with me."

"I'm not," Riley said without hesitation. "You're his uncle. You *should* be the one he wants to talk to. I'm only his babysitter."

Oz moved quickly, shifting and twisting until Riley's back hit the cushions. He hovered over her. "You aren't 'only' anything. You've spent just as much time with him as I have, maybe more."

"It's okay, Porter. Seriously. I'm just so glad he's going to open up to you about whatever's been bothering him. Just…

don't lose your mind if he tells you something you don't like. You two have come a long way, and the last thing I'd want to see is you doing something that would make him revert back into his shell."

"You think I'd do that?" Oz asked.

Riley shook her head. "Not on purpose. But if he tells you something about how he was abused in the past, maybe by one of his mom's boyfriends or something, I can totally see you losing your shit."

Oz closed his eyes in pain. Then they popped open again. "You think that's it? With all my talk about consent and all?"

One of Riley's hands came up and she palmed his cheek gently. "I have no idea. I'm just saying, whatever it is he tells you, you can't overreact."

"I hear you," Oz said, knowing she was giving him good advice. "I'll do my best, but if it's bad...I'm not sure *what* I'll do."

"You'll deal with it. That's what. Logan is a wonderful kid. He's had some tough breaks, but your sister seemed to love him and that comes through loud and clear. She might've had some issues, but that doesn't mean she loved him any less."

"I know. I'm still coming to terms with the fact that she kept my nephew from me. But I said some pretty harsh things to her the last time we talked, and she probably assumed I hadn't changed. It does make me feel a little better that she seemed to be getting her life together the last few years, and that she talked to Logan a bit about me. I'd like to think she might've reached out eventually. Especially since she lived nearby down in Austin. We were so close, and yet so far."

"You're a good man, Porter," Riley said softly, repeating what she'd told him before.

Turning his mind away from his sister and her problems, Oz took Riley in. She'd changed into a tank top when she'd gone back to her apartment. It was perfectly decent, but he'd had plenty of *indecent* thoughts about her since she'd come out of her bedroom. She had on a pair of elastic-waist pants that were extremely silky to the touch. He loved how they felt when he ran his hand down her leg, but he wanted to feel her warm skin instead. Needed it.

Lowering his head, he nuzzled the skin under her ear, and she turned her head, giving him more room. "Ummmm," she murmured.

"I can't wait to feel you under me," Oz admitted.

"What if I want to be on top?" she asked with a smile.

"I'd say fuck yeah," Oz told her. "Above, under, behind, however you want me, I'm happy to oblige."

"I don't care. I just want you," Riley said shyly.

"Time for bed," Oz announced. His cock was throbbing in his jeans and he knew he couldn't stay on the couch any longer without taking her. And he'd never risk Logan walking in on them. It would scar both him and Riley forever.

He stood and grabbed Riley's hand, pulling her to her feet in front of him. His gaze roamed down her body, and he saw her nipples were hard. His mouth watered with the need to take those buds between his lips.

He heard her chuckle as she struggled to keep up with him when he towed her down the hall to his room. Logan's door was cracked open as usual, and Oz made a mental note to do his best to keep them quiet. Then he was pushing open his door.

He shut it all the way behind them, keeping hold of Riley's hand, then turned so his back was to the bed and sat, bringing her with him. She straddled his waist, and he scooted backward, keeping Riley right where she was the entire time. His cock pressed into the vee of her legs, and it was all Oz could do not to shove up against her like a sex-starved maniac.

When he got to the middle of the bed and his legs were

no longer hanging off the edge, he turned them once more, so they were lying properly on the mattress.

"You know it's so damn sexy that you can do that," Riley said.

"Do what?"

"Move around with me sitting on top of you as if it's not difficult at all."

Oz grinned. "It's *not* difficult," he told her. "You're tiny compared to me, and you're kinda like my ruck sack."

Riley rolled her eyes. "Oh, yeah, just what every girl wants to hear."

Oz loved that they were joking with each other. He realized that he was having a good time. Yeah, he wanted her with every fiber of his being. Wanted to be inside her so bad his cock was throbbing in his jeans, but he loved that he could tease her and she could handle it.

His hands snaked under her tank top until he had both her tits in his hands. He squeezed gently, and Riley arched her back, pressing her flesh into his hands.

"I want to go slow. Make sure I don't hurt you," he said, his mouth watering.

She shifted above him, pressing harder against his dick. "For the first time in my life, I feel desperate," Riley said, looking him in the eyes as she did. "I've never felt this way about sex before. I've always kind of dreaded it. I did it because I knew it was expected of me. But with you…I *need* it. I can't wait for you to fill me up. I'm a little nervous because of how big you are, and I'm assuming that's the case all over, but I trust you not to hurt me."

Her words made precome leak from the tip of his cock. Oz could feel his boxers get damp with his excitement. She was going to make him come in his pants if he didn't move this along. "You can take me," he said, praying that was the case. He *was* a large man…all over. He hadn't had any complaints before, but Riley was smaller than anyone he'd ever been with. This was going to be a new experience for them both.

Riley smiled down at him, then reached for the hem of her tank top. She had it off before Oz could even blink. Her large tits were overflowing the cups of her bra, and he tugged at the material, needing to see her.

It took his brain a second to catch up with what he was seeing, but the second it did, he was doing a sit-up, shifting to hold Riley with one hand on her back to keep her right where she was, and the other lifted a luscious tit to his mouth. Her areolas were large and dark pink, and her nipples were puckered into tight little buds. He opened his mouth wide, taking as much of her inside as he could. Then he sucked. Hard.

Riley made a small squeaking noise, which morphed into a moan as he feasted on her breast. Before he knew what he'd done, Oz had pressed her onto her back, shifting to hover over her. Now their heads were facing the end of the bed, but he didn't care. Nothing mattered but Riley.

She didn't complain about the change in position, but she didn't lie passively under him either. Oz felt her hands slide down his body, but instead of reaching for his own shirt, she began to tug at the button of his jeans. Every time her fingers brushed against his cock, he flinched with pleasure. She was going to be the death of him.

He didn't want to take his mouth from her nipple, but he needed to be naked. Needed Riley to be naked. His mouth made a popping sound as he lifted it from her breast, and even that had his dick twitching. He brushed her hands away from his pants as he came up on his knees. "Clothes. Off," he said, sounding like a caveman of old.

But Riley didn't complain. Didn't tell him he was moving too fast. She reached for the waistband of her pants and lifted her hips to shove them down.

The sensual way she moved under him, and the feel of her thighs against his own, made pushing his jeans over his erection almost impossible. But somehow, and with some gymnastic moves that would've been highly impressive if he wasn't so desperate to get naked, Oz managed to kick his pants and boxers off.

He was in the process of removing his shirt when he felt Riley's fingers circle his cock.

He froze with his shirt just over his head, and literally all he could do was try to remember to breathe.

It was only a few seconds, but that was more than enough for Oz to grow to full length in her hands. He whipped his shirt the rest of the way off and stared down at her. He might be on top, but she was in complete control. Riley was naked except for her bra. The cups were pulled down, pushing her tits up on her chest. Her nipples were still hard, and he saw that her pubic hair was trimmed short.

She grinned shyly up at him as her small hands stroked his dick. "I was right, you *are* big," she told him.

Oz wanted to shift upward, fuck her tits, have her lick the head of his cock on every upstroke, but that could come later. He needed to get her ready to take him, and quickly, before he spurted all over her hands and belly.

"Please tell me you have a condom," she whispered, blushing.

Oz wanted to laugh. "How can you be embarrassed to talk about birth control when you've got your hands on my cock and I can smell your arousal coming from that beautiful fucking pussy?"

He forgot to warn her that when he got turned on, he had a filthy mouth.

"I don't know," she said softly.

Oz shook his head in amusement. "I've got condoms, Ri. I'd never risk you in that way. But I'm clean. I get tested by the Army on a semi-regular basis."

"Really?" she asked with a tilt of her head.

Oz inhaled as she ran one of her fingernails down the

sensitive underside of his dick. "Yeah, really," he said absently, closing his eyes and doing his best to memorize this moment.

"That's good. I...um...me too. I mean, I haven't been with that many men, but I made sure they always wore a condom, and I see my gynecologist every year."

Oz was done with this conversation—but not before he had a momentary glimpse of Riley in his mind, her belly distended, full with their child.

Oz fell to his back then pulled Riley over him. With a hand on her ass, he pushed her body forward. She laughed—until he took her hips in his hands and encouraged her to straddle his face.

"Um, Porter...I don't think—"

"*Don't* think," he ordered, looking up her body. She was so fucking beautiful. He loved this vantage point. He could smell her arousal stronger now, see the small pooch of her belly, and her nipples were still rock hard. She looked down at him uncertainly, and the thought occurred to him that it was likely she'd never had a guy do this before. At least not in this position.

Looking at her pussy, Oz licked his lips. Then he lifted his head and nuzzled her with his nose. Riley groaned.

"Quiet, Rile," he reminded her. "We don't want to wake Logan." Then he got to work pleasing his woman.

His tongue parted her folds, and he gave her one long lick. Her flavor exploded in his mouth. She was tangy and musky and he wanted more. He wanted her dripping all over his face.

He dug his fingers into the flesh of her hips and did his best to drive her out of her mind. It took a little bit for her to get comfortable with him eating her out, but once she did, Oz closed his eyes and feasted.

Her hips began to undulate above him, and he had a hard time keeping his tongue on her clit. But he persevered, loving how she began to fuck his face. She did her best to keep quiet, but little grunts and groans kept escaping her lips. She was passionate, and Oz had a feeling she'd be embarrassed when she remembered how she'd reacted to him eating her out later. But he fucking *loved* it.

It wasn't long before her thighs began to shake with the effort it took not to collapse on top of him. Oz used his arm strength to hold her right where he wanted her, and he could feel when her orgasm approached.

Her stomach muscles contracted, and she held her breath as her thighs clamped around his head. Oz flicked his tongue faster against her clit. It was swollen and sticking out from its protective hood, and he didn't show her any mercy. He wanted her to orgasm harder than she ever had in her life.

"Porter!" she exclaimed on a quiet breath, right before her entire body began to shake uncontrollably.

Watching and feeling her go over the edge was sexier than anything he'd ever seen before. And Oz *had* to have her. Had to experience all that was Riley firsthand.

When she fell to her back beside him, boneless, Oz rolled and reached for a condom in the nightstand drawer. He shifted to his knees between her legs, pushing them farther apart. He rolled the rubber down his pulsing cock and crept forward until the tip was brushing Riley's soaking-wet folds. Using one hand, he rubbed her sensitive clit with the tip.

Riley moaned and squirmed under him. "Oh, God, Porter. More. I need more."

He wanted to take off her bra. Wanted to tease her. But his cock wasn't having it. It wanted inside her. Now.

He notched his cock at the entrance to her pussy, then braced himself above her. "Look at me," he said in a low, husky tone.

Her eyes immediately came up to his and her hands latched onto his arms. He felt her widen her legs even more, telling him without words that she wanted him to continue.

"You're mine," he told her as he slowly began to push inside her body.

"And you're mine," she fired back, panting slightly.

"Damn straight," he agreed, loving the sound of that.

Then neither of them could talk as he began to fill her with his cock. It was a tight squeeze, and it took a few small thrusts before he could sink all the way inside her. But when his pubic hair finally meshed with hers, they both sighed in contentment.

"You fit," she whispered.

"Like a fucking glove," Oz whispered back.

"Why aren't you moving?" she asked.

"Because if I move an inch, I'm going to blow, and the last thing I want is to miss out on the feel of fucking you."

Riley giggled under him, and the movement made her clench down on his cock.

"Oh, shit," Oz said as his hips involuntarily pulled back and slammed forward.

Her giggle turned into a moan. "God, Porter, you feel so deep."

Every word out of her mouth turned him on even more, and Oz couldn't help but thrust into her again. He looked down as his hips continued to piston in and out, saw her copious juices coating the condom he'd put on.

He resented that bit of latex more than he'd ever resented anything in his life. He wanted to feel her wetness against his skin. Wanted to feel her hot, slick inner walls against his bare cock.

Her hips came up to meet his with his next thrust, making him forget about the damn condom. He loved that she wasn't passively lying under him. Thinking it might make him last longer if he gave her control, he leaned down and whispered "hold on" before rolling them. The sheets under them were bunched and there was a lump under his back now, but Oz ignored it. He could only concentrate on Riley as she tried to get her equilibrium back in this new position.

Her hair was tousled around her head and she had pink blotches on her chest, and she was the most beautiful woman he'd ever laid eyes on.

"Fuck me," he ordered.

A smile crossed her face—and Oz suddenly knew he'd made a tactical error.

He thought he'd be able to last longer if she was on top, if she controlled the speed of their lovemaking, but he was wrong. Seeing her naked body above him, and the excitement in her eyes as she shifted her hips, was going to be his undoing.

Once more, he did a small sit-up and reached for the clasp of her bra behind her back. He quickly undid it and pulled the straps down her arms. Now her tits hung free, and as she began to undulate over him, they swayed and bounced on her chest.

Oz had no idea what it was about women's tits that turned men on so much. Maybe it was because they were so different from their own. He didn't know. All he knew was that the sight of Riley's bouncing up and down in time with her shallow thrusts on his cock made him feel like he was fourteen again and sneaking a glimpse at a *Playboy* magazine.

His gaze wandered down her body to where they were joined. He had a hard time believing this was actually happening. That he was inside Riley. Finally. His fists clenched at his sides as he lay under her, letting her take what she wanted, needed, from him. One of her hands was on his chest, bracing herself as she took him.

When the other went between them and began to flick her clit, he was done giving her control.

"Hold on," he ordered as his hands went to her hips. It was all the warning he gave her.

* * *

Riley was lost in pleasure. She felt almost drunk and could feel another orgasm hovering somewhere deep within her. Porter was huge, and he filled her up so full, she was having a hard time processing just how amazing he felt. Every time she took him inside her body, she could feel his cock brush against her cervix. It didn't exactly hurt, but it made her very aware of him, of how big he was.

She loved that he gave her control. Loved that she could look down at his broad chest while she took him. She even loved the sounds their bodies made as they came together. But she needed more.

She brought a hand down between them and began to flick her clit. It was still swollen and sensitive from when he'd eaten her out earlier. Riley knew she'd relive *that* experience in her head over and over until she died. At first she'd been embarrassed, but he'd made her feel so good, she forgot all about the fact she was probably smothering him and had fucked his face until she'd exploded.

Her fingers brushed against his cock as he entered and exited her body, and that turned her on all the more. Riley didn't even recognize herself. She'd never been this sexual before. Hadn't needed to be filled with a cock like she felt she needed Porter's now.

She hovered on the verge of another orgasm when she felt his fingers dig into her hips.

"Hold on," he said.

Riley wasn't sure what she was supposed to hold on to, but she dug her fingernails harder into his chest and widened her legs a fraction of an inch. The strain on her inner thighs was immense, but she didn't care at the moment.

Then Porter began to fuck her. She might have been on top, but she was definitely not in charge. Not anymore. He held her still as his hips slammed upward, shoving his huge cock inside her over and over. Their skin slapped together as he fucked her, and all Riley could do was try to remember to breathe.

"Keep touching yourself," Porter ordered. "I want to feel you come on my cock. I want to feel it dripping down my balls."

God. His dirty talk was sexy as hell. And with Porter's dick inside her, making her feel things she'd never felt before? She loved it even more.

Her inner muscles squeezed hard when he pulled out of her, trying to keep him from leaving, then relaxed when he slammed inside her once again. In. Out. In. Out.

"Fuck, you're killing my control," Porter groaned.

If this was him out of control, she was more than okay with it.

Riley felt the telltale signs of another orgasm rising within her. She gasped and took the hand she'd been touching herself with and braced it on his chest.

But Porter wasn't happy with that, and he took over where she left off. His calloused fingertips roughly stroked her clit with a harder touch than she'd ever used before. It was enough to immediately send her soaring. She clamped down on his dick and closed her eyes.

"Yes! Fuck, that's it. Damn, that feels so amazing," Porter whispered.

Then he groaned quietly himself and pushed inside her even deeper than before. He held her hips tight to his and moaned long and low as he finally came.

They stayed locked together for what seemed like forever before her arms gave out and she fell on top of him. Porter immediately wrapped his arms around her and held her tightly to his chest.

After what seemed like minutes, but was probably only seconds, he asked, "You good?"

"If I was any gooder I'd be dead," Riley quipped.

"Gooder?" Porter asked with a chuckle.

"You gonna break out the grammar manual at a time like this?" she mumbled into his chest.

"Nope. Not me." She felt him kiss the top of her head before he said, "That was amazing."

"Ummmm." Riley was done. It had been a long day, and she was exhausted. And the two orgasms Porter had given her had pushed her over the edge. He moved her once more—she freaking loved how easy it was for him to manipulate her body—and while she wanted to protest when he pulled out of her, she didn't have the energy.

"I'll be right back. I need to take care of this condom and check on Logan."

"Mmm-kay," she muttered.

"Fuck, you're cute," Porter said before he rolled away from her. He straightened the sheet and covers and kissed her once more before he headed for the bathroom. The last thing Riley remembered was seeing his taut ass before he disappeared from her sight.

* * *

The last thing Oz wanted to do was leave Riley, but he wanted to make sure they hadn't woken Logan, and he did need to get rid of the condom. As he took it off his cock, he glared at it with resentment. Never in his life had he actually disliked wearing a condom. He'd always just gloved up because it was the right and smart and safe thing to do.

But with Riley? He wanted to see his come leaking out of her. Wanted to know he'd filled her up to overflowing. It was Neanderthal as hell, but he couldn't deny it was how he felt.

She was his. He'd said it, she hadn't protested, and in fact had reciprocated, telling him he was hers right back. His life had been insane lately, but being with Riley felt so right. Having Logan with him, and Riley at his side, and now in his bed...it all felt as if it was meant to be. He just needed to figure out what Logan's big secret was, deal with it, then they could get down to the business of getting on with their lives.

Oz cleaned himself with a washcloth, then headed back into his room to grab a pair of boxers before checking on his nephew. His eyes immediately went to his bed, and he saw that Riley was dead asleep. She was fucking adorable and looked so small in his huge bed. He couldn't wait to get back to her and take her in his arms. He'd slept amazingly well the night before with her there, and he had no doubt he'd do the same tonight.

Exhaustion tugged at him, but Oz pushed it back. He strode down the hall and peeked into Logan's room. The boy was fast asleep. He was starfished in the middle of the bed and he'd kicked off most of the covers. Satisfied that Logan was truly dead to the world, he eased his door shut almost all the way once more.

Then, as he usually did when he woke up in the middle of the night, Oz checked the front door to make sure it was locked, then did the same with the windows. It wasn't that he felt unsafe in his apartment, he'd just seen enough shit to want to be sure he was safely locked away from whatever crazy was lurking in the darkness outside.

Satisfied that all was right with the world, Oz headed back to his bedroom. He debated waking Riley to get her to put on his T-shirt she'd worn to bed the night before, but decided to be selfish this once. He wanted to feel her bare skin against his. He had a feeling he'd never get enough of her being naked. If he could have his way, she'd be naked all the time. But obviously that wouldn't work with Logan living there, so he had to take his pleasure where he could get it.

As much as he wanted to take off his own boxers, Oz knew it was smarter to keep them on. Even though Riley had taken him with enthusiasm, she'd probably be sore in the morning. He hadn't missed that it had been difficult for her to take him all the way, even after orgasming before he'd entered her. The last thing she needed was his cock pressing up against her impatiently all night.

Mentally telling his dick to calm the fuck down, Oz climbed into his bed. His sheets smelled like sex and Riley's musk. He fucking loved it. The second the mattress dipped, Riley turned into him. Her face landed on his chest and she sighed deeply, as if content.

His heart swelled in his chest. If this was what Trigger, Lefty, and Brain felt with their women, it was no wonder they were so anxious to get home from missions. Oz's life had been altered significantly when Logan had been dropped off on his doorstep, but that was almost nothing compared to the pivotal shift he felt at this moment.

If Riley left him, he'd probably never recover. He knew that without a shadow of a doubt. He made a mental vow to do whatever it took to keep her satisfied. Not just in bed, though that was a part of it. But with life in general. It wasn't easy to be married to a military man, and being special forces just ramped up the difficulty level tenfold. Add a kid to the mix and it was almost a recipe for disaster.

They'd need a bigger place for sure. One where she could have a home office. He'd build her a professional home studio so she could continue to do her job without distractions. He'd do what he could to cultivate her relationships with Gillian, Kinley, and Aspen. He knew from listening to his teammates that their women having friends to talk to—especially during missions—was important.

He needed to find a school where Logan could be happy as well. Riley didn't need to be rushing down to the school to defend his nephew when he'd done nothing wrong in the first place.

They all needed some stability, and Oz swore to do whatever was necessary to achieve that for them.

His eyes got heavy, and Oz did his best to turn his mind

off. His life had made a complete one-eighty in the last month, and he wasn't the least bit resentful about it. How could he be when it had brought him Logan and Riley?

Oz fell asleep with one hand on Riley's ass and the feel of her hot breaths puffing against his chest. He'd never been so content, and he already couldn't imagine a life without her in it. He was a lucky bastard. He knew it. And now that he'd found Riley, he wouldn't let anyone or anything take her from him.

Not his job. Not her ex. Nothing.

She was his. She'd agreed and had claimed him right back.

It felt fucking amazing.

CHAPTER FIFTEEN

Oz woke up feeling happier than he could remember being in a very long time. He was an early riser, thanks to years in the Army. He and Riley had shifted in the night, and now he was lying behind her, spooning her smaller body. Her ass was pressed against his cock, and he had one of her tits in his hand.

Smiling, Oz couldn't have kept his hand still if his life depended on it. He began to play with her nipple, loving how it immediately hardened under his touch.

Riley shifted in his grasp and sighed.

"Morning," Oz said softly. She fit against him perfectly, nestled in the cradle of his body as if she was born to be there.

"Morning," she replied sleepily. "What time is it? Do we need to make sure Logan is up?"

"We've got time," Oz told her. "Just relax." Then his hand moved down her body and he cupped her pussy.

Riley inhaled deeply and grabbed hold of his wrist. "Porter?"

"Relax," he said. "Let me make you feel good this morning."

"I...think I'm embarrassed to do this when it's light outside."

Oz chuckled. "Then close your eyes."

She turned her head to look over her shoulder at him. "Do you want to..." Her voice trailed off.

It was hard to believe the passionate woman from the night before was embarrassed now, but he didn't make fun of her for it. It was endearing.

"I'm guessing you're probably sore this morning," he said as he ran a finger between her nether lips.

She said, "Not really," at the same time her hips tilted away from his finger.

"I promised not to hurt you last night, and the same goes for this morning. Trust me."

"I do," she said immediately, relaxing. Her fingers loosened around his wrist, but she didn't let go.

He moved his finger up to circle her clit. He lazily caressed it, taking his time, not pressing too hard. It took a minute or two, but eventually he felt her body completely relax against him...and her hips ever so slightly start to tilt forward into his touch.

"That's it, Ri. Give yourself to me. I'll make you feel good."

"I always feel good around you," she told him, making a smile break out on his face.

He moved his finger down, gently collecting some of her wetness before turning his attention to her clit. Even with everything going on last night, he'd paid attention to what she liked and how she'd touched herself when she'd gotten herself off. He wished she was on her back and he was between her legs, touching her up close and personal, but he loved having her in his arms. He could easily feel every movement she made. When she pushed against him...when she squirmed if his touch became too much.

Her breathing sped up as his finger did, and she gripped

his wrist harder now. It felt even more intimate to have her holding onto the wrist of the hand that was pleasuring her.

"Porter," she whispered.

"That's it," he encouraged. "You're so fucking beautiful. Your nipples are like hard little rocks and I can smell your arousal. I loved how you tasted last night, and I can't get enough. The thought of you masturbating in my bed while I was gone is even more fucking exciting now. Promise me every time we have to sleep apart from here on out, you'll get yourself off. I want to imagine you here, in my bed, just like this."

She gasped for air, but didn't answer him.

"Riley?" Oz asked, as his finger stopped moving. "Promise me."

"Promise," she panted. "Don't stop! I'm almost there."

He knew she was. He was fast learning her reactions. His cock was hard now, pulsing against her ass as she undulated in his grip. He wanted to release himself, lift her thigh, and plunge into her wet pussy, but this morning was for her. And she was sore.

His finger moved again, pressing against her sensitive clit. Riley groaned and tried to widen her legs, but their positions prevented it.

Oz drew out his teasing for as long as possible, loving how sensual she was and how, when she forgot to be embarrassed, she let herself enjoy the moment. Frigid? What a fucking joke. She burned hotter than anyone he'd ever been with.

Riley tightened her hold on his wrist until it was almost painful before she began to shake in his arms from the orgasm he'd given her. It was too much for Oz, and even though he'd thought he could hold out until he'd gotten in the shower, he'd been wrong. He felt come spurt out of his cock as he ground against her ass. He should've been embarrassed, but he couldn't feel anything but satisfaction.

After a moment, she said quietly, "We're a mess."

Bringing the hand that had been between her legs up to his mouth and licking her juices off his finger, Oz merely grunted.

When he was done, he wrapped his arm around her waist and held her against him tightly.

"You came?" she asked softly.

"Yup. Right in my boxers. Couldn't help it. Feeling your ass thrusting against me, smelling your musk, and feeling you go over the edge under my touch...you were too damn sexy for me to hold out."

"Is it wrong that I freaking love that?" she asked.

"Nope. Making your man come is never wrong," Oz told her.

Riley squirmed until she was on her back looking up at him. "You scare me, Porter," she said.

It was the last thing he thought she'd say at a moment like this. He frowned down at her. "I hate that."

She shook her head. "I mean, I just...I feel so much right now. It's overwhelming. And if you decide that I'm too introverted, or not educated enough, or a million other reasons why you deserve so much more than me, I have a feeling it will destroy me."

Oz shook his head immediately. "You have it all wrong, Ri. I'm the one who should be scared. You're quickly becoming everything to me. My life is insane right now. I'm trying to figure out how to be a good role model and parent to my nephew, which isn't something most women would be willing to take on right off the bat of a new relationship. Not to mention the fact that I could get called away on a mission tomorrow for an indeterminate period of time. I'm terrified you'll get tired of coming in third behind Logan and the Army. Not that you'll ever really be third place in my life, but there *will* be times when I have to put either one of those things first."

Riley raised a hand and put it behind his head, pulling him

down to her. She kissed him then. Long and slow. When they were both panting, Oz lifted his head to stare down at her.

"I don't mind your job," she told him. "And I'm okay with Logan being your main concern. He should be. He needs you, and I think you need him too. I've got your back, Porter. As long as you want me to have it."

Oz wanted to say "forever," but he also didn't want to freak her out. Everything would be different from here on out, now that they were sexually intimate, but he was excited to see where things would go between them. He settled for saying, "Thank you."

"You're welcome," she told him softly.

"Now that that's out of the way...I really need to get up. My underwear is wet and it's uncomfortable. And I need to get Logan up and figure out what to make him for breakfast. And I've been a slacker with PT recently. Would you mind staying here with Logan while I go for a run? I won't be longer than forty minutes or so. Then you can head back to your place while I have my talk with Logan. Do you want to go look at schools with us today?"

"I do, but I can't. I have some work I need to get done," Riley said with a frown.

"I should've known that. Don't let me ever keep you from what you need to do," Oz told her. "Okay?"

"Okay. But I also don't want to feel as if I'm putting work over you guys."

"I'll never feel that way. I'm proud of what you've accomplished. You have an amazing business, and you're doing well for yourself. I don't want to do anything to hurt that."

Riley nodded.

They stared at each other for a moment before Oz chuckled. "Man, it's usually not that difficult for me to get out of bed in the morning, but I have a feeling that's gonna change now."

Riley blushed and pressed on his shoulder. "Well, go on then. Get going, you lazy bum."

Oz shook his head, once again enjoying her teasing. "Thank you for trusting me last night, and this morning. And for the record...you're anything but frigid. Anyone who can make me come in my underwear is one hot mama."

He could see his words pleased her, but she rolled her eyes. "Whatever."

Oz kissed her one last time, then rolled off the bed. He stripped off his wet boxers and threw them into his hamper, making a mental note to get a load in the washer before he left with Logan for the day. He walked toward the bathroom and turned to say something to her, but forgot what it was when he saw the way she was staring at his ass. "Are you ogling me, woman?"

"Yup," she said without any shame. "An ass like yours deserves to be ogled."

Oz leaned against the doorjamb, not embarrassed in the least that his cock was at half-mast and he was naked. "I was thinking last night that I wouldn't mind if you were naked all the time...at least when Logan wasn't around."

Riley sat up in the bed and held his sheet to her breasts. "Not happening."

Oz pouted. "Why not?"

"Because. Many women aren't as comfortable in their own skin as men are. Besides, you're much nicer to look at than all my jiggly parts."

"I like your jiggly parts," he told her. "And I can't wait until I get to inspect all those parts up close and personal again."

Riley smiled, then her eyes widened when she saw that his erection had grown. "Are you going to be able to walk around like that?" she asked.

Oz chuckled. "No. Which means I'm gonna have to take

two showers this morning. One now to take care of this," he gestured to his cock, "and another after I run. I can see being with you is gonna make me the cleanest I've ever been in my life."

Riley bit her lip, and her cheeks were pink with a blush. "I'll check on Logan while you...er...shower then."

"Sounds good. Ri?"

"Yeah?"

"I love having you here. In my bed. In my life." It was as close as he could come to telling her how he felt about her without outright saying the words.

"I love being here," she admitted.

"Right. I'm going to shower now," Oz said, and forced himself to push off the doorjamb. He entered the bathroom and shut the door firmly. What he really wanted to do was ask her to shower with him, but he knew they didn't have time. Making another mental note for his future master bathroom to have a huge shower with some sort of seat in it to make fucking her there easier, he leaned over and turned on the water.

* * *

An hour and a half later, Oz was sitting on his couch with Logan. Riley had made omelets for breakfast after he'd returned from a long, hard run. She'd done her best to make Logan laugh and relax, but it was obvious the boy had something heavy weighing on his mind.

Oz had walked her to her door, and she'd hugged him and told him to relax. "Whatever he tells you, remember he's doing so because he trusts you not to lose it."

Which was true. Somehow his support of the boy after the incident at the school had shown Logan that he could truly trust his uncle. It had taken a while, but Oz had understood his reluctance.

"Sleep okay?" Oz asked Logan.

The boy nodded. "I thought of something last night," he said.

"Yeah?"

"Why Oz? I mean, Riley calls you by your real name. Mom did too. But everyone else calls you Oz. What's it mean?"

Oz shrugged. "Back when I was younger, I listened to a lot of Ozzy Osbourne. I always had one of his CDs playing. Some of the guys I lived with at my first duty station with the Army started calling me Ozzy. It got shortened to Oz."

"CDs? I think Mom had some of those around her house."

Oz chuckled. "I'd forgotten that they're almost obsolete. Yeah, CDs. I loved to put his stuff on in my car and blast it. I'm surprised I don't have hearing loss as a result."

"Would I like him?"

"Ozzy Osbourne?" Oz asked.

"Yeah."

He shrugged. "I don't know. He's not for everyone, and his music is pretty hardcore. But you can take a listen and see what you think. I've probably got all those old CDs I listened to back in the day around here somewhere."

"Uh, I can just go to YouTube or Spotify," Logan said.

"Right. Of course. You kids and your technology," Oz teased. It wasn't that he was clueless when it came to digital shit and technology, his Delta team used that stuff quite a bit, but he was feeling a little nervous trying to make small talk when he knew Logan had something heavy he wanted to discuss.

Logan gave him a small smile then looked away.

"You can tell me anything, Slugger," Oz reassured him. "I might not have known you existed before too long ago, but I love you. I'd do *anything* for you, to keep you safe, to make sure you're happy and healthy."

"I'm happy here," Logan said softly. "And sometimes it makes me feel guilty."

"You weren't happy with your mom?" Oz asked gently.

"Not all the time. I don't remember a lot of stuff from when I was little. But I know she was doing a lot of drugs. Lots of different guys would come over to our apartment and she'd tell me to stay in my room."

"Did anyone hurt you? Touch you in private places?" Oz wasn't sure how to handle this situation. He just hoped he wasn't fucking it up too bad. He made a mental note to find a child psychologist, pronto. But for now, he'd listen to whatever Logan wanted him to know. He wouldn't judge, and he'd try to keep his shit together.

"No! Mom yelled at anyone who tried to go into my room. Stuff was hard though. I had to take care of her, make sure she ate, and sometimes I had to steal money so I could go to the store and get food, stuff like that. But things got better. The last few years were good. She didn't do as many drugs and was trying to stop. But if she went too long without them, she'd shake a lot and throw up. It made her really sick until she found some drugs again. But she was trying," Logan said defensively.

He was making Oz's heart hurt. For Logan and for his sister. Becky had always been independent, wanting to do everything on her own. If she'd reached out, Oz could've helped her. But if he was being honest with himself, he wasn't sure *how* he would've reacted. He'd already basically disowned her for doing drugs in the first place. If she came to him and asked for help getting clean, would he have done anything? He would like to think he would've, but it was a moot point now.

"That's good," he told Logan, meaning it.

"She met a guy, and I thought he was nice for a while. But then he and Mom started fighting. A lot. He didn't like that she was trying to stop using drugs. He still wanted to party and have tons of people over and stuff, and she didn't. She broke up with him, and I was happy. But he still came over a lot."

"He did? If your mom broke up with him, why was he still coming around?"

Logan swallowed hard and looked down at his hands. "Because...he wanted to see his daughter."

It took a second for Logan's words to sink in.

When they did, the ramifications struck Oz hard. "What?" he whispered.

Logan looked up into his uncle's eyes. "That's my secret. I have a sister," he whispered. "We have different dads. Her name is Bria, and she's six and a half. When Mom was killed, she went with her dad and I came here. I miss her a lot. I looked after her, protected her at our other place. And I haven't seen or talked to her since we were taken away. Do you think you can find her and let me make sure she's okay?"

Oz's head spun—and it took everything within him not to throw something.

He not only had a nephew he hadn't known about, apparently he also had a *niece*. Who lived God knows where with a guy who was a drug addict.

"Are you mad?" Logan whispered.

That was all it took for Oz to lock down his emotions. "No," he told his nephew honestly. "I'm thrilled that I've got a niece, and I'm sad that you're missing her. I know she's missing you too."

The relief on Logan's face was worth the effort it had taken not to lose his shit.

"Our plans for the day have changed," he told the boy.

"They have?"

"Yeah. We can look at schools later. Today, I want to see if I can find where your sister is living and take you to see her."

Logan's eyes widened. "Today?"

"Yeah, Slugger. You miss...Bria, that's what you said her name was, right?"

Logan nodded.

"Right. So, you miss Bria, and I bet she's probably missing you, because you're an amazing kid and I know you're an awesome brother. But I need to make some calls. Can you entertain yourself while I do that?"

Logan nodded, but he looked worried again. "You don't want me to hear you when you talk to people?"

Oz sighed. "Here's the thing—you did the right thing in telling me about your sister, but I should've been informed that I had a niece from the second you were brought to me. And I wasn't. I'm probably going to use some not-so-nice words when I call CPS. I'm trying to do the right thing by shielding you from that."

"I'm ten," Logan scoffed. "I'm not a baby, I've heard swearing before."

"I know, but you shouldn't hear it from your uncle," Oz told him.

Logan kept his eyes locked on Oz for a long moment before he nodded. Then he asked, "Can Riley come with us? I know she'd probably like Bree."

"That's what she likes to be called? Bree?" Oz asked.

Logan nodded.

"Right. First, there's no probably about it, Riley's gonna *love* Bree. And yes, I can ask her if she wants to come with us. But I'm going to wait to tell her until after I make my calls. She has work she needs to get done, Slugger. I want her to come too, but it might take a while for me to get ahold of the right people so we can go say hi to your sister. Okay?"

Oz could see his nephew thinking about that for a moment, then he nodded again. "Okay."

"Why don't you go into my room and turn on the TV in there. I'm sure you can find something to entertain you while

I try to get through the red tape that is Child Protective Services."

"Why's the tape red?" Logan asked with an adorable tilt of his head.

Oz chuckled, which was a miracle because he definitely didn't feel like laughing. "It's just a saying," he told Logan.

"It's a weird one," Logan said.

Oz reached out and put his hand on his nephew's shoulder. "Thanks for telling me your secret, Slugger. I know it wasn't easy. Can I ask you something though?"

"Uh-huh."

"Why now? Did you just get to the point where you missed Bree enough to say something?"

Logan shook his head and looked his uncle in the eye. "It's because you agreed with me that it was okay to hit Gary. I didn't know if you would even want to meet Bree or not, especially since you were mad at Mom, but when you talked about the consent thing, I knew I could trust you."

Oz closed his eyes and took a big breath in through his nose before opening them again. "Your trust means the world to me," he told Logan. "I'm not your mom, or your dad, but I'll do everything in my power to keep that trust. I want only the best for you, and your sister, and I'll always do what I think is right for you. That might not always make you happy, but in the long run, I hope you can look back and understand why I made the decisions I did. Thank you for sharing your secret. As I told you before, sometimes sharing a secret can feel really scary, but afterward, it's as if a load has been taken off your shoulders."

"I do feel better," Logan admitted.

"Good. Now go find something on TV that will rot your brain."

Logan smiled. "You're weird. Watching television won't rot my brain."

Oz stood at the same time Logan did. He watched as his

nephew headed down the hallway toward the master bedroom. He maintained his composure until the boy was out of sight, then he clenched his fists and squeezed his eyes shut. His entire body trembled. It took everything within him not to lash out, not to punch the wall or throw something. But doing anything like that would scare Logan, and that was the last thing he wanted to do.

It was unconscionable that no one had told him he had a niece! And while he partly understood why Bria would be placed with her biological father, it still angered him. He definitely didn't like the fact that her father may be doing drugs. His niece had been with the man for over a month. Oz hated to think that she might've been in a precarious situation for that long.

But maybe he was wrong. Maybe her father was thrilled to get his little girl full time and she was being spoiled living in his house.

Oz's first instinct when he had himself under control was to call Riley. He needed her. Needed her support and even-keel way of looking at things. But she had work to do, and he had to let her—because he was *definitely* going to need her when he took Logan to see his sister. And nothing was going to keep him from doing that today.

Oz walked into the kitchen where he'd left his phone after breakfast and grabbed a piece of paper and a pen. He sat at his dining room table and clicked on an internet browser on his phone. He needed answers. Now.

Three hours later, Oz had gotten the information he'd needed. It had taken several calls, and waiting way too long for someone to call him back, but he'd finally gotten ahold of the woman who'd been responsible for placing Logan and

Bria. She'd quickly informed him that she couldn't allow him to visit Bria by himself. But eventually, she'd agreed to meet him and Logan at the house where Bria was living with her father. Said she'd move up the home visit she'd been planning for next month.

Apparently, someone was supposed to visit *his* apartment as well, to make sure Logan had settled in all right and there were no problems. But Oz hadn't been informed of that when Logan had been dropped off, and he had no idea when that was supposed to happen.

So far, he wasn't impressed with CPS, but he tried not to judge too harshly. There were a lot of kids in the system and not enough employees to check on them. But that didn't mean the pit in his stomach wasn't churning and spinning.

He'd checked on Logan a bit ago and had found him asleep in the huge armchair in the corner of his master bedroom. The kid had probably slept like shit the night before, worried about revealing his secret.

Reaching for his phone, Oz shot Riley a text. He knew she might not hear him knocking on her door if she had her headphones in and was working.

Oz: I need you.

He could've explained more, but he didn't want to get into the goat-screw that the morning had been over the phone.

She responded immediately.

Riley: I'm on my way.

. . .

Oz loved that response. The second he said he needed her, she dropped everything to come to him. And that was why he hadn't bothered her earlier. She would've sat next to him, holding his hand and helping him find the right numbers to call, but he didn't want to be the reason she lost any clients.

He got up and headed to his front door. By the time he opened it, she was halfway down the hall. She hadn't wasted any time. The second she was within reach, Oz wrapped his arms around her and pulled her into him. She came willingly and held on tightly as he backed them into his apartment and shut the door.

"What's wrong? Was Logan's secret that bad? Is he all right? Are *you* all right? What can I do?"

Oz's throat got tight. He swallowed hard, then, standing right there in the short hallway, explained what was going on.

"We're okay. Logan's secret was that he has a sister."

Riley stared up at him for a second before his words registered. "Holy shit, you have a niece?"

"Apparently. Her name is Bria. She was sent to live with her biological father."

"How come you didn't know about her?" Riley asked, her ire rising. "That's bullshit! You should've been informed that your sister had two kids from the get-go."

Oz knew it was wrong, but he loved that she was so pissed on his behalf. "I know. And believe me, I made sure the poor woman who had the misfortune to pick up the phone at CPS knew that too. It took some doing, and several phone calls back and forth, before they agreed to let me bring Logan down to see his sister today."

Riley's eyes got wide. "Today?"

"Yeah. How much of your work did you get done this morning?"

"Almost all of it," she said immediately. "It seems that when I have the right motivation, I work a lot faster. And before you ask, *you're* my motivation."

"So you'll come with us?" Oz asked.

"Of course. How's Logan?"

"He's sleeping right now. I think he was probably up a lot of the night stressing about telling me his secret."

"Poor thing," Riley said with a frown.

It was obvious she was going to be a great mother. Oz pushed that thought away. They weren't at that point in their relationship...yet. "A CPS worker is going to meet us at the house down in Austin. We can stop and grab something for lunch along the way."

"Okay, I just need to grab my purse and put my shoes on, then I'll be ready to go," Riley said.

Oz looked down and realized that her feet were bare. She'd been in such a hurry to get to him, she hadn't even bothered to put on shoes. God, had he ever been with someone as unselfish? He didn't think so. "Take a breath, Rile. We've got time."

She did as he requested, then rested her forehead against the center of his chest. "You have a niece," she whispered.

"I know."

"How old is she?"

"Six and a half," Oz said.

"So that's what, first grade?" Riley asked.

"No clue," Oz admitted. "We can ask Logan for more details about her on our way to Austin."

Riley looked up at him as her hands rubbed his back gently. "How are you *really* doing?"

"Honestly? I'm pissed. It was bad enough when I found out I had a nephew I didn't know about. But this seems worse, somehow. I'm not mad at Logan for keeping it from me. He didn't trust me, and he's used to being Bree's protector. But I'm more upset at the system. Logan said he thinks he's using drugs."

"Who?" Riley asked, her brows furrowing in confusion.

"Bree's father."

Her eyes widened. "And yet she was still placed with him? That's so wrong!" she hissed.

"They can't exactly take my word that the man is an addict. I'm sure they hear all sorts of stories from people who want custody of a kid. A father is also a closer relation than an uncle," Oz said, repeating what he'd been told several times over the phone.

"I. Don't. Care. You're an Army soldier. You're employed in a respected job. You should've at least been given consideration. Not to mention the fact that they separated siblings!"

"Which is what I told the woman on the phone," Oz told her. Again, he couldn't help but love how pissed off she was on his behalf. "I'm also a single man, which worked against me. They weren't sure about placing a little girl with me."

"And that's bullshit too," Riley hissed. "Is her dad married?"

"Living with a girlfriend," Oz said.

"So how is that different?" Riley asked. It was a rhetorical question because she went on. "Just because someone is married or living with someone doesn't make them a good person, or the right person to trust with a child. And if Logan said he uses drugs, that's even worse! When are we leaving? You need to go wake Logan so we can go. I'll go grab my shit."

Riley pulled away from Oz and turned to open the door to his apartment.

He gently grabbed her arm and pulled her back against his chest. One hand went behind her head and the other to her back. "Shhhh, Ri. It's okay."

She shook her head. "It's not!" she insisted. "Logan's sister is probably scared and confused. I can't stand the thought of her wondering where her brother went. And if her dad's not looking after her properly? We need to get there to see for ourselves that she's okay."

"And we will," Oz soothed. Trying to calm Riley did wonders for his anxiety. It took him out of his own head. "Take a breath, Ri."

He felt her inhale, then slowly let it out. Oz took her face in his hands and tipped it up to his. "Better?"

She nodded but said, "No."

Oz smiled. God, she made him feel so much better, just by being herself. Then he sobered. "I need you to help me keep it together today," he said. "If I think there's been one hair on Bree's head that's been harmed, I'm going to need you to reel me in."

Riley immediately nodded.

"I mean it, Ri. Don't let me do anything that will put my custody of Logan in jeopardy."

"I won't," she vowed. "She's gonna be fine. It'll be a good visit."

Oz could tell she was doing her best to rein in her own frustration and anger over the situation, and he loved her all the more for it.

Yeah...

He loved her.

"Thank you," he said, bending down to kiss her to try to distract himself. Now wasn't the moment to declare his feelings, but he knew he wouldn't be able to keep them to himself for long. He had no problem saying the words first, but now wasn't the time or place.

Riley kissed him back, and they made out in his front hallway for several minutes. Oz finally pulled back and took a big breath. They needed to get going. "You're staying tonight, right?" he blurted.

She blinked up at him. "Why?"

"After today, I'm gonna need to hold you," Oz admitted without embarrassment.

"I'll stay if you want me to."

"I want you to."

Riley smiled up at him. "Then I guess I'm staying."

"Great. Now go put some shoes on, woman. I'll get Logan up and we'll head out."

Riley nodded and turned to the door. She turned back at the last second before she opened it. "Porter?"

"Yeah?"

"I think you're doing an amazing job with Logan. Not everyone would be as upset as you are about learning they have a niece they didn't know about. They'd just be grateful they didn't get two kids dumped on their doorstep with no warning."

"Then they'd be stupid," Oz said without hesitation. "I'm not saying having Logan has been easy, it's disrupted just about everything in my life. But he's a blessing. One I'm privileged to have. And two kids placed in my care would've been twice the disruption, but also twice the blessing."

He saw tears in Riley's eyes as she gave him a small nod, then opened his door.

As Oz turned to go wake Logan, he thought about how much his life had changed. He'd never realized how difficult it was to be a single parent, especially one in the Army. He loved his job, but the government didn't make it easy to be a parent while expecting him to give one hundred percent to his country. He'd been afraid he might have to quit Delta Force, but with the help of his teammates, and their women, and Riley, he'd become more confident in his ability to continue on with his career. Thinking about quitting Delta was as painful as losing a limb.

Pushing those thoughts to the back of his mind, Oz opened his bedroom door. It was time to reunite Logan with his sister. They'd been apart too long. And a small part of Oz hoped that maybe, just maybe, Bria might come to like him too. Maybe not immediately, it hadn't been easy to gain

Logan's trust; but down the line, she might someday call him Uncle Oz.

First things first—finding Seth Matthews' house in Austin and reuniting two siblings. Oz couldn't help thinking that if Seth—and his girlfriend, Vanessa Huff—hadn't been treating his daughter as if she was the most precious thing in their world, someone was going to pay dearly.

CHAPTER SIXTEEN

Riley's heart was beating a mile a minute. She was excited and nervous to meet Porter's niece. Logan had been talking nonstop while they drove south toward Austin.

They'd learned that she was indeed in the first grade, and that she and Logan had ridden the school bus together every day. She'd apparently inherited her dad's auburn hair, but had her mom's hazel eyes. She liked Pokémon, and Logan had been reading Harry Potter to her before their mom died.

The love in Logan's voice was easy to hear, and it was almost too painful to bear. It was obvious he missed his sister dreadfully, and that he was worried about her.

"Are we there yet?" he asked from the back seat.

Riley smiled.

"Almost, Slugger," Porter reassured him.

"I taught her to hide, you know," Logan said out of the blue.

"What?" Riley asked.

"You know, how we hid behind the couch when that guy was trying to find you?" Logan asked Riley.

"Yeah, I remember. It was very clever."

"I taught Bree that too." His voice lowered. "The day our

mom was killed, she was sick. She stayed home from school. Bree told me someone knocked on the door and Mom told her to hide. She hid where I taught her."

Riley looked over at Porter, who glanced over at *her*. She figured the disbelief on Porter's face was probably reflected on her own. "Bree was in the apartment when your mom was killed?" Riley asked Logan.

He nodded. "She was scared and only came out once the police came. She said the people who hurt Mommy didn't even know she was there."

"Fuck," Porter muttered under his breath.

Riley was thinking the same thing. As far as they knew, the investigators hadn't figured out who'd killed Becky yet. And if the little girl was in the apartment at the time, she would be a damn good source of information.

"What did she tell the police about what happened?" she asked.

Logan shrugged. "Nothing. Lots of people tried to talk to her, but all she said was that she hid and didn't see anything. She was scared," Logan said. "She wouldn't even talk about it with me. Then we were taken away."

Riley reached out and took Porter's hand in hers. He was tense and frowning. She took a deep breath. "Well, I'd say you're really good at finding hiding places," Riley told Logan.

"I am," he agreed.

Silence settled in the car after Logan's bombshell. Things seemed to be getting more and more complicated, and she felt so bad for the entire Reed family. If Porter got custody of Bria, and she really hoped he would, Riley would suggest he take her to see a child psychologist, one of those who were experts in getting kids to talk about traumatic events and crimes. But it would need to be handled with the utmost care. The last thing she wanted was the little girl being traumatized by having to relive what had happened to her mom.

It took another twenty minutes for them to arrive at Seth

Matthews' house. Riley frowned as they headed down the street. They were definitely in a not-so-good part of town. That didn't mean the people living in the houses weren't doing their best to provide for their families, but the lawns were all overgrown and full of weeds, fences were broken and falling apart, and there just seemed to be an overall neglectful vibe.

Porter pulled his Expedition to the curb in front of the address they were given. There was a white Crown Victoria parked in the driveway and a woman in a navy-blue suit was standing at the front door, obviously having an argument with a woman.

"Stay here," Porter ordered as he reached for the handle of his door.

"Breathe, Porter," Riley said as she touched his back.

He nodded, then was out and closing the door behind him.

"What's going on?" Logan asked.

"I don't know, but your uncle will figure it out. Just hang tight."

Riley watched as Porter strode up to the two women. He didn't crowd them, but every muscle in his body was tight as he listened to the exchange.

Without thought, Riley reached for her phone. She didn't know what was going on, but it was obvious this wasn't going to be the nice, congenial visit they'd hoped for. Porter needed support, maybe more than she could provide, and she couldn't think of anyone better to have his back than his teammates. It would take some time for any of them to get there, but she had a feeling they'd need the support. Mental, emotional, and possibly physical.

She clicked on the first name that she thought of. Grover.

"Hey, Ri, what's up?" he asked as he answered.

"Grover, I'm in Austin with Porter. And I think we need you."

"What's wrong? Where are you?"

She gave him a short rundown, being vague since Logan was in the car listening to her every word.

"I'm on my way, and I'm calling the guys too."

"I don't know what's going on, if anything. I'm probably overreacting."

"I'd say you aren't," Grover told her.

"All of you don't need to come. I forgot you guys were at work," she said.

"I wish we all could. There are some sensitive meetings going on right now, but we don't all need to be there. I'll call Lefty and Doc. Okay?"

"Thank you," Riley said.

"We'll be there as soon as we can. Hang on." He ended the connection without another word, and Riley let out the breath she hadn't realized she'd been holding.

"I'm scared," Logan whispered. "Vanessa looks mad."

And she did. Just then, a man with red hair and an extremely scruffy beard appeared behind the woman. Riley assumed it was Bria's father.

Logan whimpered—and the sound made Riley's blood run cold. He sounded terrified.

"Is that Seth? Bria's dad?" she asked.

"Uh-huh. I don't like it when he yells."

They could hear Seth shouting from across the yard even with the doors of the Expedition shut.

"It's okay," Riley soothed. She had to admit she didn't like it when Seth yelled either, and she hadn't even met the man. "Porter will take care of things."

She watched as Porter reached into his pocket and pulled out his phone. She had no idea who he was calling, but Riley knew the situation was seconds away from getting completely out of hand.

* * *

Oz was done.

The entire situation was bullshit. Vanessa was refusing to let the CPS employee enter the house and also refusing to let Bria come to the door. She was complaining that the visit was out of the blue, and she wasn't prepared to be inspected, which was ridiculous because that's exactly how the visits were conducted.

Then Seth Matthews came to the door, and Oz's entire body tightened. The man looked higher than a kite. He'd bet everything he owned that he was strung out on drugs. He immediately began yelling at the woman as well, saying she could come into his house when hell froze over, and he wasn't letting his daughter see *anyone*.

Oz was well aware of Logan and Riley sitting in his car behind him, and while he was satisfied they were safe for the time being, he wasn't leaving without laying eyes on his niece. His skin was crawling. Something was very wrong here. He'd never discounted his sixth sense in the past, and he wasn't about to start now.

This wasn't a mission, but the danger level was real. He pulled out his phone and dialed 9-1-1.

"Nine-one-one. Do you need police, fire, or medical?" the voice on the other end asked.

"Police."

"What's the problem, sir?"

Oz gave the operator the address and briefly explained what was going on. He emphasized that the CPS worker was in danger, and possibly a child's life, as well. He also made sure to tell the woman that he suspected Seth was on drugs. No, he didn't know if there were weapons involved, but he wouldn't be surprised.

The operator told him to stay on the line, but Oz hung up. He needed to be completely focused on what was happening in front of him. He could subdue either Vanessa or Seth, but not both at the same time. For the time being, he would stand by and try not to escalate the situation, but he couldn't stop wondering where the hell Bria was, and if she was all right.

Oz realized that he should've asked one of his teammates to come with him, but it was too late for that.

Several tense minutes later, with Seth shouting the entire time, Oz breathed a sigh of relief when he heard sirens approaching.

Unfortunately, Vanessa and Seth heard them too. It set them off big time.

Vanessa tried to slam the door in their faces, but the CPS officer threw her hand out and stopped it from shutting all the way.

Oz moved on instinct. There was no way he was going to let this turn into a hostage situation. The pair could hole up in their house for hours while the police did their best to convince them to come out. In the meantime, his niece would be trapped with two very unstable and unhappy people.

Not happening on his watch.

He flew past the protesting CPS worker and added his strength to the door, keeping Vanessa and Seth from closing it.

"Let go!" she screeched.

"No way in hell," Oz told her. "Bring my niece out here and we'll go away," he said, lying through his teeth. This had gone way too far for them to turn around and leave now. It was obvious the couple was hiding something.

"Get your fucking hands off my property!" Seth growled as he added his weight to his girlfriend's on the door.

Straining, knowing if they got the door shut, this situation would be even more fucked, Oz held his ground.

The sweetest sound he'd ever heard was that of car doors shutting and voices yelling for everyone to back the hell up.

"Come outside with your hands up!" the cop yelled.

Oz heard the Child Protective Services woman explaining what was going on to the nearest officer, and he was grateful. The last thing he needed was to be shot while trying to find Bria.

"I've got nonlethal," one officer behind him told his partner.

He was all about someone Tasing either Seth or Vanessa, but they needed to hurry the hell up. Doing his best to move to the side to give the cops some room so they wouldn't accidentally hit him, Oz pushed harder on the door, widening the gap so Seth was clearly visible.

"Come out here, now!" one of the officers yelled.

"Fuck you!" Seth shouted.

A second later, Oz heard the sound of the electrical current going through the Taser. When Seth fell to the ground with a loud thump, it was easy enough to slam the door open. Vanessa fell backward over her boyfriend, and then the officers were there.

Oz backed off with his hands out to the sides, doing his best to show that he wasn't a threat in any way. But obviously the officers had been in touch with the 9-1-1 operator, because they seemed to know he wasn't the aggressor.

Seth fought with two officers, even with the Taser barbs still embedded in his chest. Vanessa had gone from fighting mad to hysterically crying. She had to be dragged out of the house by another officer.

Oz hated that Logan was witnessing this fucking mess, but his concentration was on finding Bria.

The yard seemed to be swarming with police now. It ultimately took three people to subdue Seth, who continued to scream obscenities and accuse the cops of violating his human rights. That they had no right to go into his house and he was going to sue everyone.

"Can you tell me what's going on?" a female officer asked

after Seth was subdued and in the back of one of the squad cars.

Oz did his best to explain why they were there, then asked, "Please, can I go inside and find my niece?"

The woman looked sympathetic, but she shook her head. "I'm afraid not."

"Can the CPS worker go in, then? Or one of you? My niece could be inside freaking out. Or she could be hurt."

The woman nodded. "We're on it. We have to clear the house to make sure there isn't an additional threat inside. We'll find your niece. Just please back up and let us do our jobs."

Oz ground his teeth together. This was taking too long. He'd hoped this would be an uneventful visit, although he'd already been dreading having to leave Bria behind. He knew it would devastate Logan. This was even worse than anything he could've imagined.

He backed up and heard the doors opening on his Expedition. Then Riley was there. She curled into him on one side, and Logan pressed against him on the other. Putting his arms around them both, Oz did his best to get himself under control.

"Well, that didn't go well," Riley said softly.

Amazingly, Oz found himself grinning. "Ya think?" he asked.

"Oz, where's Bree?" Logan asked.

"I don't know, Slugger, but the police are gonna go in and find her."

Logan nodded, but he tightened his arms around Oz's waist.

Oz was relieved that his nephew had turned to him for comfort, even while he was pissed that he had to in the first place.

The three of them watched as a handful of police officers entered the house with their weapons drawn.

"They aren't going to shoot Bree, are they?" Logan asked, his voice shaking.

"No," Riley said before Oz could. "They just want to make sure there aren't any other adults in there who might hurt anyone."

Keeping his eyes on the front door, Oz expected the officers to exit the house with Bria any second. But with every minute that passed, and they didn't reappear, he began to get more and more nervous.

One officer came out and gestured to the CPS worker. She entered the house, and still Bria didn't appear.

Then the same officer exited the house once more and walked over to where the three of them were standing. He said in a low, concerned tone, "We found the girl, but she's scared and won't come out."

"I'll get her," Logan said. "If she sees me, she'll come out."

Oz was clenching his teeth together so hard, it felt as if he would crack a tooth. He didn't know *why* Bria wouldn't come out, but nothing about this situation was sitting well with him.

"I'm sorry, but no," the officer told Logan gently.

"I'll go," Riley offered.

"No. I'm her uncle, *I'll* go," Oz said. If there were drugs in the house, or who knew what else, he didn't want Riley or Logan exposed. And he could tell by the officer's demeanor that whatever was happening in the house wasn't good. Clearly the officer didn't want Logan to witness it. If the boy's sister was hurt, it was the last thing that needed to be stuck in his head.

"Follow me," the officer said.

Logan grabbed the hem of his shirt, and Oz looked down.

"Something's wrong," he whispered.

Oz kneeled in front of Logan and put his hands on his shoulders. "I know," he told him, not wanting to downplay the obvious.

"Sometimes I played hide-and-seek with Bree. Usually when Mom had some scary people come over. I'd tell her she wasn't allowed to come out until I said the magic words."

"And what were those?" Oz asked.

"I'd tell her the Easter Bunny was there," Logan said. "I know it's stupid, but she always wanted to catch him in the act. I think she knew he wasn't really there, but she'd always come out when I said that. And it wasn't something anyone would accidentally say."

"I don't think it's stupid at all," Oz told his nephew. "I think it was extremely smart of you. I'm going to bring your sister out. Can you be brave for just a little while longer and stay here with Riley?"

Logan nodded.

Oz leaned forward and kissed Logan's forehead. It was the first time he'd done anything like that, but the boy didn't recoil from his touch. Instead, he threw himself into Oz's arms and desperately held on for a long moment. Then he pulled away and wiped at a tear. "I'm okay."

"I know you are, Slugger." Oz stood and kissed Riley too. He needed her brand of softness and caring, but he didn't have time to soak it in. He turned and jogged after the officer, taking a deep breath before he entered the house.

It was worse than he ever imagined.

There was trash everywhere. Stacks of newspapers. Milk cartons with sour milk spilling from them. He could even see rat shit littering the floor everywhere he looked. The place wasn't fit for *anyone* to live in, but especially not a little girl.

He walked by a bathroom where an officer was taking pictures of powder on the floor and on the toilet seat. It wasn't hard to guess what Seth had been doing while Vanessa was stalling the CPS woman at the front door.

The farther into the house he went, the worse it smelled. It was obvious one, or both, of the inhabitants were hoarders. There were stacks of clothing and boxes everywhere. He and the officer had to climb over piles of junk in order to get to the back bedroom.

The CPS employee was on her knees in front of what looked like a dog crate.

A fucking cage!

When she saw them, she stood, and the pain in her eyes was easy to see.

While Oz was happy that the woman still seemed to care about the children she was responsible for, he couldn't help but feel bitter. If she'd checked on Bria before today, maybe all this wouldn't have happened. He wondered how much longer the girl would've been forced to live like this if he hadn't called, wanting Logan to have a chance to see his sister. He knew the system was overloaded, but this was unacceptable.

"She's scared," the woman told him unnecessarily.

Oz nodded and braced himself before kneeling on the floor in front of the cage.

Nothing could've prepared him for what he saw.

A tiny little face stared back at him from the back of the cage. It was filthy, and the stench coming from the crate was almost overwhelming. Bria's fingernails were black with dirt and it didn't look like her hair had been brushed in days. Weeks. The auburn locks were matted and greasy, hanging around her face as if she were a shaggy little dog.

"Hey, Bree," Oz said softly, pushing back his revulsion and hatred for Seth and Vanessa. This precious girl was all that mattered right now. "I'm Oz...your uncle."

Bria simply stared at him, not moving an inch.

"I know you're scared, and I can't blame you. This house is really scary. But your dad and his girlfriend can't hurt you anymore. They got arrested."

Bria shifted, turning her face away from him—and Oz saw the chain around her ankle for the first time.

His anger almost got the best of him, and he had to close

his eyes to try to gain control of his emotions. He couldn't lose it now. Logan, Riley, and Bria were counting on him. He was well aware of the officers and CPS employee standing behind him. He needed to get Bria out of there. Now.

"Do you want to know why I came here today?" he asked when he had himself under control. It didn't matter that Bria wasn't looking at him, he knew she could hear him. "Logan missed his sister. And the kicker is that I didn't even know he *had* a sister. I know, that's crazy, right? How could I have a niece and not know about her? Especially one as adorable as you. It took a while, but Logan finally decided he could trust me. He told me all about you this morning. And here we are. I got here as soon as I could. I'm sorry I didn't get here before now."

He saw her eyes peer out at him from behind the mess that was her hair.

"Nothing would've kept me away if I knew you were here. And you know what else? Logan is here. He's outside waiting to see you. He's missed you like crazy."

He heard a quiet whimper from inside the crate.

Feeling as if he was making progress, Oz shuffled forward a little bit until his head was just inside the cage. He lowered his voice as if he was telling her a secret. "And you know what else Logan told me?"

Bria shook her head, and Oz inwardly rejoiced. She was interacting with him. "He told me the Easter Bunny is here."

At that, Bria turned to face him head-on. The look of hope on her face made his eyes tear up. Oz didn't bother to wipe the tears away as they fell down his cheeks.

"I know, I was skeptical too. I mean, it's not even close to Easter. But that's what Logan told me to tell you."

One of his niece's hands reached toward him, and she touched the wetness on his cheeks. "Why're you crying?" she whispered. "Are you hungry too?"

God, she was fucking killing him.

Oz shook his head. "I'm crying because I'm so happy to meet you. Your mom was my sister, and we got mad at each other a long time ago and stopped talking. Logan said your mom talked about me. I miss *my* sister so very much. Just like Logan misses you. Will you come with me to see him? And see if we can find that Easter Bunny?"

Oz was never so thankful to Logan for telling him about his code words as he was in that moment. "Mommy told me about Uncle Porter."

"That's me," Oz told her, backing up slightly and holding out a hand.

The second Bria reached for him, Oz was a goner. This little girl had him wrapped around her little finger in seconds. He vowed to do whatever it took to make sure no one ever hurt her again.

He took hold of her hand and waited patiently as she shuffled forward on her knees toward him. The chain around her ankle clanked against the hard plastic of the crate as she moved. Seth and Vanessa hadn't even bothered to put so much as a blanket inside the cage.

Not caring that she needed a bath, Oz lifted her into his arms as soon as she got close enough. She wrapped her arms around his neck and buried her face in his neck.

Oz felt and heard one of the officers come forward and cut the chain off Bria's little leg. He stood without any trouble, as his niece weighed nothing at all. He began walking back through the house with Bria clinging to him desperately.

"You're tall," she whispered.

"I am, but I won't drop you," Oz reassured her. He frowned when she held on even tighter. Shit, he'd said the wrong thing. He hadn't meant to scare her. But she didn't try to get out of his arms or flinch away from him, so Oz kept walking. He needed out of this house. Needed *Bria* out of this house.

He was holding on to his shit by the skin of his teeth. All

it would take is one thing to push him over the edge, and he knew it. He was seconds away from stalking to the car holding Seth and beating the shit out of him. The only thing holding him back wasn't the threat of being thrown in jail, but Bria and Logan. They needed him.

And he wasn't fucking leaving without his niece. No fucking way.

When he walked out into the sunlight, Oz took a deep breath. He brought a hand up and stroked Bria's hair. "You're free, baby girl."

She lifted her head and stared into his eyes. "Promise?" she whispered.

"Promise," Oz told her.

"Bree!"

Oz turned to see Logan running toward them. He knelt on the ground and put Bria on her feet, keeping a protective arm around her. He caught Logan gently by the arm and said, "Easy, Slugger."

Logan's eyes widened and it was easy to see the anger he was struggling with. But the kid was a trooper, and he pulled himself together.

He gently hugged his sister, then he drew back. "Are you hungry? I saved you some of my Happy Meal that we got on the way down here. This is Oz, he's our uncle. He's good. You can trust him. And that's Riley," he said, pointing behind him. "She's awesome too. She lives next door and she's Oz's girl-friend. She stays the night, and they don't yell at each other at all. She makes the best breakfasts, although Oz makes better-shaped pancakes. Oz got me a baseball and glove, and I'm gonna join a team!"

"You don't have to tell her every single thing that happened since you last saw her," Oz chided gently.

Then Logan broke his heart when he said, "But I don't know when I'll see her again."

Oz knew he shouldn't say what he was about to say...but

he did anyway. "She's coming home with us. She's gonna live with us from here on out, so you don't have to overwhelm her with everything right this second."

"I am?" Bria asked, the hope in her voice almost painful to hear.

"She is?" Logan echoed.

"Um, we need to talk about this, sir," the CPS employee said from next to them.

Oz shook his head and stood, keeping a hand on both Logan's and Bria's shoulders. "No, we do not," he said, emphasizing each word.

"There's protocol we have to follow. You can't just decide you're taking her and that's that."

"She's my *niece*," Oz said between clenched teeth. "You kept the knowledge of her existence from me, and I'm not very happy about that. And now that her father has shown himself to be a piece of trash, I want custody."

"Be that as it may, we have to investigate the situation, and she might have other relatives who want custody."

"Investigate?" Oz asked incredulously. "She was chained inside a damn dog crate," he bit out. He took a breath to continue to berate the woman, but he felt a hand land on his arm.

Riley.

"Breathe, Porter," she whispered. Then she turned to the CPS employee. "Please excuse Porter, today has been very trying. He wants what's best for his niece, and right now he's a little raw."

The woman's face lost some of its belligerence. "I think we all are."

Riley nodded. "He's still reeling from learning that he even had a niece, then finding her in this condition...it's a lot. I'm sure there will be paperwork and investigations, but he's willing to do whatever's necessary to keep his niece and nephew from being separated again."

God, she was being so diplomatic, and Oz was even more thankful she was at his side.

An ambulance pulled up at the curb the same time as a pickup truck. Grover, Lefty, and Doc exploded out of the truck and headed straight for them.

Oz could only stare at his teammates in disbelief. He had no idea what they were doing there. He'd obviously been inside the house with Bria longer than he'd thought. And Lefty must've driven like a bat out of hell to get down to Austin as fast as he had.

Oz looked at Riley and knew she'd called them. God, the knowledge that she had his back and was looking out for him settled deep in his bones.

He wasn't letting her go. Not ever.

"Bria needs to go to the hospital," the CPS employee told him. "Then we need to talk to her...we've got a licensed and very competent psychologist who's standing by."

Oz didn't want to be separated from Bree. He'd just found her, and the thought of her being sent off to be poked and prodded by strangers didn't sit well.

"You can go with her," the woman added, and Oz breathed a huge sigh of relief.

"Me too?" Logan asked.

Oz looked down and saw that he was holding his sister's hand tightly. He didn't seem to care that she was dirty and smelly. He was obviously just happy to be back with her. And Bria was more than content to have her brother by her side too.

"You too," the woman said with a smile.

Oz knew she was doing her best, but he couldn't help thinking it was too little, too late.

"I'll follow the ambulance to the hospital," Riley told him softly.

Oz regretted that she couldn't come with him, but knew that wouldn't be allowed. She wasn't related to him or the kids in any way. And that thought made a pang of regret shoot through him, but he pushed it back. He had to focus on the here and now.

"I'll drive Riley," Grover said, obviously hearing the tail end of the conversation. His eyes were glued to Bria, and Oz could see the anger in his face. Lefty and Doc were also more than pissed as well, but just having them here helped Oz keep a handle on his temper.

"Thanks," he told his friend.

"She's a little liar!" Vanessa screamed as an officer opened the back door of the car they'd stashed her in. They pulled her out to move her to a different squad car, and she continued to spew her vile words.

"She had to be taught not to lie! Bria lies about *everything*! Her imagination is out of control. You can't believe anything she says!"

Her words only made Oz more determined to take anything Bria said *more* seriously. Vanessa was a little too desperate for everyone to think the little girl was a liar. The question was...why?

He caught Riley's eye, and saw she was thinking the same thing as him.

"They did it," she whispered in disbelief.

Oz nodded grimly. He was pretty sure Seth had killed the mother of his child. He didn't know why, didn't really care at the moment, but it was obvious Vanessa was in on it as well.

He felt Bria lean against his leg and looked down. She was staring at Vanessa in terror, and it killed him. He got down on his knees and put a finger under Bria's little chin, turning her head so she was looking at him. "You look like a very honest little girl to me," he told her. "I'll believe anything you tell me, and you can trust the policemen and women to also believe you. Don't be scared now, you're safe, and I'm gonna make sure you stay that way."

He wasn't sure she believed him and was relieved when Logan chimed in.

"I'll believe you too, Bree. It's you and me together, right?"

She nodded.

"Sir?" an EMT asked from a respectful distance.

"How about taking a ride with me?" Oz asked Bria.

"Logan too?"

"Logan too," Oz told her. He had no idea if that was allowed, but he wasn't going to separate the siblings. They needed each other right now.

"I'm gonna go get my Happy Meal for her!" Logan exclaimed.

"Hang on, Slugger, I think we need to wait for that, but we'll get her a fresh one as soon as we can, okay?"

"Say the word and I'll bring whatever you need to the hospital or police station," Lefty said.

Oz nodded at him in appreciation.

"I'm gonna pick you up again, Little Red, okay?"

Bria nodded, and Oz leaned over and sighed in content-ment when she wrapped her arms around his neck once again. Logan grabbed hold of his sister's foot and stuck right by his side as he walked to the ambulance.

After he'd reassured Bria and handed her to the EMT, he turned to Riley.

She immediately snuggled into his chest, hugging him hard.

"How can I love her so much after just meeting her?" Oz whispered.

"Because you're you," she told him. "She'll be all right. She has you now. You've got this."

Her trust and belief in him was overwhelming. And exactly what he needed. Oz looked up at his teammates. "Look after her for me?"

"Of course, man," Grover said. "We'll see you at the hospital."

He owed his friends. Huge. Leaning down, Oz kissed Riley briefly. "I love you," he whispered.

Her eyes widened, and she immediately said, "I love you too."

This wasn't how he thought they'd share their feelings for each other for the first time, but it felt right. She'd shown how levelheaded she was in the middle of a crisis. It made him feel amazing to know that she was as strong as he'd always assumed she was.

"If you need anything, just text me," she said.

"I will."

"I'll stop and get Bree some clothes on the way to the hospital."

Oz hadn't even thought about that, but he nodded gratefully.

"And you need some too. That shirt is done for."

Looking down at himself, he saw his polo was smeared with dirt, and he had a feeling Riley was right. If nothing else, he'd never be able to wear it again without thinking about this day, which probably wasn't a good thing.

"I'm sure the guys know what size you are, so they'll help me," Riley went on. "Go. Make sure she's okay. I'll talk to the CPS lady and the cops about our suspicions. There's no *way* they'll let that little girl go home with anyone else when I get done with them."

Oz smiled. *Fuck*, he loved her. "I'll see you later."

"Tell Logan I said he's an amazing kid. He held it together really well, Porter. I was proud of him."

"I will."

"Sir?" the EMT asked. "We're ready to go."

Riley backed up and gave him a brave smile. "Love you," she whispered.

"Love you too. Later." Then Oz stepped into the ambulance. Bria looked incredibly small on the gurney. The EMT had taken off her shirt, and the bruises on her chest made anger rise up within Oz once more. But then he saw Logan looking scared and worried, and he knew he had to do whatever he could to comfort his nephew.

He sat in the chair the EMT nodded toward and picked up Logan's hand. As the ambulance began to roll, he squeezed the small hand in his. They'd be all right. All three of them. He'd make sure of it.

CHAPTER SEVENTEEN

Oz had no idea what time it was. All he knew was that he was beyond tired. He felt as if he'd been awake for days.

After Bria had been examined in the hospital—and found to be dehydrated, suffering from bruises all over her body, and severely underweight—a nurse had taken her to get clean. Then they'd changed into the new clothes Riley had brought and been driven to the Department of Child Protective Services headquarters downtown.

Oz had only had a minute or two with Riley, but he'd needed that short amount of time. She kept him grounded. Kept him from leaving the hospital to break into the jail and kill Seth and Vanessa.

The couple had been arrested for child abuse. Drug and gun charges were pending, based on a much more thorough search the cops were conducting on their house. And he hoped first-degree murder charges weren't far behind.

Oz knew Grover had driven Riley to the CPS building, but he had no idea where she was now, or if she was even still there. Bria had fallen asleep on the way to the building, and Oz had insisted the counselors let her sleep. She'd woken up a few hours later and eaten another meal with her brother.

Miraculously, the little girl seemed to be mostly all right. As long as her brother was near, she smiled and laughed, and had no problem talking with strangers. But one counselor had made the mistake of asking Logan to leave, and Bria lost it. She began to cry and shake, and only Logan sitting on the floor and pulling her onto his lap made her calm down.

Oz had to watch it all go down from behind a one-way glass, and it made his anxiety spike. He needed to hold that little girl. Needed to make everything better, and he couldn't.

Once Logan was allowed to stay, Bria had opened up to the counselor. The woman was skilled, making it seem as if they were having a casual conversation, not recounting all the abuse the little girl had suffered since being placed in her father's custody.

She'd told the woman, and her brother, that she'd been living inside that dog crate for a "long time." She hadn't been back to school. And Vanessa and her dad hadn't let her eat much. She was allowed out of the cage once a day to use the bathroom, but sometimes she couldn't hold it and had to clean up her own urine and sometimes poop when she had an accident.

It was all completely horrifying, and Oz couldn't understand why they'd done it. Apparently the counselor had the same question, and she asked Bria why her dad and Vanessa would do that.

"Because they wanted me to tell them what I saw the day Mommy was killed," Bria said, sniffling a little.

"And did you?"

Bria shook her head. "No. I was scared to tell them. They got mad when I wouldn't tell."

"Tell them what?"

Bria had looked at Logan, and he'd squeezed her hand. "It's okay. I'm here now. You're safe."

And that was apparently all Bria needed to hear before telling the counselor everything she'd heard that fateful day.

She'd heard her dad pounding on the door, and her mom had told her to hide. So she'd gotten behind the couch like her brother had taught her, and then she heard her dad yelling at her mom some more. She'd heard fighting. Heard him tell Vanessa to grab a cord. She'd heard her mom begging for her life...and then her mom stopped talking.

Then her dad and Vanessa had gone through the house, looking for something, and they'd left without knowing she was there the whole time.

Oz had walked away briefly at that point. He'd gone outside, and luckily Doc had been there. He'd prevented Oz from getting into his car and doing something stupid. The thought of his fragile niece hearing her own father kill her mother was overwhelming.

After more time talking with the counselor, with her brother by her side, Bria seemed to be doing all right. Oz figured he'd need to keep a close eye on her and have her continue to see a therapist for a while, just to make sure.

Oz also learned after talking to the detective who'd interviewed Seth and Vanessa that after discovering Bria hadn't been at school the day her mom was killed, they'd been scared she would tell someone that she saw or heard them kill her mom, so they'd locked her up in their small house to make sure that didn't happen. It was essentially a confession and Oz was hopeful the two would spend the rest of their lives in prison.

The fact that Bria was doing as well as she seemed to be after her ordeal was a miracle. It also sucked...because it probably meant her life *before* her mom had been killed wasn't exactly ideal. Oz had heard enough from Logan to figure out that much.

Logan's confession that Bree had been in the house the day her mom was killed had been passed on to the detective who was investigating Becky's death, and he'd come to CPS headquarters to listen to the counselor's conversation with

Bria. He had more questions, which the counselor had to ask. The back and forth was done in a gentle way, so as not to traumatize either Logan or Bria any more than they already were.

Then Oz had to meet with more CPS officials to get approval and permission to take Bria home to Killeen. They had to get in touch with his commander and get a reference. He'd also learned from the detectives that Seth and Vanessa had pawned everything they'd been able to get their hands on from Becky's apartment. It made him sad that he wouldn't be able to get any mementoes of their mom for Bria and Logan, but he'd do anything possible to make sure they never forgot her.

Becky wasn't the greatest mother, but she'd done her best, and it seemed as if she'd been doing what she could to clean herself up in the last few years. Oz had to respect that.

Oz had been dealing with the aftermath of what had happened to his niece and his sister for hours by now, and finally, just five minutes ago, he'd been given the green light to take Bria home. It was dark outside, and Bria was barely awake as he picked her up.

"We're going home," he told both her and Logan.

"Both of us?" Logan asked.

"Yeah, Slugger. Both of you."

"You promised," Bree said.

"I did," Oz agreed.

"Riley too?" Logan asked. Then he turned to his sister. "You're gonna like her. I told you all about her, and she's amazing. She smells like flowers."

Bria smiled weakly at her brother. It was clear she wasn't completely sold, but Oz knew she'd come around. How could she not? Riley *was* awesome.

"I'm not sure," he told Logan. "It's late, and we've been here a long time. Riley has probably gone back to Killeen by now."

He finished his sentence just as they walked into the large waiting room at the front of the building. Oz stopped in his tracks and stared at what he saw.

The waiting area was full of people. Not only were Grover, Lefty, and Doc still there, they'd been joined by the rest of the team. Trigger, Brain, and Lucky stood as they entered the room.

Gillian was there too. As was Kinley, Aspen, and Devyn.

Aspen put her finger to her lips and said quietly, "She finally fell asleep."

Oz looked to where she'd indicated with a nod of her head, and saw Riley slumped in a chair. Her head was resting against the wall and she was sound asleep.

"Hang out here with your sister for a second, Slugger?" Oz asked Logan.

"Okay."

Oz walked toward Riley, stopping to hug each and every one of his friends along the way. He was feeling extremely emotional after the long day, and seeing the support he and his family had was almost overwhelming.

But seeing Riley there, exhausted from running around making sure he, Bria, and Logan had what they needed, made him want to bawl his eyes out. He hadn't felt this off kilter in a very long time, if ever.

His friends talked quietly behind him, but Oz only had eyes for the woman who owned his heart.

He knelt in front of her, and he almost smiled thinking about how often he'd been getting on his knees lately. Being tall was a pain in the ass when you had to get eye-to-eye with kids to reassure them.

He put a hand on Riley's knee, hoping to wake her gently, but the second he touched her, she bolted upright and looked around in alarm.

"It's okay, Ri. It's me."

"Porter. Where're the kids?"

"They're here. We're ready to go home."

"Bria too?"

"Bree too," he reassured her.

Then Riley burst into tears. It was as if she'd been holding back her emotions all day and only now, knowing all was well, allowed herself to break. Oz gathered her in his arms and stood. He'd never been so grateful for his height and strength as he was right this moment. His woman needed him, and he was happy to be there for her. Today, and every day from here on out.

"I'm okay," Riley muttered against his chest.

"I know you are," Oz told her. "Ready to go home?"

"Yes," she said emphatically. "Put me down, I can walk, Porter."

"I know you can," he told her. He lowered her feet to the floor but kept his arm firmly around her waist. Riley leaned heavily against him as they headed for Logan and Bria.

"Riley?" Logan asked as Oz got close.

"She's okay," Oz told his nephew. "She's just so happy we're all going home. Together."

"Me too," Logan said.

Keeping his arm around Riley, Oz reached down and took Logan's hand in his free one. His nephew grabbed his sister's hand, and they walked out into the night. Oz might not have thought this was how he'd get a family, but he wouldn't change it for the world.

* * *

The trip back to Killeen was quiet. Riley had been exhausted earlier, but now she was wide awake. Logan and Bree fell asleep almost the second the door shut behind them, and it felt right to just hold Porter's hand as he drove. They didn't talk, they just existed in the moment. Happy to be together.

Once home, Porter carried Bria up the stairs and Riley held Logan's hand as they entered the apartment.

"She can have my room," Logan told Porter after the door had shut behind them. "I can sleep on the couch, just like you did when I first got here and you let me have your bed."

Riley's eyes filled with tears. It was obvious Logan paid very close attention to *everything* his uncle did, and he couldn't have a better role model.

Porter didn't say a word, but he carried Bria into Logan's room and lay her on the full-size bed. She didn't take up much room at all, and Riley's mind was spinning with all the things she wanted to feed the little girl to help her get back to a normal weight for someone her age and height.

Then Porter took Logan by the hand and led him out into the living room. He sat him on the couch and took a seat next to him. "Here's the thing, Slugger. As you know, I've only got two bedrooms here. I appreciate you being willing to give up your room, but I don't want you sleeping out *here* either. I'm going to look for somewhere more appropriate for us to live, but do you think in the meantime, you'd be willing to share a room with Bree? My room is bigger, so we can move you both in there, and I can take your room. I know it's not ideal to share a room with your little sister, but I promise I'm gonna find us a bigger place."

Logan's eyes widened. "You'd give us your room?"

Porter nodded. "Absolutely," he told his nephew.

Riley held her breath. God, she loved this man. She didn't know many people who would give up the comfort of their bedroom for kids they hardly knew, related or not.

"What if we got bunk beds? I love my big bed, but it takes up a lot of room. If we got bunk beds, it wouldn't take up as much space and I could have the top and Bree could have the bottom," Logan said. "You wouldn't have to give up your room. I'm not sure you and Riley would fit in mine."

Riley's heart just about stopped beating. She couldn't

believe Logan had thought about *her* in all this. Porter's eyes came up, and he met hers. She could see emotion blazing in them, and it was all she could do not to go to him right then.

"You're a good kid," Porter told Logan. "And I think bunk beds are a great idea. I'll see if one of the guys can store your bed until I find a new place. That way, you can have it back when we move. Okay?"

"Okay," Logan said, then yawned huge.

"For now, you gonna be okay sharing a bed with Bree?" Porter asked.

Logan nodded. "Yeah, we shared in our apartment we lived in with Mom. I'm good."

"Okay, Slugger. I know it's been a long emotional day, but don't forget to brush your teeth. You don't want them to rot and fall out."

Logan smiled. Then he reached out and gave Porter a hug. "Thank you for saving my sister."

"I didn't save her, *you* did," Porter said, wrapping his arms around his nephew's much smaller body. "If you weren't brave enough to share your secret, I wouldn't have brought you to see her, and we wouldn't have gotten her out of that house."

"Why are people so mean?" Logan asked when he sat back.

"I don't know," Porter said. "But the good thing is that Bree has *you* to have her back. And I have *your* back. And Riley has mine. We're going to be okay."

And with that, Logan nodded. As if his uncle's words were law. He stood and headed toward the hallway.

"I'll be in to check on you guys in a minute or so," Porter told him.

Logan nodded and disappeared into the hallway.

"Come here," Porter said as he held out his arm to Riley.

She immediately walked to him and straddled his lap right there on the couch. Porter held on to her as if she was the only thing keeping him from falling into a hundred pieces. "It's okay," she murmured. "She's safe."

"It was horrible," Porter said in a tortured tone of voice.

"I know." And she did. Riley hadn't seen Bria in that cage firsthand, but she'd heard enough from the officers at the scene about how bad it was. "Don't fall apart yet," she told Porter. "You need to say good night to Logan. Then come to bed, and I'll hold you while you let it all out."

Riley didn't know where her strength was coming from. All she knew was that she hated to see Porter hurting. And it was obvious he was in pain.

He nodded against her and pulled back. "I love you," he said. "Today was awful, but saying that we loved each other is one moment that I never want to forget."

Riley smiled. "I love you too. So much it kinda scares me."

"Don't be scared of me," he ordered. "Do you love me enough to take me as I am...two kids and all?"

She frowned at him. "I can't believe you even asked that," she scolded.

"It would be too much for some women," Porter said.

"I'm not some women," Riley retorted.

"No, you aren't. I thought you might've gone home," he said. "I wouldn't have thought less of you if you had."

"I wasn't leaving you. No way," Riley said. "And if you tell me I should've, I'm gonna get mad. Go say good night to your nephew and niece," she ordered.

"Bossy," Porter observed. "I like it."

He stood suddenly, and Riley kept herself from screeching at the last second, not wanting to wake Bria.

Porter grinned as he let her legs drop. "Thanks for being with us today."

"Nowhere I would've rather been," she said honestly.

He walked her down the hall, holding her hand, only letting go in front of Logan's room. Then he kissed her forehead before she continued to his room.

She quickly got ready for bed and was slipping under the covers when Porter joined her. He disappeared into the bathroom and came out a minute or so later. Riley watched as he stripped off his clothes and put on a clean pair of boxers. He was so comfortable in his skin, had no problem getting naked in front of her. She wasn't there yet, wasn't sure she ever would be, but she loved being able to ogle him.

Then he was under the covers, pulling her into his arms. They were plastered together from chest to ankle...and it wasn't long before she felt Porter's body begin to shake.

He soaked her shirt as he cried, letting out all the heavy emotions he'd kept in check all day. Riley held his head to her chest and stroked his hair as he broke. She murmured words of love and praise for how he'd handled everything that day.

Eventually, his sobs resided and his tears dried up. He lay against her, and Riley had never felt as close with anyone as she did to Porter right that moment.

"Thank you for being there today. And for calling my team. And for helping me keep my shit together. I don't know what I'd do without you."

"I'm not going anywhere," she told him.

"Damn straight you aren't," Porter said. Then he shifted, moving farther up the bed and onto his back before taking her into his arms.

Riley lay her head on his chest and heard his heart beating under her cheek.

"I have no idea what the future holds," Porter said. "I have to find a school these kids will like, tell my commander I'm now the father of *two* kids, not one, and redo my family care plan. I need to find a bunk bed, buy clothes appropriate for a first grader, figure out how to get my niece not to be terrified of being alone with me, and find a child psychologist for her to talk to so she doesn't turn out to be a serial killer fifteen years from now.

"I *still* haven't managed to take the woman I love on a

proper fucking date, and I have no idea if and when that'll happen now. But what I *do* know is that I want you in my life. It's going to be crazy, and I might not be able to give you the attention you need between the kids and my job, but I don't want to lose you, Riley. Tell me what I need to do in order to make that happen," he demanded.

"Love me," Riley told him softly. "That's all I need."

"Done," Porter whispered. "Don't let me take advantage of you," he told her. "You are not my housecleaner, cook, or babysitter. I know I can be clueless when it comes to a lot of things, and I don't want you to resent me if I get too complacent with you doing that stuff for me all the time."

"I won't. And for the record, I love spending time with Logan, and I know I'll love being with Bria just as much. I'm happy to keep things as they are. With me hanging out with them after school until you get home."

"I'm a lucky bastard," Porter told her.

Riley grinned. "I think I'm the lucky one. I always wanted a large family, and you're giving me just that."

"I'll give you all the babies you want," Porter said seriously. "Just say the word."

Riley's heart lurched. "Um...I think we need to get the hang of the two kids you have before we decide to start throwing babies into the mix."

"You didn't completely reject the idea though," Porter said with a smile. "I can work with that."

"You're crazy," Riley told him.

"My life has been completely thrown upside down in the last couple months, and I can't help but think how lucky I am. And I'm more than aware that I never would've been able to do this without you."

"Wrong," Riley countered. "You would've been fine. Porter Reed is a badass Delta Force special forces soldier who isn't afraid of anything." She smiled up at him to let him know she was teasing. But he didn't smile back.

"I'm terrified of losing the best thing that ever happened to me," he said seriously. "You." Then he lifted his head and kissed her long, hard, and hot.

He pulled back and pressed her head back to his chest. "Sleep, Ri. It's fucking late. I have no idea what time it is, but I know it'll be time for us to get up sooner rather than later."

Riley adored that Porter wanted her there for more than sex. He wanted to sleep with her in his arms. And it gave her all the warm fuzzies. It made her love him all the more.

"Love you, and I'm proud of the man you are," Riley said.

"Love you too," Porter replied.

She wanted to stay awake, to treasure the moment, but she was too tired. Feeling completely safe in Porter's arms, Riley was asleep within minutes.

CHAPTER EIGHTEEN

The next few days were extremely hectic. Riley spent each night with Porter, then after breakfast, went back over to her apartment to get as much work done as she could. She'd explained the situation to her clients and most had been supportive. It helped that she was still able to deliver their transcripted documents. For the few people who needed big jobs done as soon as possible, she gave them the name of a trusted friend she'd made in the business, who was very thankful for the references.

At lunchtime, Riley went back over to Porter's apartment and got caught up on what everyone had done each morning, then they'd run errands. Porter had brought Bree to see a child psychologist twice, and the sessions seemed to go well. The psychologist told Porter that he thought Bria was a remarkable little girl, and while she might have a bit of PTSD, having her brother with her was working wonders for her mental health.

They'd gone to the base and had gotten Bree her own ID card, which she couldn't stop showing off to just about everyone they met. They went grocery shopping, clothes shopping, toy shopping, and one afternoon, Logan helped his uncle put together the bunk beds he'd bought for him and his sister.

They'd even found time to hang out at Brain and Aspen's house one evening. All his teammates had been there, and of course the women. Even Brain's ninety-something-year-old neighbor, Winnie, had come over, with her granddaughter and her boyfriend. It was a packed house, and Riley had been proud of both Logan and Bree. They'd been polite to all the adults and didn't seem all that bothered to have everyone around. When it was time to head home, Bria was sound asleep in Winnie's lap.

Today, they were all headed to Gerry Linkous Elementary School. Porter had taken the job of finding Logan a new school very seriously. Even though he only had a little bit of time left in elementary school, it was important to find a place where his nephew would be comfortable. Not to mention, Bria would be there for several more years.

Gerry Linkous seemed to have a good reputation. Porter knew they'd had an active shooter at the school years ago, but he'd been impressed at how the entire situation had been dealt with. He'd even called Fletch to get his thoughts on the place, since his daughter Annie had attended the school.

"I liked the school on post," Porter told Logan as they drove toward Gerry Linkous, "but I think this one might be a better fit. It's in the same district as the high school with the best baseball team."

Riley turned around in time to see Logan nod from the back seat. He looked worried.

"What's up, Slugger?" Porter asked, alternating his attention from the road to the rearview mirror so he could see his nephew.

Logan shrugged. "I don't know. I just haven't had luck with school."

Riley hated the fear she heard in his tone. Bria wasn't sure if she should be excited or terrified, and kept looking at her brother for cues on how she should feel.

The little girl had also latched onto her uncle very quickly. Maybe it was because he'd been the one to take her out of the nightmare she'd been living in, or maybe because he was male, like her brother, but Bree adored him. Riley was determined to get the little girl to like her just as much. No matter how long it took, she wanted Bria to trust *her* too.

"I think you're looking at it the wrong way," Riley said quietly. "If you hadn't been in your other school, what do you think would've happened to poor Lacie? You stuck up for her and I know she appreciated that."

Logan shrugged.

"I have a good feeling about this school. Your uncle told me there's a retired Army soldier who teaches gym. I bet she's awesome." Riley turned to Bria. "And Mr. Santoro is one of the first-grade teachers, and he's won lots of awards. Maybe he'll be *your* teacher."

Bria's eyes sparkled, but after a look at her brother, she copied his uninterested shrug.

Sighing, Riley turned to face forward. She'd tried. Hopefully the day would go all right.

An hour later, they'd dropped Bria off in Mr. Santoro's class. She was going to sit in on the class while they visited with the principal, Jane Allen. She had a doctorate degree, but she didn't use her title when she'd introduced herself. She seemed down-to-earth and approachable, which was a nice change from Mr. McClain.

After introductions, Riley sat in a chair off to the side of the large, welcoming principal's office while Logan and Porter took the chairs nearest to the desk.

"It's good to meet you, Logan. Can you tell me why you want to change schools after you've only been in town a few weeks?"

When Logan didn't answer, Porter prompted, "You were asked a question, Slugger."

Logan's shoulders were slumped and it was obvious he was uncomfortable. Porter had warned him he was going to have to explain why he'd been suspended, and why he wanted to go to a new school, but Logan wasn't very happy about having to do so.

"I was suspended," he said after a moment.

Bless Ms. Allen, she didn't seem alarmed in the least.

"Tell her why," Porter encouraged.

"I hit Gary Wittingham," Logan said so softly, it was hard to hear him.

"Why?"

Riley relaxed. The other woman asking for details was already a lot more than Dr. McClain had done.

"Because he was touching Lacie, and she didn't want to be touched."

Ms. Allen rested her elbows on her desk and leaned forward as she said, "Ah, I see. And I'm guessing the other school had a zero policy on physical violence."

Logan nodded.

"Right, we have the same policy here. But, we also take into account what happened before and after the violence occurred. We don't condone children hitting each other, but I think it's important to know what provoked the altercation. Do you think you might've done something differently if you knew about the consequences of your actions?"

Logan thought about that for a minute, then said, "I probably could've gotten between Gary and Lacie, so he couldn't touch her anymore."

"That sounds reasonable," Ms. Allen said, nodding. "Now, your uncle tells me that you like baseball, is that true?"

Logan looked up at the principal in confusion.

"What?" she asked.

"I...are we done talking about me hitting Gary and being suspended?"

The principal smiled. "Yes. It wasn't right what you did, but you did so because you were defending someone else. I would much rather have a class full of students who want to protect others than a class full of bullies. So...baseball?"

It was as if a weight had been lifted off Logan's shoulders. He sat up straighter in his chair and began to tell Ms. Allen all about Shin-Soo Choo, who was, in his opinion, the best outfielder in the world.

Riley shared a quick look with Porter and couldn't help but be relieved. It looked like they'd found Logan and Bria's new school. Even though she wasn't related to either child, she was just as invested as Porter in finding a good fit for his niece and nephew.

On the way to Whataburger for lunch, Logan and Bria babbled nonstop in the back seat. Bree was telling her big brother all about her time in Mr. Santoro's class and how much she liked the other kids. Logan had briefly met the fifth-grade teachers and some of the kids. He was obviously withholding judgement on the other children, but all in all, things looked promising.

Porter reached over and grabbed her hand. He looked tired, which worried Riley. He was working extremely hard and wasn't used to being a dad to one kid, let alone two. But he never complained. He was getting up at five in the morning to go work out with his team and get a few quick meetings in before coming back at eight to have breakfast with the kids and to entertain them while she worked for a few hours.

His commander had been amazing over the last week, giving Porter as much time off as he needed. But the time was coming for all of them to get back into a normal routine. The kids needed that as much as Porter did.

Arrangements had been made for Logan and Bria to start

school the next day. They'd take the bus together in the morning and afternoon. Riley could catch up on her work and Porter could get back into the swing of whatever it was he did during the day on post.

They all climbed out of the Expedition at the fast food restaurant—and Riley was shocked when she felt Bria's hand slip into her own as they walked toward the door.

She'd never been as happy as she was right that moment. She had the most amazing boyfriend, Bria was beginning to trust her and had come out of her horrific ordeal relatively unscathed, and Logan's personality was really starting to blossom.

Porter's arm wrapped around her waist and he pulled her into him, bending down to kiss the top of her head. He didn't need to say anything, but it was obvious he was also happy with how things had turned out.

Later that night, after Porter had to go into the kids' room and tell them to hush, that it was late and time to sleep, he came back into the master bedroom smiling. He climbed into bed next to her and snuggled up close. "God, who would've thought I'd be happy to have to yell at my kids?"

"Yell?" Riley questioned with a smirk.

"Okay, there was no yelling, just a request for them to shut the hell up," Porter clarified.

"I love hearing you call them your kids," Riley told him.

He nodded. "They *are* my kids. I might not have been around for the beginnings of their lives, but I'll damn well sure be around from here on out. And no one will hurt them as long as I'm alive. Bree's been through too much shit as it is. And Logan feels responsible. I'm gonna give them the best life I can."

"I know you are," Riley told him, overcome with love for this man. Some people would've felt irritated and inconvenienced by having a kid dumped in their lap. But it seemed with the addition of Bria, Porter was even more serious about protecting, nurturing, and loving his nephew and niece.

With the news that Seth and Vanessa would be staying in jail for a very long time on child abuse and first-degree murder charges, and with the decision about school done and behind him, Porter seemed more relaxed tonight. Less as if the weight of the world was on his shoulders.

Listening hard, Riley didn't hear anything from the kids down the hall.

They hadn't made love since Bria had moved in, but suddenly Riley *needed* Porter.

She pulled out of his arms and moved down his body, stopping to suck on a nipple as she went.

"Ri," Porter moaned, and the sound of lust in his voice encouraged her to keep going. She'd given blow jobs before, but had never been all that enthusiastic about it. Now, she couldn't wait to get her mouth and hands on Porter's cock.

She didn't hesitate when she got to his boxers, she slipped her hands under the elastic and pushed them down. Porter lifted his hips to help, and she had his dick in her hand before he could kick the material off.

"Shit, Ri," he moaned as she grabbed the base of his half-hard shaft and lowered her mouth over the tip.

Riley didn't know what had come over her, but she felt like if she didn't get him into her mouth right that second, she'd die. Her confidence rose as he quickly hardened under her touch. She sucked on the tip, running her tongue along the sensitive ridge on the underside. She felt goose bumps break out on his thighs, and his reaction made her feel extremely powerful.

She came up on her knees between his legs and began to bob her head up and down on his cock, slurping and sucking as she did her best to drive him crazy.

"Holy fuckin' shit!" Porter swore, and Riley smiled as she continued to suck him off. She could feel her pussy dampen as she worked him. She felt strong and sexy, and when he shoved both hands in her hair and held her head still as he began to gently fuck her mouth, she couldn't help but moan. She palmed his balls, rolling them in one hand as she held herself over him with the other.

She caressed his perineum, and a squirt of precome landed on her tongue.

"Do that again," Porter ordered.

She did, and was rewarded with another burst of tanginess in her mouth.

"Enough," he told her, moving his hands to her shoulders. He had her turned and on her hands and knees before she knew what was happening.

"I wasn't done," Riley complained.

"I was *about* to be done," Porter returned. He shoved her sleep shirt above her ass and groaned when he realized she wasn't wearing underwear. She felt his cock brush against her pussy, as if testing her readiness. Then his fingers were there, flicking against her clit.

"Porter, I'm ready, please," she told him, shifting under him, wanting him inside her now.

They both moaned as he sank into her tight, wet sheath.

Then Porter held himself very still, and swore.

"What? What's wrong?" Riley asked.

"Condom," Porter said as he pulled out of her body.

She wanted to tell him not to worry about it. To take her bare. But she knew that wasn't responsible. Hell, it wasn't smart for him to even *enter* her ungloved. She wasn't on birth control and he was leaking precome after her blow job.

She waited impatiently as he leaned over and grabbed a condom from the drawer next to the bed. She heard the wrapper crinkle, then he put a hand under her belly and guided his dick back inside her.

"Damn, you feel so good," he told her. "But that one stroke inside you bare ruined me for life. I'd fucking kill to be back there, fucking you skin on skin. Filling you with my come, filling your belly with my baby."

Riley shivered. She loved when he got so turned on, he started talking dirty. And she wasn't upset with the thought of him coming inside her. Her muscles gripped his cock as he slowly fucked her from behind.

"You like that thought, Ri?" he asked. "You want babies with me?"

"I want it all with you," she blurted.

"Fuck yeah," Porter said as his hips began to move faster. "Touch yourself. I'm not gonna last. Not looking down at this luscious ass and remembering how you took my cock in your mouth. I've never seen anything sexier than you getting off on blowing me."

Resting her weight on one shoulder, Riley moved a hand down her body and strummed her clit as the man she loved more than she ever thought she could love *anyone* fucked her hard. His balls hit her hand with every thrust and she took the time to play with him as he thrust in and out.

"Stop fucking around," he ordered. "Make yourself come so I can too."

She loved that he wanted to wait to orgasm until after she had. She'd never been with anyone who was so attuned to her desires and pleasure.

Knowing it wouldn't take long when she started manipulating her clit, Riley got to it.

She heard Porter telling her how hot she was, how good she felt, and how much he loved her, but tuned him out as her body demanded more. The second she began to shake under him, Porter held onto her hips and fucked her harder than ever. His hips slapped against her ass and sounded loud in the otherwise quiet room. It only took four thrusts before he held himself as far inside her as he could and groaned softly.

Riley moved her fingers down to where they were joined

and stroked his perineum once more. He pushed even farther inside her and said, "Holy fuck!" as he jerked.

Smiling, more satisfied than she could ever remember being after sex, Riley waited until Porter got himself under control.

"You're lethal," he mumbled as he pulled out. But instead of letting her off her knees, Porter stayed behind her. His fingers played with her folds, and then they entered her still swollen sheath.

"Porter?" she asked nervously.

"Trust me," he said softly.

She did, but she still jerked as he touched her clit with his other hand. She'd barely come down from her first orgasm before Porter was sending her climbing once more. He fucked her with two fingers as he played with her clit, and soon she began shaking.

"I fucking love seeing this," Porter said from between her legs. "Come for me, Ri. I want to see your come dripping out of your pussy."

God, his dirty talk would be the death of her, and Riley had no choice but to do exactly as he said. She arched her back and came again. It felt as if the only thing holding her up was his hands.

Then he shocked the shit out of her by leaning down and licking the fluid that leaked from her body.

Shivering, Riley knew she was going to fall over. "Porter," she warned.

He lifted his head and said, "I know. You're so fucking beautiful, and I love you so much."

He helped her lie down on her side and was headed for the bathroom before she could blink. He was back in seconds, climbing in behind her. The shirt she'd put on was still up above her boobs, but she couldn't find the energy to pull it down. One of Porter's arms shoved under her shoulders, and the other covered her still-throbbing pussy.

She gasped when the heel of his hand brushed against her clit, and he said, "Easy, Ri. I'm done."

Sighing in relief, she still jerked in surprise when he raised one of her legs and propped it up on his thigh, opening her to his hand. He gently ran his fingers over her soaking-wet folds.

"What are you doing?" she asked a little shyly.

"Imagining what this will feel like after I come inside you."

"Porter!" she protested.

"What?" he asked.

"That's...I don't know what that is."

"It's sexy as fuck," he said without hesitation. "I know it was irresponsible of me to slide inside you without a condom, but damn, Ri, you have no idea how amazing it felt. I've never been inside a woman bare, and I'm glad you're my first. And last. Knowing Aspen is pregnant, and seeing how happy and proud Brain is...it makes me want that too. I know it's crazy. We haven't been together that long, and it's not as if I don't already have my hands full with Bria and Logan, but I want more. I already love being a dad, even though it's scary as hell and I'm afraid every day that I'll fuck those kids up. I love you, and I want to have kids with you."

Riley wasn't sure what to say. She wanted that too, but something held her back from admitting it. Her past, probably. The uncertainty that Porter would still want to be with her a year from now.

"You're thinking too hard," he accused. "Whatever it is you're thinking, unless it's how much you love and trust me, is bullshit."

She couldn't help but chuckle.

Porter sighed against her neck, then lifted her leg off his thigh and reached for the covers. He pulled them up and over their bodies and moved his hand to cradle one of her boobs. He held her to him, and she closed her eyes in contentment. She'd been fucked to within an inch of her life, her boyfriend loved her and admitted to wanting kids with her, and his nephew and niece seemed to be settling in to their new life. Everything was great.

So why did she feel a little uneasy?

Maybe it was because in the past, when things seemed to be going well, the rug was always pulled out from under her. She didn't know how she'd survive losing not only Porter, but his two adorable charges as well.

"I love you," she whispered.

"And I adore you beyond words," Porter responded. "Thank you for being you."

Riley sighed. She had no response to that. She just hoped being who she was would be enough for him in the long run. Time would tell.

CHAPTER NINETEEN

A week later, Oz was having a hard time concentrating on the meetings he was having with his teammates. He loved waking up with Riley every morning, and Bree and Logan kept him entertained as he got them fed and ready for school.

Logan had told him last night when they were outside in the park, throwing a baseball back and forth, that he really liked his new school, and that he'd made a friend in his class who liked baseball as much as he did.

Bria was also settling in well. She had moments where she showed evidence of the abuse she'd suffered, but with her brother by her side, she was blossoming.

And then there was Riley. Oz had never been as happy in a relationship as he was with her. She worked hard, never complained, and seemed just as happy with their routine as he was. Oz had no idea what he'd do without her. He'd probably muddle by, but she made his life so much easier, and fulfilling, just by being herself.

She met Logan and Bria in the afternoons when they got off their bus and kept them entertained until he got home. Gillian, Aspen, and Kinley had been taking turns coming over to help Riley with the kids too. They'd gone to the park and had done crafts, and generally anything they could to help Riley keep them occupied until dinnertime.

He was a lucky man. The more time he spent with Riley, the more time he *wanted* to spend with her.

"You're feeling it, aren't you?" Trigger asked as they sat in a conference room waiting for their next debriefing to start.

Not embarrassed in the least that his teammates were all shamelessly listening to their conversation, Oz nodded. "Being scared to death that something will happen to her when I'm not there? As if the day can't be over soon enough? That if she ever left me, I'd be nothing but a shell of the man I used to be? Yeah, I feel it."

Trigger grinned. "It's awesome, isn't it?"

"You didn't think it was awesome when you thought Gillian had been shot and you literally freaked out like a newb soldier who was seeing blood for the first time," Lucky teased.

"Fuck you," Trigger told his friend and threw a pencil at him. "Wait until you find a woman and she cuts a finger or something. You'll want to faint in panic too."

Lucky grinned. "Not gonna happen. Any woman who ends up with me will have my good luck rub off on her."

"Oh, shit," Brain said. "Famous last words."

"And since you're interested in my sister, you obviously have no clue. Devyn's a terror. She'll keep you on your toes, and I guarantee you'll puke your guts up the first time she tells you she wants to go bungie jumping off the side of a mountain."

Lucky actually paled, and Oz couldn't help but chuckle.

The door opened, stopping the conversation. A major entered the room and set a folder down on the table before sitting.

Any teasing and joking the Delta team had been doing

was immediately stopped, as it was obvious the man wasn't happy about something.

"There's been a series of kidnappings in Afghanistan," he said solemnly. "It looks like Abdul Shahzada has taken over for Mullah Abbas Akhund."

"The asshole that we killed," Lefty said.

"Yeah, him. We were pretty sure Shahzada was the true head of the organization, but he was letting Akhund take the lead for some reason. We were right. Now there've been a few contractors who've gone AWOL from the base, and none of their loved ones have heard from them. There's reason to believe that Shahzada may be responsible. But he's still a ghost. We have no intelligence on the man, except that he's been gaining power. Word on the street is that he's practicing his torture techniques before striking hard against the Army units who are over there protecting the area."

"What's the plan?" Doc asked.

"Nothing as of now. We're watching and waiting."

"And the missing contractors?" Grover asked.

The major sighed. "Our hands are tied. Their employers have hired private investigators to try to track them down, but we're in a wait-and-see holding pattern."

"That's bullshit," Grover complained. "The contractors are there serving their country just like the active-duty men and women."

"I know, and I agree. But politics being what they are, we haven't been approved to move in and see if we can find them as of yet."

"One of the food contractors hasn't answered my emails since our last deployment to Afghanistan," Grover said, the tension easy to hear in his voice. "Is she listed as one of the missing?"

"What's her name?"

"Sierra Clarkson."

The major shuffled some papers in front of him and Oz could see Grover's impatience as he waited to see what the officer would say.

"No one's heard from Sierra Clarkson," the major said. "It looks like she left not too long after Akhund was killed. All her personal belongings were gone along with her."

"It's bullshit to think that she just up and left," Grover said angrily. "Especially when other contractors have gone missing. No one just goes AWOL from Afghanistan."

"Some people have married locals," the officer said.

"Sierra hadn't been in the country long enough to meet anyone at the time of her disappearance," Grover growled.

Oz knew if Grover continued to antagonize the major, he might push him too far, and while he was also worried about Sierra, he wasn't sure what they could actually do about her disappearance at this point. Before he could think of something to say to deflect the attention away from his stressed-out and obviously upset teammate, Lucky spoke.

"How many more have to disappear before we're approved to do something about it?"

"I have no idea. Hopefully none," the major said.

The man sounded stressed, and Oz believed him when he said he hoped no one else had to disappear before they could figure out what the hell was going on.

"Moving on," the officer said, "Venezuela is still an extremely volatile hot spot."

Trigger snorted but didn't comment further. He didn't need to; they all remembered the last time they were in that country, when Gillian's plane had been hijacked, and the fallout from that event.

Oz listened carefully as they discussed the various places the United States was keeping an eye on. As the major listed country after country, he realized one of the things he liked best about his new life was how...*normal* it was.

Bria refused to eat hotdogs, but loved chicken nuggets. Logan could talk baseball stats all day and night, and Riley was always there with a kind and encouraging word. His home life was so completely different from his job as a Delta, where he dealt with conflict and strife all day.

He was a *damn* lucky man, and Oz knew it. Now that he'd seen the kind of life he could have with Riley, he wasn't going to do anything to fuck it up...he hoped.

* * *

Miles Bowen sat in his gray Kia Rio and glared hatefully at the apartment complex across the street. Why he'd ever gotten involved with Riley fucking Rogers was beyond him. Probably because she'd been convenient. A way to stay under the cops' radar. But then she'd gone and broken up with him, kicking him out.

No one broke up with Miles. He was the breaker-upper, not the breakee.

But that wasn't what was pissing him off right now. He didn't give a shit about Riley. Didn't even like her—but he needed that disk he'd left in her apartment. If she'd just let him back in to get his shit, he'd be long gone by now.

He'd assumed she'd roll over when he started texting, demanding to be able to come get his stuff. Then she'd told him that she'd gathered it all up and left it in a box in the fucking laundry room! He'd about lost his shit, thinking about what someone might find if they stole that box before he could get to it. But then he'd realized there was no way his game was in the box.

Because it wasn't a game, of course. It was a video he'd burned onto a disk and hidden in her apartment. A video that could send him to jail for the rest of his life, and would essentially be a death sentence.

Miles knew how child molesters were treated in prison. He wouldn't last a week.

But it wasn't his fault that he was attracted to kids. It wasn't! It was just who he was, how he'd always been. But that video could be his downfall, and he needed it back.

As he sat in his car, a school bus pulled up to the edge of the parking lot and kids streamed off. Miles straightened. Some of the kids were too old or young for his liking, but there were several who were perfect for what he liked. Needed.

As he watched, Miles was shocked to see none other than his ex, Riley, come out from the building and open her arms in greeting. A cute little boy with brown hair went running toward her, giving her a big hug. A smaller red-haired girl smiled shyly up at Riley as she approached.

Miles was surprised. He had no idea who these kids were, but it was obvious they were close with Riley. Did she have kids he didn't know about? He shook his head. No. No way. They had to be her nephew and niece or something. Maybe she was babysitting other people's kids now for extra money.

His eyes stayed glued to the boy. He needed to get his disk back. That's why he was here. He'd decided to break in, was just hoping to see Riley leave at some point. He'd hidden the disk inside one of her DVD cases, where it was unlikely she'd find it unexpectedly...but he couldn't control his excitement at seeing the boy.

If he was important to Riley, he could break into her place, get his disk back—and whatever else he could get his hands on—and hurt Riley even more by taking the boy. She'd fucking regret dissing him and ignoring his texts and calls.

No one ignored Miles Bowen.

Looking at his watch, Miles thought of how much time he'd need to get into Riley's apartment, take care of her, grab his disk, then meet the kids at the bus stop.

Kids were dumb. He knew enough about Riley to fool them into going with him. And it would be fun to terrorize her with his plans. She'd realize anything that happened to them would be *her* fault, not his.

He couldn't wait.

CHAPTER TWENTY

Today was going to be a good day. There was a high school baseball scrimmage late that afternoon that they were all going to. Porter was going to come home a little early from work so they could get there before the game started. Logan had been so excited that morning before leaving for school, it was hard to get him to concentrate on anything other than the upcoming game.

Riley sometimes couldn't believe how easily she'd gotten into a routine with two kids and a very serious boyfriend. She enjoyed making breakfast for everyone then doing her best to find all their school stuff and get the kids out the door. Then she and Porter usually had about thirty minutes to themselves. A couple of times he'd taken her back into his room and made fast, hard love to her. Other times, they sat on the couch and talked about their upcoming day.

She enjoyed having the one-on-one time with Porter, but she also loved hanging out with Bria and Logan. She literally loved *everything* about the Reeds. Bree was still a little shy, but was taking her cues from Logan and her personality was becoming more and more evident. She was very sensitive to others and always wanted to please them. She didn't talk back and generally did what she was told without complaint. Riley knew when she got older that would most likely change, so she was enjoying it while it lasted.

After Porter went to work at the post each morning, she went back to her apartment to get some work done. Her life was so much more well-rounded now than it had been before. She was getting out more, and Riley loved having friends. Yesterday, she'd talked on the phone for twenty minutes with Aspen, chatting about how her pregnancy was progressing and the details on her courthouse wedding ceremony.

It was safe to say Riley was very content with how life was going.

"I should be home by four," Porter told her as they stood in front of his door. He was getting ready to go to work. Riley loved seeing him in his uniform. It wasn't anything fancy, but there was just something about a man in uniform that did it for her. No, that wasn't true. There was just something about *Porter* in his uniform that did it for her.

"That sounds good. That'll give the kids about an hour after they get off the bus to have a snack and get started on their homework. The game starts at five, right?" she asked.

"Yeah. I don't think it's going to be a full nine innings since it's a scrimmage. It's just a chance for the team to play in front of an audience and to introduce all the players," Porter said.

Riley nodded. She knew nothing about baseball, but she had a feeling she'd be getting quite the education on the sport if Logan's interest in it continued.

"You're so not excited about this, are you?" Porter asked with a smile.

Riley shrugged. "Doesn't matter if I am or if I'm not. If Logan wants to watch baseball, then that's what we'll do."

"Fuck, I love you. Bree might get bored, so feel free to take her and wander around if you get bored too," Porter said.

She would never get tired of hearing him say those three

words. "I love you too. And don't worry about us. We'll be fine."

"Have a lot of work to get done today?" he asked.

Riley smiled. It seemed as if he was stalling, and she loved that he didn't want to leave. "Not too much. Enough to keep me busy most of the morning though."

"I should let you get to it."

"You're in meetings today, right? No training?"

"Right. I think we're scheduled to be out in the field the rest of the week, but today we've got briefings all day."

Riley wrinkled her nose.

Porter chuckled. "Yeah, that's what I think too. But having intelligence is good. It helps us figure out how to stay safe when we go on missions."

"I know, but still. I know you like to be active. You can hardly sit still when you're at home. Having meetings all day isn't your thing."

Porter smiled down at her.

"What?" she asked.

"You know me well," he said simply. "Now I really *do* need to go. The guys are gonna give me shit if I'm late...again."

"You're getting a bad reputation," she told him.

"Naw, they understand. Lefty, Trigger, and Brain were the same way when they started seriously dating their women."

Riley knew she was blushing but couldn't help it.

"And between you and me, Lefty told me he was done fucking around—his words—and he bought tickets for him and Kinley to fly to San Francisco to get married."

Riley smiled. "That's awesome!"

"Yeah, I think he was kinda upset that Brain beat him to it."

"You guys are so competitive," she mock complained.

"Yup. When we decide to do something, we do it."

Riley couldn't decide if she could hear a hidden message in his words, but she smiled at him anyway.

"Have a good day," Porter said with a small smile of his own. "And if you're good, maybe we can try out my shower tonight. I know it'll be a tight fit for us both, but I'll just need to be creative."

Riley could only nod enthusiastically. They'd had plans to shower together before now, but life kept getting in the way. It wasn't as if she thought the sex would be better in the shower, but she'd never done it, and she wanted to experience everything with Porter.

She stood on her tiptoes and he met her halfway. Her intended brief goodbye kiss turned into something much more, and when they finally pulled apart, Porter had quite the tent in his pants and Riley could feel how wet her panties had gotten.

"Fuck, you're gonna be the death of me," Porter said with small shake of his head. "Have a good day."

"You too," she told him.

She followed him out of the apartment and headed to her own place after he'd locked the door behind him. She waved one more time as he headed down the hall. She went inside her apartment, locking the deadbolt, and headed for the kitchen. She poured herself a large glass of orange juice and noticed that her refrigerator was actually quite empty. Which wasn't exactly a surprise, since she spent breakfasts and dinners over at Porter's apartment.

She had just enough in her pantry and fridge for lunches. It occurred to Riley that her apartment was essentially an office space now. She'd moved quite a few of her clothes over to Porter's place, and slowly but surely, with his encouragement, more of her things were migrating over there as well. Blankets, pillows...he'd mentioned that he liked one of the pictures on her wall, and she'd brought that over too. CDs, DVDs that were appropriate for the kids, books...if she wasn't careful, she'd be completely moved in before she realized what had happened.

Would that be so bad?

She didn't think so, and she was pretty sure Porter wouldn't think so either. He'd been very clear that he wanted children with her...and he wouldn't say that if he wasn't thinking long term.

Smiling, Riley picked up her OJ and carried it into the second bedroom in her apartment that she'd set up as an office. She had no idea how big of a space Porter was thinking about, but they'd need at least four bedrooms, two for the kids, one for them, and one for her office. Porter had no intentions of asking her to stop working, thankfully. He understood how important it was for her to contribute to the household and for her own mental well-being.

She sat down in front of her computer and thought about how much space they'd need and recalculated in her head. If Porter wanted kids, they'd need five or six bedrooms. She could probably set up an office in the basement or something.

"You're getting way ahead of yourself," she said out loud as she shook her head. "You have no idea if this thing with Porter will work out."

Of course, she *hoped* it did. She loved Porter, flaws and all. She could deal with his not being able to just sit and relax, or with his obsessive need to watch or read the news, or what a mess he made in the kitchen whenever he cooked. She wasn't perfect either, not even close.

Taking a deep breath, Riley did her best to push all thoughts of having babies with Porter to the side and turned on her computer. She checked her emails and saw she'd received three jobs for the day. Two were from repeat customers and one was new.

Thankful for the work to keep her mind occupied, she picked up her noise-canceling headphones and slipped them over her head. She propped her phone next to the computer screen so she would see the strobe if someone called or sent her a text, she pulled up the first audio file and a blank Word document and got to work.

* * *

Miles didn't have much of a plan. He knew when the children would be getting off the school bus and wanted to time the retrieval of his disk with the bus arriving. He was well aware of how nosey Riley's neighbors were. The last time he'd been there, casing the complex, someone had called the cops on their cell phone, not even bothering to hide the fact they were reporting him. So he'd have to be extra careful today. He had to get into her apartment without making a lot of noise and alerting the damn neighbors. He already knew Riley wouldn't simply let him in if he knocked.

He knew she'd be in the spare bedroom of her apartment with her headphones on. She was a creature of habit, it was one of the things that drove him crazy about her. She wasn't spontaneous at all. She was content to sit at home all fucking day. She was boring as fuck.

His plan was to get in, get his disk and whatever else he thought he could pawn for cash, then find Riley and fuck her up a little.

He'd only dated her to have a place to go during the day. He'd been living in his vehicle at the time, and hanging out in her air-conditioned apartment, eating her food, was preferable to sitting in his hot, cramped car. Before she'd decided she didn't want him hanging around all day, it was an ideal situation for sure. She'd left him alone to do whatever while she typed shit up in her office. He hadn't even had to worry about fucking her; Riley was frigid and uninterested. He'd made a half-hearted attempt once, but hadn't even been able to get it up.

Luckily, she was content with kisses after that. He felt absolutely nothing when he kissed her, and had no problem making Riley believe their lack of a sex life was because of *her*.

But really, she just wasn't the kind of person he was attracted to; she was too old. And the wrong gender.

Miles used to worry about his sexual preferences, but over the years, he'd come to terms with them. Humans were all made differently, and besides, he didn't take any of the boys he dated by force. No, he wooed them. Just like he would a woman, if he was into that sort of thing. He deserved love, just like everyone else.

The boy who'd be getting off the bus in an hour or so was younger than anyone he'd dated, but Miles would keep him around for a while. He'd take him away, groom him to be the kind of boyfriend he wanted most. In a year or so, he'd be ready for a sexual relationship. Maybe they'd live happily ever after...and Miles wouldn't have to constantly watch over his shoulder for the authorities.

Satisfied with his plan, ignoring the fact that it was morally and legally wrong, Miles pushed the crowbar from his trunk up the arm of his long-sleeve shirt. It was awkward, but the last thing he wanted was one of Riley's fucking neighbors getting suspicious again.

But he needn't have worried. When he went into the apartment building, he didn't run into anyone. Miles was aware of the cameras in the entryway and did his best to look nonchalant as he strode inside. Since it was the middle of the day, most of the residents were at work. It would make what he was about to do much easier.

He walked up to Riley's floor and glared at her neighbor's door as he went by. He *hated* that asshole. The Army guy thought his shit didn't stink. Miles still remembered how he'd stood in his doorway with his arms crossed as Riley threw him out. He was sure he could kick the guy's ass—but he'd settle for taking his kid.

He'd finally put two and two together. The day he'd tried

to get his shit back, she'd been in *his* apartment. Had probably been dating the guy behind his back the entire time. He knew the boy wasn't Riley's, so that meant he had to be the neighbor's brat. The guy probably had a dozen kids out of wedlock with different women. Why chicks wanted soldier dick so bad was beyond him.

Concentrating on the job at hand, Miles slid the crowbar out of his sleeve and jammed one end where the lock met the wall in Riley's door. It didn't take much to break the deadbolt, the damn thing was cheap as hell and only extended an inch into the doorjamb.

"Should've done this way before now," Miles muttered as he entered Riley's apartment. He shut the door behind him. It wouldn't latch, but he didn't want to leave it standing open as he grabbed his disk.

He went straight to Riley's DVD collection, his heart stuttering in his chest when he saw about half the boxes were missing. But he sighed in relief when he saw the movie he was looking for. *Spice World*. When he'd asked why the hell Riley had the movie, she'd laughed and said it was on sale and she'd bought it on a whim. She'd also admitted that she'd only gotten halfway through it before she'd called it quits. When he'd asked why she still had it in her collection, she'd shrugged and said she might try to watch it again someday.

He'd felt pretty safe hiding his own disk behind the DVD, and sure enough, he'd been right. Miles released a long breath when he opened the case and saw the CD that had caused him so many problems was still safely nestled inside.

He stood and turned—only to stop in his tracks.

Riley was standing in the hallway, staring at him in shock.

"Hi, Riley," Miles said jovially, adrenaline and excitement filling him.

"What are you doing here?" she asked. "Get out!"

"I came for my game," he told her. "And if you'd have let me come and get it before, you could've gone on with your pathetic little life and wouldn't have seen me again. But you pissed me off, called the cops on me."

"I didn't call the cops," she protested.

Miles narrowed his eyes, and he dropped the light tone. "You almost got me arrested. And you're gonna pay for that, bitch."

* * *

Riley couldn't believe Miles was standing in her living room. She had no idea how he'd gotten in, but every muscle in her body tensed the second she saw him. She'd finished up with her work and was hungry because she'd skipped lunch. Looking at the clock, she'd been relieved that she had just enough time to make herself a sandwich before going downstairs to get the kids, then getting them ready for their outing that evening.

But when she'd gotten to her living room, she'd seen Miles squatting by her DVD rack. Her first inclination was to tell him she didn't have his stupid game, but he stood with one of her movies in hand and turned before she could say anything.

When he lowered his voice to a menacing drawl and told her that she was going to pay for getting him arrested, her muscles finally obeyed the message her brain had been screaming...*run!*

She turned and sprinted for her bedroom, but Miles lunged after her, grabbing her arm before she could get there. Fighting with everything she had, Riley kicked, hit, and scratched her ex as he forced her back into the living room. He threw her to the floor and climbed on top of her, straddling her stomach and holding her down with his weight. She opened her mouth to scream, but he covered it with one of his hands. He pressed down so hard on her skin, she could feel her teeth biting into her inner lips.

Panting, Miles hovered over her. His brown, stringy hair

brushed against her cheek, making her shiver. He smelled as if he hadn't showered in a week or more and his clothes were dirty. She'd never been scared of Miles when they'd been seeing each other, but this seemed like a completely different man.

"You're dumb as a box of rocks," he sneered. "Why would I be so desperate to get a fucking game back? That's just stupid! It's not a game. It's a disk. With a video on it that I couldn't risk falling into the wrong hands. And I knew if you ever saw it, you'd turn me in without a second thought."

Riley's mind raced. A video? Of what?

The questions in her head must've been expressed in her eyes. "You ever wonder why I didn't push you for sex? Why I couldn't get it up that one time?" he asked.

Riley shook her head as best she could from under his hand. She was scared of what he'd do if she continued to fight him, but just as scared to do nothing.

"Because tits don't do it for me. Or body hair. Or curves."

Riley's eyes widened. Was he saying...

"I see it's finally dawning on you. I wouldn't have been able to get an erection no matter *what* you did. I used you, bitch. For your food. Your roof. Your TV. And those few times you let me stay the night on your fucking couch? I masturbated to my video, watching better times with a partner more to my taste."

Riley wanted to throw up. She couldn't believe she'd dated this man. This...sicko. She tried to tell him to take his fucking video and get the hell out, but all that she managed was a mumble behind his hand.

"I've been watching the complex, trying to figure out the best time to come take back what's mine...and I saw you with those kids," Miles said. "If I'm not mistaken, they should be coming home before too long. I'm between partners right now—and that boy is beautiful."

Riley *did* fight now. She shook her head frantically and did her best to thrash and squirm, trying to get out from under Miles.

He removed his hand from her mouth and wrapped it around her throat instead. His other hand came up to join it, and he began to squeeze. Hard.

She desperately gasped for breath but couldn't get any air into her lungs. He was strangling her.

"Here's the thing. I can't have you going to the cops, and I know that's exactly what you'd do the second I let you up. You'd turn me in, and I'd have to deal with that bullshit. I haven't been caught yet, and I won't ever be. That's why I had to get my disk back. I'm not going to jail. I know what happens to men like me there. So, there's only one thing I can do."

Riley fought harder than she'd ever fought in her life. Miles was going to kill her. Leave her dead body right there on the floor and go get Logan, and possibly Bree too. They hadn't ever seen Miles, wouldn't know he was a bad man.

She didn't want to die. She wanted to live. Wanted to have a wonderful life with Porter. Wanted to have his babies. The family she'd always dreamed about.

But Miles wasn't letting go.

Riley continued to thrash. She reached up and scratched his face, but all that did was piss him off. His hands tightened. His face got red as he leaned all his body weight down on hers. "Die, bitch! Just fucking die already!"

Those were the last words she heard before her world went dark and she fell unconscious.

* * *

Miles kept his hands around the bitch's throat for a moment after she went limp, just to make sure she wasn't faking. Then he quickly stood and looked for the DVD case. His dick was hard as a pike, and he looked down at it in surprise.

"Huh. Who knew?" he said out loud, smiling.

It was wildly interesting that he could get it up not just by thinking about and fucking boys, as he'd thought. But also while killing someone.

He wondered if it would be even more exciting to do both at the same time?

Maybe he wouldn't keep the boy as he'd planned. Maybe he'd experiment with this new knowledge instead.

Looking at his watch, Miles realized he was running out of time. He had to get downstairs and meet the bus.

Not looking back at the body on the floor, Miles exited the apartment, closing the door as best he could behind him. Then he whistled absently, as if he hadn't a care in the world, as he strode back down the hall.

Logan was excited. He was going to get to see a baseball game! He'd watched plenty of games on TV, but this would be live and in person. School had seemed to go by extremely slow, and he waited impatiently for Bria as she climbed off the bus behind him.

"Come on, Bree," he whined.

She smiled at him and jogged the few steps to get to his side. She reached for his hand and Logan immediately clasped his fingers around hers. He knew some people wouldn't like to hold their sister's hand, but he'd missed her a whole lot and was happy to have her living with him again.

He didn't even mind sharing a room with her. Their bunk beds were cool, and they were both so much happier than they'd ever been. Logan still felt guilty about that. He loved his mom, but it was hard living with her. He'd had to find food for Bree, and sometimes his mom too. He'd had to lock them inside their room when people came over and take care of his mom when she got too sick to get off the floor.

Living with Oz and Riley was…easy. They made him food, washed his clothes, and helped him with his homework. They played with him and laughed a lot. He had chores, but they were easy compared to what he used to have to do. He regretted not telling Oz his secret about his sister earlier, but was happy they were all together now.

They walked hand in hand toward the apartment complex, and Logan frowned when he didn't see Riley waiting for them. They hadn't been riding the bus from the new school long, but she'd been there every day so far.

A man approached them, and Logan instinctively moved so he was in front of Bree. The stranger had greasy brown hair that looked as if it hadn't been brushed in a while and his clothes were really wrinkled. He had big scratches on his face that looked like they had to hurt.

"Hi!" the man said in a friendly voice as he approached. He stopped a small distance away, making Logan feel better that he didn't crowd them.

"Hi," he responded, not wanting to be rude.

"I'm sure you're wondering where Riley is. One of her friends had an emergency and she had to go to them. She asked if I would take you to her."

"Gillian?" Logan asked, not sure which friend the man was talking about.

"Yeah. She was hurt in an accident and is in the hospital. Riley was super worried about not being here when you got off the bus, so she asked if I would meet you and bring you to the hospital."

"Where's Oz?" Logan asked, looking around.

"He's at the hospital waiting for us," the man said without hesitation. "My name is Mark. I live on the first floor." He gestured to the building behind them. "Riley's known me a long time."

"How come she hasn't mentioned you before?" Logan asked suspiciously.

"Because we're just neighbors. We see each other here and there, but don't actually hang out. But she was really upset when she left. Was crying and everything. She begged me to pick you guys up and bring you to her."

"What happened to your face?" Logan asked, trying to give himself time to think.

"I've got a cat, and she got me good this morning," the man said without hesitation.

Logan bit his lip. He hated that Gillian was hurt. He liked her. Liked all the women Oz was friends with. And he really didn't like that Riley was crying. She was usually pretty happy all the time. He was also upset that it looked like the plans to go to the baseball game were probably out, but he knew people's lives were more important than a game.

"Okay," he said slowly.

Mark smiled huge. "Great. My car's over here. I'll get you dropped off quickly. I have to come back here and meet my wife when she gets home from work."

Hearing that the man was married made Logan feel better. "Come on, Bree. Let's go find Riley and Oz."

His sister nodded trustingly and followed him toward Mark's car. It was a smaller four-door that had seen better days. The man held open the back door and Logan climbed inside. He wrinkled his nose at the garbage on the floorboards. It smelled funky inside too. Bria sat on the seat next to him, and the man shut the door.

He smiled at them through the window and got into the driver's seat. He started the car and began to drive. Logan wasn't paying attention at first, as he was helping Bria get her seat belt fastened, but when he looked up, he didn't recognize where they were going.

Then Mark turned onto the interstate and accelerated, driving faster and faster.

"Um, mister...I don't think this is the way to the hospital."

The man didn't answer. Logan could see a smirk on his face, but he didn't even turn around.

Logan's belly rolled. He'd messed up. He knew it immediately. This guy wasn't a friend of Riley's, and she wouldn't send someone he didn't know to get him. She would've had Kinley, or Lucky, or one of the other guys come and get them.

He wanted to throw up, and his entire body shook with fright. He'd been hearing all his life about stranger danger, and he'd gone and climbed inside this car without a second thought. Just because the guy *said* he knew Riley didn't mean he really did. He probably didn't even live in the apartment complex.

He was so stupid! And now both he and Bree were in danger.

The man driving leaned over and turned on the radio. Loud music filled the car, and it hurt Logan's ears. But he was glad for it because it gave him a chance to talk to Bree without the man hearing.

He had to think of a plan. Had to get Bree out of this situation. Had to protect her...like he'd done her entire life.

* * *

Oz was in a great mood as he walked up toward his apartment. He couldn't wait to spend the afternoon and evening with the people he loved most. He unlocked his apartment, ready to be bombarded by an impatient Logan and to see Riley's smile. But when he walked inside, the place was quiet. There was no sound of the kids talking and laughing and no scent of food cooking.

Even though Oz was pretty sure the apartment was empty, he still searched it from top to bottom, his gut churning. He even checked behind the sofa, Logan's favorite hiding spot. No one was there.

Oz pulled out his phone and dialed Riley's number. He

sighed in relief when he heard her ringtone through the thin walls between their apartments. For some reason, Riley had obviously brought the kids next door to her place while waiting for him to get home.

Feeling foolish that he'd been so worried, Oz headed for the door once more. Not bothering to change, and wanting to see his kids and Riley more than he wanted to get into comfortable clothes, he headed down the hall for Riley's apartment.

But the second he saw her door, all the anxiety he'd had a moment ago returned. This time even worse. Her apartment had been broken into. Someone had pried the lock open, splintering the wood.

Oz knew he should've called the cops right then and there, but he could *not* just stand in the hallway while he waited for them to show up. Riley had to be in there. He'd heard her phone. She didn't go *anywhere* without her phone. She'd told him that she wanted to be able to be reached just in case the school called. Or if Gillian, Kinley, Devyn, or Aspen needed her. She'd gotten very close with the other women, and they all texted back and forth constantly.

His took his K-BAR knife out of the holster at the small of his back and carefully pushed the door open with his elbow, trying not to contaminate any fingerprints on the door from whoever had broken in.

"Ri?" he called out. Nothing but silence greeted him. He slowly stepped over the threshold, the stillness unnerving. If Logan and Bria were there, they should've heard him. He glanced into the living room as he entered—and froze.

Riley was sprawled on the floor, not moving.

Oz knew he needed to clear the apartment. Make sure whoever had hurt Riley wasn't still lurking inside. But he literally couldn't stop himself from rushing toward the woman who owned his heart. She was lying so still on the floor. Lifeless.

He could see bruises forming on her throat, as if she'd been strangled. There wasn't anything lying nearby that could've been used to strangle her, but that didn't mean the perpetrator didn't take it with him.

A sob caught in Oz's throat as he kneeled next to Riley. He was scared to touch her, but he knew if she was still alive, he needed to help her.

Moving slowly, as if he were in quicksand, Oz reached forward with his left hand. His other still held the knife at the ready. He placed two fingers on Riley's wrist, trying to feel for a pulse. He knew if she had one, it would be more easily detected at her throat, but again, if the bastard who hurt her had used his hands to strangle her, he didn't want to contaminate the DNA he'd surely left behind.

It took a second, but then he felt it. Blood pumping through her veins.

She was alive. He had no idea how, by what miracle, but he was so damn thankful.

"I'm here, Ri," he told her, torn between wanting to take her in his arms and search for his kids.

As if the sound of his voice roused her, Riley moaned. Oz put down his knife and took her hand in his, noticing the blood under her nails. She'd scratched the hell out of whoever had done this. Good. There'd be more DNA evidence there.

"Can you hear me, Riley? It's Oz...Porter. I'm here. You're okay." He pulled out his phone and dialed 9-1-1.

"Nine-one-one. Do you need fire, medical, or police?"

"Medical and police. I just found my girlfriend on the floor of her apartment. Looks like someone tried to strangle her. My nephew and niece are missing too." Oz knew he didn't need to search the apartment for Logan and Bree. They weren't there. They would've come out when they heard his voice. He knew that without a doubt.

"Okay, sir. What's your address?"

He gave it to the operator.

"What's your name?"

"Porter Reed."

"And your girlfriend?"

"Riley Rogers."

"Okay, is she breathing?"

"Yes. But she's got bruises around her throat."

"Porter?" Riley whispered. Her voice was scratchy and didn't sound anything like her.

"Yeah, I'm here," he assured, hunching over her.

"Miles," she whispered.

"What?" Oz asked.

"What's she saying?" the operator on the phone asked.

But Oz ignored her, straining to understand Riley.

"It was Miles," she repeated. "His game was child porn. Was going to get Logan and Bree..."

Oz's blood ran cold. His voice hardened. "I'm gonna get them back," he told Riley.

Her eyes opened into slits. "I'm sorry."

He shook his head. "No. You have nothing to be sorry about. *Nothing*. Hear me? This wasn't your fault. Okay?"

She swallowed and winced.

"The police and ambulance are on the way."

"Go find them," she pleaded. "Now!"

Oz was torn. He needed to find his kids, but he couldn't leave Riley. He looked down at the phone in his hand and ended the call with 9-1-1. He knew he was supposed to stay on the line, but he had to call his team.

Trigger answered on the first ring.

"I need everyone," Oz told him. "Riley's been attacked and the kids are gone. She said it was Miles. Police are on the way, but I need you guys." His voice cracked on the last word.

"I'm on the way. I'll call the others. Is Riley okay?"

"I think so," Oz told him. "But the bastard tried to strangle her. He must've stopped when she went unconscious and didn't make sure he'd killed her."

Just saying the words made Oz feel sick. How he could be repulsed and relieved at the same time was insane. He'd never felt like this before. Even when on missions, when they'd been in the middle of a firefight, he hadn't felt like this...as if his skin was too tight and he was going to throw up from fright.

"We'll be there in ten minutes," Trigger said. "Hang on, brother." Then he hung up without another word.

Oz was so scared for his kids right now. If Miles really was a pedophile, they were in extreme danger.

He felt Riley's hand on his arm. "Go," she ordered.

"I will. When the guys get here."

She nodded.

"You're okay. He's not going to get away with this. I love you, Riley."

"Love you." Her eyes filled with tears that spilled over onto her temples.

Oz felt helpless as he waited for the cavalry to arrive. All he could do was sit there holding Riley's hand and watching her chest move up and down, reassuring himself that she was still breathing. Was still alive.

Footsteps walking quickly down the hall had never sounded so good. He could hear whoever was moving toward the apartment telling dispatch that they'd arrived. "They're here. You're gonna be okay," he told Riley.

"Go get our kids," she ordered.

Our kids.

Fuck yeah, they were.

As much as Oz wanted to stay—wanted to go to the hospital with her—he couldn't do anything other than obey. He had no doubt Gillian and the other women would be there soon. They'd go to the hospital with Riley.

He and his team had a kidnapper to hunt.

CHAPTER TWENTY-ONE

"You understand what to do?" Logan asked Bree.

She nodded. Her face was pale and her cheeks were wet with tears, but Logan knew she'd do what he'd told her. He had no idea if his plan would work or not, but he had to take a chance.

"Mister?" he asked, but the music was too loud for the man to hear him.

Clearing his throat, Logan tried again. "Mark?"

The man heard him that time. He leaned forward and turned the music down. "What?"

"I gotta pee," Logan said.

"Hold it," the man said.

Logan shook his head. "I can't," he whined. "I drank a lot before I left school and I really gotta go. I'm gonna pee all over the seat if you don't stop."

The man swore under his breath. Logan couldn't hear all his words, but the ones he did hear, he knew were some of the *really* bad words he wasn't supposed to say.

But it seemed as if his plan was working. The man pulled off the interstate and headed down a country road.

Shoot. Logan had hoped he would pull into a gas station,

but it didn't look like there were any around. All he saw here were a few farmhouses and lots of scrub brush, with some trees in the distance.

"Go to the trees," Logan whispered to Bria.

She nodded, and Logan squeezed her hand. He held on as the man pulled off onto the side of the road. There were some spindly trees on the side they were parked on, but off in the distance, to their left, there were much larger and thicker trees. Logan gestured to the left with his head, and Bria nodded.

"Well, come on. You had to go so bad a second ago, what'cha waiting for?" the man asked gruffly.

Logan opened the door on his side and left it partly open as he walked around the car to the small trees. The man followed him with a weird smile on his face. This was working better than Logan had hoped, but he still didn't like that the man was following him so closely.

"I'll be right back," he said.

The man shook his head. "I'm not lettin' you out of my sight, boy-o. You go right here while I watch."

Logan shivered. He didn't like the way the man was looking at him. And he definitely didn't want to pee in front of him.

Out of the corner of his eye, he saw Bria cross the street and take off running as fast as she could across the field on the other side of the road.

Unfortunately, the man who called himself Mark saw her too.

"Shit!" he swore, taking a few steps toward the car, as if he was going to run after her. Logan got ready to run in the other direction, but then the man stopped himself and stalked back to where he was standing. He grabbed Logan's arm and started dragging him toward the car. Logan struggled, but he was no match for the man.

A car drove by, and Mark froze, staring at the vehicle.

Then he swore again and stalked around to the driver's side. He slammed the back door Bria had exited and threw Logan into the front. "Climb over, and don't even think about doing anything to piss me off."

Scared at the man's tone, Logan did as he was told. He climbed over the center console and huddled in the front passenger seat. He was scared to death, happy Bria had gotten away, but now he was left alone with this crazy man.

Mark slammed his door and hit the door locks. Then he pulled back onto the road and did a U-turn. He pressed on the gas and the car shot forward. All the while, the man mumbled under his breath about pain-in-the-ass kids.

As they drove back toward the interstate, Logan did his best to memorize the area they were in. He desperately looked for landmarks and street signs. He'd told Bria to run and hide, and not to come out until the Easter Bunny came for her, their secret words so she'd know she was safe. He refused to think about what would happen to her if he wasn't able to come back.

"You're going to pay for that," the man said, before reaching for the knob on the stereo once more. He turned the heavy metal music up even louder than it had been before. Logan brought his hands up and covered his ears, trying to mute the sound a little. Tears fell from his eyes as he stared out the window. He was scared to death and afraid he'd never see his sister again. Or Oz. Or Riley.

* * *

Oz sat in the front seat of Lefty's truck and frantically scanned each driveway they passed. Grover had overheard the officers discussing the last known address for Miles Bowen, as well as what kind of car he drove. The police had put out an Amber Alert for Bria and Logan, but Oz wasn't willing to sit around and wait for a stranger to call in a tip. He had to be out looking.

He'd heard from Gillian not too long ago that Riley was going to be all right. She was sore, and scared to death, and the doctors in the emergency room had said the fact that she was alive was a miracle.

Oz wanted to be with her, but Riley had told Gillian to tell him under no circumstances should he come to the hospital. She was all right. He needed to find their kids. So that's what he was doing.

Although, he and his team had a hell of a lot less information than when they went out on missions. It was like looking for a needle in a haystack, and Oz was absolutely terrified.

"A tip's been called in," Lucky said from the back seat. He'd been on the phone nonstop, calling anyone and everyone for information. He'd received a call a moment ago, but Oz hadn't even noticed. Every time he hung up, the phone immediately rang once more. Oz had never been so glad for all the connections on the police force the team had made over the years. Whoever was passing information to Lucky probably wasn't supposed to be sharing, but he was relieved someone was helping them.

"Someone saw the Amber Alert notice on the billboards on the interstate and called in. Said they saw a gray Kia on the side of the road about ten miles north of Killeen. A man was pulling a boy toward the car."

"What road?"

"I don't know."

"What about Bree?"

"Nothing was said about a girl," Lucky answered.

"Fuck!" Oz swore.

"It's something," Doc soothed from the back seat. "It's more than we had before."

Lefty stepped on the gas and headed out of the neighborhood they'd been searching and turned his truck toward the interstate.

Oz held his breath, feeling helpless.

"The cops have spotted a gray Kia Rio on the interstate," Lucky informed them. He'd opened a scanner app on his phone and was tapped into the frequency used by the cops searching for Miles.

"What direction?" Lefty asked.

"North."

Oz saw the speedometer climb up to eighty-five Then ninety. Lefty wasn't fucking around, and Oz couldn't have been more thankful. He wished Trigger hadn't sold his Porsche. He would've liked to have its speed right now. Lefty wasn't driving like a grandma, but the Porsche would've let them go even faster. And right now, he needed to get to his kids as quickly as possible.

The landscape flew past, and Oz didn't think he even breathed as they raced north, hopefully toward Logan and Bria.

"Miles isn't stopping. He's trying to outrun them. They put out spike strips a mile down the road... Fuck! He went around them and almost wrecked in the median, but gained control again. His Kia is no match for the cop cars. They're right on his ass."

Oz decided it was worse knowing what was going on, but not being able to do a damn thing to help.

"How far ahead of us are they?" Lefty asked.

Lucky looked for a mile marker. "Less than five miles."

Oz couldn't talk. His mouth was dry as cotton. He was usually extremely levelheaded in emergencies, but he was completely useless right now. All he could do was hold on and pray his kids wouldn't be hurt when this chase came to an end. And it *would* come to an end. They all knew that. It was just a matter of how.

Peacefully or in a fiery crash.

"Okay, they're backing off a bit, giving him some room, they're gonna try the stop sticks again another mile or so north of where they are."

Lucky sounded excited, but Oz couldn't find one damn thing to be excited about. Yeah, the stop sticks could pierce Miles's tires, but that would just make the car more unstable at high speeds.

"They're in place...he's approaching...boom! Got him! All four tires! He's on rims now, and the tires are smoking bad... he's slowing down..."

Lucky went silent.

Lefty continued to tear up the interstate, trying desperately to catch up to the chase.

"What? What's happening?" Doc asked.

Lucky held up a finger, telling Doc to wait.

Oz turned around to stare at his friend, trying to read his face. Had the car crashed? Were the kids okay? Was Miles in custody, or had he tried to use Logan or Bree as a hostage? But Lucky's face was completely blank, not giving away anything.

Oz wanted to grab his friend by the collar and force him to talk, or grab the phone out of his hand and demand to know what the fuck was happening.

Then Lefty began to slow down.

Oz turned and saw what seemed like a company's worth of police cars and lights ahead. Smoke turned the air hazy around the Kia, and he struggled to see what was going on. Cars were stopped in front of them, but Lefty simply pulled into the median and continued forward.

Oz felt as if his teeth were going to rattle out of his head, but he didn't tell his friend to slow down. Instead, he mumbled, "Hurry."

They stopped just behind where the police cars had

blocked off the interstate, and Oz didn't hesitate to leap out of the truck. He began to run toward the still-smoking Kia, now facing the wrong way in the middle of the road. It was surrounded by at least six cop cars, and all the police officers had their weapons drawn and were pointed toward the driver's seat.

Movement from the left of the car caught his attention—an officer was running away from the Kia carrying a small body.

All the air left his lungs, and the only thing Oz could think was that he couldn't be so lucky a second time. Riley had survived—but maybe losing one of his kids was penance.

Then he saw the officer kneel down behind a police car... and put the child on their feet.

Oz might've been frozen in fear before, but now he moved. He ran toward the man and boy, only stopping when the officer raised his weapon and pointed it at him. "Stop right there!"

He fell to his knees and tried to catch his breath. The boy turned and, before the officer could get ahold of him, ran straight for Oz. He held out his arms just as Logan slammed into him.

"Oz!"

"Oh my God, Logan!" Oz breathed out.

"He's okay, he's the kid's uncle!" one of his teammates yelled from behind him, but Oz couldn't concentrate on anything but Logan. He pulled back and held his nephew at arm's length, running his eyes up and down his body. "Are you okay? Did he hurt you?"

"I'm okay," Logan said, tears streaming down his face.

"Are you sure?"

"I'm sure," Logan said.

Then Oz crushed him to his chest once more.

"You need to get out of the middle of the road," an officer said.

Oz nodded and stood without letting go of Logan. He carried him into the grass in the median and knelt back down when Logan squirmed in his grip.

"Bree!" his nephew said in a choked-up tone.

"What about her? Where is she?" Oz asked. "Is she still in the car?"

He knew he had a circle of people around him now, both his teammates and police officers, but he kept his gaze on Logan's.

Logan shook his head and said miserably, "No. I told Mark I had to pee and he stopped. I told Bria to run when I got out. She did. I lost her!" he wailed.

Oz assumed Mark was the name Miles had given to Logan and Bria, but his mind immediately moved on. His heart broke for his nephew, but he gently shook his shoulders. "You didn't lose her, you *saved* her," he said, believing his words one hundred percent. "We just have to go back to where you were when she ran."

"B-But I don't know where it was!" Logan cried.

"Take a deep breath," Oz ordered. He wanted to cry himself, but knew he had to stay calm so he could get his nephew to concentrate.

Logan did as he was ordered, his little chest filling with air as he inhaled deeply.

"Good, and another."

He watched in approval as his kid, who had already been through so much in his young life, did his best to get control of himself.

"Look around you, Logan." Oz waited as Logan did just that. His eyes widened as he took in the number of police officers, and Lucky, Lefty, Doc, and Grover. Trigger and Brain had escorted the women to the hospital and were looking after Riley until Oz could get back to her, with their kids in tow.

"You see all these people? They're here because of you.

Because they knew you were smart and brave. That you'd hold on until they could get to you. And you did. You not only got your sister out of an extremely dangerous situation, you stalled that guy enough that we could all catch up."

Logan nodded.

Oz pulled his nephew into his arms once more. He could barely remember the time before this kid was in his life. It was crazy, as he didn't even know of his existence not too long ago, but Oz's life had changed for the better the second he'd seen him walking down the hallway of his apartment complex all those weeks ago.

"Close your eyes," he told Logan, leaning back enough to see his face.

He did.

"Now, think about where you were when you pulled over. What did you see?"

"I was hoping he'd go to a gas station and Bree could get help, but there was nothing on the road he got off on. Houses in the distance, and trees."

Oz's stomach clenched with worry, but he kept encouraging Logan. "What else, Slugger?"

"I got out and left the door open and told Bree to run across the road to the trees in the distance."

"Smart."

Logan's voice got stronger as he concentrated. "Mark wasn't happy when he saw her running, and he pulled me back to the car. Someone drove by, and I think that scared Mark."

"I think that person called the cops," Oz said. "Did you come straight back to the interstate then, Logan?"

"Uh-huh. There was a fireworks store. It was red, white, and blue. We turned a couple times, but I think I saw a sign that said Elm on it."

Oz closed his eyes in relief. It had to be enough. It just

had to. He opened his eyes and looked up at his team. Lucky was on his phone already, and he saw two of the police officers scrolling on their own phones.

"Got it," one of the cops said a minute later. Oz stood, keeping his hand on Logan's shoulder. "There's an exit that has an American Fireworks Superstore right at the corner. And the name of the street is Elm Street."

The officer turned to head back to his car, and Oz was right on his heels.

"We're coming with you," he informed him.

"No, you need to stay here," the officer said.

Oz looked at the man's name tag and shook his head. "Officer Myers, I didn't get to introduce myself. I'm Porter Reed, US Army Delta Force. My niece is probably scared to death, and you're gonna need me when you find her."

"And me," Logan said from next to him.

Oz squeezed his shoulder in support.

"I can show you where we stopped. And we have a code word. Bree won't come out without it," Logan added.

"Delta Force?" Officer Myers asked.

Oz nodded.

"Fine, but you need to do what we say."

Oz agreed immediately. "Those are my teammates. They'll be following us."

Officer Myers headed for his cruiser with Oz and Logan following him. Lefty went back to his truck with the rest of his team. Oz was well aware that the officer didn't have to take them with him. That he was making an exception. He was just relieved the man seemed to be as eager as he was to get to the area where they'd hopefully find Bria.

Not wanting to think about how scared she was, Oz helped Logan into the police car and crawled in after him. He wasn't thrilled to be in the back seat of a cruiser, but he didn't care *how* he got to Bree, just as long as he got to her.

From the corner of his eye, he saw Miles in another vehicle. He'd been taken into custody without incident. He'd surrendered like the coward he was. Oz couldn't even think about the future right now—court dates and if Logan would have to testify. All he could do was be thankful that Logan was all right and focus on finding Bria. Everything else was secondary.

As they took off, and the officer communicated to the others on the radio what was going on, Oz looked down at Logan. He was sitting as close to Oz as possible and had both his arms around his torso.

"Slugger?"

Logan looked up at him.

"This is the one and only time you'll ever be in the back seat of a police car. Understand?"

Logan's lips twitched. "Got it."

"You did good, and I'm so proud of you," Oz said softly.

"I shouldn't have gotten in the car with him," Logan said sadly. "I knew better."

"It's easy to know what the right thing to do is after the fact. I bet he had a really good excuse," Oz said.

Logan shrugged. "He said Gillian was in the hospital and Riley had gone to be with her. He said he lived in our apartment complex, and she asked him to bring me and Bree there."

Oz inhaled deeply. It *was* a good excuse. Miles might be an asshole, but he wasn't completely stupid.

"I know Riley would be worried about Gillian, but she wouldn't ask a stranger to pick us up. I was stupid."

Oz lifted Logan's chin so he had to look at him. "We all make wrong decisions, Slugger. Even me. But the thing is, you went with him because you were worried about Riley. And Gillian. That's not entirely a bad thing. And, not only that, but you did what you had to do in order to get your sister to safety. I'm thinking we need a family safe word or phrase, like you have with your sister. Just in case something like this ever happens again."

Logan nodded. Then said with a sniffle, "Bree's probably scared."

"No doubt. But she would've been more scared if she'd still been in the car when the police stopped it and pulled their guns. And she would've been scared if that man took you to some strange house, right? All I'm sayin' is that you did what you had to do to protect your sister, and both Riley and I are more than proud of you."

"Where is Riley?" Logan asked.

Oz's belly tightened. Shit. Logan would find out what had happened to her eventually, but maybe once they'd found Bria he wouldn't be as upset about it. But he needed to be upfront with his nephew. "She's okay," he said.

Logan's lip trembled.

Oz decided to treat this like a Band-Aid, rip it off and get it over with. "The man who took you and your sister hurt her. He was her ex. The guy who scared you when he banged on my door, and you hid behind the couch. But she's okay. She's in the hospital and badgering the doctors to let her go home so she can see you and Bree."

Logan stared up at him for a long moment. "You aren't lying? She's really okay, not dead like my mom?"

"She's not dead," Oz whispered. Even saying the words hurt. "I wouldn't tell you she's okay if she wasn't."

Logan thought about that for a second, then he gave Oz a small smile. "I bet she's not happy to be stuck in the hospital. She's pretty protective."

"She is," Oz agreed, and he knew he'd never take that for granted in the future. She could be as protective as she wanted and he'd go with it. He'd build her a fucking moat around a house if she wanted one.

"This is the exit," the officer told them from the front.

Logan straightened and his eyes lit up. "This is it! It really is! I told you there was a red, white, and blue fireworks place!"

"I'm going to drive slowly, you let me know when something looks familiar," Officer Myers told him.

Logan craned his neck trying to see out the front of the car, and Oz looked out the back window. There were at least ten cars trailing them. He saw Lefty's truck, and the rest were law enforcement vehicles. Texas Ranger, Highway Patrol, and Killeen Police Department. Everyone was there hoping to be able to lend a hand in finding a lost, kidnapped little girl.

"There!" Logan shouted.

The officer immediately slowed further.

"See those trees?" Logan asked, pointing to his right, almost whacking Oz in the face. "That's where the man wanted me to pee. I stood over there, and Bria ran that way." He moved his hand to point in the other direction.

Officer Myers cut the engine and got out, immediately opening the back door for Oz and Logan.

Oz stared across the field toward the trees, and his heart sank. The area was huge. Bria could literally be anywhere.

"We've got a bird on the way," Officer Myers said.

"With FLIR?" Oz asked hopefully.

"Yes."

"What's fleer?" Logan asked. "Why aren't we going to find Bree?"

"FLIR stands for forward-looking infrared camera. It'll spot where your sister is hiding without us having to beat every bush and tree. She'll show up as bright white, when everything else is black and gray. The guys in the helicopter will guide us right to her, Slugger."

Logan still looked worried, but the trust he was showing in him humbled Oz.

"What are we waiting for?" Lucky asked as he ran toward them. The area was fast filling with law enforcement personnel, and it was obvious his Delta team was more than ready to head out to find Bria.

"Chopper's on the way with FLIR," Oz told Lucky.

"Thank God," his teammate breathed.

Doc, Grover, and Lefty arrived in time to hear the news about the chopper.

Everyone waited on the side of the road with bated breath to hear from the helicopter camera operator. They heard the rotor blades before they saw the bird, and when they finally did spot the chopper, it was the most beautiful thing Oz had ever seen in his life.

"How long will it take to find her?" Logan asked, shifting impatiently on his feet.

"I don't know, Slugger. But they're doin' their best," Oz soothed. Truth was, he wanted to ask the same thing. Wanted to whine that it was taking too long, but he remained patient. He felt Grover's hand land on his shoulder, and it helped to know his friends had his back.

After seven and a half minutes—Oz knew exactly how long it had been, because he was closely watching the time— they heard over the radios the police officers were holding that the FLIR had spotted something they thought might be Bria.

"You all need to stay here," Officer Myers told them.

Oz was shaking his head before the man had finished his sentence.

"Not happening," he told him. "I understand that you have a job to do, but I guarantee I've seen more in my life-time than you have. I *have* to be there when you find her."

"But does he?" the officer asked, nodding at Logan.

Oz was torn. The last thing he wanted was Logan to see his sister if something bad had happened to her, but he honestly didn't think anything had. Bria was smart, even if she was only six and a half. He had a feeling she'd done exactly what her brother had told her to do. Ran like hell and hid until he could come get her. And he knew she'd need Logan to feel safe.

"No, but I have faith in my niece. She's okay. Scared to death, but waiting for her big brother to make good on his word and come get her."

The officer sighed, but he finally nodded. "All right, but you all stay behind me. I mean it. I'll have you locked up so fast your head will spin if you so much as step one inch out of line."

"Yes, sir," Oz said immediately. He wasn't happy to be relegated to the back of the group of officers searching for Bria, but he was being allowed to accompany them. He'd do whatever he was told.

His teammates had also been able to talk their way into entering the field with the search party, and they all jogged across the dry weeds and grass toward the trees. The officer in the lead was talking to the person in the helicopter running the infrared camera. He was making a beeline for a particularly thick strand of trees.

"Good girl," Oz said under his breath.

When they arrived, Oz could hear the officer being directed to a spot right in front of them.

"Stop. She should be right there, a little to your right. She's lying down."

Oz couldn't see anything but scrub brush. He itched to plunge into the undergrowth and find Bree. He understood why she hadn't immediately shown herself. She was probably scared. And she'd learned the hard way that many adults weren't trustworthy.

He just prayed that she wasn't wounded, or worse.

No, she was fine. She had to be. He couldn't have been lucky enough to have Riley and Logan spared, only to lose her.

Logan had been standing silent next to him, but before

Oz could stop him, he slipped away and went up to the officer who'd been calling his sister's name.

Without asking permission, Logan said, "Bree? It's me! Logan. It's okay, you can come out. I brought the Easter Bunny with me, just like I told you I would."

Oz held his breath—and within seconds, a frightened Bree poked her red head out from the middle of a bunch of sticks and debris. "Logan?"

"Yes!" Logan said excitedly. "You're okay! I found you!"

Oz went to his knees in relief when Bria bolted out of her hiding place and practically tackled Logan. He watched as brother and sister greeted each other tearfully and with relief.

He felt his teammates slap him on the back in support. He wanted to thank them for being there for him. For doing everything possible to get the most precious people in his life back. But he couldn't. All he could do was stare at Bria and Logan. He was crying, but barely felt the tears on his cheeks.

As if knowing what his uncle needed, Logan took Bria by the hand and pulled her over to where Oz was kneeling.

"Look, Oz! I found her!" he said.

"I see, Slugger," Oz said softly. He barely heard the helicopter flying away or the police officers congratulating each other. He only had eyes and ears for his kids.

"You okay, Bree?" he asked quietly.

She nodded. "I was scared," she told him. "But I knew Logan would come get me. And he did!"

"Yes, he sure did. He loves you very much, and you're lucky to have him for an older brother. I love you too. I know I haven't known about you very long, but I love you, kiddo. So much."

She dropped her brother's hand and walked right up to him. She stepped between his knees and wrapped her small arms around his neck and hugged him.

Then she looked into his face and said seriously, "Boys aren't supposed to cry."

"Says who?" Oz asked.

Bria looked confused. "I don't know."

"Right. Well, boys *do* cry. There's nothing wrong with showing your emotions, no matter if you're a boy or girl, man or woman."

"Are you sad?" Bria asked as she reached up and wiped his cheek with her dirty hand. Oz knew she was probably smearing dirt across his face, but he didn't care.

"Not anymore," Oz told her. "You and your brother are safe. Riley too. The three people I love the most in this world are okay, so I can't be sad."

"Oz?" Bria asked.

"Yeah, sweetheart?"

"I'm hungry. Can we go home?"

Oz chuckled, and he heard others laughing around him. "Yes. Although we might need to make a stop first." He looked up and back at Grover. "Has someone called Riley? Told her?"

"Yeah, Lucky's been on the phone with her ever since we stopped."

Oz nodded in relief. He wasn't surprised one of his team had made sure Riley was kept up-to-date. He owed them all. Big time. "Has she been discharged yet?"

"I'm not sure the hospital wants to let her go home," Lefty said.

Oz looked at Doc. "What do you think?"

"I think if she's not experiencing any complications, it should be safe. She was lucky."

Oz knew that.

"We're going to need to talk to the little girl," one of the officers said from nearby, obviously overhearing his conversation.

Sighing, Oz nodded, then slowly stood. He felt shaky and weak, but knew it was from the adrenaline dump his body had just experienced.

"I'll get Trigger and Brain to bring Riley to your place," Lucky said. "I just need to make some calls."

"Thank you. You've been a godsend," Oz told him. And he had. Oz had no idea how he'd made the kind of connections they'd needed today, but he wouldn't forget it. Lucky truly *was* lucky, and he'd take luck over skill any day of the week... not that his teammate didn't have some amazing skills as well.

Oz felt a tug on his pants and looked down. Bree was standing at his side, and when she saw she had his attention, she held up her arms. Oz bent and picked her up, and Bree's head immediately went to his shoulder. He closed his eyes in relief.

Logan leaned against his other side, and Oz wrapped his arm around his shoulders. They walked back across the field that way, as a family, very thankful to be together. All that was missing was Riley, and soon enough she'd be with them.

Oz wasn't a very spiritual man. He'd seen too much hatred and violence to put much stock in a higher power doing what was right for mankind. But right that minute, he was sure he'd had someone looking over his family. Logan survived a kidnapping and high-speed chase, Bria had managed to escape a potentially deadly situation and didn't seem too fazed by the entire thing. And Riley...

Oz swallowed hard, trying to keep from crying—again. She shouldn't be alive. They both knew it. Miles had done his best to choke the life from her. But somehow he'd managed to screw that up too.

Looking into the bright blue Texas sky, Oz sent a prayer of thanks upward. Thanks to whomever or whatever might've been looking after the three people he loved most in this world. He didn't know what he would've done if even one of them hadn't survived this hellish day.

"We missed the baseball game," Logan said quietly from next to him.

Oz couldn't help but smile. "We did," he agreed. "But the

good thing about baseball is that the season is really long, and there will be plenty of games we can go see."

Logan seemed to perk up at that. "True."

Oz couldn't believe he was smiling, but it felt good. Damn good. Now he just needed Riley. They all did.

CHAPTER TWENTY-TWO

"We must've been going two hundred miles an hour! Then there was smoke everywhere and I couldn't see anything! The car stopped and there were a hundred policemen pointing their guns at us. Then I was pulled out and Oz was there! He cried. Then we got to ride in the back of a police car and a helicopter came and I told Bree our code words and she came out! Oz cried again and then we got to eat Whataburger and when we got home, *you* were here!"

Riley smiled at Logan. He was recounting what had happened earlier that day. It was late, the sun had long since set, but she wasn't the least bit tired.

She was wearing a turtleneck sweater even though she was lying in bed, so the kids didn't freak out about the bruises around her neck. Over the last few hours, they'd really begun to darken. The sight of Miles's fingermarks on her neck made even her a bit queasy. She was stiff, and pale, but she thought she looked pretty damn good for almost dying earlier that day.

She was sitting on Oz's bed with Bria snuggled in her arms, Logan sitting at her feet, and Oz's arm around her. He was supporting both her and Bria's weight, and she'd never felt as relieved as she did right that minute.

Miles was in jail on quite the laundry list of charges. Along with kidnapping, attempted murder, and fleeing from police, he was also facing child pornography charges. After all the trouble he'd gone through to get his disk from her place so the cops wouldn't find it, they'd confiscated it from his car. She'd been told his case would be a slam dunk, that they had more than enough evidence to put him away for a really long time.

But Riley didn't want to think about Miles. She was just so thankful to be alive. That Logan and Bria were all right.

"It sounds like it was quite the adventure," she told Logan.

"It was. But...Oz told me that was the only time I was ever allowed to ride in the back of a police car."

Riley smiled. "He's right. And how are you doing, Bree? You've had a rough couple months," she said gently.

Bria shrugged. "I'm okay. I was scared but Logan told me to hide, and I knew he'd be back to get me."

Riley felt Oz shiver under her. They both knew so many things could've gone wrong. If Logan hadn't been smart enough to look for street signs and other distinguishing landmarks from where Bria had run, she might still be out there waiting for her brother to come back for her. In the dark. They'd all been so very lucky.

"Are you really all right?" Logan asked. "That man hurt you."

Oz's arms tightened. He'd been very quiet since they'd gotten home. He'd helped her change and had examined her from head to toe, wanting to see for himself every bruise and scrape she'd gotten at Miles's hands. They needed to talk, but they would take care of the kids first.

"He did," she agreed. "But I'm okay. Here's the thing, I could cry and stay in bed for a month, but that won't change what happened. I can either decide to move on with my life and be happy, or I can fall apart. I've got too much to do to fall apart. We have baseball games to go to, Bree has a music recital with her class coming up in a month or so that she's excited about, and I have customers who are relying on me to get their jobs done on time."

Logan nodded as if everything she'd said made perfect sense, but Bria turned to look up at her. "I wanna be happy. Sometimes I remember that scary cage and how hungry I was, but now I'm with Logan. And I like you. And Uncle Oz."

Riley hugged her. "Good. And it's okay to talk about what happened to you, like you've been talking to the psychologist. I'm not saying I won't remember being hurt, but I've got you guys, and Porter, how can I *not* be happy?"

Bria snuggled back into her as she nodded.

Riley felt Porter kiss the top of her head and she sighed. Today had been the worst day of her life, but lying here in Porter's arms, with Bria and Logan safe and healthy, she couldn't help but be utterly content.

No one said anything for a long moment, then Porter said quietly, "I think Riley needs some sleep. And so do you guys. It's been a long, eventful day. I think we're all going to take a sick day tomorrow. Maybe go down to the big park on the Army post and throw a baseball around. Bree, there's an awesome obstacle course there that you might find fun."

"Yay!" Logan exclaimed.

It was obvious Bria wasn't sure what her brother was so excited about, but she let out a happy whoop too.

"Sounds good," Riley said softly.

"*You* will sit on the sidelines and watch," Porter told her quietly. Then louder, he said, "Come on, kids, let's go get you ready for bed."

Riley watched the trio leave the room and leaned back on the pillows behind her with a sigh. She closed her eyes and must've dozed, because the next thing she knew, Porter was back, sliding into bed and pulling her into his arms. He held her as if she was the most precious thing in his world.

This was the first time they'd been alone since he'd found her on the floor of her apartment, and she had to say what she'd been thinking about since she awoke and became aware of what had happened.

"I'm so sorry—"

"No," Porter said firmly.

"What?" she asked, turning her head to look back at him.

"No apologizing. You did nothing wrong."

"How can you say that?" Riley asked incredulously. "I messed up in so many ways with Miles, I can't even begin to list them all."

"No, you didn't. You wanted to find a nice guy to date, and you thought Miles was him. He played you from the start, used you for a place to crash. Took advantage of your gentle and loving demeanor. He belittled you, verbally abused you, and tried his best to tear you down.

"But it didn't work. You got rid of his ass. Maybe we shouldn't have ignored him when he started to harass you, but that's on us both. We didn't know he'd go *this* crazy. We should've taken precautions. Taken out a restraining order, not that it would've prevented him from breaking into your apartment, but still. Rile, he's the one who almost strangled you to death. He's the one who kidnapped our kids. He's the one who put Logan's life at risk by driving like a lunatic. You have nothing to apologize for. It's all on him. Do *not* take this on yourself."

It took Riley a moment to be able to speak. The lump in her throat was almost overwhelming. "How did I get so lucky?" she whispered.

"I think that's my line," Porter said. "I admit that I didn't think I was so lucky when Logan showed up, but now I can't imagine not having him in my life. And then finding Bree? She reminds me so much of my sister, it's almost uncanny. I miss her. I'm sorry that I didn't get the chance to mend our bridges, but she gave me two of the best gifts I've ever gotten. Three, if I include you." He leaned in and sighed against Riley's neck. "You scared the shit out of me," he admitted. "When I saw you unconscious on the floor, I thought you were dead."

Riley wasn't sure what to say. She knew it was only because Miles was in a hurry, and an idiot, that he hadn't finished the job. She *should've* been dead on that floor, and it wasn't something she liked to think about.

"I can't live without you," he whispered.

"And I can't live without you," she returned. "I'm going to be a mess when you go on missions. I hate to even admit that because it puts a lot of pressure on you, but...please be careful."

Porter rolled her so she was on her back looking up at him. He brushed a lock of hair off her forehead. "I've never really thought too much about death before. I knew it was a possibility every time we went on a mission, but I've got too much to live for to let some asshole take me out. I honestly think the fact that Trigger, Lefty, Brain, and I have found women we want to spend the rest of our lives with, we're actually more cautious than we were before."

She loved hearing that he wanted to spend the rest of his life with her.

Deciding that they'd been morose long enough, she said, "Well, if we're going to be together forever, we definitely need a bigger place. Not to mention, I have a feeling things with the powers that be in the Army would be easier if we were actually married, and I wasn't just the neighbor who babysat the kids."

She was completely kidding, and awkwardly trying to lighten the mood.

"Yes," Porter said without hesitation.

"Yes? Yes, what?" she asked.

"I accept your marriage proposal," he told her.

Riley blinked up at him. "I didn't propose," she protested.

"Yes, you did. And I accepted. So now we're engaged. Did you get me a ring?" he teased.

Riley wasn't sure what had just happened. Was he kidding? She wasn't sure.

"No matter," he said, then rolled away. He opened the drawer in his nightstand and pulled out a small black box. "If you don't like it, I can get you something else."

He opened the box to reveal a simple diamond solitaire ring. The stone was emerald cut, and it sparkled in the overhead light they hadn't turned off yet. She stared at it, then back up at him, speechless.

"I love you, Riley. I really do want to spend the rest of my life with you by my side. I have a feeling nothing about our lives will be calm and sedate, but I can't wait for what tomorrow brings. Will you marry me? Have more kids with me?"

"Oh, Porter," Riley said.

He smiled and took the ring out of the box and picked up her hand. He slipped the ring down her finger. It was a bit big. "I wasn't sure of your size, but I was too impatient to have you agree to be my wife to get it sized properly."

"When did you get this?" she asked, still in shock.

"A week ago." He shrugged. "I know it's fast, but fuck it. I love you. You love me. The kids adore you. And after what happened today, after almost losing you all, I'm especially glad I already bought it so I could ask you right this second to marry me."

Riley had never felt as happy as she was at this moment. "You know, when I get pregnant, I'll gain weight. I think this ring might fit perfectly if my fingers swell up."

She saw the flare of lust in Porter's eyes at her words.

"Fuck," he swore quietly. A hand went down her body to rest on her belly. "I can't wait for you to be pregnant. I know that's probably weird, but I can't help it. Now that I know how awesome kids are, I want more."

"They don't come out being ten or six. Babies are loud. And they're quite a disruption to life as you know it," she warned.

"Don't care," he said as he lay down next to her. She was still wearing her sweater and sweatpants, but she didn't have the energy or desire to get up and change. Porter's hand slipped under her sweater and rested on the bare skin of her belly.

"Thank you for being so strong and not giving up," Porter said softly.

"Thank you for finding our kids."

"Love you."

"Love you back," Riley said.

The light was still on, she was still almost fully dressed, and she'd almost died that day. But Riley had never slept better as she did that night.

EPILOGUE

"Porter, I can't see where I'm walking!" Riley complained with a laugh.

Oz held a finger to his lips for Logan and Bria. They were giggling and skipping around him and Riley. He'd blindfolded her and brought her here for a surprise. He had his arm around her waist, guiding her so she didn't fall.

It had been three months since Riley had almost died and his kids had been kidnapped, but everyone seemed to be thriving. Bree was hilarious, and Oz loved seeing her personality come out more and more. She absolutely loved her teacher at Gerry Linkous Elementary, Mr. Santoro. And it seemed as if she had an affinity for the obstacle course on the Army post. An interest her gym teacher, Mrs. O'Brien-Santoro, cultivated.

Logan was thriving in his class as well. He'd move on to the middle school next year, but he'd made tons of friends in his new school. Baseball league was also a hit, and he couldn't wait to get home on the days he had practice.

Oz hadn't wasted any time in making Riley his wife. She'd been right in that being married made things a lot easier as far as red tape and the military went. He didn't have to worry about a family care plan anymore, and she was able to get medical insurance and all the other perks that went along with being a military spouse. They'd gone down to the courthouse, and then his teammates had thrown them a huge party at Brain and Aspen's house.

Lefty and Kinley had flown to San Francisco the very next day, Lefty saying he wasn't going to be the only guy living in sin with a woman. He'd been kidding, but Kinley was more than happy to finally get married. His parents had put together a quaint wedding in their backyard, and Lefty had said it was actually perfect.

Aspen was now showing, and Brain couldn't seem to keep his hands off her pregnant belly. Whenever they were standing next to each other, he was fondling her stomach. The guys made fun of him for it, but Logan couldn't blame him. He and Riley had stopped using birth control, and he prayed every day that he'd knock her up. He didn't think it was normal for a guy to be so excited and impatient for his woman to get pregnant, but he didn't give a shit. He wanted a baby with Riley. Now.

On top of everything else...Miles had hung himself shortly after being imprisoned, while awaiting trial. It was surprising, as Oz hadn't thought the man had the balls to do something so...permanent. And he was secretly glad. Yes, he would've liked to have seen him pay for what he'd done to his family, but Bree and Logan would no longer have to relive what they'd been through during a trial, and it was a relief.

And now...today was a special day. He'd worked hard to keep what he'd been doing a secret from Riley. Oz felt a little guilty that he'd been coming home late for a while now, but Riley, being as sweet as she was, never complained. She took Logan to his baseball practice, played with Bree, helped them with their homework, and made sure they were fed.

She'd never gone back to her apartment after she'd been

attacked. Oz didn't blame her, and was more than happy that she'd moved in with him without a fuss.

He'd been in her apartment a few times, to help his teammates and their wives pack up her stuff, and it gave him the heebie-jeebies. He couldn't stop looking at the spot on the floor where Riley had been lying motionless. Bless Doc, Grover, and the others, they'd stepped up and done all the moving for them.

But afterward, his apartment was packed to the gills with their stuff. A two-bedroom was way too small for four people and all their belongings. He and Riley had been talking about trying to find a three-bedroom apartment to tide them over until they could house hunt, but they hadn't actually had the time to get it done.

And now it was time to show Riley his surprise.

The kids ran ahead, and Oz made sure Riley was safe and secure as he guided her forward. He stopped after a few more steps and took a calming breath. "You ready?" he asked.

Riley laughed again. "Porter, I've been ready for whatever this surprise is for what seems like forever. I know you've been up to something, but I haven't asked about it. Let's get this over with before you explode."

Oz burst out laughing. He should've known he couldn't keep anything from his very observant wife. "Right. Okay, hang on," he told her as he fumbled with the tie at the back of her head. He got it loose and it fell around her neck as she blinked in the sudden bright light.

"Surprise!" Logan shouted.

"Happy new house!" Bree added.

Riley stared up at the large house in front of her in shock. "What? How... Oh, Porter!"

He smiled down at her. "Welcome home," he said softly into her ear. "It's got six bedrooms. Plenty of room to expand our family, and there's an office downstairs that will be perfect for you. The kitchen's been redone and the master bathroom is to die for...especially the oversized shower. I've already found a housecleaner who can come every other week, because I know this place will be a bitch to keep clean. Bria and Logan have already claimed their rooms."

"Can we go in, Oz? Can we?" Logan shouted from the porch.

"Go!" he told them.

With a whoop of excitement, their kids disappeared through the front door.

"I can't believe you bought a *house*!" she exclaimed.

"I've been saving money for a long time. And doing what I do pays well when you're single."

"What if the Army moves us?" Riley asked nervously.

"We'll cross that bridge when we get to it. We can talk about renting it out or something, but I want us to live here. Raise our family here. I won't always be in the Army, and I really like this area of Texas. Logan loves his school and his baseball team. I see good things for him in the future."

"Six bedrooms?" Riley asked with a laugh.

Oz shrugged. "Go big or go home," he said.

Riley turned, wrapping her arms around his waist and tilting her head back to look at him. The creamy skin of her neck was unblemished, and there wasn't a mark left from her ordeal with her ex. Every time Oz looked at her, he thanked his lucky stars that she was still here.

"I guess it's a good thing that we have so many bedrooms. I mean, in less than a year, we'll have filled four of them."

Oz nodded absently—then frowned. "Wait, what?"

"I'm pregnant," Riley said softly. "Surprise!"

Oz was speechless. "Seriously?"

"Yes. I wouldn't lie about it. Not with how hard you've been working to knock me up. Although...maybe I shouldn't have told you just so I could enjoy your efforts for a few more months."

Oz let out a yell and picked her up and spun her around in a circle before kissing her.

They were still making out when they heard Logan's voice from the house. "Are you guys ever gonna stop kissing and come check out the house?"

Oz pulled back and stared down at the woman in his arms. He was at a loss for words.

"I love you," Riley said.

"I didn't fully know what those words meant, not really, until this year," Oz told her.

Riley beamed at him. Then she said slyly, "When are we going to get to christen the new house?"

"Trigger and Gillian said they'd babysit tomorrow night," he answered with a smirk.

"I love a man who plans ahead," she said.

"And if you think I'm not going to fuck you as much or as often as I did when I was attempting to put my baby in you, you're wrong. I need to make sure my son or daughter knows who their daddy is."

Riley laughed. "I'm not sure it works that way."

"Are you complaining?" he asked with a quirk of his eyebrow.

"Nope. No complaints here," Riley said.

"Good. Now come on. Come examine your castle, my queen."

* * *

Lucky watched Devyn from across the yard. They were all at Oz's new house, breaking it in with a rousing housewarming party slash wedding receptions for Lefty, Brain, and Oz. Logan and Bree were running around the yard, hyped up on too much sugar from the s'mores they'd made on the firepit earlier.

Everyone was there. Trigger, Gillian, Lefty, Kinley, Brain,

Aspen, Doc, Grover, and Devyn. Winnie, Brain's ninety-one-year-old neighbor, had shown up with her granddaughter, and her new husband, Rocket. There were even some of Oz's new neighbors in attendance as well.

The mood was relaxed and festive. The Deltas all did their best to enjoy their downtime because they never knew when they'd be called to head out on a mission. Things in the world seemed more volatile now than they had in a very long time. Skirmishes were breaking out all over the world, and tensions were high across borders.

Drugs were out of control, terrorists were ramping up to wreak havoc against their supposed enemies, and North Korea was always a threat. Sometimes Lucky despised his job, hated seeing the lack of respect for human life, but the times they got to rescue people, or make a difference in a significant way, made it all worthwhile. And he'd been lucky enough to be on more missions with positive outcomes than negative ones.

Lucky might be "lucky" in life, and with his job, but he was definitely striking out when it came to love. He wanted what his friends had. And there was only one woman he wanted it with.

Devyn Groves. Grover's sister.

She'd come to Texas a while back now, but as much as he tried to get close to her, she'd kept him at arm's length the whole time. Lucky didn't know why, but it depressed him.

Devyn was everything he wanted in a woman. Oz might love his petite wife, but Lucky tended to be attracted to taller women. And at five-eleven, Devyn was the perfect complement to his six-two. She was slender but muscular, and he knew she worked out often. She kept herself in shape so she could wrangle the animals she helped care for as a vet tech.

She was also smart, empathetic and kind, but wasn't afraid to say what she thought, especially when it came to her big brother. It was obvious the two had a good relationship, and Lucky loved watching them together.

Yes, Devyn was pretty much a perfect package in his eyes. Good-looking and with a fantastic personality to boot.

But he could see the constant wariness in her eyes, and it killed him. He wanted to slay all her dragons, or at least stand at her side while *she* slayed them, and she refused to give him a chance.

If he hadn't been watching Devyn so closely, he would have missed what happened next.

She was talking with Gillian when she received a phone call. She reached into her pocket and answered it without looking to see who was on the other end. The frown on her face alerted Lucky that whoever had called her wasn't exactly welcome.

She said something to Gillian and walked away. Then, with her back to the others, she had a short phone conversation. After she hung up and put the phone back in her pocket, Devyn headed around the corner of the house without a word to anyone.

Lucky stood. Was she leaving? Just like that?

He was on the move before he thought about what he was doing.

"Where are you going?" Grover asked as he passed him inside the house. Lucky was going to try to head Devyn off before she could actually leave, and the quickest way to get to the front of the house was to cut through it.

"Devyn got a call from someone, and she's not happy about it," Lucky told his friend.

Grover sighed. "Shit. I told Spencer to call later *tonight*."

Lucky stopped to glance at his friend. "Your brother?"

"Yeah. He's been bugging me to get Devyn to talk to him. I guess they had a disagreement before she left Missouri, and she's been avoiding him. And Mom too. He asked for her new number, and I gave it to him. I mean, he's our brother. Why wouldn't I? I don't know what's going on, but I want them to kiss and make up so we can be the close-knit family we've always been. But I told him we were having this party today. I asked him to wait until later to call her."

"I wasn't close enough to hear who she was talking to, but I'm guessing he didn't wait," Lucky said.

Grover looked devastated. "I hate not knowing what the hell is going on with them."

"I'm on her," Lucky told him.

"I appreciate it," Grover said.

Lucky nodded and opened the front door. He wasn't looking after Devyn as a favor to his friend. He was doing it because he admired Devyn. Liked her a hell of a lot. She was a great friend, a hard worker, and funny as hell. Anytime he was around her, Lucky felt as if the pressures of his job simply disappeared. She made him feel...grounded. He'd never felt that way about any woman before. He was relieved Grover hadn't pulled the "don't go near my sister" crap that so many men did. He was all for Lucky dating Devyn. Which was great—except Devyn didn't seem to be interested in dating *anyone*.

Firming his resolve, Lucky headed straight for her. She was fumbling with her keychain, trying to unlock her car door.

He came up next to her and wrapped his hand around her keys. "I got it," he said softly.

As a testament to how upset she was, she didn't protest. She let go of her keys, giving them to Lucky.

"I'm driving," he told her, pushing his luck.

But again, Devyn simply nodded and headed around the front of her car to the passenger side. Lucky unlocked the car and they both got in.

"Do you want to talk about it?" Lucky asked after he'd started the engine.

"Just take me home," Devyn said softly, shaking her head.

Lucky wanted to press the issue, but he wouldn't force this woman to do anything. He wanted her to come to him when she needed help. When she was happy and wanted to share her excitement. When she was sad and needed comforting. He wanted *everything* with Devyn, and he'd do whatever it took to prove she could trust him, that they were perfect for each other.

For now, he needed to get her home. Where she felt safe. Then he'd do what he could to get to the bottom of whatever was going on. She'd always accused Grover of being stubborn, but she had no idea. She was about to see exactly how stubborn *this* Delta Force soldier could be. As much as he didn't like the fact that Devyn was avoiding her mom, and now Spencer, Lucky couldn't help but be relieved he had a legitimate reason to push Devyn harder than he had before.

But if Spencer thought he could come into their house, so to speak, and ruffle some feathers, he was wrong. No one messed with their inner circle, not even someone related by blood.

* * *

Sierra Clarkson lay in the dirt in the back of the cell she'd been thrown into and tried to figure out how long she'd been a captive. It was impossible; she'd spent too much time in the dark recesses of this mountain in Afghanistan to mark the passing of day and night. She'd been moved from house to house and finally had ended up here. In a cave in a mountain. It was an unconventional prison cell, but the bars that had been erected across the entrance to the alcove she was in were as strong as any in any conventional jail.

Not only that, but it was obvious the men who'd taken her from the military base where she'd worked had finally tired of using her as a punching bag. She was mostly forgotten now, lying by herself in the dark and trying not to feel guilty for actually being bored.

Bored. What a joke. A few months ago—at least, she thought it was a few months—she would've welcomed a chance to be bored. The first month or so after she'd been captured, Shahzada and his followers had taken turns torturing her. Discovering what made her cry. How they could inflict the most pain. She'd figured out pretty quickly that the faster she "broke," the sooner they stopped the beatings and threw her back in her cell.

There had been a couple other prisoners who'd joined her in this hell since then, and now her captors concentrated on torturing *them*, trying to get information about the military operations on the base.

It was stupid, really. The contractors they'd kidnapped didn't know the ins and outs of what went on at the base. Not the important stuff Shahzada wanted to know, at least. She'd tried to talk to her fellow captors when they were left alone, but they wouldn't answer her. Were too freaked out and scared to death.

One by one, they'd disappeared. Sierra didn't know what happened to them, but she assumed it couldn't be good.

And she didn't understand why *she* was still here. What Shahzada wanted with her.

She didn't want to bring attention to herself, but when they forgot to feed her or bring her a fresh bucket of water, she had no choice but to cry and carry on until someone remembered she was back here and brought her something to eat.

Mostly she was in limbo, and it sucked. But Sierra had always tried to be positive. Things could definitely be worse. She could still be getting tortured every day. She could've been raped. And she could be dead. But she wasn't. She was alive, and with every day that went by, her resolve to stay that way increased. Someone would eventually have to find her.

Maybe because they were looking for someone else who'd disappeared. Or maybe Shahzada would finally mess up and the military would go after him.

So she had to keep hanging on until that day came. In the meantime, she needed to do whatever it took to survive. Sierra had already learned how to cut short any beatings she might receive, and she'd begun to wonder what else she could manipulate her captors into doing.

Closing her eyes, Sierra sighed and did her best to turn her mind to better things than the hellhole she was currently stuck in. Her favorite choice since the kidnapping was Fred Groves, known as Grover to his friends. He didn't look like a Fred in her eyes, so she'd always thought of him as Grover too.

She was amazed when he'd seemed to take an interest in her. Usually no one noticed her, except to comment on how short she was. But *he* had. And when he'd asked if he could keep in touch with her after his deployment, she'd been thrilled. She'd only gotten to write him one letter before Shahzada had snatched her from base.

She often wondered what had become of that letter. Had Grover gotten it? Had he written her back? Did he even think about her? She didn't know, but picturing the strong, handsome soldier in her mind was better than thinking about her empty belly or worrying about what might happen tomorrow.

* * *

Poor Sierra! How much longer will she be a captive? Will Grover be able to find her? You'll have to wait a bit longer to find out because next up is Lucky and Devyn's story, *Shielding Devyn*. :)

. . .

Lucky has to get to the bottom of what's going on with Devyn and Spencer, convince Devyn that she can trust him, and get her to see that he's more than just her brother's teammate. I have a feeling he's got his work cut out for him. Get *Shielding Devyn* now to find out how it all shakes out!

Want to talk to other Susan Stoker fans? Join my reader group, Susan Stoker's Stalkers, on Facebook!

JOIN my Newsletter and find out about sales, free books, contests and new releases before anyone else!! Click HERE

Want to know when my books go on sale? Follow me on Bookbub HERE!

Also by Susan Stoker

Delta Team Two Series
Shielding Gillian
Shielding Kinley
Shielding Aspen
Shielding Jayme (novella)
Shielding Riley
Shielding Devyn (May 2021)
Shielding Ember (Sep 2021)
Shielding Sierra (TBA)

SEAL of Protection Series
Protecting Caroline
Protecting Alabama
Protecting Fiona
Marrying Caroline (novella)
Protecting Summer
Protecting Cheyenne
Protecting Jessyka
Protecting Julie (novella)
Protecting Melody
Protecting the Future
Protecting Kiera (novella)
Protecting Alabama's Kids (novella)
Protecting Dakota

SEAL of Protection: Legacy Series
Securing Caite
Securing Brenae (novella)
Securing Sidney
Securing Piper
Securing Zoey
Securing Avery

Securing Kalee
Securing Jane (Feb 2021)

SEAL Team Hawaii Series

Finding Elodie (Apr 2021)
Finding Lexie (Aug 2021)
Finding Kenna (Oct 2021)
Finding Monica (TBA)
Finding Carly (TBA)
Finding Ashlyn (TBA)
Finding Jodelle (TBA)

Delta Force Heroes Series

Rescuing Rayne
Rescuing Aimee (novella)
Rescuing Emily
Rescuing Harley
Marrying Emily (novella)
Rescuing Kassie
Rescuing Bryn
Rescuing Casey
Rescuing Sadie (novella)
Rescuing Wendy
Rescuing Mary
Rescuing Macie (novella)

Badge of Honor: Texas Heroes Series

Justice for Mackenzie
Justice for Mickie
Justice for Corrie
Justice for Laine (novella)
Shelter for Elizabeth
Justice for Boone
Shelter for Adeline
Shelter for Sophie

Justice for Erin
Justice for Milena
Shelter for Blythe
Justice for Hope
Shelter for Quinn
Shelter for Koren
Shelter for Penelope

Ace Security Series

Claiming Grace
Claiming Alexis
Claiming Bailey
Claiming Felicity
Claiming Sarah

Mountain Mercenaries Series

Defending Allye
Defending Chloe
Defending Morgan
Defending Harlow
Defending Everly
Defending Zara
Defending Raven

Silverstone Series

Trusting Skylar
Trusting Taylor (Mar 2021)
Trusting Molly (July 2021)
Trusting Cassidy (Dec 2021)

Stand Alone

The Guardian Mist
Nature's Rift
A Princess for Cale
A Moment in Time- A Collection of Short Stories

ABOUT THE AUTHOR

New York Times, *USA Today* and *Wall Street Journal* Bestselling Author Susan Stoker has a heart as big as the state of Tennessee where she lives, but this all American girl has also spent the last fourteen years living in Missouri, California, Colorado, Indiana, and Texas. She's married to a retired Army man who now gets to follow *her* around the country.

She debuted her first series in 2014 and quickly followed that up with the SEAL of Protection Series, which solidified her love of writing and creating stories readers can get lost in.

If you enjoyed this book, or any book, please consider leaving a review. It's appreciated by authors more than you'll know.

www.stokeraces.com
www.AcesPress.com
susan@stokeraces.com

facebook.com/authorsusanstoker

twitter.com/Susan_Stoker

instagram.com/authorsusanstoker

goodreads.com/SusanStoker

bookbub.com/authors/susan-stoker

amazon.com/author/susanstoker

CPSIA information can be obtained
at www.ICGtesting.com
Printed in the USA
LVHW052146080121
676101LV00010B/848

9 781644 990513